The Girl
at the
Last House
Before
the Sea

BOOKS BY LIZ EELES

LIZ EELES

The Girl
at the
Last House
Before
the # Sea

bookouture

Published by Bookouture in 2022

An imprint of Storyfire Ltd.
Carmelite House
50 Victoria Embankment
London EC4Y 0DZ

www.bookouture.com

ISBN: 978-1-80314-235-7
eBook ISBN: 978-1-80314-234-0

For Tim, with love

PROLOGUE

It was the only photograph she had from that time so long ago. The only image that hadn't been destroyed. It said so much, and yet nothing at all.

Kathleen traced her fingers across the picture that had faded over the years. The sea had been bluer that day, the sky brighter, and the house's white-washed walls more vivid against the emerald of the clifftop.

Her emotions had also been heightened. She could still remember the bitter taste of betrayal and the spearing pain of a broken heart as she left that place – though she wondered for how long. Her memory was no longer what it used to be, and maybe one day soon she would forget it all. Every joy, sorrow and regret. That was a day she anticipated with relief and dread in equal measure.

But what would be, would be. Hadn't that always been the way with affairs of the heart? It was devastating, that he'd wanted nothing more to do with her, and all that had followed on from his deception, but she had survived.

Kathleen pushed the photograph to the back of her bedside

table drawer and closed it firmly. This was her secret and she would take it to her grave.

1

FREYA

'Happy birthday to me,' sang Freya under her breath. She put down her suitcase and brushed hair from her eyes. A quick glance around confirmed that no one had overheard her, thank goodness.

There was no point in advertising the fact that she was in Heaven's Cove on her thirty-ninth birthday with no one here to wish her many happy returns. No one except a half-sister she hadn't seen for three years, who'd probably forgotten it was her birthday anyway.

Freya picked up her suitcase and started walking again, cursing the cobbles which caught at the heels of her black boots. Cobbles which made it impossible to wheel her case, which weighed a ton.

It was a pretty place, Heaven's Cove, but not terribly practical, she decided, consulting the map on her phone again. At least the phone signal wasn't too bad here, down by the sea, which was lapping against the stone quayside. The air was filled with an acrid tang of fish, and, above her, seagulls wheeled and screeched.

Pushing her phone back into her pocket, she stopped for a

moment to take in the view. To her right, a gentle headland curved into the blue water, and to her left, a high cliff marked the edge of the village. A house stood alone on top of the cliff, Freya noticed. Its windows were catching the March sunshine and twinkling like stars.

What fortunate person lived there, with the village laid out before them? she wondered, walking on until she reached a row of tidy, white-washed cottages just off the seafront. One of them had a noticeboard hammered into a garden flowerbed, carefully placed so it could be seen by passers-by. Pinned behind glass were the dates of parish council meetings, details of a whist drive in the village hall, and a flyer appealing for the return of a ginger cat named Claws.

This looked like the home of a pillar of the local community, thought Freya, squinting at the cottage door to confirm that it was number five. Yes, this was definitely where Belinda lived.

The last time the two of them had met was at a cousin's wedding, when Belinda had talked non-stop about how involved she was in village life. Freya had found it hard to get a word in edgeways and had found her sibling, as always, rather overwhelming. But here she was, offering Freya a way out of the mess she was currently in – and for that, Freya would be forever grateful.

Taking a deep breath to steady her nerves, she hauled her suitcase up the path that wound through the neat garden, and knocked on the door. Seeing her sister always made Freya nervous, but the door was pulled open immediately, before she had time to gather herself and plaster on a smile.

'Freya! How good to see you after all this time.'

'Hello, Belinda. You too.'

'It's been absolutely ages.'

'It has. About three years, I think.'

'Something like that.' She pulled the door open wider. 'Well, come on in. Don't just stand there on the doorstep.'

Freya stepped into the cottage and put down her case. Belinda hadn't changed much since they'd last met. She was a little greyer and a little rounder. But her brown eyes were as inquisitive as ever as they took in Freya's faded denim jacket and her fair hair pulled into a ponytail that had partly fallen down. With any luck she wouldn't notice the stain on Freya's trouser leg, where she'd dropped her sandwich on the train.

Greg certainly wouldn't approve of her current appearance. He preferred it when Freya looked 'polished', like one of the gems in the upmarket jewellery store he owned. And he'd looked at her in horror when she'd dissolved into a tear-streaked state a few months ago. Though what had he expected when their marriage was falling apart?

If he could see her right now, he'd tell her that she looked a complete mess. Or perhaps he wouldn't care enough to tell her anything at all.

Pushing aside thoughts of her soon-to-be ex-husband, Freya gave her sister as wide and bright a smile as she could manage.

'You have a lovely home, Belinda, in a beautiful part of the country.'

'Thank you. Heaven's Cove is aptly named.' She frowned, deep lines scoring the gap between her eyebrows. 'Or it would be if it weren't for hordes of tourists descending on us daily, leaving their litter. Some of them shoplift locally, and do worse. As chair of the parish council, I felt it was my duty to speak to two women last summer who were sunbathing topless on the beach, which was totally inappropriate. They were rather rude to me, actually.'

'Gosh,' managed Freya, when Belinda paused, clearly waiting for her reaction. It had been a long, upsetting day and her sister's list of complaints was making Freya's head spin.

'Gosh, indeed. Being harangued by half-naked women isn't pleasant, I can tell you. But local people rely on me to uphold standards within the village so what else could I do?'

She tutted, before pushing Freya's suitcase behind a coat stand. Then, she ushered her guest into a sitting room where pale sunlight was shining through latticed windows and pooling on a cream rug.

'Please do excuse the rather overpowering odour, Freya. Jim decided to cook himself an early tea, even though I said you were due to arrive at any moment.'

Belinda pursed her lips but Jim, sitting on a beige sofa while tucking into a hot dog, simply smiled and waved. And he kept on smiling, even when his wife took the plate from him and placed it firmly on the dining table at the back of the room.

'How are you, Freya?' he asked, wandering over to the table to finish his tea. 'I don't think we've seen you since Kerry's wedding.'

'No, it's been quite a while.' Freya smiled. 'I'm OK, thank you. How are you two doing?'

'We're doing fine and keeping busy. Well, Belinda keeps busy and I just do as I'm told.'

He gave Freya a wink and brushed breadcrumbs from his lips. He'd lost more hair since she'd last seen him, and his face sported more lines. But his dark eyes still sparkled with warmth, just as she remembered.

'It's very kind of you both to let me stay,' she told him, her nose prickling. Belinda was right; the air was laced with a strong smell of caramelised onion.

'You're very welcome. You are family, after all and—'

'How could we not step in when we heard what had happened?' cut in Belinda, tilting her head. 'You poor woman! While I don't like to speak ill of your husband, it must be awful to be cast aside like that. It's unspeakable behaviour.'

Freya forced herself to carry on smiling. Belinda hadn't grown any more tactful over the years.

'It was a joint decision,' she said quietly. 'It's very sad and unfortunate, but it's just one of those things.'

One of those very sad and unfortunate things that changes the whole direction of your life, thought Freya, her face still stretched into a ridiculous grin.

'I see. Well, you seem to be coping with it all right,' muttered Belinda, sounding rather disappointed. 'And as for letting you stay, we're happy to have you. You're only here for one night, anyway.' She tutted again and bent to pick up a shred of dropped onion from the carpet. 'After that, we'll get you all settled in at Kathleen's.'

'If I get the job, that is,' said Freya quickly.

Belinda raised an eyebrow. 'If? I think you mean *when.* Kathleen, poor woman, is in dire need of some support in her home and you are eminently qualified to provide that. So I'm absolutely certain that you'll get the job and your new life can begin.'

Her new life. Freya felt her smile falter. She didn't particularly want a new life, thank you very much. She was happy enough with her old one, until a year ago. Until everything changed.

That was when the easy banter between her and Greg had turned into arguments, their love life had dwindled to nothing, and once companionable silences had become charged and uncomfortable. Even so, Freya had been prepared to hang on in there, to fight for a better relationship. And it had broken her heart that Greg hadn't. He'd preferred to move on to something new. Or someone new, maybe? As their marriage had imploded, he'd received a flurry of calls from Erica, the immaculately dressed blonde who headed his sales team at work.

Freya shook her head, trying to dislodge her suspicions. What was the point in torturing herself and making a bad situation even worse? Their marriage was over and it was time to move on.

'You really are being very brave,' said Belinda, adding a pout of sympathy to her empathetic head tilt. 'Not only do you have the trauma of a shattered marriage to cope with, I obviously heard all about your care home closing recently and you losing your job. That must have been the final straw.'

'Mmm,' answered Freya, not trusting herself to speak. She and Belinda hardly ever saw each other, but her sister seemed very well informed about Freya's recent car crash of a life – and not averse to bringing it up.

'Remind me, how long had you been working there?'

'Almost five years.'

'Really? That long? You must have felt a part of the furniture. How sad for the staff.'

'It was very upsetting for everyone who worked there, but far more devastating for our residents.'

They, several of them with dementia, had been shipped off to other homes across the county. Freya blinked to ward off tears as she remembered the startled incomprehension on their faces as everything familiar was stripped away.

And now, looking through Belinda's sparkling-clean windows, at the churning sea and an unfamiliar headland in the distance, she understood even more how scared they must have felt.

It'll be fine, she repeated in her head, like a mantra. Hoping that maybe if she said it to herself often enough, it would come true.

At first, losing her job had seemed almost fortuitous, once the initial awful upset was over. Getting away from the small industrial town where she and Greg had made their home seemed like a good idea. She wouldn't have to live in fear of bumping into him and perhaps she would start sleeping through the night again. Lying awake at three in the morning, going over and over what had gone wrong in their relationship, was as pointless as it was exhausting. A new job and home somewhere else in the country would signal a new start. She could build herself a brand new life.

But now she was here, in an unfamiliar place with a much older sibling she hardly knew and an interview lined up for a care job that she wasn't sure she wanted anyway, everything felt far worse, rather than better. And the mantra, still swirling round her head, was doing a rubbish job of quelling the panic she could feel bubbling under the surface.

The truth was, she missed Greg, and she missed the care home residents who had come to feel like family. Working at the home had been so much more than just a job to her. She'd loved listening to residents' tales of the past and had felt honoured to be entrusted with their precious memories as their lives drew to a close.

Jim stared at Freya, as though he could read her mind, before giving her a sympathetic smile. He'd dropped ketchup down his jumper, she noticed.

'Why don't you show our guest to her room, Belle? She must be tired after all that travelling.'

'Of course. Where are my manners?' said Belinda, ushering Freya back into the hall to collect her suitcase. 'You do look tired. A little peaky, in fact. But don't worry,' she declared brightly as she started climbing the stairs. 'I'm well known and, dare I say, respected in Heaven's Cove as a superb fixer. If something needs fixing, they call for me. So you've come to the right place and the right person to get your life sorted out. Just shout, by the way, if you need Jim to carry your case.'

Freya sighed quietly and followed her sister, hauling her suitcase up one step at a time. She wasn't sure she wanted Belinda to fix her.

The spare bedroom was small, with a single bed taking up much of the space. But it was beautifully presented. A floral duvet cover and cream curtains contrasted with the dark beams running across the ceiling. A bath towel sat on a chair next to a pine wardrobe, and a vase of pink chrysanthemums had been placed on the bedside table.

Belinda had certainly done what she could to make her sibling feel welcome and Freya *was* grateful. Belinda did seem to care about her, and maybe the undercurrent of hostility she sometimes sensed from her sister was imagined and simply a case of her being over-sensitive.

According to Greg, Freya was too sensitive for her own good, and sometimes, she had to admit, that was true. Being sensitive had a positive side because it made her a good listener and an excellent keeper of secrets. All of her life, people had told Freya things – hidden things – and seemed to know instinctively that she would keep their emotional outpourings to herself. But being over-sensitive sometimes made her doubt people when they were merely being kind.

Freya looked again around the bedroom that had been made so welcoming, and gave her sister a warm smile.

'I really do appreciate you helping me out and letting me stay,' she said, forgiving Belinda her incessant questioning as they'd climbed the stairs. *What is Greg doing now? What are your long-term plans?*

They were questions Freya was doing her best to avoid asking herself, and she'd deflected them as politely as she could.

'That's all right. Like Jim said, you're family,' said Belinda gruffly. 'Oh, I saved you some coq au vin from lunch, by the way, so there's plenty to eat if you're hungry. It's my special recipe and tastes rather good, if I say so myself. It'll be nicer than Jim's hot dogs, at any rate.' She ran her hand across the duvet cover to smooth out a crease. 'Why don't you unpack and come down in a few minutes? I can tell you more about the village and the locals, including the woman two doors down who's just been charged with stealing money from the gift shop where she worked. I knew there was something shifty about her but Jim wouldn't have it.'

She folded her arms across her large bosom before giving a nod of vindication.

'Some food sounds lovely. Thank you.' Freya hesitated before asking, 'How's your mum doing these days?'

Belinda tensed, the lines around her mouth becoming more pronounced.

'She's still living alone in her bungalow in Birmingham, although we've suggested she move to Devon to be closer to us. She's in her eighties now and still no happier. I don't suppose she ever will be.'

'That's a pity,' said Freya, feeling a familiar wash of shame over what had happened all those years ago – and all because of her.

'Well, there you are. It is what it is.' Belinda bent over the bed and straightened the pillow before heading for the door. 'Settle in and I'll see you downstairs in a minute.'

After she'd gone, Freya went straight to the window. Leaning out, she gulped in a lungful of salty air and gazed at the sea. A fresh breeze was whipping across the water and the waves were tipped with white. Bands of green and grey stretched past the headland towards the horizon.

It was very different from the view that she and Greg had shared for the last few years, since they'd moved to a flat in the middle of town. He loved their urban landscape and being at the centre of things, and she'd found the constant buzz of traffic and humanity energising.

But today, a sea view was just what she needed, because the endless movement of the water was calming. Life might disintegrate into an unholy mess but the waves would roll on.

She stayed at the window for a few more minutes, relaxing her tense shoulders, before unzipping her suitcase and taking out the clothes that were more likely to crease. And as she spread clothing across the bed, she realised that the story of her failing relationship with her husband was there, laid out in front of her. Practical trousers that she'd worn to work were still bundled up in her case, while tailored dresses and smart skirts were draped across the duvet.

Freya was more of a jeans person – always had been – who never felt completely comfortable in anything more tailored. Greg had been the same once, practically living in sweatshirts and combats. But he'd swapped them a while ago for cashmere sweaters and chinos when his jewellery business had begun to attract an upmarket clientele. He'd also started telling people his name was Gregory and glared at Freya if she ever forgot and called him Greg in company.

Freya had tried to fit in with her husband when he'd joined networking groups and hobnobbed with local VIPs who might be 'good for business'. She'd updated her wardrobe and worn the posh clothes when she needed to. But it had always felt as though she was playing a part and would never measure up to what Greg expected of her.

In the great scheme of things, the difference in their clothing tastes seemed immaterial. But it highlighted a painful truth: that she and Greg had grown apart and wanted different things out of life.

Freya picked up the fitted dress in mint-green silk that her husband had chosen for her two years ago. It was beautiful, but dry-clean only which made it impractical to wear very often. And where would she wear it anyway? After a while, she'd rarely been invited to the endless networking events that Greg – Gregory – attended.

Perhaps she should have insisted that he take her with him. She should have made more of an effort to be the sort of polished, glamorous woman that he wanted her to be. A woman more like Erica from his sales team, with her blonde hair, flawless make-up and designer wardrobe. A woman whom Freya had always found rather unfriendly and faintly intimidating.

Freya pulled her make-up mirror from the suitcase and peered into it. Her hair, though thick and shiny, could best be described as mousey and wayward, her face was almost make-up free, and her only concession to fashion today was the ankle boots that had been so murderous on the cobbles. The trainers packed away in her case would have been a far more sensible choice.

Greg wouldn't be seen dead in trainers. When they'd first got together twelve years ago, he'd almost lived in them. But now his footwear of choice was tasselled loafers in soft Italian leather, handmade in Siena. He'd swapped his comfy Renault for a sports car and turned his nose up at any wine that wasn't vintage and hideously expensive. Recently, Freya had found herself looking at him and wondering if she knew him at all.

Freya turned away from the window with a sigh. Below her, she could hear Belinda clattering about in the kitchen. She'd be heating up the coq au vin and preparing to regale her sister with tales of errant locals.

That was the last thing Freya wanted right now. She'd rather crawl under the duvet and sleep – sleeping obliterated the sharp stabs of panic about her future and the memories of her marriage that taunted her, at least for a while.

But Belinda had been kind enough to let her stay and arrange the interview tomorrow that might help to put her life back on track. Plus, Freya had to acknowledge, she owed her sister big-time and always would after what had happened years ago. So the very least she could do in the circumstances was eat Belinda's food and listen to an hour of gossip.

Freya re-did her ponytail, plastered on a smile and went downstairs into the kitchen.

'There you are.' Belinda looked up from the steaming chicken and vegetables she was ladling onto a plate. 'Go and grab a seat at the table with Jim and I'll bring this in for you. We can have a catch-up while you eat.'

Freya did her best to do justice to Belinda's 'special' coq au vin. It was delicious and she should be hungry. She'd had nothing to eat, other than a soggy sandwich, all day. But it was an effort to get each mouthful down.

'You're not on a diet, are you?' asked Belinda disapprovingly, after telling her at length about the village hall fundraising committee that she chaired. 'You're a little chunky in places but not bad at all for your age.'

Chunky? Freya blinked at Belinda's blunt assessment. 'No, I'm not dieting, and this is really delicious, but I think all the travelling has taken the edge off my appetite.'

'I expect that's it,' said Belinda, giving Freya a searching look. She sniffed. 'Emotional upset can play havoc with the digestion too. It might help to tell me what happened between you and your husband. I promise that I won't tell a soul.'

Jim's eyes opened wide and he gave an almost imperceptible shake of the head. But Freya already had the measure of Belinda's grasp on discretion.

Keeping secrets was important to Freya. It got a bit hairy sometimes, remembering which friend had told her what, and what information she could tell people and what she couldn't. But she managed it well, unlike Belinda, who seemed keen to collect people's secrets so she could share them later.

'Honestly,' said Belinda, leaning forward across the table. 'Talking always helps and you can tell me absolutely anything.'

'I'd really rather not talk about it at the moment, if you don't mind.'

'Are you sure?' Belinda's face fell. 'I'm a very good listener so do feel free to tell me all about it whenever you like.'

'Thank you. I will. But I'm honestly fine.'

Freya smiled to prove the point and pushed food round her plate.

'Hmm. If you say so but there's a lot going on in your life. It's very challenging for you right now.'

'Challenging' was one word for it. Her past was upsetting, her present was unsettling, and her future... well, who knew?

Freya speared a pallid mushroom and shoved it into her mouth while Belinda watched.

As soon as she could, Freya escaped upstairs with the excuse of finishing her unpacking, although she wasn't planning on unpacking anything else at all. What was the point when tomorrow, if all went to plan, she'd be in a new home, living with a woman she'd never set eyes on before?

She moved her laid-out clothes onto the chair and lay down on the bed. Then she started taking deep breaths, determined to quell the panic that was making her feel sick. What had she done? She'd left behind everything familiar to come to a tiny village in Devon on the say-so of a sister who didn't always seem to like her that much.

It'll be fine, she repeated over and over in her head. *Smile, be brave and get on with it.*

A sudden tap on the bedroom door interrupted her thoughts, and Belinda poked her head into the room.

'You ran off so quickly, I forgot to give you this.'

When she pushed the door fully open, Freya saw she was carrying a small sponge cake on a plate. 'I didn't want you to think I'd forgotten or was ignoring your birthday.'

'Thank you.' Freya swung her legs off the bed and sat up. 'That's really kind of you.'

'Well,' said Belinda, her cheeks colouring as she placed the cake on the bedside table. 'We are family, after all.'

After her sister had gone downstairs, Freya pushed her finger into the cake filling and licked off the sickly-sweet cream. Then she began to cry.

What finally pushed her over the edge on such a difficult day wasn't leaving home, the pain of heartbreak, or a sense of loss. What brought her to tears was a homemade Victoria sandwich with a dripping pink candle stuck in the top.

2

FREYA

Freya woke early the next morning and lay still for a moment, wondering where she was. She and Greg would wake each morning to the sound of lorries being loaded at the warehouse opposite and trains pulling into the station nearby.

Here, she'd been roused from sleep by the mournful cry of seagulls and a faint boom of waves hitting the rocks that edged the village.

The crashing realisation of where she was, and why, made her stomach sink. With Greg leaving her, and the care home closing down, the last few months had felt like a nightmare that continued when she opened her eyes. And now she was miles from home and about to embark on a new life – as long as Belinda's friend, Kathleen, liked the look of her.

Nothing felt familiar. Even the half-sister who had stepped in to 'fix' her life was almost a stranger. But it was too late to back out now.

Freya forced herself to swing her legs out of bed and walk to the window.

Below her, Heaven's Cove was waking up. Boats were bobbing on the water and a brightly painted wooden caravan had been parked on the front. A woman in a striped apron was putting out a chalkboard that read: HEAVENLY COFFEES. BACON BREAKFAST BUNS. CLOTTED CREAM PORRIDGE.

Beyond her, the headland jutted into the sea and Freya vowed to walk across it as soon as she could. Exercise and fresh air always made her feel better.

In spite of her nerves, Freya's stomach was rumbling and she broke off and ate a piece of yesterday's birthday cake. It was dry and stuck to the roof of her mouth, but the sugar rush helped. Then she went along the landing to the bathroom and had a quick shower before going downstairs.

Belinda, in a pink velour dressing gown, was wiping down the kitchen counters.

'Well, you're an early riser,' she said, nodding with approval. 'I've just made a pot of tea if you'd like a cup? Help yourself.'

Freya poured herself a cup and sat at the small table that filled a corner of the room. Putting down her cloth, Belinda picked up her tea and joined her.

'I hope you slept well on your first night in Heaven's Cove.'

'I did, thank you,' lied Freya. 'It's a very comfortable bed.'

'We bought the best, even though it's not often used.' Belinda sniffed before taking a sip of her drink. 'I've told Kathleen that we'll be with her shortly after nine o'clock. She's anxious to meet you.'

Not as anxious as I am, thought Freya, pushing her hair behind her ears. 'What if she doesn't like me?'

'Of course she'll like you,' tutted Belinda, as though even asking the question was letting the side down. 'I've vouched for you and my word carries weight in these parts. It'll do both of you good. You need a job and Kathleen needs care. It's a perfect combination, and Kathleen will love you.'

Would she? It took time to build up a relationship with someone, especially if you were in their home. Freya finished her tea and dutifully ate the piece of toast, slathered in butter, that Belinda placed in front of her.

'Is that what you're wearing?' Belinda frowned as she eyed Freya's clean jeans and neat blue jumper.

'Um...'

'Only Kathleen is a very traditional type. A rather dyed-in-the-wool, old-fashioned woman with high standards. And this is a job interview, albeit a fairly informal one.'

'They're new jeans, but it's not a problem. I can change if you think that will help.'

'I do. After all, we're family and you don't want to let the side down. I have a reputation in the village to uphold so you need to look smart.'

She laughed to soften her words. But Freya, feeling suitably admonished, slipped back upstairs to change into the mint-green silk and to put on some make-up.

She dabbed concealer on the dark shadows under her big grey eyes and wished she'd got round to booking the gold high-lights that Greg had bought her some time ago, at a posh salon – he liked having a blonde wife. But it was one more thing that had slipped as her life had changed, so her natural shade of mouse would have to stay. Greg said a member of his staff had recommended that particular salon. Erica, maybe?

Freya's fingers automatically went to her fourth finger where her wedding ring used to be. She checked her mobile phone but there was no message from Greg. No 'hope you're OK' or 'good luck in your new life'.

The realisation that he didn't care clutched at her heart and made her feel even more unsteady. She and Greg were defi-nitely over. And even though she'd accepted that sad fact a while ago, acceptance didn't make his indifference towards her hurt any less.

She sat on the bed and was taking deep breaths when Belinda tapped on the door and called out: 'If you're ready,

Freya? You don't want to make a bad impression by arriving late on what will be your first day if Kathleen wants you to start work immediately.'

Her first day. It was like going to a new school where you knew no one. *It'll be fine,* she repeated over and over in her head as she put on a slick of pink lipstick before going downstairs.

3

FREYA

Kathleen's cottage was a little larger than Belinda's, but not as well maintained. The window frames were weathered and the navy-blue front door needed a coat of paint.

The building was made of the same white-washed stone and also faced the sea. But it stood several streets back from the front and overlooked the village green, a weather-beaten war memorial, and an old church with a stubby tower. Rays of sunlight were glinting on the church windows and giving the stone a reddish glow.

Belinda brushed her fingers across flaking paint on the front door before whispering loudly: 'Kathleen has a bit of money stashed away, I'm sure, but she doesn't seem that keen on spending it. Anyway, are you ready?' Her fingers were already curled around the brass door knocker.

When Freya nodded, feeling ridiculously nervous, Belinda rapped sharply.

'Watch out for her awful cat. It'll scratch you as soon as look at you. And bear in mind that Kathleen can be a little deaf at times so you'll need to speak up. Though her deafness can be rather selective. She never seems to hear when I'm on the lookout for volunteers to help at the village hall. Did I tell you that I chair the hall's fundraising committee too?'

'You did mention it.'

Freya had heard all about Belinda's work heading that committee, and the group who organised the monthly village market. She'd also heard about several local inhabitants whose affairs, shopping habits, or even choice of interior design, didn't meet with her sister's approval. Belinda was very judgemental, and an even more incorrigible gossip than she'd thought.

Belinda knocked on the door again, more loudly this time. 'I do hope Kathleen hasn't gone out to spite me. She can be a stubborn old bird.'

'Why would she go out to spite you?' Freya frowned. 'She is happy about you bringing me round to meet her and talk about the job, isn't she? You can be a little... um...'

'A little what?' asked Belinda, whipping her head round to stare at her sister. There was a hint of hostility in her brown eyes.

'A little... assertive at times.'

'Well, someone needs to be assertive around here or nothing would ever get done,' muttered Belinda, rubbing her fingers together until the flakes of door paint stuck to her skin fluttered to the floor.

'Are you sure that Kathleen is definitely on board with your idea?' repeated Freya, more anxious than ever. Her sister had a way of steamrollering people into submission.

'Of course I'm sure,' said Belinda, bending down to peer through the letterbox. 'She's dying to meet you.' She straightened up. 'Here she comes at last. I'm surprised Kathleen's son hasn't got to grips with the repairs around here, to be honest. Mind you, there's a tale to tell about him. His wife died in the most terrible accident so now it's just him and his daughter.'

Trust Belinda to turn a sad story about a widowed man into a piece of gossip. Fortunately, her tale came to an abrupt halt when the door was pulled open by a woman with snow-white hair twisted into a bun at the nape of her neck.

'Come inside,' she urged, shepherding Freya and Belinda into the hallway. 'Did anyone see you?' Then, with a glance down the narrow lane, she closed the door behind them. The only sounds in the cottage were the rumble of a washing machine in the distance, and the plaintive miaow of a black cat sitting on the bottom stair.

Freya's heart sank because Kathleen didn't seem keen to meet her at all. The elderly woman breathed out slowly before looking Freya up and down.

'So this is your sister, then, Belinda.'

'Half-sister,' chorused Belinda and Freya in unison.

'Sister, half-sister.' Kathleen shrugged. 'You're family so what does it matter?'

Her accent was different from the Devon burr that Freya had heard from locals during their walk to Kathleen's cottage. It had a faint Irish lilt that made Kathleen sound warm, even though her expression was far from friendly.

She led them into a sitting room that overlooked the church and gestured at a brown leather three-piece suite that was shiny with age.

'Do take a seat, both of you.'

Freya had a chance to study the older woman as she and Belinda sat down on the sofa and Kathleen moved to the chair opposite them. She looked smart, in navy trousers and a cream jumper. To all appearances, a proud woman who could take care of herself.

But Freya spotted a few signs that all might not be quite as it seemed. Kathleen wobbled slightly when she walked to her chair, and grasped the arms tightly as she lowered herself onto the cushion. And when she pulled at the high neckline of her jumper, which looked as if it might be on back to front, Freya noticed a large red burn that puckered the skin on the back of her hand.

Kathleen met Freya's gaze for a moment before looking away, a port-wine birthmark across her right cheek accentuating the green of her eyes.

'How are you, Kathleen?' asked Belinda, her eyes darting around the room, which was cluttered with furniture but cosy, with pictures on the walls and cheerful yellow tiles lining the fireplace.

'Ah, you know. Getting by. And yourself?'

She lent down to stroke the cat, which had wandered into the sitting room and was sitting at her feet, staring at the interlopers.

'I'm mad-busy as always, Kathleen, because everyone seems to want a piece of me. Honestly, I'm not sure how I manage to fit everything into my day.'

The two women made small talk while Freya studied two silver-framed photos on a table near the window. One was of a man and a woman with a baby in the man's arms. The other showed the woman on her own, her face almost filling the frame.

She was stunning, thought Freya, wondering if this was Kathleen's daughter-in-law who had died in the accident. She looked full of life as she smiled into the camera, her skin luminous, her teeth pearly-white and her hair a glossy chestnut. She looked the sort of 'polished' woman who would pass muster with Greg.

'Has Belinda told you what I'm apparently in urgent need of, Freya?' asked Kathleen, cutting through Freya's thoughts.

Apparently? Freya's heart sank even further. Kathleen had definitely been press-ganged into seeing her, which meant she'd come all this way for nothing – and she really needed a job right now.

'Belinda mentioned that you could do with some company

and support around the house,' answered Freya, trying to sound upbeat.

'That's right. Your sister thinks it's for the best.'

There was an edge to her voice that Freya recognised from the care home residents she'd encountered who were treated as children by their well-meaning relatives.

Freya leaned forward. 'But what do *you* think is for the best? That's what really matters.'

Kathleen paused, her head on one side. 'Thank you for asking me.' She glanced at Belinda, who was tapping her fingers on the arm of the sofa. 'I think that, in spite of what others might say, I'm not past it yet.'

Freya smiled. Kathleen reminded her of several of the older people she'd supported in the home, who were proud and terribly scared at the prospect of their independence being taken away. 'I can very much see that, and this is your home so you make the decisions.'

'That's right. I do.'

'Do you feel that company and support at home might be helpful?'

'I must admit...' Kathleen gave Belinda another glance. 'I must admit that the thought has crossed my mind, but I don't think it's necessary yet. However, Belinda suggested rather forcefully that I should see you, and she's told me all about your circumstances.'

Had she, indeed? That wasn't surprising. She and Belinda were no doubt alike in some ways – their shared genetic heritage made that almost guaranteed. But their approach to other people's personal information was radically different.

Belinda shifted on the sofa and gave a tinkly laugh.

'That's true, Kathleen, but I told you everything about Freya in absolute confidence. You know me, I never gossip for gossip's sake.'

Freya felt her jaw drop and made a deliberate effort to close her mouth.

'I dare say, and you don't need to worry about me keeping quiet. I can keep a secret.' Kathleen stared out of the window as though she'd forgotten that she had guests. Moments passed, broken only by the ticking of the clock on the mantelpiece.

Belinda glanced at Freya and raised her eyebrows before asking loudly, 'Kathleen? Are you still with us?'

The elderly woman turned her attention from the window. A beam of sunlight was playing on her wrinkled skin and she suddenly looked worn out.

'I'm sorry for your troubles, Freya. Life can be unkind sometimes.' She breathed out slowly. 'Belinda tells me that you used to work in a care home.'

'I did. For five years.'

'Were you sacked?'

Freya grinned at the woman's bluntness, which was softened by her gentle accent.

'No, the home closed down through no fault of the staff. The building itself was deemed unsafe so I lost my job at short notice. I do have a very good reference from the home owners. I'm trustworthy and hard-working and... and kind,' she finished rather limply.

Kathleen smiled for the first time at that. 'Kindness is everything in life, don't you think? Were you close to the people you looked after?'

'I was. They'd become friends and I miss them. I provided all kinds of personal and practical care for them, but mostly I miss the chats we had.' She swallowed, willing herself not to dissolve into tears.

'What did you chat about?' asked Kathleen gently.

'Their families, their lives, their hopes and fears. Everything that they wanted to tell me. Some of them were quite lonely.

Their families rarely visited and their friends had either passed away or were too far away to call in.'

'Gosh, you must have heard all sorts,' interjected Belinda, sitting up straighter on the sofa. 'What kinds of things did people tell you?'

Freya thought back to the many confidences people had shared. She'd had the privilege of sitting with people at the very ends of their lives, when they were sometimes desperate to share their secrets and regrets while there was still time.

Belinda would lap up their tales of lost love and missed chances, but they weren't Freya's to share. She shook her head. 'I don't think it would be appropriate for me to talk about them.'

'Oh, come on. It's only us, and they'd never know that you'd spilled the beans.'

'Maybe not, but I would.'

Belinda narrowed her eyes at Freya, who held her gaze. In the unlikely event she ever did share deathbed secrets, the last person in the world she would share them with would be her loose-lipped sister.

Fortunately, any intention Belinda had of continuing to wheedle secrets out of Freya was thwarted when the cat jumped up onto the sofa and curled itself onto Freya's lap.

'Good grief!' Belinda shifted along the sofa, putting more space between her and her sister. 'You're honoured. Kathleen's cat doesn't like me much.'

'Rocky doesn't like anyone much but the two of you seem to be friends,' said Kathleen. 'Are you much of a cat person, Freya?'

'Not really,' said Freya, stroking the silky fur on the cat's head. 'I like animals but I've never had a pet before. Rocky's an unusual name for a cat.'

'His real name is Shamrock but my granddaughter chris-tened him Rocky and it stuck.' Kathleen smiled and sat back in her chair. 'You've obviously made a good impression on Rocky, and me too. You seem like a lovely young woman, Freya, and I must admit that I do get lonely here sometimes.' She shook her head. 'But I'm not sure about this. Having a stranger in my house is... well, it's too much.'

'But Freya has travelled all this way,' said Belinda, tapping her fingers more loudly.

Freya tried not to wince. This meeting wasn't about how far she'd travelled. It was about Kathleen and what she wanted in her own home.

'I realise that,' said Kathleen stiffly, 'and I'm sorry for it. You were rather persuasive at the time, Belinda, and it seemed like it might be a good idea. The solution to a difficulty. But I've had a rethink since then and, now it's happening – rather more quickly than I'd expected – I'm afraid I no longer think so. It's nothing against you, Freya. But I'm not sure I'm ready to have someone else living in my home.'

Belinda began to remonstrate again but Freya interrupted her.

'That's fine, Kathleen. I totally understand.'

She did understand but she couldn't help the disappointment flooding through her. She didn't want to stay in this unfamiliar cottage if Kathleen didn't want her here. But the truth was, she had nowhere else to go and no job to go to. She'd have to go home. Back to the apartment, filled with memories, that was currently on the market.

'I'm sure that you and I would get along, but I don't need extra help at the moment. It's nothing against you,' insisted Kathleen.

'I realise that.'

Though, irrationally, it did feel like a rejection, thought Freya. Just a little bit. She hadn't measured up. First, with her husband and now with a total stranger.

'I still think you're making a mistake, Kathleen,' said

Belinda. 'You need support and my sister is the perfect person to provide it. I can vouch for her.'

'Thank you for your concern, Belinda. I know you mean well but I can look after myself. I'm perfectly safe here.'

'That's not what I've heard. You're quite the topic of conversation in the village.'

'Really? What have you heard?'

'People are concerned about you living here on your own, and heaven knows how your son is going to cope. Though I'm surprised he hasn't stepped up to the plate already.'

'Please, Belinda, let it go,' murmured Freya, spotting Kathleen's expression harden.

She hated her sister being so pushy and was about to insist they leave Kathleen in peace when she noticed something strange. The room had begun to smell of burned food and the acrid odour was getting stronger.

Before she could mention it, the piercing wail of a smoke alarm cut through the room.

'Oh my!' exclaimed Kathleen, pushing herself up from her chair. 'Not again.' She hurried to the door and opened it but stopped in her tracks. 'Oh dear,' she mouthed.

Belinda jumped to her feet and rushed over to join Kathleen. Then the two of them stood frozen in the doorway, like statues. What on earth was going on?

Freya gently pushed Rocky onto the sofa before going to have a look for herself. At first all she could see was the hallway – a small square space, painted white to maximise the light, with a telephone table against the wall, near the stairs. But then she saw the smoke. Dark tendrils were curling from the edges of a closed door and wafting up to the ceiling.

'You're on fire,' yelled Freya, above the din of the smoke alarm.

She pushed past the women and ran to the closed door. The doorknob was cool when she closed her fingers around it. That was a good sign, wasn't it? Maybe the fire was small at the moment, but it might spread before the fire service arrived, and the cottage had a thatched roof. The whole place would go up and Kathleen would lose everything.

With one last glance at the two frozen women watching her, Freya took a deep breath and pushed open the door.

The smoke was thicker in here and it stung her eyes, but she could see flames coming from a cooker.

Coughing, she ran through the room, bumping hard into a table on the way, and pulled out the cooker's grill pan. Two slices of blackened bread were belching smoke and the greasy foil they were sitting on was alight.

Flames twisted into the air as Freya dropped the grill pan onto the hob and grabbed a tea towel from the worktop. She pushed the towel into the washing-up water in the sink, wrung it out and threw it over the flames. Mercifully, they sizzled and died as Freya threw open the back door and shoved the kitchen windows wide open to let out the smoke.

After gulping in deep lungfuls of fresh air, she rushed back into the cottage and pushed past Kathleen and Belinda, who'd made their way to the kitchen doorway. Both women looked pale and horrified.

'Belinda, take Kathleen into the garden,' shouted Freya, before grabbing a coat draped over the bannisters and flapping it under the screeching alarm. At last the dreadful wailing stopped and she slumped against the wall with relief. This was one job interview she wouldn't forget in a hurry.

While she was catching her breath, the cat slipped out of the sitting room and gave her a disdainful stare as it marched past.

'It wasn't my fault,' muttered Freya, watching the cat stalk off with its tail in the air. It seemed the two of them were no longer friends.

'Freya!' yelled Belinda from the garden. 'Is everything all right?'

'Everything's fine,' Freya shouted back though, actually, nothing was fine at all. Her marriage had disintegrated, her overbearing sister was trying to 'fix' her, a prospective new job had come to nothing, and even Kathleen's cat was giving her the cold shoulder.

But looking on the bright side – as she was trying so hard to do these days – at least this ancient cottage would survive to see another day and no one had been hurt. That would have to do for now.

Kathleen and Belinda watched anxiously as Freya walked towards them across the grass. They'd taken refuge in wicker chairs as far from the cottage as possible.

'Is the fire out?' asked Belinda. She patted Kathleen's hand when Freya assured her that it was, and spoke slowly and clearly to the elderly lady, as though she might not understand. 'Everything's OK now. You don't have to worry. Well, that was quite an excitement.'

Kathleen nodded, her face pale in the sunlight.

Freya sat on a low border wall nearby and looked across the small walled garden. It was a glorious profusion of climbing plants and spring flowers waving in the breeze, and felt beautifully calm after the chaos inside the house.

'Honestly, the whole of Heaven's Cove must have heard that alarm and be wondering what's going on,' said Belinda.

She smiled slightly and Freya realised she'd enjoy telling everyone exactly what had happened. Poor Kathleen.

'Some toast had been left under the grill. That's all. It's easily done,' said Freya briskly.

'But there was so much smoke. I thought the whole house was on fire.'

'I think the build-up of heat had caught the rubber seal around the grill a little. But there's no long-term damage done,' said Freya, noticing again how very pale Kathleen looked.

A man's head suddenly popped up over the wall. 'Is everything all right?' he asked, his silver hair shining in the sunshine.

'It is now, thank goodness.' Belinda laughed. 'Kathleen here tried very hard to set fire to her cottage but it's all sorted, thanks to my sister here.'

She put her arm briefly around Freya's shoulders as Freya realised that putting out a fire had promoted her to a full sibling in Belinda's eyes.

'It's lucky you were there,' said the man. 'That alarm goes off quite regularly. We do worry about it, especially as our cottages are connected. The thatch would go up like a tinder-box. Anyway, I'm glad all's well.'

He frowned before disappearing back into his own garden.

Kathleen still hadn't said a word. Freya sat beside her. She recognised the same look of distress she'd seen in the residents of the care home when its closure became common knowledge.

'Perhaps you could get Kathleen a glass of water,' she said to Belinda.

'I don't think she needs one and—'

'Please, Belinda. I think the smoke has mostly gone now.'

Reluctantly, Belinda went back into the kitchen.

'Everything's fine now,' said Freya to the elderly woman, patting her arm. 'The flames are out and the smoke has almost cleared, thanks to the breeze. There's no harm done.'

'Only because you were here,' said Kathleen, biting her lower lip. 'I forgot about the toast when you knocked on the door.'

'We've all done it.'

'And I'm ashamed to say that I completely froze when I saw so much smoke in the hall.' She paused. 'It's not the first time that I've almost set fire to my home, as you might have gathered from Ted next door. I'm becoming quite the liability.' Kathleen looked towards the kitchen where they could hear Belinda banging through cupboards, searching for a glass. 'Don't tell your sister that she's right, but I rather fear that I can't cope with living on my own for much longer. Not without razing the cottage to the ground.' Her face crumpled but she pulled back her shoulders and continued. 'I really can't bear the thought of having to go into care, Freya. I can't move away from Heaven's Cove.'

She glanced up at the cliff that towered above the village. Seagulls were white dots in the sky as they swooped over the house that stood alone on the clifftop – the impressive house that Freya had noticed when she first arrived in Heaven's Cove.

'Of course you don't want to leave because Heaven's Cove is your home. Do you think that your son might be able to help out?'

'I know that Ryan will help as much as he can but he has a young daughter and... it's complicated. He has quite enough to cope with and I can't add to his difficulties.' Kathleen shifted in her seat and her bright green eyes met Freya's. 'It seems I'm in rather more of a pickle than I'd thought, or had been willing to accept.' She drew in a deep breath. 'So will you stay here with me?'

'I... I don't know.' Freya swallowed. 'It's a bit of a strange arrangement, to be honest. You don't *really* want me here. And you know nothing about me.'

'That's all true enough, but Belinda has vouched for you, you seem kind and very experienced, and... and I don't quite know what else to do. I'm rather frightened that I *will* burn the cottage down next time, and Ted would be rather angry with me.' She gave a wobbly smile. 'And from what Belinda says, you're in dire straits yourself at the moment. I have a good feeling about you. You seem like a decent person and Rocky is rarely wrong when it comes to first impressions. Do you have somewhere else to go?'

Freya shook her head. 'Not really. I could go home but...'
When she petered out, Kathleen gave her a sympathetic smile.

'You'd rather not?'

'Mmm, something like that.'

'Then why don't we help each other out? You could stay for
a month and we can see how it goes?' She glanced up at
Belinda, who was bustling through the garden with a glass of
water in her hand. 'We can sort out the arrangements later.
Please,' she urged quietly. 'I can't leave this place.'

'What are you two whispering about?' asked Belinda,
pushing the water into Kathleen's hands. 'What did I miss?'

Freya glanced at Kathleen. 'Nothing, really. We were just
having a chat and...' She paused for a moment before making up
her mind. '...we were arranging for me to accept the job working
with Kathleen, and move in for a while.'

'Oh, but that's wonderful!' Belinda sat down on the wall
with a thump. 'I'm so glad you've both listened to me and seen
sense. This is going to be marvellous for both of you, I can tell.'

Was it really? Kathleen had begged her to stay, but only
because she'd just filled her kitchen with smoke and was
panicking about the future. She might feel very differently
about the whole thing tomorrow.

Freya breathed in the scent of the flowers, wondering what
she'd let herself in for, as Kathleen took a sip of her water and
went back to gazing up at the cliff in the distance.

4

RYAN

The acrid smell of smoke was unmistakable when Ryan opened the front door of the cottage, and his heart started to beat faster.

Last month, his mum had flooded the kitchen after leaving a tap running and he'd found her ankle-deep in water. Before that, she'd slipped on the bottom stair and he'd found her lying in the hall. Fortunately, she'd had nothing but a few bumps and bruises, but one of these days... He felt nervous every time he put his key in the front door lock.

'Mum? Are you here? Are you all right?'

He knew he sounded panicky but he was too tired to care. Work was a pain – he was horribly behind and had spent the morning trying to catch up, Chloe was being argumentative about doing her homework, and now his mother was apparently trying to burn her house down. He really couldn't cope with much more.

'I'm fine, Ryan.'

When his mum's voice drifted down the stairs, he sighed with relief and his shoulders dropped. There didn't seem to be any smoke, or signs of a fire, and his mother was still alive. Maybe his day wouldn't be so bad after all.

'Wait in the hall a moment, will you,' called his mum. 'I'll be down in a minute.'

Ryan took off his jacket and hung it over the bannisters. Then he glanced in the hall mirror and frowned. His hair was more grey than brown these days, he could do with a shave, and his jumper had seen better days. What would Natalie think of him if she were still here?

He used to scrub up well – he'd even been quite a hit with the ladies, once upon a time. Though he'd never say as much to his daughter or she would accuse him of being disloyal, even though his womanising days had been long before Natalie, and there had been no one since. Other than Isobel from the village of course, who for some reason seemed to be keen on him – despite his best efforts to avoid her.

He was thinking about Isobel as he walked into the kitchen. He should really be upfront with her, rather than continuing with his rather sad avoidance tactics. But right now what he needed was a strong cup of coffee to wake him up and get him through the afternoon.

He stopped abruptly when he spotted a stranger at the sink, up to her wrists in soap suds.

She spun around, dripping water over the kitchen tiles and over her totally impractical green dress, which looked like silk. Silk that was now scattered with dark water spots.

'Who are you?' he asked.

'I'm Freya.'

Was that supposed to mean something to him? He scoured his memory. Was she a friend of his mother's? No, she was far too young. And he was sure he would remember if he'd met her before, with her big grey eyes, full mouth and fair hair pulled into a ponytail.

'Freya,' she said again, as though that would help. She wiped her hands on the tea towel at the side of the sink. 'You must be Ryan.'

'That's right. But I'm afraid I'm still not sure who you are.'

'Really? Oh no, your mum hasn't said anything to you about me, then.' Colour flared in her pale cheeks as she pushed tendrils of hair from her face.

'Said anything about what?' asked Ryan with a sense of foreboding. His mother's behaviour was increasingly erratic these days. He sat down heavily at the kitchen table. His back was aching after hours spent hunched over his computer. 'I'm afraid I don't know what on earth you're going on about.'

'Right. Well, that's a bit awkward, then.'

'Awkward in what way?'

The kitchen door suddenly banged against the wall as his mum hurried into the room. She seemed nervous when she glanced between him and the woman at the sink – Freya.

'Ryan, I told you to wait for me in the hall.'

'Why? What's going on? And why is it so cold in here?'

The windows and back door were flung wide open, even though today's pale spring sunshine was tempered by a stiff breeze blowing off the sea.

'I left some toast under the grill this morning and the place still smells rather...' She hesitated. '...singed, so the kitchen is having an airing.'

'I knew I could smell burning when I came in. You need to be more careful when you're cooking, Mum.'

'I am. I just get a bit distracted sometimes. But there's no need to fuss because everything's grand, thanks to Freya, who put out the flames.'

Flames? Ryan's blood ran cold as he nodded at the woman who was still standing dripping at the sink.

'Thank you for that. Um, so who are you, exactly?'

'I'm Freya.'

'Yes, I know that much already.'

That came out more sharply than he'd intended but life seemed overwhelming these days and he really was exhausted.

He felt mean though when the woman's cheeks flared pink again. She looked awkward and out of place in her posh dress, with her hands shoved into his mother's pink Marigolds.

'I think your mum had better explain what's going on and...' She trailed off, biting her lower lip.

'It was a bit of an impulsive decision,' piped up his mum, and Ryan's heart sank.

His mother's last impulsive decision had involved buying a mega-load of ingredients to make beef and Guinness stew. She'd made gallons of the stuff, most of which was still sitting in his freezer. Chloe refused to touch it because it had onions in it, and he wasn't much of a meat eater. So it would probably sit there, frozen solid to the bottom of his freezer, until the end of days.

'What sort of decision?' he asked warily.

'Freya has moved in.'

'Freya has... what?'

Of all the things he'd expected his mum to say, that wasn't one of them.

'She's moved in,' repeated his mum.

'Moved in where?'

'Moved in here, of course.' She jutted out her chin as she always did when she felt backed into a corner.

'Why?'

'It's just for a while, to help me out in the house.'

'But I help you out in the house,' said Ryan flatly, thinking of the time he spent juggling parenthood, work and caring for his mother.

'I know you do, and I appreciate everything you do for me. But you're busy working and bringing up Chloe, so employing somebody properly to help me out is a better solution all round.' His mother didn't sound that convinced herself but she frowned when she saw his expression. 'It's only for a trial period. Freya and I have agreed on a month, to see how it goes.

As long as I don't burn down the cottage in the meantime, of course.'

Ryan ignored his mother's attempt at black humour.

'Why didn't I know anything about this?'

'It was only suggested a day or two ago and I didn't think that I was going to agree to it. But Belinda brought Freya round this morning.'

'Belinda? What has Belinda got to do with any of this?'

The woman at the sink – the stranger who was now apparently living with his mother – pulled off her rubber gloves.

'I'd better leave you two alone to discuss this. I'll be in the garden.'

She hurried through the open back door and Ryan watched while she walked as far away from the house as she could. Which wasn't very far because the garden, like most gardens in Heaven's Cove, was what local estate agents described as 'bijou'. The cottages were crammed too close together to allow for much outside space.

'Who on earth *is* she?' asked Ryan once she was out of earshot. 'And how is Belinda involved?'

'Freya is from up country – the Midlands somewhere. She used to work in a care home and needs a job so I said she could work here instead. She'll live in and help me with the cooking and cleaning and keep me company. It's a good idea.'

'But I told you that Chloe and I can do that. We've been talking about us moving in with you.'

'I know you have, and I appreciate it, but I don't want you giving up your life to move in with me.'

'We don't mind moving in,' said Ryan, pushing down the doubts he felt whenever he thought about the idea. 'And I haven't got much of a life to give up, to be honest.'

He'd meant that as a joke, to lighten the strained atmosphere, but his mum just looked sad. She obviously didn't think he had much of a life either.

'What about Chloe?' she asked. 'What does she think about the idea?'

'She's absolutely fine with it.'

When his mum raised an eyebrow, he found it hard to catch her eye. Twelve-year-old Chloe had told him exactly what she thought about moving in with her 'ancient' grandmother.

No way! My friends will think I'm a loser.

'So what's Belinda's involvement in all of this?' he asked, to move the conversation on.

'Freya is Belinda's sister.'

'You have got to be joking!' Ryan jumped to his feet and started pacing the small kitchen. 'This is ridiculous, Mum. Not only are you, totally out of the blue, moving in a woman you've never met before, she also happens to be related to the biggest gossip in the village.'

'Don't exaggerate, Ryan. Belinda's not so bad.'

'Not so bad? She's dreadful. And if her sister's living here in this house, all our family business will be bandied around Heaven's Cove and, to be honest, I've had quite enough of that already.'

He sat down at the kitchen table and put his head in his hands.

Heaven's Cove was a beautiful village with a good sense of community and it had seemed like paradise initially, when he and Chloe had moved in two years ago – a couple of years after they'd lost Natalie. The constant ebb and flow of the ocean was soothing. And it was peaceful here, especially in the winter months when storms blew in off the sea and the tourists all but vanished. He and Chloe had been able to gather themselves back together and face the future.

But the village had felt more stifling recently, especially now tourists were returning with the arrival of spring.

He sometimes contemplated moving on to somewhere new, though even thinking about it was pointless. Heaven knows why his mother had moved to this village after his dad's death, or why she'd become so wedded to the place and this cottage in particular. But there was no way she'd ever move on to anywhere else now, which meant he couldn't either.

She was getting older and needed him nearby. And then there was Chloe, who was settled in the local school and had already had enough changes to cope with in her young life. So he was stuck here in paradise, whether he liked it or not.

'I know you're not happy about it, Ryan,' said his mum, putting her veined hand on top of his. Her skin felt papery smooth. 'But things are sorted now so let's give this a go. Having Freya here will take a weight off your mind because you won't have to worry about your poor old mammy any more. I'm sure that'll be a relief to you.'

Ryan looked around the kitchen and noticed brown burn marks on the cupboard that butted up to the cooker. The flames his mum mentioned had left their mark and could have done far worse if she'd been alone in the house.

But he couldn't be here, and work and look after Chloe, all at the same time. It was physically impossible. And the other option, if his mum got even more absent-minded, would be a care home, and neither she nor he could face that. She loved this dark, draughty cottage and leaving it would break her heart.

'I'm sure my plan will work out just grand,' said his mum, giving his hand a squeeze.

'Your plan or Belinda's?'

'It might have been her plan to begin with, but the final decision was mine. So what do you say?'

'I don't know. I... I need to speak to this woman. To Freya.'

'Of course, go ahead. But please don't frighten her off. She looks rather worn down by life and as if she might startle easily.'

Ryan walked into the garden, his head reeling from his mother's latest impulsive decision.

Daffodils and crocuses were waving in the flower beds but

Freya was still at the very end of the garden, making a great show of inspecting the ivy that clung to the back wall.

She didn't notice him at first as he walked across the grass, so he had a chance to inspect her properly. It was hard to believe that she and Belinda were related. Belinda was short and round with grey hair and a fashion taste that Chloe had once described as 'tragic'. Whereas, Freya was younger and prettier, with more delicate features. There were dark shadows beneath her grey eyes, that she'd tried unsuccessfully to disguise with make-up.

She jumped when she noticed him approaching.

'Have you spoken to your mum?' she asked with a nervous smile. 'I didn't realise that she hadn't told you about me coming round today.'

'Did you come on your own or did Belinda come round too?'

'Belinda came too because she'd recommended me to your mother, but she didn't twist her arm to make her say yes.' Freya winced. 'Well, not really. I'm sure no one could make your mother do what she didn't want to do.'

'And you know her so well, do you, after what, a couple of hours?'

He was being impolite. He knew he was, and he hated himself for it, but he felt done in and this was the final straw. He didn't want to move in with his mother. Who wanted to be living with their mother in their mid-forties? But he'd reconciled himself to it and Chloe was finally coming around to the idea – sort of. And it was his job, after all. He was an only child, and it was what his dad would have wanted. But now it seemed that this total stranger was moving in instead. What kind of a rubbish son did that make him?

'Do you have references?' he asked coldly.

Freya nodded. 'I have a reference from my last employer, and I can give you my CV, which shows I have many years of

experience in providing care for older people. There's also the
paperwork for my qualifications, including a level three diploma
in health and social care, which I'll of course be providing to
your mother – and you.'

'So what exactly will you do for my mother?'

Freya shrugged. 'As much as she'd like me to do. Your mum
decides. I can help her to live as independently as possible
while ensuring that she's safe. I can cook and clean and shop for
her, provide any personal care she might need, and keep her
company too if that's what she'd like.'

'We already do most of that.'

'I'm sure you do all you can but it can't be easy.'

'What can't be easy?'

Freya's eyes sparked with alarm. 'Belinda mentioned that...
that it's just you bringing up your daughter. You must be so
busy.'

So Belinda had been gossiping about him already and Freya
knew about Natalie. Ryan pushed down his annoyance because
Freya was trying to be kind. He could tell by her sympathetic
smile, but she really had no idea how hard it was bringing up a
child on your own while living with the terrible guilt that had
become a part of him. He took a deep breath and changed the
subject.

'So what brings you to Heaven's Cove?'

She hesitated at that and her smile faded. 'Life,' she said
quietly. 'The tricky bits of it.'

It was the tricky bits of life that had brought him to this
village too. Chloe had been pining the loss of her mum two
years earlier, and his mum had been the best person to help fill
the gap that Natalie had left behind. The move to Heaven's
Cove had been a good decision, initially. The two of them –
grandchild and grandparent – had forged a deep bond, but
recently Chloe seemed to be pulling away.

Was it her age? There was something wrong in Chloe's life,

Ryan could tell that much. But he wasn't sure exactly what. His attempts to talk to her about it had been stonewalled, and googling 'single parenting an adolescent girl' had only served to make him realise how out of his depth he was. At least she had a friend in Paige, Isobel's daughter, though he got the impression that Paige called the shots.

'Look,' said Freya, cutting across his thoughts. 'I appreciate that this has come as a total surprise to you, and I'm sorry you didn't know about it. Would you like some time to think about it?'

Ryan glanced at his mother, who was standing in the doorway, watching them.

He could send this woman packing but he wasn't quite ready to move in yet. And what if his mum was more successful next time at burning the house down? She'd probably set light to the whole row of thatched cottages, endangering herself and her neighbours. If that happened, he'd never forgive himself – and he couldn't cope with any more guilt.

Ryan sighed. 'Mum said something about a trial period.'

'That's right. We agreed that a month was a good idea – to see if she likes me, and if I like it here too.'

Ryan thought quickly. A month would give him time to firm up his own plans to move in here with Chloe, if that's what he decided. But he would need to set down a few ground rules first.

'I'd need to see your references and CV and review any arrangements regarding payment and bed and board that you make with my mother.'

Freya nodded. 'Of course. I can get that to you later today.'

'You'd better have my email address.' Ryan fished in his trouser pocket and brought out a dog-eared business card that Freya took without a word. 'And all financial issues regarding my mother will need to be handled by her or go through me if she prefers.'

'Of course. Whatever your mother wants,' said Freya with a straight stare.

'Also, please respect the fact that my mother is a private person who doesn't like being talked about.'

Freya frowned. 'I'm very good at keeping personal information confidential and I have no intention of talking about your mother to anyone.'

'Not even to your sister?'

'Especially not to my *half*-sister.'

When she raised an eyebrow, Ryan glimpsed the same disdain that he often spotted in Chloe these days, whenever he asked when she'd be home or urged her to turn her music down.

He thought for a moment. Half-sister explained the disparity in age between Freya and Belinda, and the difference in their looks. Though it didn't mean that they weren't of a similar gossipy nature.

But a faint smell of burning was wafting from the cottage, and his mother was still staring at them with her arms folded. He didn't have much of a choice.

He nodded. 'OK. Let's give it a month.'

5

FREYA

Freya watched Ryan go with a sense of relief tinged with curiosity. She was relieved that he was leaving – their whole exchange had been tense and, on top of meeting Kathleen and then putting out a fire, it had been almost too much.

But she was curious about him. He seemed troubled and sad, which wasn't surprising when his wife had died and he was bringing up their child alone. Not, she supposed, that he'd be alone for long if he wanted company. He was a good-looking man, with dark hair greying at the temples and bright green eyes like his mother.

She watched him as he had a word with his mum at the back door before kissing her cheek and leaving.

It was a shame that Kathleen hadn't told him about this morning's interview and about employing her, which meant the whole thing had come as an unwelcome surprise. Belinda appeared to tell everyone absolutely everything but it seemed that Kathleen was the opposite – a woman who kept her cards close to her chest.

It was the same in the care home. Most residents were an

open book and Freya soon knew everything about them and their families – sometimes far more than she wanted to know. It was hard to behave normally with their nearest and dearest when she'd been told embarrassing stories about them.

But a few of the residents kept themselves to themselves. They were polite but gave very little away. She provided intimate personal care for them and yet knew hardly anything about their lives.

'Did my son give you a hard time?' asked Kathleen, wandering over through the garden. 'He's only looking out for me, and his life has been rather difficult since Natalie died so tragically.'

Freya shook her head. 'Of course, I understand. Is that his wife in the photo in the sitting room?'

'Yes, that's her. She was a beautiful soul and perfect for Ryan in every way. He idolised her and has never got over her loss. I'm not sure that anyone else could ever measure up to her.'

'How did she die?' asked Freya gently. She wouldn't normally pry but Kathleen had been the first to mention Natalie's death.

Kathleen bent and pulled a weed from the flower bed before answering. 'She died about four years ago in a car accident. It was a tragic case of wrong place wrong time, I'm afraid.'

Freya blinked hard to ward off tears. She'd been feeling emotional since arriving in Heaven's Cove, and the thought of Ryan and his daughter coping with such enormous loss made her incredibly sad. Of course he'd been abrupt with her. It made sense that a man who had lost his beloved wife out of the blue would not take kindly to surprises being sprung on him.

'Are you all right, my dear?'

Freya smiled when Kathleen lightly touched her arm. 'I'm fine, thank you. I'm probably still a bit tired from the travelling yesterday.'

'Then why don't you go and unpack and settle in. Jim called round with your suitcase while you were kindly doing the washing up for me and I asked him to put it in your bedroom. While you're doing that, I'll go and have a sit down. It's been a busy old morning.' She paused. 'Thank you for putting out the fire and for saying that you'd stay. To be honest, I'm not sure how this is going to go.'

Freya placed her hand on top of Kathleen's, which was still resting on her arm. 'It's all a bit strange, isn't it. But let's take it day by day and see if we can still stand each other after a month.'

Kathleen threw back her head and laughed. 'Oh, you'll do. We'll give it a go – two wounded souls together.'

What wounds had Kathleen suffered? Freya wondered as she watched the elderly lady walk back to the kitchen. She'd lost her daughter-in-law and presumably her husband too, and who knew what other affairs of the heart had caused her pain over the years?

Freya made Kathleen – her new employer – a cup of tea and set it down by her armchair with a smile, before climbing the narrow staircase. The landing was brighter than she'd expected in such an old cottage. Light was flooding through a latticed window, pooling on the seagrass carpet and highlighting the bumps and notches in the beams that crossed the ceiling. There were four doors, all of them closed.

Freya cautiously opened the first door, which led to a small bathroom, with just enough space for a toilet, a small basin and a walk-in shower. A long, floral dressing gown was hanging on a hook on the wall, and an old-fashioned shower cap was resting on the edge of the basin.

The second door led to a box room piled high with books and various pieces of bric-a-brac, and the third to a small, dark bedroom that overlooked the back garden. This room was almost entirely taken up with a double bed, a bedside table and a dressing table. Freya stepped inside, sure this must be her room, but her case was nowhere to be seen.

She made her way along the landing and poked her head around the fourth door. This bedroom was much nicer – it was far larger, with bright sunshine streaming through the window. She walked across the sanded floorboards and looked out over the village that was her new home. There was a fabulous view of the green and the church and, in the distance, she glimpsed a flash of blue sea.

The double bed was covered in a colourful eiderdown and there, in the centre of it, was her suitcase.

The sound of creaking floorboards came from the landing and, when Freya went to investigate, she found Kathleen standing there. She was puffing slightly from the exertion of climbing the stairs.

'Don't mind me while you get yourself sorted,' she said in her soft Irish lilt. 'I forgot my book so had to come up for it. Do you think you'll settle in here all right?'

'I'm sure I will. It was very kind of Jim to bring my case over but I'm afraid he's put it in the wrong bedroom.'

'Really?' Kathleen walked into the smaller, gloomy bedroom and Freya followed. 'No, it's not in here.'

'Jim put it in the larger bedroom, at the front of the cottage.'

'That's all right, then.'

'Oh, I thought that room must be yours.'

'No, this is my room. You'll be all right in the front room, won't you?'

'Yes, definitely. It's a lovely room. I just thought you'd have chosen the larger one with the better view.'

'This room has the view that I want,' said Kathleen, moving to the window. 'So that's that.'

Freya looked past her at the world outside. The view from

this back bedroom took in myriad cottage rooves, all higgledy-piggledy, and towering above them, the cliff at the edge of the village. It was a perfectly pleasant view but nothing like as impressive as the green, scattered with trees, and the ancient churchyard.

'What's that house up there?' Freya pointed at the white building standing alone on the clifftop. It looked like a sentinel, standing watch over the village and its inhabitants, and was starting to intrigue her.

'That's Driftwood House.'

'What an amazing location! Whoever lives up there must have a fabulous view.'

'I... I suppose,' said Kathleen in a quiet voice. Then she turned so quickly from the window, she lost her balance and Freya put out an arm to steady her. The elderly woman's face was ghostly white.

'Are you all right?' asked Freya with concern. 'Do you want to sit on the bed for a minute?'

Kathleen shook off Freya's steadying hand. 'No, thank you. I'm perfectly fine and there's no need to make a fuss. You really should be unpacking and I'll go and sit downstairs.'

She left the room quickly, without taking her book that was on the bedside table.

Freya took the novel down to Kathleen before going back to her new bedroom and unpacking. The dresses and skirts, that she'd probably never wear, fitted with room to spare in the large wardrobe.

Then she changed into her jeans and picked up the business card that Ryan had handed her in the garden. He was a freelance copywriter, she noted, as she emailed him her CV, references and proof of her qualifications. And his email address, four years after the death of his wife, was still ryanandnat@.

How would she be feeling four years post break-up, she wondered, when the split from Greg wasn't so raw? How would he be feeling? Freya doubted he would still have any reminders of her.

Ryan had obviously adored his wife and loved her still, but these days Freya sometimes questioned whether Greg had ever really loved her at all. It was hard to remember the good years they'd spent together. The only images that came to mind right now were of their final few months, which were filled with furious arguments followed by painful silences.

Freya kicked off her shoes and lay on the bed, with its patchwork eiderdown that smelled of washing powder. She allowed herself a few minutes of sadness about Greg and anxiety about her new life with Kathleen. Then she gave herself a good talking to in a bid to shake off the self-pity that was threatening to overwhelm her. This was a new start and she needed to make the most of it. She had a new job and it was time to move on from Greg and her old life. However scary that might be.

'So just get on with it,' said Freya out loud, swinging her legs off the bed. The specifics of what kind of assistance she would provide for Kathleen still had to be agreed on, so she could go and chat to her about it right now – as well as check on how she was feeling after her near-fall.

Freya went out onto the landing but stopped when she reached the open door to Kathleen's bedroom. On tiptoes so as not to make the floorboards creak too much, she crossed to the window and stood looking for a moment at the house on the cliff. It seemed benign enough up there, under a pale blue sky scudded with cloud. But Kathleen had seemed spooked when Freya started talking about Driftwood House. Almost as if the place scared her.

As seagulls swooped and Ted next door started mowing his back lawn, Freya shook her head. As well as accusing her of being over-sensitive, Greg also reckoned she had too active an imagination, and he had a point. Sometimes she read too much into situations and got the wrong end of the stick.

Perhaps his relationship with Erica had always been innocent, Driftwood House was just an impressive building on a cliff, and Kathleen's sudden distress had been about nothing more than having a stranger in her home.

6

FREYA

Freya closed the front door quietly and stood for a moment breathing in the briny scent of the sea. A stiff breeze was blowing and there was a faint boom in the distance as waves, whipped by the wind, hit the quayside.

Pulling her jacket more tightly around her, she set off towards the centre of the village, keen to spend an hour exploring her new home.

Kathleen, who was taking a mid-afternoon nap, had urged Freya to take a break seeing as she hadn't stopped over lunch. Instead, she'd spent time sorting out laundry and arranging for Kathleen to see her GP about her arthritic knees.

In fact, it had been all go since Freya had moved in and started the job yesterday morning. But it felt rewarding to be immediately useful to Kathleen. They were still feeling their way around their new arrangement, but so far so good.

Freya yawned as she walked across the green, past the church and into a cobbled lane. She'd slept badly in her new bed. The house was filled with strange noises that had kept her awake into the small hours.

Freya's over-active imagination meant that she deliberately

never read or watched ghost stories because they spooked her. Yet, here she was living in a centuries-old cottage that screamed *haunted* from every beam, inglenook and shadowy corner. Greg would laugh at her.

She shook her head to banish thoughts of him and tried to focus on the village, which was bustling today with tourists. Several of them were wearing shorts, even though it had rained on and off all morning and the sky was covered in a blanket of grey cloud.

Freya walked past the ice-cream parlour, village hall and tourist office until she reached the edge of the village, where the land rose steeply. She glanced at her watch. Kathleen would expect her back in forty-five minutes. But she was keen to take in the view from the top of the cliff and also to see Driftwood House properly.

The white building, visible from much of Heaven's Cove, intrigued her, perhaps because it mirrored her situation here – the house was a part of the village and yet separate from it.

Though it was early days, she told herself as she started climbing the cliff path. She felt like an interloper at the moment, a guest in Kathleen's cottage. But hopefully she would soon settle in and Kathleen would take to their arrangement. Ryan too, or her days in Heaven's Cove were numbered.

At least all had gone well so far. For last night's meal, Kathleen had insisted on still doing her own cooking, but Freya had helped and surreptitiously turned off the gas rings that the older woman had left on. She'd also cleared out-of-date tins from the food cupboard and had made a list to re-stock with groceries. Next, she was going to tackle the airing cupboard, which was a tangle of sheets and towels.

Freya, concentrating on future plans, stumbled on loose stones and went hot and cold at the thought of falling into the sea that was pounding the rocks below. Would Greg go to her funeral? An image of Greg in a dark designer suit, with Erica on his arm, swam into her mind.

'Stop it,' she said out loud, turning to look at the village far below her. People looked like ants in the narrow lanes, and Freya spotted Kathleen's cottage, its thatched roof dark against white stone. That was her new home, at least for the next month, and dwelling on the past wouldn't help her to settle in.

At last Freya reached the top of the cliff. It was beautiful up here. Wild flowers, scattered across the stubby grass, were waving in the breeze and noisy seagulls cried overhead as they wheeled in the air currents. The sun had peeped from behind grey cloud and was throwing beams of light onto the sea, which was a churning mass of grey and green with white-tipped waves. And there was the house that Kathleen could see from her bedroom window.

Up close, the house was even more impressive than Freya had imagined. The large, imposing building had stone pots of bright flowers flanking its front door, and there was a sign outside: DRIFTWOOD GUESTHOUSE.

What a wonderful place to stay in the spring and summer, when the wild flowers were in bloom and the house was bleached by heatwaves. Though in autumn and winter, it would be battered by fierce storms blowing in off the sea. Freya shivered, suddenly imagining being up here alone in the midst of a storm, or at night in the pitch black.

The sun disappeared behind a cloud and, suddenly plunged into gloom, Driftwood House looked less like a holiday home and more like an old building filled with secrets.

Freya shivered again. The wind was dropping but traces of warmth in the air had all but disappeared. She started making her way back to the cliff path, and noticed a small group of girls halfway down it. A large boulder stretched out from the path towards the sea and one girl was standing on it.

She was awfully close to the edge and, as Freya got nearer,

she realised that the girl, whom she judged to be in her early teens, was wearing a swimsuit. Surely she wasn't thinking of jumping? It sounded, as Freya got within earshot, as if the three girls with her, all in school uniform, were egging her on.

'Hey,' called out Freya. 'Is that safe?'

'What do you think?' asked a tall girl, flicking her hair behind her shoulders. The two girls standing next to her giggled and stared at Freya defiantly.

'I think it looks pretty dangerous.'

'What would you know? Do you live round here?'

Freya glanced at the smaller girl who was still perched precariously on the cliff edge. There were goosebumps on the pale skin of her arms.

'I've just moved into the village.'

'So you don't know anything about this place or what's safe and not safe,' said the taller girl, turning to smirk at her mates. 'Everyone jumps off Clair Point. Everyone with a bit of backbone.' She turned back to the girl on the cliff edge. 'So are you going to do it or not?'

The girl glanced nervously at the sea churning twenty feet below her. If she mistimed her jump, as the waves retreated, surely the water would be too shallow to break her fall?

'I really think you should at least wait for calmer weather,' said Freya. When the tall girl sniggered, Freya spoke directly to the girl on the cliff edge. 'Do you really want to jump?'

Behind her, the other girls laughed.

'Are you a boring scaredy cat?' one of them called.

The girl on the boulder glanced at them over Freya's shoulder and her mouth set into a thin line.

'It's none of your business.'

'You don't have to jump if you don't want to,' said Freya softly, moving closer. The girl's brown eyes locked onto hers and Freya saw a flash of fear. She was scared of launching herself into space and falling into the churning water below.

'Come on,' called the tall girl. 'Have you got the guts to do this or not? We can't stand here all day.'

The girl turned away from Freya and looked towards the horizon.

'I don't want to see you get hurt, that's all,' said Freya gently, inching closer towards her.

'You don't care about me,' said the girl, her words carried back to Freya in the wind.

'I do care and I don't think you should jump.'

The girl looked round at that. 'Well, you're not my mum so it's nothing to do with you,' she said, taking a deep breath and launching herself high into the air.

Flora felt her heart stop – she was too late to do anything. Behind her, the girls cheered and high-fived as the child fell through space towards the waves, her red hair flowing behind her.

7

CHLOE

Right up to the moment her feet left solid ground, Chloe wasn't sure she was going to jump.

It's dangerous, said a voice in her brain that sounded very much like her dad. *You're going to die.*

But the yells of the girls nearby meant she couldn't think straight. And she wanted to be accepted by them, didn't she? Especially Paige, so pretty with her long blonde hair. Paige, whose mum seemed keen on her dad.

What if they all ended up living in the same house one day? She needed Paige's respect or life would be unbearable. Even more unbearable than it was right now.

Chloe glanced at the woman who'd appeared out of nowhere and was poking her nose in. She could give her a perfect way out of this. Chloe could step back from the edge and claim that the woman had put her off. But in her heart she knew it was too late. Paige and her friends would never let her live it down if she chickened out.

'Well, you're not my mum, so it's nothing to do with you,' said Chloe to the woman, before turning and stepping into space.

The wind whistled in her ears as she dropped towards the ocean, panic rising in her chest. Was this how her mum had felt just before she died? Just before a lorry hit her car and crushed the life out of her?

She wished she could remember her mum better. She wished she hadn't jumped.

Her body hit the sea and the sudden cold felt like a hammer blow as she sank beneath the waves. Salt water was in her eyes and up her nose and she couldn't breathe. Was this how it would end?

She pictured her dad's face when he was told the news and had to identify her body. Another body for him to cry over. That wasn't fair. She couldn't do that to him. Pushing her arms above her head, she started scrabbling towards the sky and, at last, her head broke through the waves and she could breathe.

The cheers of her friends floated down from the cliff while she blinked to clear her eyes of seawater and looked up. The woman who'd tried to persuade her not to jump was still there, peering over the edge with a look of horror on her face.

At least she'd cared enough to try and dissuade her, thought Chloe, swimming towards the base of the cliff and feeling a stab of shame at how rude she'd been to her. It was just as well the woman was a stranger because the last thing she needed was her dad finding out about this and getting all stressy. She'd be grounded for the rest of her life.

Scrabbling onto the rocks, she waved up at Paige, who waved back, as though she belonged. Paige had pulled a towel from her backpack and was shaking it at her.

Carefully, she picked her way along the rocks until she reached a narrow path which led back up to the cliff top. The path was slippery and treacherous but Chloe pulled her shoulders back. How could navigating a path be scary when she'd just jumped from Clair Point? She made her way back up as quickly as she could, ignoring the stones that scratched her bare feet.

She shivered in the breeze when she reached the top of the cliff. The nosey woman who'd tried to stop her from jumping was still there, though she'd moved away from Paige and her friends, who were cheering her arrival.

'Are you all right?' she mouthed above the girls' whooping. Then she turned and walked away after Chloe gave her a tight nod.

'Gotta admit, I never thought you'd do it,' said Paige, draping a towel around her shoulders before stepping back with her hands on her hips. 'You've always been a strange one and we all thought you were a coward.'

When the other girls laughed, Chloe tried to disguise her wince with a smile. Paige could be unkind at times but things would be different if they were proper friends.

'What would your dad say if he knew what you'd just done?' asked Paige, narrowing her eyes.

'Hopefully he won't ever find out,' said Chloe, trying to stop her teeth from chattering. 'Though if he does,' she added quickly, with what she hoped was a swagger, 'he'll just have to put up with it.'

'Too right.' Paige grinned. 'You'd better not tell him though, and we'll keep our mouths shut. It's our secret. See you later, and you can sit with us at the disco if you like.'

With that, Paige and the other girls wandered off down the cliff towards the village but Chloe stayed put. She'd better dry off properly before she ventured into Heaven's Cove or her dad would get suspicious.

Chloe shivered as she rubbed her hair and body with the towel. Above her, seagulls screeched and below her the sea pounded into the rocks that she'd only just missed as she fell through space.

She'd just done something really, *really* stupid. Chloe knew that in her heart of hearts and she was freezing up here. Her skin was red and pitted with goosebumps. But inside, she felt warm in the knowledge that she and Paige shared a secret.

And best of all, Paige had said Chloe could sit with her at the school disco – the dance that Chloe was desperate to go to and kind of dreading at the same time. Paige wouldn't have said that unless she was happy to be friends with her and didn't care who knew it.

Chloe breathed out slowly, her body juddering with the cold. Maybe things wouldn't be so bad after all.

8

FREYA

Freya placed a bowl of treacle sponge on the table in front of Kathleen and closed the kitchen window. It was only early evening, and now it was mid-March the days were starting to draw out. But grey clouds were coating the sky, and dusk was swiftly falling across the garden.

'You're spoiling me! This is a real treat,' said Kathleen, digging her spoon into the pudding that Freya had made before her walk to Driftwood House. 'I don't think I've had home-made treacle sponge since I left Ireland, and that was such a long time ago.'

She stared into space for a moment, as though, in her mind, she was back in her childhood home. Freya recognised her expression – some of the home's residents she missed so much would spend hours sitting quietly, lost in the past.

'Treacle sponge was always a favourite in the care home. A lot of the residents said it reminded them of their childhood.'

'Me too because my mam used to make it. Did you learn how to make it from your mother?'

Freya shook her head. 'No, my mum wasn't much of a cook.'

Not much of a mother either, thought Freya, looking through the glass at the pale outline of a crescent moon.

The gathering gloom mirrored her mood. She'd felt almost anaesthetised from her troubles over the last day or two, as she'd fitted into a new home in such a beautiful village. But this evening she felt miserable all of a sudden. It had hit her that here she was, in a house that wasn't hers, with a woman she hardly knew and no firm plans for the future.

She still felt shaken, as well, by the girl's leap from the cliff that she'd witnessed that afternoon. It was such a dangerous thing to do, and the girl hadn't really wanted to jump, she was sure of it. She'd been egged on by her friends.

Kathleen leaned forward, her eyes searching Freya's. 'Is your own mammy still around? I hope you don't mind me asking but it would be nice to get to know you a little better, seeing as we're living together now.'

'I don't mind at all.' Freya smiled, although it was an effort. 'My mum's still around but she's in Greece.'

'On her holidays?' Kathleen pushed the spoon into her mouth and closed her eyes, savouring the taste.

'No, she lives there, not far from Athens. She moved abroad when I was ten.' Freya hesitated, myriad memories flooding her mind. 'I... I decided to stay with my dad.'

'I see.' Kathleen's green eyes were filled with kindness. 'That was quite a decision to make.'

A decision that no ten-year-old should ever have to make, thought Freya, experiencing a rush of grief and abandonment even after all these years. She swallowed to steady her voice.

'It was difficult at the time, but Dad and I got along well. He was a good father.'

A father who would have fallen apart without her. She'd known, even at ten years old, that she couldn't leave him, even though her mother could.

'Where is he now?' asked Kathleen, licking custard from her spoon.

'He died almost ten years ago. He was a lot older than my mum when I was born. He'd already had one family before I came along.'

'Ah, I presume that's where Belinda comes in.'

'That's right. Just Belinda. There were no other children from his first marriage, and no others from his marriage to my mum.'

Kathleen was quiet for a moment. 'Ten is such a tender age. Did you resent your mother leaving you?'

Gosh, that was blunt. Freya blinked but Kathleen was too busy scraping her bowl to notice.

'I was upset at the time,' replied Freya carefully. 'But she'd met another man – the man who became my stepdad – and she had plans for a new life that didn't seem to include me. Not in my mind, anyway.'

'That's sad. Do you get on well now?'

Freya shrugged. 'Well enough, I suppose. Though we don't see each other very often.'

'Could you go and live with her now, or nearer to her, at least?'

'Maybe one day. Who knows?'

Actually, her mother had suggested she move to Greece after Greg left. But it had been too much of an upheaval following the loss of the man she'd thought she would be with for ever. The rapprochement offered by her mother was too little, too late.

At that time, anyway, she'd craved familiarity and wanted to stay put. So it was rather ironic that she was now here, feeling very out of her comfort zone.

'What about you, Kathleen – whereabouts in Ireland were you brought up?' asked Freya, to change the subject from herself.

'I was raised in County Kerry and lived there until I was nineteen. Have you ever been?' Kathleen smiled when Freya shook her head. 'It's a beautiful part of the world. Mountain peaks, ancient woodlands, wonderful countryside – you've never seen so many shades of green – and the wild ocean stretching all the way to America. Then I moved to England and lived in London with my sister, Clodagh, until I got married.'

'Did you go back to Ireland on holiday?' asked Freya, coming to sit at the table.

She'd always wanted to visit the place herself. But Greg always preferred more exotic destinations where hot weather was guaranteed and he could work on his tan.

'No, I stayed in London. Clodagh went back to live in Kerry but I was too busy building a life over here with Frank to ever go back.'

'You must have missed your family.'

'Not so much,' she said, running her fingers across the table top. 'Frank and I were fine, just the two of us, and then Ryan came along and our family was complete. Frank was traditional in his ways and rather religious, but he was good to the both of us.'

'Is that your husband?' asked Freya, pointing at a framed photo on the dresser.

A grey-haired man was pictured, sitting in a garden chair with a china mug resting on his lap. His head was tilted back towards the sun and his eyes were closed. He looked asleep and at perfect peace.

Kathleen nodded. 'Yes, that's Frank in his favourite place, the garden. He had green fingers, that man.'

'It doesn't look like your garden here.'

'No, it's our garden in Cambridgeshire, where Ryan grew up. Frank never saw my garden in Heaven's Cove. I only moved to the village eight years ago, after he'd passed away.'

'So I guess you're the gardener now,' said Freya, wondering how Kathleen coped with her arthritic knees. The cottage garden was small but must still need a lot of work.

'I do what I can but Ryan does the lion's share these days. He's inherited his father's green fingers but he never has much time to spare. He's always so busy.'

Though not too busy to call in, thought Freya. He'd already nipped round three times today on various pretexts. It was obvious he was checking up on her, making sure she wasn't murdering Kathleen in her sleep or stealing the family silver. Of course he was. He was a loving son and, although she had an impressive CV and references, he didn't know her from Adam. But his impromptu visits were making her nervous.

'What brought you to Heaven's Cove?' asked Freya, keen to know more about her new housemate.

'Ah, this and that. I'd heard that the village was a wonderful place and I wanted to live by the sea again before I died, so' – Kathleen shrugged – 'here I am.'

'You'd heard? Hadn't you ever visited Heaven's Cove before?'

Kathleen paused a moment before answering. 'No, I'd never been to the village before Frank died.'

'That was brave, upping sticks and coming here on your own,' said Freya, marvelling at the elderly woman's determination to build herself a new life in a brand new place.

'No braver than what you're doing,' murmured Kathleen. 'And I'm lucky because Ryan and Chloe moved to the village to be near me a couple of years ago. Ryan's a good son.'

A better child than she was? Freya felt a pang of guilt. Her mother was getting older and had a few health problems these days. Perhaps that was why she'd suggested Freya move to Greece to be near her.

'So what do you think of Heaven's Cove?' asked Kathleen, taking a sip of the tea she'd insisted should accompany her pudding. 'You must have visited Belinda here a few times in the past.'

Freya shook her head. 'No, never. This is my first time in Heaven's Cove and I think it's lovely. Everything's so old here, the village is like a living museum, and I like being by the sea more than I thought I would. It makes me feel as though I'm on holiday. Does that feeling last?'

'Sort of, though real life has a habit of poking its nose in wherever you are.'

'That's true, though I imagine your granddaughter must love being brought up here.'

Kathleen frowned. 'Chloe's reached that time of life where it's hard to tell. Twelve is such a difficult age, don't you think? You're on the cusp of being a teenager and more independent but you're not quite there yet. But she seems to have settled into the village well enough since they arrived. And since she lost her mother.'

She glanced at Natalie, staring out from her silver frame that stood next to Frank's.

'You must all miss Natalie terribly.'

'We do. Especially Ryan, of course. He's never got over the loss of his wife, though I pray he will one day. His daughter needs a mother and he needs a companion. He's lonely, you see.' Tears suddenly filled the old lady's eyes and Freya leaned across the table to pat her arm. Kathleen gave a shaky smile. 'But what about your young man, Freya? Do you mind if I ask?'

'No, of course not.' Freya breathed out slowly. 'Greg and I were together for twelve years and married for nine, but separated a while ago. We grew apart. I hate that phrase, but in our case it's the truth.'

Kathleen shook her head sadly. 'It can happen, but I'm sorry to hear that. No wonder you were in need of a change of scene.'

'What with that and losing my job, I was feeling a bit... lost.' Freya bit her lip, unsure whether she should be saying this kind of thing to Kathleen, her employer. She'd never have told the owner of the care home that her life was a mess.

But Kathleen nodded. 'It's hard when you lose your footing in life. That's when you need people around you who care. But you'll be grand here, Freya. I know you will be. The beauty and peace of this little village has been a source of great comfort to me, and I'm sure it will be for you too if you get out and explore.'

'I had a look around this afternoon, actually, while you were having a nap.'

'Where did you go?'

'I went through the village, right to the edge, and then I walked up to the top of the cliff. The view from up there is stunning, and you're right, it *was* comforting to sit and watch the sea.'

She didn't mention the girl with the red hair, who'd leapt from the cliff into the sea below. *That* hadn't been a particularly comforting sight.

'Did you see Driftwood House?' asked Kathleen, her words almost lost because her head was bent over her lap. She picked a piece of fluff from her skirt and pushed it into her pocket.

'I did. I noticed it's being run as a guesthouse.'

'That's right.'

'It's very impressive, alone up there with nothing but sea in one direction and countryside in the other. It must be quite a place to stay.'

Kathleen said nothing. She just sat very still, staring through the window at the shadowed garden. The atmosphere had shifted and Freya wasn't sure what to say next.

Fortunately, she was saved from saying anything at all by the bang of the front door closing and a murmur of conversation in the hall.

Kathleen's head jerked round. 'Oh, who's that now?' she

asked, though it was obviously Ryan, here to see his mother – and to check up on Freya for the fourth time today.

Freya plastered on a smile as the door opened and Ryan came into the kitchen. He ran a hand through his hair that glinted silver under the light. He was a good-looking man, Freya had to admit, with his square jaw and bright green eyes that matched his mother's. But he always looked at her with a measure of irritation, as though she was the hired help he'd never have hired himself.

'Hi, Mum.' He nodded at Freya. 'Sorry, I don't want to interrupt your tea.'

'We've more or less finished, and it's good to see you,' said Kathleen. 'Is that my gorgeous granddaughter I can hear?'

'Hey, come on, Chloe,' Ryan called into the hall. 'Put your phone away and come and say hello to your gran.'

A girl, all gangly arms and legs, came and stood in the doorway, pushing her phone into her jeans pocket.

'Hey, Gran. How are you doing?'

She waved at Kathleen and then her eyes fell on Freya, who had stopped breathing. It was the girl from the cliffs. The girl who'd told her to mind her own business before leaping into the sea.

'This is Freya,' said Kathleen. 'The lady who's living with me for a while. And Freya, this is my wonderful granddaughter, Chloe, who I've been telling you about.'

'Yeah,' said Chloe, her eyes still fixed on Freya's.

'Hello, Chloe,' said Freya getting to her feet. 'It's lovely to see you.'

'Yeah,' said Chloe again.

Ryan looked between them. 'Have you two met already?'

Chloe continued to stare, a touch of panic now in her big brown eyes.

But panic turned to relief when Freya answered, 'No, I don't think so.'

There was no point in dropping her in it with her family, reasoned Freya. Chloe had survived jumping from the cliff and was surely unlikely to do it again. And it would hardly get her off to a good start, with any of them, if the first thing she did was tell tales.

Belinda would be all over it like a rash, thought Freya. Telling everyone who bothered to listen that Ryan's daughter had risked injury or worse by jumping into the waves. But she was nothing like her sister. She could keep a secret.

～

It was just her luck that the woman who'd seen her leap from Clair Point was her gran's new carer. It was typical, thought Chloe, because bad luck followed her around like a stalker. Losing her mum to a freak accident was a case in point. Though at least it looked as though Freya might keep quiet.

Chloe gave this new woman a once-over. She looked nice enough and she had a smiley kind of face, though her jeans were a disaster – tight all around her ankle. Paige said skinny jeans were *so* over. Though they looked OK on her, and the woman could certainly cook.

Chloe licked custard from her spoon and dug it straight back into the home-made treacle pudding that Freya had presented her with. One of Paige's favourite sayings was 'no carbs before Marbs', but Chloe wasn't going to Marbella any time soon and this pudding tasted so good.

'Hello. Do you mind if I sit with you?'

Chloe looked up in alarm. She'd been so busy filling her face she hadn't noticed Freya approaching. They'd all moved into the sitting room, and her dad and Gran were in the corner, talking about politics or something equally boring.

'No, that's fine,' said Chloe, feeling fluttery. Was she

supposed to say thank you for not dobbing her in to her dad? She better had or Freya might change her mind.

'Thanks for not saying anything about... um.'

When Freya smiled, her eyes twinkled in the lamplight. 'It's our secret so long as you promise me that you'll never do anything like that again. It really is dangerous, jumping from there into the sea. You could have been seriously hurt.'

Chloe shrugged. 'It wouldn't matter if I was.'

'Of course it would matter.' The woman looked shocked now. 'Your dad and your gran would be devastated if anything happened to you.'

'They'd get over it.'

That sounded snarky and it made Freya frown.

'No, they wouldn't, and I'd be upset too.'

'Why? You don't know me.'

'Not yet. But I hope I'll get to know you better.'

Did she mean it, or was she just currying favour with the granddaughter of the woman who'd just given her a job? Chloe decided it didn't really matter. Either way, Freya was being nice to her and wasn't going to tell her dad about her leap, which Chloe had no plans to repeat anyway.

'I won't do that jump again. I promise,' she said quietly, so her dad wouldn't hear. Sometimes she thought he had sonic hearing, like a bat. Wherever he was in the house, he always heard when she opened the fridge for another can of Coke.

'That's good then,' said Freya, looking relieved and sitting back in her chair. Rocky had wandered over and was winding himself between Freya's legs as if she was a witch and the daft cat was her familiar.

'Are you going to be here for long?' asked Chloe, feeling emboldened by the secret that she and Freya now shared.

Freya wrinkled her nose. 'To be honest, I don't know. We both want to see how things go, but I really like your gran and your dad seems nice.'

'He's all right, I suppose.'

When Freya laughed, she looked kind. 'That's high praise indeed,' she said. 'Well, I'd better go and clear up the kitchen. Treacle pudding might taste great but making it creates a terrible sticky mess.'

She walked across the room and through the door to the hall and, Chloe noticed, her dad watched Freya every step of the way.

9

RYAN

Ryan checked his watch and quickened his step. He had a Zoom meeting in half an hour with a potential new client and he needed time to smarten himself up – that was the trouble with Zoom; you couldn't make an important call in your oldest, comfiest sweatshirt. He also needed to factor in time for making sure his WiFi was properly up and running.

Working from home was a godsend for single parents. Being home-based meant he could nip out to collect Chloe from school when the weather was bad, keep an eye on her when she was ill, and do a quick trip to the grocery store when she was eating him out of house and home.

But relying on the dodgy internet connection in Heaven's Cove wasn't good for his stress levels. He'd lost count of the work calls that had cut out partway through. He'd broken one phone by hurling it at the wall in frustration. No wonder he was going greyer by the day.

He glanced in a shop window to check out his current grey quotient – about fifty-fifty – and spotted Isobel approaching in the reflection.

It was hard to miss Isobel. She was platinum-blonde,

whereas Natalie's hair had been chestnut-brown, but, just like his dead wife, Isobel turned heads wherever she went. She was extremely attractive, with a dazzling white smile. Her face was always expertly made-up and not a hair was ever out of place.

Ryan had thought of her while watching *Mary Poppins* with Chloe the other night. Isobel, he'd decided, was 'practically perfect' – and she appeared to be interested in him, which was flattering, but pointless after what had happened with Natalie. Men like him didn't deserve to be happy, which was why he'd rather pathetically started trying to avoid Isobel. But, here she was.

'Hey, Ryan,' she said in her breathy voice. 'I haven't seen you for a while. How are you doing?'

'I'm fine, thanks. And you?'

'Oh, you know. Being kept on my toes by Paige. We single parents have to do double the parenting work, as I keep telling Kieran, who thinks he deserves a medal when he has his daughter to stay overnight.' Her expression soured momentarily, as it always did whenever she mentioned her ex-husband. Then, she smiled again. 'Is Chloe getting excited about the school dance – or "rave" as Paige called it this morning? It's all she and her friends talk about these days.'

Ryan nodded. 'She's looking forward to the disco. Let's hope it's not a rave. I don't want the kids spending the night in a drug-fuelled haze being deafened by terrible music.'

Dear Lord, he'd tried to make a joke but ended up sounding like an out of touch old fogey instead. Chloe would be embarrassed. But Isobel gave a bright smile that accentuated her cheekbones.

'I'm sure it'll all be terribly, *terribly* tame,' she told him, moving closer and touching his arm reassuringly. 'I know you're big and strong and protective, Ryan, and I love that about you. But we can't protect our girls from the big bad world for ever.'

'I guess not,' said Ryan, determined to give it a damn good try.

Isobel moved closer still, until their bodies were almost touching, and looked up into his face. A cloud of her perfume enveloped him.

'Actually, it's rather good that I've bumped into you because I was wondering if you fancied going to the pub sometime? For a little drinkie. Or maybe even two.'

Here it was. He'd been trying to avoid what felt like this inevitable question from Isobel for a while. Because so much more than a couple of drinks was on offer. That was obvious from the way Isobel was prettily biting her lip while gazing into his eyes.

Ryan hesitated because her offer was tempting. Sometimes he felt so lonely he could cry and, on the face of it, there were no complications. Isobel was free, now she'd split up with the antiques dealer he knew she'd been seeing in nearby Callow-field, and he'd been alone since Natalie's death.

What would be the harm in enjoying comfort in the arms of a beautiful woman? It had been so long since he'd been held. And Chloe, who got on well with Paige, would probably accept him being in a relationship with Isobel – once she'd stopped telling him the very idea of him dating anyone was gross.

But the guilt that had seared through him for four long years was a huge complication that he could never voice.

'Come on, Ryan,' urged Isobel, giving him a pout. 'You know you want to.'

'I'm pretty busy at work at the moment,' he said, hating himself for coming up with such a lame excuse. 'And I don't go out much these days.'

He winced. It was going from bad to worse and Isobel was staring at him as though he was crazy for not leaping at her offer. He knew lots of men who wouldn't hesitate, but they were probably better men than him.

'Oh, I think that's Freya. Hello there,' he called out, giving a jaunty wave to his mum's carer, who, fortuitously, had just turned into the narrow lane. 'How are you today? Are you out shopping?'

'That's right,' she called back, glancing at the prominent shopping bag that was hooked over her arm. 'Um... I'm fine, thanks. Hope you are too.' She raised her hand and gave an awkward wave before disappearing into Stan's tiny grocery store.

Ryan cringed inside. Not only had he used a lamentable excuse to turn down Isobel's invitation, he'd just thoroughly confused his mother's new carer. After being polite but distant with Freya over the past week when calling in to check up on her, he'd just greeted her like a long-lost friend. He was forty-five years old and so rattled by Isobel's invitation, he'd made a total arse of himself.

At least he'd distracted Isobel from her proposed pub trip. She stepped back, and folded her arms.

'Who was that?'

'That's Freya. She's staying with Mum for a little while to give her a helping hand.'

Isobel's mouth fell open. 'Is *that* Belinda's sister? I heard she was in the village but she's much younger than I thought. I rather imagined she'd be like Belinda – all grey and round with sensible shoes.'

'They're half-sisters, apparently, which is why Freya looks so...' Ryan paused, searching for the right word. *Fresh-faced? Glowing? Pretty?* Any of them would be true, but he decided on 'different' in the end. 'She and Belinda don't look much alike.'

Isobel sniffed. 'I hope she's not a dreadful old gossip like her *half*-sister.'

'I hope not too.'

'So,' said Isobel, giving Ryan a sideways look. 'Is she living in?'

'Yes, at the moment. It's a bit of an experiment really, to see if Mum needs more help at home.'

'Your mum's a tough old bird so I wouldn't have thought she'd want someone in her home all the time.'

'She's still getting used to it,' said Ryan, grateful that his mum wasn't around to hear Isobel's description of her.

'Surely she's got you and Chloe to look after her?'

Isobel's perfect pearly teeth bit down gently on her lip again as she gave Ryan a straight stare. He shifted uncomfortably. Would people think he was shirking his responsibilities?

'We do what we can but we thought Mum might benefit from some live-in help.'

'So how's it going so far?'

'It's early days but fairly well, really.'

He sounded surprised because he *was* surprised that, though Freya had only moved in a week ago, he'd noticed beneficial changes in his mum already. She seemed more content and at ease now she had company in the house. He'd even heard her laughing when he arrived yesterday morning – the first time he'd heard his mum laugh for some time. And for the last seven days, she hadn't set fire to the cottage, flooded the bathroom or thrown herself down the stairs.

Ryan was also surprised how more relaxed he had begun to feel, knowing that his mother wasn't on her own. A stranger moving in with his mum wasn't what he'd wanted – especially one related to blabbermouth Belinda. But, at least for the time being, it did seem to be improving life for his mother and making his life easier into the bargain.

'Let's hope it continues to go well,' said Isobel. 'She looks innocent enough but you can never tell what someone's like underneath, can you? And I'd hate for Kathleen to come to any harm.'

Had Isobel spotted something in Freya that he couldn't see? Ryan gave himself a mental shake. She'd only glanced at his mother's new carer from a distance so there was no concrete reason for her to suggest that his mother might come to harm. But it worried him, nonetheless. Freya seemed to be fitting in well, but she was still a stranger who'd arrived out of the blue.

He did his best to brush off Isobel's comment and glanced again at his watch. 'I really must go because I've got an important work call in twenty minutes.'

Isobel ran a hand through her long blonde hair, a slight line appearing between her eyebrows. 'Of course. You run along and maybe I'll see you in the pub soon.'

'Mmm, maybe.'

Ryan hurried off towards home, wishing he'd never left his desk at all this morning.

10

FREYA

Freya stepped down off the stool and leaned her feather duster against the wall. She was tackling the silvery cobwebs in the corner of her bedroom that taunted her at night, when she turned out the light. The thought of giant spiders running across the ceiling didn't make for good quality sleep. What with that and thoughts of Greg and Erica snuggled up together somewhere, she hadn't had a good night's sleep in the two weeks since she'd arrived.

The days were fine. She and Kathleen were settling into a routine – Freya was helping out with household tasks and was also starting to help with more personal care, such as assisting Kathleen with getting dressed, which was difficult for her when her arthritis was playing up. There had been no more cosy chats since the bonding over the treacle sponge but the two of them were getting on well.

Freya was also getting used to Ryan's still-frequent visits, which weren't *so* bad. He was very caring to his mum and he rarely stayed for long. Plus, he was easy on the eye, though she felt guilty that she'd even noticed, as though finding another man attractive was betraying Greg – which was crazy in the circumstances.

She picked up the duster, ready to do battle with the spiders once more, but stopped before clambering back onto the stool.

'Freya! Freya!'

Someone was calling her name from the back of the house. Freya rushed onto the landing and heard the calls again, more urgent this time and coming from outside. She ran into the bathroom, peered out of the window and caught her breath. A white sheet was on the washing line, flapping in the breeze, and Kathleen was lying on the grass, a tangle of newly washed bedclothes around her legs.

By the time Freya had run down the stairs and into the garden, Kathleen had managed to pull herself up and was sitting with her back to the washing-line pole.

'Don't move. Are you all right?' asked Freya, kneeling down beside the elderly woman, who was rubbing at her knees. A hole had been torn in her tights and the edges of the nylon were stained with blood.

'I tripped over my own feet. What a stupid thing to do.' Kathleen shook her head while Freya ran her hands along the old woman's legs. 'There's no need to fuss! I'm grand. I don't think I've done any major damage, but I'm afraid I can't get up on my own.'

'You've grazed your knees but does anywhere else hurt?'

'Not really. I went down with a thump but luckily I landed on the grass.' She wrinkled her nose. 'Which is wet, by the way, so it would be good to get up as soon as possible.'

'Maybe we should get you checked over before we try to move you. We need to make sure you haven't damaged your hip. In the care home we never moved anyone until—'

'That was different,' said Kathleen, cutting across her. 'No offence, but they were old dears and fragile, whereas I'm living in my own home and perfectly capable of taking care of myself.

Well…' She looked at Freya and rolled her eyes. 'More or less, with a little help. If I can just sit still in my armchair for a while, I'll be grand. I promise you.'

When she held up her arms, Freya put her arm around Kathleen's waist and helped her get to her feet. The elderly woman wobbled slightly and winced.

'Are you sure you're OK?'

'Absolutely. It's only my knees that are stinging, and my pride. I hope Ted next door wasn't looking out of his bedroom window. Oh, I'd kill for a cup of tea.'

Freya helped Kathleen into the sitting room and sat her in her favourite armchair. She leaned her head against the headrest and closed her eyes for a moment. Then she leaned forward, her face screwed up in annoyance.

'Honestly, Freya, I'm so cross with myself. All I was doing was hanging out the washing but I tripped on the edge of the path and fell forwards.'

'Are you sure you didn't bang your head?'

'No, my head's fine. It's just my knees, and my hands from where I put them out to save myself.'

She held out her palms, which were red and grazed.

'I would have hung out the washing for you,' said Freya, pulling a clean tissue from her pocket and dabbing at Kathleen's bloody knees.

'I know you would, but you're doing so much already, I thought I'd give you a hand. Though now I've made even more work for you.'

When Kathleen's face fell, Freya put an arm around her shoulders.

'Don't worry about it. These things happen, but I'd better get you cleaned up.'

'Before Ryan arrives or he'll be angry with me for trying to do too much.'

Or angry with me for letting you, thought Freya, as she

searched through kitchen cabinets for the sterile gauze and plasters that Kathleen swore were there. All the while, she berated herself for not preventing the fall from happening. If only she hadn't nipped upstairs to tackle the damn cobwebs.

Fortunately, Kathleen seemed much recovered when Freya went back into the sitting room with a bowl of water and the gauze and plasters she'd found shoved behind a mini-mountain of tinned tomatoes. And she sipped calmly at the tea Freya had made, while her wounds were cleaned.

'Do you have any antiseptic cream?' asked Freya, dropping the bloodied gauze into a plastic bag. 'I think I've got all of the dirt out of your knees but you can never tell.'

Kathleen thought for a moment. 'I think there's an old first aid kit in the drawer in my bedroom. There might be antiseptic cream in that, though I can't swear to it. I am sorry to be causing such a fuss.'

Freya patted her hand. 'You're no fuss at all. These things happen. I'll nip upstairs and see if I can find it.'

Kathleen's bedroom was as gloomy as always, even on a bright day like today. Outside, the sheet that had caused so much trouble was flapping on the line, above a basket of wet bedding that was now upended in the mud. Those sheets and duvet covers would need another wash.

Puffing out her cheeks, Freya went to the small dressing table and pulled open the drawer. It was crammed full of photographs. Her eye was immediately drawn to a photo of a chubby baby with a gap-toothed grin, presumably Chloe. Next to it was a colour photo of a middle-aged Kathleen standing next to her husband. He was handsome, and looked taller than the stooped man with white hair standing next to an older Kathleen in a picture frame downstairs.

Freya ran her fingers across the picture, realising that she and Ryan had something in common – they'd both lost their fathers, and that was a hard loss to bear.

It had been ten years since her own father's death, but grief still had a habit of taking her by surprise. A few bars of his favourite music could move her to tears. And recently, she'd cried in the Co-op when the man ahead of her in the queue had on the same kind of polo shirt her dad used to wear. For one bittersweet second, she'd thought it was him before the reality that she'd never see her dad again had come crashing in. The young lad at the till had reddened with embarrassment when she handed over a five-pound note while tears dripped off the end of her nose.

Freya spotted a photo of Ryan, taken some years ago, and picked it up for a closer look. His hair was longer and darker, with no hint of grey, and he looked happier. He looked handsome, like his father, and less weighed down by life.

Standing beside him was Natalie, and Freya peered curiously at this woman from the past. She was so pretty with her long dark hair and she was smiling into the camera, totally oblivious to the tragedy that lay ahead.

Freya shivered as she returned the photo and closed the drawer. For all her snooping – well, what felt like snooping – there was no antiseptic cream in there. Only memories of a time before life had changed for ever.

She looked around the room. The only other possibility was Kathleen's bedside table, which had two small drawers beneath it. The top one contained a jumble of belongings including a man's silver watch, an old mobile phone and a pair of men's glasses whose lenses were filmed with dust. They must all have belonged to Frank, thought Freya, a lump in her throat. He'd been dead for eight long years but here, in Kathleen's bedroom, it was as though he'd just stepped out for a moment, leaving his belongings behind.

Freya was about to close the drawer, feeling she was intruding on another person's grief, when she spotted another faded colour photo. The woman gazing unsmiling into the camera – and from the drawer directly at Freya – was young, probably in her late teens, with a trailing yellow scarf tied around her flaming red hair. She was wearing a simple cotton dress, belted at the waist, and the dark pigmentation of a birthmark was spread across her cheek.

It was Kathleen, and she was standing in front of Driftwood House.

Freya pulled the photo from the drawer and examined it properly. The location was unmistakeable. Kathleen was on the clifftop, her bright hair blowing in the breeze and the waves below her tipped with white. And behind her stood the magnificent house, looking much as it did today, even though the photo must have been taken well over half a century ago. The stone was white-washed and Freya could make out seagulls circling above the russet-tiled roof.

Kathleen must have visited Heaven's Cove as a young woman. Who took the photo? wondered Freya. And why did Kathleen look so sad?

Freya glanced out of the window, at the cliff in the distance and Driftwood House perched on top of it. Kathleen seemed drawn to this view of the isolated, weather-beaten house, and here she was, standing in front of it decades ago.

Freya pushed the photo back where it had been. She was making something out of nothing and seeing mysteries when there were none. People often looked serious in old photos, didn't they? And although Kathleen had told her she'd visited Heaven's Cove for the first time after her husband died, maybe she'd simply forgotten a long-ago trip.

Freya pulled open the second drawer in the bedside table and there, amongst a heap of colourful silk scarves, was a battered green box marked with a red cross. Inside was a small pair of silver scissors, a bandage yellowed with age and a small pink tube of antiseptic cream. It was old but better than nothing. She'd nip to the shops for new supplies once she was sure Kathleen was OK to be left alone.

Freya tried to put the photograph out of her mind when she went downstairs with the cream and dabbed it on Kathleen's knees, before covering the wounds with large plasters.

Kathleen stretched her legs out straight. 'There you go. Right as rain again. Ah, no.' She grimaced at the sound of the front door opening. 'I thought we'd got away with it but here comes trouble.'

11

FREYA

Ryan was tired. Freya could tell from the drooping of his shoulders when he walked into the sitting room. But he smiled at his mother before catching sight of her knees and frowning.

'Mum, what on earth happened?'

'Nothing, really. Don't fuss now. I tripped over my own feet in the garden, that's all.'

'Did you fall over?' Ryan knelt down to inspect her battered knees. 'You need to be more careful, Mum.'

'I'm absolutely fine, Ryan. My knees are a little bruised, and so is my pride. Fancy falling over my own two feet!'

'You're lucky that you didn't break something. Are you sure you're OK?' When Kathleen nodded, Ryan glanced at Freya. 'Were you there when Mum fell over?'

'No, I was upstairs but I heard Kathleen calling from the garden.'

'Freya heard me straight away and she's been absolutely marvellous with sorting me out and cleaning me up,' said Kathleen briskly, but Ryan ignored her and addressed Freya again.

'I thought you'd moved in to stop this kind of thing from happening.'

Freya, feeling guilty enough already, opened her mouth to reply but Kathleen jumped back in.

'Cop on to yourself, Ryan. That's not fair. Freya can't be watching over me twenty-four hours a day. Sure, if it wasn't for her, I'd still be lying in the garden, getting cold. Or even worse, having to holler for Ted to pick me up. Just think what a fuss that would have caused.'

'That's one small mercy, I suppose.' He rubbed his eyes. 'Sorry. It's only half past two, but it's been a long day already. A work appointment fell through and Chloe's going through a particularly challenging phase.'

'Is she all right?' asked Kathleen, shifting in her chair and wincing when she moved her legs.

'She's all right, I think. Just secretive and abrupt – which is typical behaviour for a twelve-year-old I guess.' He shrugged. 'If you're sure you're OK, Mum, can I get myself a cup of tea? Would you like a top-up?'

'No, thank you. But you have a drink and a digestive. Freya filled the biscuit tin this morning, and I expect there's still tea in the pot.'

After making sure Kathleen was settled comfortably in her chair, Freya followed Ryan into the kitchen. He was standing with his hands on the worktop and his head bent as he waited for the kettle to boil.

'The tea's lukewarm so I'm making some more,' he said, glancing round. 'Would you like a cup?'

'Yes, thank you. That would be great.' She hesitated. 'Are you all right?'

'Yeah, fine. Why wouldn't I be? The tea won't be long.'

While Ryan poured boiling water into the pot, Freya nipped into the garden, picked up the muddied sheets and bundled them back into the washing machine. Then she sat at the kitchen table, wishing she'd turned down his offer of a drink. This was going to be awkward. Ryan didn't approve of her being in his mother's house. He'd made that plain enough over the last couple of weeks. And Kathleen's fall had presumably cemented his low opinion of her.

She'd hoped he might be thawing a week ago, when he'd waved to her in the village. But since then he'd gone straight back to being cool and distant whenever he called in – which was still several times a day. Quite what he thought she was going to do to his mother, Freya didn't know. But he obviously felt he needed to keep an eye on things. And after today's fall, who could blame him?

Ryan placed Freya's cup of tea on the kitchen table and then, to her alarm, brought his own cup to the table and sat down opposite her. *Right, get in first*, thought Freya, folding her fingers around the hot china.

'I'm very sorry about your mum's accident. I didn't realise she'd gone into the garden and was trying to hang out the washing. I'd have helped her if I'd known. I promise you I've never had a client fall on my watch before, even though many of the residents in the care home were very wobbly on their feet. However, I realise that's little comfort to you so I promise to keep an even better eye on your mum in future.'

Ryan stared at her for a moment, before sitting back in his chair and breathing out loudly. 'Don't worry about it. I know I sounded accusatory in there because I was worried about Mum. But realistically, I know she often tries to do more than she should.'

Freya's shoulders dropped from around her ears. 'It's pretty normal. I saw it in the care home all the time.'

A memory slammed into her mind of an elderly lady, Phoebe, riddled with arthritis but grimly determined that she could still dress herself. And she had, right up until she'd died a few months ago, with Freya holding her hand.

Freya blinked to ward off tears for lovely, determined Phoebe, whom she missed. 'It's hard accepting that you can't do the things that you always used to do. It can be hard to come to terms with the fact that you're getting old and won't do some things ever again.'

Ryan nodded slowly. 'I saw that with Dad, who pushed himself when he shouldn't have. He tried to take down the Christmas tree without any help, slipped and ended up spending his last couple of weeks in hospital with a broken hip. At least Mum is still in her own home and sleeping in her own bed with all her things around her.'

'Exactly. And I'm here to help her stay in this cottage and to make her life easier and safer. Apart from the um... the falling in the garden thing.'

Freya winced but Ryan shook his head.

'Mum seems all right and at least bashing her knees isn't as bad as almost setting fire to the place.'

'No, that was a bit scary. But don't worry. I don't let your mother go within ten paces of the cooker and I've hidden all the matches.'

There was a beat of silence during which Freya wondered if she'd totally misjudged Ryan's lighter mood, and her month-long trial with Kathleen was about to end prematurely.

But to her relief, amusement twinkled in Ryan's eyes and he smiled – not the strained, polite smile she'd grown accustomed to, but a proper smile that lit up his face. It made him look younger and less severe.

'Keeping my mother away from fire sounds very wise. How is it really going around here?'

She grinned back at him. 'Falls aside, it's going pretty well. At least, I think it is. It's not easy having someone new in your home but your mum seems to be adapting well, and I really like her. She reminds me of some of my favourite residents at the care home. She's very spirited.'

Ryan raised an eyebrow. 'That's one way of describing her. Bloody-minded is another. My mother can be very stubborn at times and, unfortunately for me, I think her granddaughter is following in her footsteps.'

He picked up his cup and took a sip of tea.

'It must be difficult, bringing up a child who's almost a teenager on your own,' ventured Freya, remembering her adolescent years. She'd driven her poor dad to distraction with her loud music and combative attitude. The transition from child to adult had been very difficult, perhaps more so because, like Chloe, she'd had no mother to guide her through the hormonal upheaval.

'She's not even a teenager yet! And it's certainly more challenging than I thought it would be,' admitted Ryan, tracing his finger along a scratch in the kitchen table. 'To be honest, I don't really know what I'm doing.'

He said the last bit so quietly, Freya hardly caught his words and wasn't sure she was supposed to. But she wanted to keep the conversation going. Ryan looked as if he needed someone to talk to, and at least he wasn't interrogating her about her treatment of his mother.

'How's Chloe getting on at school?' she asked.

'Why?' Did Mum say something?'

'No, it's just...'

I think she's in with the wrong crowd. I saw her jump from the cliffs into the sea.

She couldn't say it. She'd made a promise to Chloe, and Ryan already looked as though the weight of the world was on his shoulders. His daughter's ill-advised leap would have to remain a secret, albeit one that Freya would rather not keep.

She shrugged. 'School can be tough at Chloe's age. Life in general can be hard when there are a lot of hormones starting to swoosh around.'

'Hormones! Heaven help me. And that can only get worse, right?' Ryan puffed out his cheeks. 'It's at times like this that she really needs a mother.'

Ryan looked so done in, Freya had an urge to scoot round the table and put her arm around his shoulders.

Instead, she waited a moment before asking, 'I don't mean to intrude, but does Chloe get on well with Isobel? Your mum told me that her daughter and Chloe are great friends, and that you and Isobel are... quite friendly.'

Were Ryan and Isobel in a relationship? Kathleen didn't seem wholly sure, but Freya assumed it had been Isobel she'd seen with Ryan in the village a week ago. The striking blonde woman had been standing so close to him, one step forward and she'd have been in his arms. Freya was taking a gamble with this conversation. But Ryan genuinely seemed to need help.

'Do you think Chloe should talk to Isobel?' he asked.

'I don't know Isobel and I don't know how Chloe feels about her. But if they get on well, perhaps she might be someone for Chloe to confide in.'

'Yeah, maybe,' said Ryan, not looking wholly convinced. 'Though I think she's more likely to talk to Paige, Isobel's daughter, about how she's feeling. They're thick as thieves.'

Freya hoped not, if Paige was the tall, blonde girl who'd been encouraging Chloe to jump from the cliff below Driftwood House. But she couldn't say that to Ryan. She couldn't say anything about the very first time she'd met his daughter.

Ryan put down his cup. 'I'd better get back to work because I have a marketing brochure to write. Then I'll be peeling potatoes for tonight's tea and spending my evening trying to convince my daughter that I'm not the enemy.'

'That sounds like fun.'

'Oh yeah, my life is a heady round of non-stop excitement.'

He gave a rueful smile and looked at Freya. His eyes were tired but they were the most beautiful shade of green, like the emerald in her mother's engagement ring. Freya knew she was staring but she couldn't look away as his eyes locked onto hers. She could hardly breathe.

Suddenly, the kitchen floor started moving as the washing machine began to grumble and shake. Freya jumped up in alarm but Ryan got to his feet slowly.

'It does that sometimes. I think it's on its last legs but Mum doesn't want to get another one. Perhaps you can persuade her.' He put his cup into the dishwasher and paused at the door. 'I'll check on Mum on my way out. Let me know if there are any problems with her, and I guess I'll see you soon.'

Freya knelt down by the washing machine as Ryan went into the sitting room and she heard the door close behind him. Her emotions felt as tangled as the muddied sheets twisting round and round.

One minute she was apologising to Ryan for his mum's fall and feeling awkward. The next, she was staring into his eyes and little shocks of desire were shuddering through her. Honestly, all he'd done was drop his general arseyness and reveal a hint of vulnerability and she'd been ready to fling herself at him. And just for a moment, she'd imagined he felt the same spark between them.

When the machine started to move even more violently on the tiles, Freya stood up and pressed her hands down on it. The pressure calmed the mini earthquake but sent shockwaves up her arms that made her teeth rattle.

I need a good shake, thought Freya. I need to concentrate more on my job and less on flights of fancy. Because the truth of it is, I'm a carer, recently separated from her husband, who's been employed to look after Ryan's mother, and he's a single parent who's still madly in love with the ghost of his dead wife.

That did the trick. A dose of reality made Freya feel much steadier, in spite of the washing machine shockwaves still juddering through her – steadier but just a tiny bit disappointed.

12

FREYA

Great swathes of greenery stretched towards the purple horizon. The land was littered with chunks of grey stone that had tumbled from the nearest tor – a raised outcrop of rock that punctuated the wide open countryside. And a family of short, big-bellied ponies were picking their way along the banks of a fast-rushing stream.

'It's amazing,' murmured Freya, mostly to herself. But Kathleen, sitting in the passenger seat next to her, nodded in agreement.

'I thought you'd like it. Ryan knows how much I love Dartmoor so he brings me out here often. There's something about the wildness of the place that reminds me of growing up in Ireland. It's a shame about the weather.' She chuckled. 'Though that reminds me of home too.'

Freya turned on the windscreen wipers to clear the drizzle that had started to fall from a leaden sky.

She and Kathleen had managed a short walk before the rain set in, Kathleen leaning on her arm as they made their way across the moor. But Freya didn't mind the weather. A mist had lowered and was starting to shroud the top of the tor, making the ancient landscape even more atmospheric. It truly was breath-taking.

'Thank you for bringing me out here,' said Kathleen, giving her knees a rub.

'Are you sure you didn't walk too far?'

'We hardly walked at all.' Kathleen sounded faintly disapproving. 'In my heyday, I could have walked for miles.'

'It's good to keep active whatever your age, but I don't want you to do too much. It's only ten days since your fall and it can take a while to fully recover.'

'And now you sound just like Ryan.'

When Kathleen pursed her lips, she reminded Freya of Greg at the few networking events they'd attended together. He'd been paranoid that she would say something 'inappropriate', though she wasn't quite sure what. She was hardly likely to swear loudly or insult someone's fashion sense. But his apprehension had made her nervous about saying anything at all, so she tended to be quiet, which he found equally irritating.

Freya tried to focus on Ryan rather than her ex-husband. She seemed to be thinking less and less of Greg these days.

'Ryan worries about you,' she told Kathleen. 'And he was kind enough to put me on his insurance so I could take you out for a drive.'

Kathleen smiled, her irritation short-lived. 'He's a good boy. Children are a blessing, don't you think?'

A pang of sorrow for the children she'd never have surged through Freya but her voice was level when she replied: 'I imagine they are. How long had you and Frank been together when Ryan was born?'

Kathleen didn't reply. She was gazing out of the rain-streaked windscreen, lost in thought. As heavier rain started to patter on the car roof, Freya settled back into the driver's seat. It was strange sitting here, where Ryan often sat, surrounded by his belongings.

A bottle of de-icer and a folded map were in the pocket of the car door, and a half-eaten packet of chocolate Hobnobs was on the back seat – possibly a bribe to improve Chloe's mood.

She could imagine Ryan negotiating the narrow lanes of Heaven's Cove behind this steering wheel. Listening to the radio which, she'd noticed, was tuned to a station that played hits of the nineties. She wondered if he took Isobel out for drives, to Dartmoor or to other beautiful isolated places where they could be alone.

Freya hadn't been alone with Ryan for over a week, not since they'd talked in the kitchen after Kathleen's fall. She went a bit hot and cold when she remembered that afternoon. The fact that Ryan had opened up to her was great. He'd also stopped checking up on her so much recently. But the strong attraction she'd felt towards him wasn't ideal. It was a complication she didn't need, and she only hoped that Ryan hadn't picked up on what she'd been thinking.

'You can have a biscuit if you want,' said Kathleen, snapping Freya out of her reverie. 'I'm sure Ryan won't mind. He's always got a stash of biscuits hidden away somewhere. Just like his father, who couldn't go more than a couple of hours without a snack. He'd get very bad-tempered, otherwise. What do young people call it nowadays? H, something?'

'Hangry,' said Freya, turning on the ignition and reversing very slowly out of her parking place.

It *was* very good of Ryan to lend her his car but she was nervous about pranging it and had never driven so carefully. It was a slightly battered Volvo, nothing new or fancy, but she didn't want to batter it any more.

The sky cleared when they drove away from Dartmoor towards the coast. And as the car crested a hill and Heaven's Cove lay ahead of them, Kathleen asked: 'So what do you think of it around here? Do you think you'll stay?'

Freya glanced at Kathleen, who was staring straight ahead.

The end of their month-long trial period was getting closer and Freya had wondered if Kathleen would mention it.

'Would you like me to stay?' she asked.

'I believe I would. It's very helpful having you around, and I think we're muddling along pretty well.'

'I think so too,' said Freya, pulling over to the side of the lane to let an approaching tractor trundle past.

'Good. Shall we just carry on as we are then, for the time being? Once the month is up, I mean.'

Freya smiled. 'That sounds fine by me.' She'd grown fond of the elderly lady over the last three weeks and was charmed by the pretty seaside village. She'd very much like to stay.

'Excellent. That's sorted then.'

Kathleen gave a small nod before pulling sunglasses from her handbag and putting them on.

Heaven's Cove was bathed in early April sunshine and looked absolutely beautiful. Ancient cottages huddled together with the tower of the church poking above them. The ruins of Heaven's Cove castle were just visible at the far edge of the village and, where the land ended, the blue sea sparkled as if it was encrusted with diamanté.

'Let's not go straight home,' said Kathleen, sitting up straighter. 'Why don't you drive up onto the headland? The views will be wonderful on a day like today and I haven't been up there for ages.'

'Sure,' said Freya, doing a swift right-hand turn onto the narrow track that led to the top of the cliff.

'What are you doing?' asked Kathleen sharply.

Freya glanced at her passenger who sounded panicked.

'I thought you wanted to go to the top of the headland.'

She swore under her breath as the car lurched in and out of a pothole.

'Not this headland. This is the cliff. I meant Cora Head, the headland that's over there, beyond the castle.'

Kathleen jabbed her finger towards the piece of land at the far end of the village that jutted out into the ocean. The headland that Freya had seen from Belinda's window on her first day in Heaven's Cove.

'Sorry, Kathleen. I didn't realise. I thought you wanted me to drive up here.'

'No. You need to turn around. Now.'

Freya looked at the bumpy narrow track rising steeply ahead of them. It wasn't doing the car any good, and the rough ground that edged it looked even more likely to take out the car's suspension.

'I'm not sure I can turn around.'

'Please. You have to.'

Kathleen was sounding very panicky now but there was nothing Freya could do.

'If I go to the top, I'll be able to turn around,' she said, her voice wavering as the car hit another pothole.

She didn't envy people staying at the guesthouse who had to negotiate this track frequently. It looked as if efforts had been made to repair some of the holes, but Freya expected it was a losing battle on this exposed, weather-beaten cliff.

Kathleen grew quiet as the car finally reached the top of the cliff. It was even more spectacular up here than Freya had remembered. A swathe of wildflowers had bloomed since her first visit over three weeks ago – that fateful trip when she'd encountered Chloe and Paige, and had ended up with a secret to keep from Ryan.

Then, the cliff had been starkly beautiful under a grey sky. Today, the landscape had exploded with colour. The grass was dotted with clumps of yellow gorse, tall bluebells and violet spring squill. And Driftwood House stood alone, its walls crispwhite against the azure of the sea.

'It's very pretty up here, Kathleen. Do you want to stop at all, to take in the view?'

Kathleen kept her eyes on her hands, neatly folded in her lap. 'No. I'd rather go home now.'

Freya suddenly remembered the photo she'd found of Kathleen, standing in front of Driftwood House as a young woman. She'd put it out of her mind ever since, not wanting to pry. But it had definitely been her – those striking green eyes and her distinctive birthmark were unmistakeable.

As Freya did a bumpy three-point turn, Kathleen didn't lift her eyes once to look at Driftwood House. She'd deliberately chosen a bedroom that overlooked this house, and the photo Freya had found showed she'd once stood in its doorway and gazed across the ocean. But now it seemed that she could hardly bear the place.

Freya bumped back down the track until they reached the lane again that led into Heaven's Cove.

'We can go through the village to the other headland if you'd like and take in the view from there. I'm sure it would be just as good.'

'No, thank you,' said Kathleen primly, her hands still twisted together in her lap. 'If you don't mind, I'm rather tired all of a sudden and would rather go home.'

Freya drove back to the cottage in silence, hardly noticing the tourists thronging the pavements.

She'd misunderstood Kathleen's suggestion and had taken the wrong road to the top of the wrong cliff. It was a simple mistake that had turned out to be a terrible faux pas, though she had no idea why.

13

FREYA

Freya wasn't sure what woke her. At first she thought it was the wind, whistling around the church outside, or the faint boom of waves being whipped up by the breeze and slamming into the stone quayside.

She slipped out of bed, padded to the window and pulled back the curtain. It was still dark but a pale dawn was breaking over the sea. As she watched, shivering in her pyjamas, the golden curve of the sun peeped over the horizon, spreading rays of light.

The flowers that lined the plinth of the old war memorial were swaying in the stiff breeze. But it wasn't the wind that had woken her, she realised. The sounds that had disturbed her were coming from inside the cottage. Small sounds that bounced off the old, thick walls.

Pulling on her dressing gown, Freya went onto the landing and stood still. There was nothing now. No noise apart from the faint creak of old timbers, and she was about to go back to bed when she heard it again. A sniffling sound. She listened for a few moments. Someone was crying.

When Freya knocked gently on Kathleen's door, the sniffling stopped. Should she leave it and go back to bed? Kathleen had been a little quiet since they'd returned from their Dartmoor trip two days ago, but she seemed well enough. The traumatic visit to the top of the cliff hadn't been mentioned at all.

She was holding something back, Freya could tell. But didn't most people have secrets they'd rather not share?

Freya had collected dozens of them over the years, very few of them her own. She couldn't sit next to someone on a bus or in the waiting room at the doctors' surgery without hearing their life stories and secrets. There was something about her face that made people want to open up and share all sorts with her.

But Kathleen was different. She rarely spoke about anything personal, including her childhood in Ireland. Which was totally fine. Freya was only there to listen if people wanted to talk.

She'd turned to go back to her room when she heard a sob that brought her up short. Kathleen was breaking her heart, all alone.

Freya knocked on the door again. Kathleen could tell her to go to hell if she wanted, but she couldn't walk away from someone who was so obviously upset.

There was a pause before Kathleen called out tremulously, 'Come in.'

Freya opened the door and poked her head around it. Pale dawn light was peeking under the curtains and Kathleen was lying in bed, her long white hair spread out around her on the pillow.

'I'm so sorry to disturb you, Kathleen, but I heard a noise and wanted to make sure that you're all right.'

'I'm fine,' sniffed Kathleen, rubbing a hand roughly across her cheek. 'I'm sorry if I woke you.'

'I was already stirring, and I wouldn't normally intrude but you sounded upset. Are you feeling ill?'

'No, I'm perfectly well.' There was a catch in her voice when she added: 'I'm afraid I'm just being a silly old woman.'

'You're certainly not silly, and I reckon you're wonderfully mature, not old.'

The ghost of a smile flitted across Kathleen's face as she fished a tissue from beneath her pillow and dabbed at her cheeks. 'You're very kind, Freya. I could tell that the first time we met.'

'And I could tell that you're a strong woman who I'm sure will get through whatever it is that's upsetting you. I'm here if you'd like to talk but I totally get it if you'd rather not.'

Kathleen ran her fingers through her long hair. 'You're not like your sister, are you.'

'Belinda? No, not really. At least I hope I'm not.' Was that terribly disloyal to her sister? Freya felt a pang of guilt that was familiar but irritating none the less. Of course she didn't want to be gossipy and intrusive like Belinda. 'Look, I'll leave you in peace and get back to bed but please call me if you need anything.'

'I will. Thank you, and it's nothing to worry yourself about. Really.' Kathleen hesitated. 'It's the date, you see. April the sixth reminds me of someone I lost who meant a great deal to me.'

'I'm so sorry. Anniversaries can be very painful.' Freya thought back to bereaved Clara in the care home, who would sob on the twelfth of each month as it marked another month without her husband.

Every month takes me further away from him, she would tell Freya, tears in her eyes. *How can I live without him by my side?* She couldn't, it turned out. Clara joined her beloved husband less than a year after he'd passed away.

Kathleen was staring at the small framed photo of Frank on her bedside table.

'Is April the sixth the day that your husband passed away?' asked Freya gently.

Kathleen startled and stared at Freya as though she'd forgotten she was there. Then she blinked and pulled herself higher in the bed.

'That's right. Frank was getting more fragile and then he broke his hip, which was more than his body could cope with. He died in hospital.'

'That must have been heart-breaking.'

'It was.' Kathleen drew in a deep breath and gave a no-nonsense shake of the head. 'But it was a while ago now and life must go on. I'm so sorry to have woken you up, Freya. Get yourself back to bed before you get cold. I dare say I'll drowse on and off until the sun's fully up. But,' she added, just before Freya disappeared, 'thank you for your concern. It's good to know that you care.'

Freya went back to her room and got into bed, glad to feel the warmth of the duvet around her.

She felt so sorry for Kathleen, grieving alone for the man she'd lost. Losing Greg was hard enough but at least she knew he was still breathing somewhere. *He's probably in bed right now with perfect Erica,* said the little voice in her brain. But she was getting better these days at ignoring it so it wasn't her own destructive thoughts that kept her awake until her alarm went off.

Something was niggling at the edges of her brain. Something was off in her exchange with Kathleen, something that Freya couldn't quite put her finger on.

14

RYAN

Ryan picked Chloe's jacket up off the floor and hung it on the coat hooks under the stairs. Then he tidied up her shoes and pushed her abandoned backpack into the downstairs cupboard.

Her new skirt, bought during a shopping expedition with Paige, was still draped unworn over the banisters, and he placed it on the bottom step to take up later. It was quite short, far shorter, he was sure, than her mum would have liked. But Natalie wasn't here, and he couldn't face another row with Chloe, who seemed to take offence at everything he said these days.

Once they'd been as thick as thieves. It was him and Chloe against the world from the moment Natalie died. But recently their relationship had changed. His daughter – their daughter – was more secretive these days and definitely more liable to throw a strop and storm off.

It was normal, he supposed. She was almost a teenager and he wasn't her mum, but that didn't make it any easier. Heaven knew how things might deteriorate once her adolescence got into full swing. He'd been quite a handful in his teens, and that was with the steadying influence of both parents to guide him.

'I'm sorry I'm getting it all wrong, but what should I do?' he said, to the photo of Natalie that was hanging on the hall wall.

Then he felt foolish. Who asked their dead wife for advice? Natalie's soulful eyes seemed to follow and chastise him as he picked the post off the doormat and placed it on the hall table.

He'd started rifling through the envelopes when someone knocked on his front door. When he opened it, Freya was standing on his doorstep. She fidgeted as though he made her nervous, which made him feel awful. Was he really so scary?

It was his own fault, he realised. He hadn't wanted Freya to move in with his mother. He'd thought the whole idea was bonkers so he'd been rather unwelcoming.

But recently, he'd started to appreciate the benefit of having someone keeping an eye on his mum. And Freya seemed to be doing a good job. His mother was eating better and she'd even seen the doctor to talk about her worsening arthritis, which Ryan had been trying to persuade her to do for weeks. The more her joints hurt, the more unsteady she was on her feet.

'Is everything OK?' asked Ryan, suddenly worried that his mum might have had another fall.

'Yes, there's nothing to worry about,' said Freya in a rush. 'I'm here because your mum asked me to drop this in to you. She found it behind the back of the sofa and thought Chloe had left it at our house.' She corrected herself. 'At her house.'

Ryan took the jumper that Freya pulled from her straw basket. 'Yep, that's Chloe's. Thanks for delivering it. How is Mum doing?'

'She doesn't seem too bad. Her knees aren't bothering her too much.'

'I meant generally, really. How do you, as a professional, think she's doing?'

Freya relaxed at that and gave a smile that made her face light up. 'She has some mobility issues as you know – the fall proved that. But overall she's doing remarkably well. We had a nice walk up on Dartmoor a couple of days ago. She leaned on me the whole time but honestly, it's impressive to see her up and about and keen to be active.'

'That's my mother for you.' Ryan hesitated. 'What are you doing now?'

'I'm going for a walk into the village during my lunch break. Your mum's having a nap and said she didn't need me for a while.'

'I thought you might be heading for the beach while the sun's out.'

'That's a good idea. I've only managed to get to the beach twice since I arrived, and it was drizzling the first time and foggy the second, so I didn't see it at its best.'

'You can't beat Heaven's Cove beach in the sunshine.' Ryan drew in a deep breath of air that smelled of the sea. 'Actually, I'm going to Liam's farm, which is out that way, so why don't I walk with you?'

Why had he said that? Freya's expressive grey eyes widened slightly but then she nodded. 'Great. If you're going that way anyway, why not?'

Ryan grabbed his jacket and closed the front door behind him. Well, this was going to be awkward, thanks to that strange moment between them when they were drinking tea in the kitchen after his mum's fall. Unless he'd just imagined it, of course.

That kitchen conversation, when Freya was so warm and understanding, had been the moment when he'd started to trust that maybe she was the right person to look after his mum. But then things had turned awkward, or they had in his mind, at least. And now this walk was going to be mega-awkward too.

Oh well. He only had himself to blame. Ryan zipped up his jacket and strode off towards the centre of Heaven's Cove, with Freya by his side.

After a while, once he began to relax, he started pointing out some of the village's highlights.

'Chloe loves the ice-cream parlour, Pauline's tea shop does a mean cream tea, and that, over there, is the best chippie on the Devon coast. Not that we're obsessed with food in Heaven's Cove.'

When he laughed, he noticed Freya glance at him and smile. She looked nice when she smiled. Less worn down by life. He knew very little about what had brought her to Heaven's Cove, but he recognised damage when he saw it. Someone or something had hurt Freya badly. He gave his head a slight shake. Not that it was his problem or, indeed, his business. All he cared about was that she took good care of his mother.

That's not quite true, said the little voice in his head that tormented him in the early hours with talk of Natalie and what he'd done. He felt some kind of pull towards Freya that he couldn't explain. Whatever it was, he had to ignore it. She worked for his mother and she didn't know what kind of a man he was.

Did Isobel feel a similar pull towards him? he wondered. She still seemed keen for them to go on a date, even though he'd continued to dodge her requests. His gentle rejection only seemed to make her more determined. And he couldn't deny that she was an extremely attractive woman.

She's a stunner, mate! I would. That was Jamie's comment when she'd sashayed into the pub, just after her split from her antiques dealer boyfriend. Jamie would, but he didn't have a dead wife and a shedload of guilt to put the brakes on.

Jamie didn't fear that, deep down, he was not the sort of man any woman should be with.

As though thinking about her had conjured her up, Isobel suddenly appeared around the corner of Stan's grocery shop. She waved when she saw Ryan and walked over, her blonde hair swinging around her shoulders.

'Hello, stranger. Long time no see.'

Ryan nodded, even though he'd bumped into Isobel in the newsagent's just yesterday. He was bumping into her so often these days, sometimes he wondered if she was stalking him.

'Who's this?' asked Isobel, looking at Freya. Her wide, bright smile had slipped slightly.

'This is Freya, who's staying with my mum for a while. Don't—'

Don't you remember that I waved to her? Ryan didn't finish the sentence. He'd waved at Freya after responding like an idiot to Isobel's loaded invitation to go for a drink. He really didn't want to remind her of that.

'Don't what? Frighten her off?' Isobel laughed. 'It's nice to meet you, Freya. I'm Isobel, Ryan's good friend.' She smiled up at him before turning her attention back to Freya. 'Tell me, how is Kathleen doing these days? I haven't seen her for a while.'

'She's absolutely fine, thank you,' said Freya, taking a step away from Ryan.

'That's good. So you've moved in with her to... what? Have little chats?'

Isobel was still smiling but Freya tensed beside him. 'We do chat, and I'm enjoying keeping Kathleen company. She's an interesting woman to talk to. I'm a qualified and experienced carer, so I'm able to provide a range of care. Whatever Kathleen needs to make her life easier.'

'Excellent. It sounds like you're just the woman for the job.'

'I hope so,' said Freya, side-stepping a child on a bicycle who was weaving along the pavement.

'How long are you here?' Isobel glared at the child, who wobbled off obliviously.

'I'm not sure.' Freya glanced up at Ryan. 'It depends how things go.'

'Let's hope that things go really well, then,' said Isobel, not sounding terribly sincere. 'So where are you two off to?'

She aimed the question at Ryan but Freya answered.

'I'm going to the beach and Ryan was walking the same way so he's kindly pointing out some of Heaven's Cove's best bits.'

'Is that right?' Isobel put her hand on his sleeve and folded her fingers around his arm. 'You really are a pushover, Ryan. I don't think tour guide features in your list of responsibilities as an employer, does it?'

A pushover? Ryan felt his hackles rise but forced himself to answer politely. 'Technically, it's my mother employing Freya, not me.'

'Of course. I should have realised that Kathleen is Freya's boss.'

Ryan was starting to feel very uncomfortable. There was a strange atmosphere between the two women and he wanted to get away, but Isobel was hanging onto his arm for dear life.

She raised an eyebrow. 'Well, I do hope you won't both be stripping off on the beach. The sun's out but it's still pretty chilly. We don't want you getting hypothermia, Freya, when you've only just arrived in the village.'

Freya gave a tight smile. 'I only have time for a quick look at the beach because I have to get back for Kathleen.'

'So we'd better get on,' said Ryan swiftly.

'Right.' Isobel loosened her grip on his arm. 'It was absolutely lovely to meet you at last, Freya. And I'll see you in the pub soon, Ryan.'

She gave him a wink before walking off towards the village hall. Ryan watched her go with relief. He could be oblivious. Natalie had often told him he was hopeless at reading the room, especially when it came to women. But Isobel seemed very put out by Freya's presence in the village and in his life. Did she think he was going to fall for his mum's carer?

The encounter put an end to the small talk between him and Freya, and they walked on through the village in silence and onto the lane, flanked by high hedges, that led to the beach.

When they reached Cove Farmhouse, Ryan stopped.

'I'm nipping in here to pick up some veg. As you know, the beach is at the end of the lane, if you walk straight on.'

'Oh, of course. Thanks. I'll head off then.'

When a pink stain flushed across Freya's cheeks, Ryan wondered if she'd expected him to go to the beach with her. Should he go with her? Part of him would like to.

'Hey, Ryan.'

Liam was waving from the farmyard. He put down the hosepipe he was using to spray the yard and walked over with his dog, Billie, bounding at his heels. There was a new spring in Liam's step these days, ever since he'd taken up with Rosie Merchant at Driftwood House. The two of them seemed ideally suited – Ryan often saw them walking hand in hand through the village, and he envied them that first flush of love when anything seemed possible. Before real life stuck its oar in.

Ryan gave himself a mental shake. He was in danger of becoming a cynical and bitter old man if he didn't watch it. Not everyone's love story ended as tragically as his.

'Earth to Ryan!'

Liam was talking to him. 'Sorry, what did you say?'

Liam laughed. 'I said how are you and are you after some of my amazing produce?'

'I'll take some carrots, and a very large cabbage if you have one? I'm still trying to get Chloe to eat her greens.'

'Sure. There's plenty in the barn.' Liam tilted his head to one side and looked at Freya. 'Who's this, then? Are you two out for a walk?'

'Sorry, I should have introduced you. This is Freya, who's just moved to the village.'

'Ah, so this is the famous Freya. I've heard all about you from Belinda.'

Freya blinked, presumably wondering what her loose-lipped sister was going round telling everyone.

'She said you're staying with Kathleen for a while to help her out. Is your mum OK, Ryan?'

'I think so. Just getting older.'

Liam rolled his eyes. 'Tell me about it. My mum and dad are starting to creak a bit, and Dad's getting more forgetful by the day.'

He said it lightly but Ryan knew how much Liam worried about his father. Only last week Robert had been found wandering around the village, unable to remember how to get home.

It was good that Liam still lived here in the handsome farmhouse with his parents. Though he spent most of his free time at Driftwood House, if Belinda's gossip was to be believed. Ryan stole a glance at Freya, who was standing on tiptoes, trying to glimpse the sea at the end of the lane. It really was hard to believe that Freya and Belinda were related.

'How's Rosie these days?' he asked. 'I haven't bumped into her in a while.'

Liam beamed. 'She's great, thanks, and her business is starting to take off.'

'Rosie is Liam's fiancée and she runs the guesthouse on the cliff,' Ryan told Freya. He was only including her in the conversation to be polite so he was surprised when Freya's eyes opened wide.

'Is that Driftwood House?'

'That's right. Do you know it?' asked Liam, bending to pat Billie.

'I've been to the top of the cliff a couple of times and seen the house from a distance. It looks amazing.'

'It really is.'

'How old is the building?' asked Freya, sounding very interested in the place.

Everyone knew Driftwood House. It was the first building

you spotted when you drove towards the village from Dartmoor, and it was a landmark for local sailors.

Liam shrugged. 'I'm not sure. Rosie would know because she's got the deeds for the place.'

'How long has it been a guesthouse?'

'Not long. Just a few months since Rosie took on the house after her mum died. Her mum lived there for years,' replied Liam, his mouth lifting in amusement at Freya's enthusiasm. 'Why do you want to know?'

Why indeed, thought Ryan, wondering why Freya seemed so animated about the house that was a white smudge on the cliff from here.

Freya's cheeks flushed as she laughed. 'Sorry to bang on about the house. I was just curious about the people who've lived there over the years. It's an intriguing place, up there on its own.'

Liam bent down to pat Billie again and nodded. 'Rosie loves it and so do I. Mind you, the whole of Heaven's Cove is pretty special. Do you like it?'

'I do, very much, and it's lovely to be so near the sea.' Freya smiled. 'I'm heading for the beach right now, actually. Ryan offered to keep me company on the way.'

'The beach is great, especially on a day like this.' Liam rubbed his muddy hands down his thighs. 'Why don't you go too, Ryan, and you can pick up the veg on the way back? I'll have it ready for you.'

Ryan hesitated. He hadn't planned on accompanying Freya to the cove but Liam had already turned and was heading towards the barn. He gave them a wave and disappeared inside.

'OK.' Ryan took a deep breath, not sure why he felt so flustered about spending another ten minutes alone with Freya. 'Let's go and see the beach, then.'

15

RYAN

They walked on in silence to the end of the lane. The worn tarmac turned to sand and suddenly they were at the edge of the cove that formed a perfect semi-circle.

'Wow!' exclaimed Freya, looking around in wonder.

That had been Ryan's reaction when he'd first seen the secluded cove bathed in sunshine, and Chloe, younger then and less cynical, had loved it too. Even now, in her grumpiest moments, she never criticised the beach. And it was gratifying to see Freya's delight when she saw it on a beautiful day for the very first time.

'Not bad, huh?' he said, savouring the warmth of the spring sunshine on his face and glad that Freya was seeing the beach at its spring-time best.

The cove was particularly picturesque in spring and summer, when the sea was as blue as the Mediterranean. But it looked amazing too when winter storms rolled in and seagulls were caught in air currents as waves crashed onto the sand.

'Not bad?' said Freya, turning towards him. 'It's absolutely fantastic!'

Her face was glowing; all traces of the defensiveness he'd

spotted in her had disappeared. She looked happy, and very pretty.

Ryan swallowed hard. What was the point in being attracted to Freya? He wasn't much of a catch – a single parent with a stroppy daughter who was barely holding things together. And she wouldn't be interested in him anyway. Not if she knew what he'd done. He suddenly realised that Freya was talking to him. He was making a habit of not listening properly to people today.

'Sorry, what did you say?'

'I asked how long you've lived in Heaven's Cove.'

'Only a couple of years. Chloe and I stayed living in Worcester for a while after Natalie died. But we wanted to move closer to Mum, and Heaven's Cove seemed a great place to bring up Chloe.'

Truth be told, he had to move. He couldn't cope with the guilt every time he drove along the winding piece of road where Natalie's accident had happened. It was a major A-road that he wasn't always able to avoid.

Freya nodded, still gazing at the crescent of sand and sparkling blue sea. Huge boulders had fallen from the red-tinged cliffs that rose at the farthest edge of the cove, and a few small children were splashing in rock pools, looking for crabs. He'd brought Chloe here with her bucket and spade often enough, but nowadays she preferred to go into Exeter shopping with her friends.

Of course she did. She was growing up, and he missed her. He still had her loud, door-slamming physical presence about the house, but he missed her unconditional love. Once she'd believed him capable of achieving anything. Now, more often than not, she rolled her eyes with exasperation when he did or said something that was apparently 'old and out of touch'.

Freya was looking at him strangely. She smiled, concern sparking in her grey eyes.

'Don't worry about showing me the beach if you've got things to do.'

Ryan shrugged. 'I'd rather be here than Zooming with my clients, to be honest, or picking Chloe's clothes up off the floor.'

And it was true, he realised, as Freya took off her trainers and socks and sank her toes into the soft sand. He rarely did the same these days. He rather feared that Chloe's opinion was right and he was becoming stuffy and old. So he slipped off his shoes and socks too and enjoyed the feeling of sand between his toes.

'Shall we walk a little way?' asked Freya. 'I can't be too long because I need to get back for your mum.'

'Sure.'

Together, they walked across the sand until they reached the far end of the cove. The tide was out and the boulders at the base of the cliffs, underwater at high tide, were drying in the sun.

Freya sat down on a large boulder and dipped her feet into the rock pool formed by a hollow in the stone.

'Brrr, it's freezing.' She laughed, but continued to trail her toes in the water as Ryan sat down beside her. Without thinking too much about it, he dipped his feet into the water too and juddered as the cold went through him.

They sat in silence for a few moments, both gazing towards the tide, which was turning. Several people were scattered across the sand but no one was braving the water, which hadn't yet been heated by summer sun.

'This really is a wonderful place to bring up a child,' said Freya at last.

'It is, in many ways. Where were you brought up?' he asked. Getting to know more about Freya seemed easier while they were together in this beautiful place.

'I was raised in the middle of a city, so it was nothing like this. I had the chance to go and live abroad, by the sea, when I was about Chloe's age but, well, it didn't work out.'

'Do you regret that?'

'Sometimes, but I got to stay with my dad so that was good.'

'So it was your mum who you'd have moved to live with if...?' Ryan trailed off, feeling awkward, but Freya nodded.

'That's right. She moved from the UK to Greece after finding the love of her life, who, it turned out, wasn't my dad.'

Ryan winced. 'That sounds messy. So where does Belinda fit into all this?'

'My dad was Belinda's dad too and he left her mum to be with my mum because my mum was the love of *his* life. Ironic, huh?'

Ironic and quite a mess for Freya to navigate as a child. Ryan suddenly wanted to know lots more about this woman who had dropped into their lives from nowhere.

'So what made you think of Heaven's Cove when you were looking for a job? Did you want to live closer to your sister?'

'Half-sister.' Freya took her feet out of the rock pool. 'Not particularly, but I needed a job and Belinda told me about your mum.'

'It must have been difficult for you when the care home closed down.'

'It was, but the home had to close. There was no other choice because the building was damaged. Cracks had started appearing in the plaster and there was some catastrophic failure with the foundations. So me losing my job was nothing to do with the quality of my work.' The defensive tone in her voice was back. 'I outlined my qualifications and experience on my CV,' she continued, 'and I gave you a contact number for my old boss. Did you ring her?'

'I did,' said Ryan quickly, keen to reassure her, 'and she had nothing but good things to say about you. I wasn't implying that losing your job was your fault. But with all your experience I'd imagine finding another job would have been relatively easy. Couldn't you have got a job that was more local to you?'

'Possibly. Probably. But I needed to move away for a while.'

'Why's that?'

He knew he was asking too many questions but he had to know for sure why this woman, who was living in his mother's house, had chosen to come to Heaven's Cove. Even so, he felt like a complete heel when she turned to him, her eyes bright with unshed tears.

'I wanted to get away because my marriage broke up. I was hoping for a fresh start.'

Didn't everyone deserve one of those? She started rubbing at the fourth finger on her left hand, which Ryan had already noticed was ring-less.

'I'm sorry,' he said, feeling totally ineffectual.

Freya sniffed. 'It was for the best, really, though it was hard at the time. Greg and I had been together a long time but we'd grown apart.'

'Do you...?' Ryan hesitated but he'd already started going down this route. 'Do you have any kids?' He assumed not. None had ever been mentioned. But maybe she'd been a very young mum.

Freya stuck out her chin and gazed towards the horizon. 'Nope, kids never happened. I was keen but Greg got busy with his career and his enthusiasm for children waned rather.'

Ryan felt a wave of sadness for this woman, whose fair hair – he couldn't help but notice – was shining gold in the sun. Much as Chloe drove him mad sometimes and filled his life with worry, he wouldn't be without her. How lonely would he have been after Natalie died? How could he have coped with the feelings that threatened to overwhelm him?

'Sorry,' he said again, wishing he'd steered clear of personal subjects but grateful nonetheless that she'd been so candid.

Freya shrugged and shifted round to look at him, her toes leaving damp prints on the rock.

'That's all right. It's just one of those things. I think I'd have been a pretty rubbish mum anyway so it's probably for the best.'

She stopped speaking, and Ryan hesitated. Having seen how caring Freya was with his mother, he doubted her damning prediction of her own parenting skills. But there was no point in saying that, not now he'd upset her.

Change the subject, change the subject, you idiot. 'So tell me more about how Mum is after her fall,' he gabbled.

'She's much better, though today's a sad day for her because of missing your dad.'

Ryan frowned. 'She misses my dad *every* day.'

'Of course, but it must be extra poignant today with it being the anniversary of his death.'

'No, it's not.' He felt rattled now. 'Dad died at the end of January.' He remembered the phone call from the doctor at the hospital as though it was yesterday. *I have some unfortunate news.* That's what the doctor had said, sounding young and embarrassed to be calling about his father's death in the early hours. 'What made you think that the anniversary was today?'

Freya opened her mouth and closed it, then her eyes opened wide. 'Oh, of course. You told me your poor dad passed away soon after he fell while trying to take down the Christmas tree.'

'That's right. He only lived for a couple of weeks or so after he broke his hip.'

'I'm sorry.' Freya, pushed her hands through her hair and turned her face towards the sun. 'I must have misunderstood something your mum said earlier. She seemed a bit low.'

'Mum always gets low at this time of year but she'll never say why so I've given up asking her about it.'

Freya nodded, and they sat in silence for a few moments, lost in their own thoughts.

'So, Ryan.' She turned to him and smiled brightly, the tears that had threatened to fall now gone. 'What are the must-visit places around here, then?'

This was safer territory. Ryan outlined the top tourist attractions and threw in a few places that only the locals knew about. It was relaxing here, sitting on a boulder as waves washed onto the sand, with a woman who didn't know him at all.

After ten more minutes of small talk, Freya glanced at her watch. 'I'd better be getting back or your mum will wonder what's happened to me.'

Ryan got to his feet and brushed sand from his jeans. 'I suppose I'd better go and pay Liam for the cabbage that Chloe will push round her plate later.'

'Ah well, it's worth a try. Getting vegetables into your mother is no walk in the park either.'

Ryan laughed. 'Mum's eating habits have definitely declined since she's lived alone. That's why I'm glad you're there to force-feed her.' Why on earth had he said that? It sounded like he was into elder abuse. 'I don't literally mean...'

He tailed off, feeling ridiculous, but Freya caught his eye and smiled. 'Of course not. Thank you for showing me the beach in the sunshine. It's really beautiful here.'

With one last look around, she clambered off the rock and walked off over the sand. Ryan watched her go, her hips swinging as she crossed the cove.

16

FREYA

Freya could feel Ryan's eyes on her back as she walked across the sand. He'd seemed sorry to see her leave, or perhaps she was imagining things. He'd certainly been attentive and, once she'd relaxed, he was easy to talk to as they'd sat watching the ocean – it was the most at ease she'd felt since arriving in the village.

The frisson of attraction she felt for Ryan was still there. She couldn't deny it – especially when he sat, his handsome face in profile, gazing out to sea. And he'd been pretty sympathetic about her messy life.

But she wasn't kidding herself. Ryan had been press-ganged by Liam into taking her onto the beach and was probably just being polite when he'd asked about her life. Or maybe he was pumping her for information to make sure he hadn't allowed a serial killer to move in with his mother.

Freya suddenly felt sad. The break-up with Greg had dented her self-confidence and made her question people's motives. She was at risk of turning into a wary middle-aged woman. Or Belinda, if she didn't stop asking questions about Driftwood House.

Freya left the sandy beach behind and started walking

along the narrow lane that led back to the village. Ryan seemed a decent man, but he was worn down by life. She could see it in the worry lines around his eyes and hear it in the slightly flat timbre of his deep voice.

Though Isobel seemed keen to bring more fun into his life. Freya could tell by the way Isobel had looked at Ryan earlier, and at her as though she was a threat.

Isobel was wrong. She wasn't a threat, but she was deceptive – she was deceiving Ryan by keeping a secret from him. Not for the first time, Freya wished she'd never come across Chloe leaping into the ocean. His daughter's ill-judged jump and her own promise to stay quiet about it had played across her mind when she and Ryan were talking about children. That, and the fact that Paige, Isobel's daughter, was definitely the blonde girl on the cliff who'd been egging Chloe on. The facial resemblance between mother and child was unmistakeable.

'Bye, Freya. Nice to meet you,' called Liam from the doorstep of his handsome farmhouse, his dog jumping and barking at his heels.

Freya jumped, startled by his voice when she was deep in thought. 'Thanks,' she called out. 'You too.'

She waved, hoping that all the villagers would be as welcoming as handsome Liam. Rosie was a very fortunate woman to have Driftwood House, and Liam to warm her bed.

As she walked back towards the village, Freya's thoughts strayed to her conversation with Kathleen that morning. She'd known there was something off about their exchange but couldn't put her finger on it. Now she knew for sure.

Kathleen had lied to her about the anniversary of her husband's death. It wasn't a big lie, as lies went – Freya had heard worse. Among them the lies that people often told themselves when they shared their innermost secrets with her.

'He'd understand if he found out.' 'I had no choice.' 'I'm coping with it really well.'

Kathleen's lie didn't hurt anyone else. But the truth clearly hurt her and Freya couldn't help wondering who she'd really lost on the sixth of April. It was someone who could still break her heart. A lover, perhaps, who'd once lived at Driftwood House?

Whatever the truth behind it, Freya felt sure that Driftwood House was involved somehow. Why else would Kathleen have kept a photo of herself standing on its front doorstep all those decades ago? And why now would she be too distressed to visit the clifftop, where the house kept watch over the village?

Freya glanced up at Driftwood House, sitting alone under a grey cloud that was about to blot out the sun.

What had happened up there? she wondered, as the stone walls of the isolated house were plunged into shadow. Heaven's Cove seemed a picturesque, benign kind of place, but who knew what secrets were swirling around the village?

Freya was so deep in thought, walking past the castle ruins, she didn't notice Belinda until she almost fell over her.

'Penny for your thoughts,' said her sister, setting her shopping bags down like a barrier in front of Freya's feet. She smoothed down her sensible tweed skirt and folded her arms.

'Hello, Belinda. How are you?' asked Freya, immediately feeling wrong-footed by her sister.

The two of them had spent very little time together since Freya had arrived in Heaven's Cove. This was mostly because Belinda was always busy with her commitments in the village, but Freya was secretly relieved. Making small talk with her sister was never particularly easy.

'I'm well, thank you,' said Belinda, glancing at Freya's jeans, which were smudged with sand. 'What have you been up to?'

'I've been having a look around.'

'Shouldn't you be working?'

Freya groaned quietly. She'd encountered this before –

people thinking that carers should be 'caring' twenty-four-seven, with only the occasional bathroom break allowed.

'I am working but Kathleen's having a nap so I nipped out to do an errand for her and to get some air.'

Belinda leaned forward conspiratorially, her voice laden with sympathy. 'How is dear Kathleen doing after her fall in the garden? That was unfortunate, an accident happening so soon after you'd moved in. I'm not sure that's the way to win Kathleen's heart.'

Freya let the criticism go, focusing instead on how Belinda could possibly know about the fall. It had happened almost two weeks ago now and, as far as she knew, Kathleen hadn't told anyone about it. She seemed rather embarrassed about the whole thing.

Would Ryan have said something to her sister? Probably not. Freya remembered his involuntary wince when he'd mentioned Belinda's name on the beach.

'How did you hear about Kathleen falling over?' asked Freya, deciding on the direct approach for her direct sister.

Belinda tapped her nose. 'I have my sources. I can assure you that very little happens in Heaven's Cove that I don't know about.'

Belinda would be a fabulous recruit for MI5, thought Freya, deciding that Kathleen's fall would not become gossip fodder.

'Kathleen's doing really well,' she told her sister with a beaming smile. 'There's absolutely no need to worry.'

'Did she hurt herself? Elderly people break so easily when they fall over. Has Kathleen been falling a lot recently? Is she unwell?'

Why did Freya get the feeling her sister was trawling for juicy details?

'Not as far as I'm aware,' she told her, adding quickly, 'So where are you off to?'

'I was having a quick stroll and doing some shopping, before the rain sets in later. But I've just been summoned to the village hall because there's a problem with the boiler. Honestly, I don't know what they'd all do around here without me.'

'You're a local VIP,' said Freya, trying to be kind because Belinda, for all her puffed-up self-importance and incessant prying, had found her a job and a home with Kathleen.

'I suppose I am. I'm a local celebrity, if you will.'

Belinda gave a self-satisfied smile as Freya wondered if people, seeing them together, would guess that they were related.

There was a fifteen-year age gap between them and their hair and eyes were different colours. But they had the same oval jawline and their eyes were a similar shape. Perhaps they'd looked more alike as children but Freya had never seen a photo of young Belinda.

Growing up, she'd often wondered about her father's first family and worried that one day he might leave her behind too. But any questions she'd asked about his life before her were brushed aside by her parents.

It was a shame really, thought Freya. Perhaps if she and Belinda had known one another from an early age their relationship now would be less strained. Freya's guilt might have eased, and Belinda might have lost the undercurrent of resentment, overlaid with politeness, that made the back of Freya's neck prickle whenever they were together.

'So how is life going at Kathleen's generally?' asked Belinda. 'I want to hear all about it. Every little detail.'

Behind her a middle-aged couple, locals presumably, spotted Belinda and crossed in double-quick time to the other side of the cobbled street. The woman gave Freya a sympathetic smile when they went past. Freya turned her attention back to her sister.

'There's nothing much to tell. I'm still finding my feet but all's going really well.'

'With the whole family?'

Absolutely. Apart from the completely inappropriate crush I seem to have developed on my employer's son. And apart from the pact I've made with my employer's granddaughter to keep a secret from him.

Freya blinked, aware that Belinda was staring intently at her, as though she knew her sister was keeping secrets.

'I think Ryan and Chloe are adjusting to me being there.'

Had Belinda heard differently? Freya breathed a sigh of relief when her sister nodded.

'And what do you think of our beautiful village?'

'I think it's an amazing place. Ryan and I just went to the beach, which is wonderful.'

'Did you, indeed? The two of you?' said Belinda, raising an eyebrow while Freya kicked herself for mentioning his name and turning their trip to the cove into potential salacious gossip.

'That's an amazing house up there on the cliff,' said Freya, in a bid to stop Belinda putting two and two together and coming up with six. She pointed at Driftwood House, which was again bathed in sunlight, its windows sparkling like diamonds. 'Do you know much about it?'

'It's a guesthouse now, run by Rosie Merchant. It was lived in for years before that by her mother, who died a while ago. Poor Sofia had a stroke out of the blue. It was absolutely tragic.' She shook her head. 'Rosie lived abroad and never came home to see her mother. Not until it was too late.'

'And what about before that? Who lived there before Rosie's mum?'

Belinda frowned. 'I have no idea. Twenty years ago, when Jim and I moved to Heaven's Cove, Rosie's parents, David and Sofia, were living there with a young Rosie. Why?'

'No particular reason. I'm interested in its history because it's such an intriguing-looking building, up there on the cliffs. I'm interested in the whole village really, not just the house.'

Did Belinda believe her? She narrowed her eyes and stared again but thankfully didn't ask any more questions. Instead, she pointed over Freya's shoulder. 'A brand new Heaven's Cove history and culture centre is opening at the weekend in the village hall, over there. Lettie, the young woman who's set it up, has various information about the village's history that you might find interesting. There's a grand opening ceremony on Saturday morning if you're interested in going along.'

Freya felt a rush of excitement at her sister's news about the centre – a place where she could learn about the history of Heaven's Cove, and maybe even of Driftwood House. She was sure that Kathleen was hiding something about that lonely house on the cliff. And while she didn't want to be too inquisitive, if something was public knowledge, wouldn't that make her interest a little less... Belinda-ish? She hoped so.

'Do you think you might go to the opening?' urged her sister.

'Yes, I think I probably will.'

Belinda smiled with satisfaction. 'I've been involved, of course, every step of the way. In fact, the project would never have got off the ground if I hadn't put Lettie in touch with Claude, an old fisherman who lives on the quayside. I happened to know that he had a cellar crammed full of old village documents and photos. Honestly, a cold, damp cellar and he refused to move them in spite of me telling him they should be somewhere safer. I could tell you a few things about Claude. He has a new lady friend, Esther, who...'

Freya enjoyed the warmth of the sun on her face, hardly listening to more gossip about people she didn't know. She took a deep breath of briny air and imagined she was back sitting on the beach with Ryan. He looked tired and worried much of the time but when he laughed his whole face lit up and he looked more handsome than ever.

Freya suddenly became aware that Belinda was talking about Ryan.

'Sorry, I missed that. What did you say?'

'I said, here comes Ryan now.'

She waved at Ryan, who had just come into view, clutching a large cabbage to his chest. He spotted the two of them and gave a weak smile before waving back.

'How's your dear mother?' shouted Belinda above the screeching of seagulls as Ryan got closer. 'I heard she fell over in the garden and damaged her knees, poor thing.'

Ryan glanced at Freya and his mouth tightened, his smile more forced. 'She's fine, thank you,' he called back.

'It's so easy to fall when you get to a certain age, and so lucky that Freya was there to help her. She might have saved your mother's life. I mean, who knows what would have happened if she hadn't been found?'

Belinda turned her palms to the sky, obviously imagining Kathleen coming to a sticky end, while Freya cringed inside.

'Kathleen wouldn't have come to any harm because her family call in regularly,' she said, but Ryan had walked on and she wasn't sure that he'd heard.

Great, thought Freya. *He thinks I've been gossiping to Belinda about his mother, and bigging myself up in the process.*

'Who *did* tell you about Kathleen's fall, Belinda?'

'Pat, who heard it from Isobel,' said Belinda, waving to someone else over Freya's shoulder. 'Have you met Isobel yet? Tall woman, one daughter, belongs to the village book club but never comes to meetings. She's always very well turned out and she's enjoying her divorce, if you know what I mean. She's had quite a few boyfriends, including an antiques dealer a few miles along the coast whose sister once shouted at me in the street.'

Freya blinked, not sure how to respond to that. 'I've met Isobel briefly,' she managed.

'Oh, you'll see a fair amount of her if you're around poor Ryan.'

'Are Isobel and Ryan together?'

I hope not, thought Freya. Isobel didn't seem right for Ryan. Though why she thought that when she hardly knew Ryan and knew Isobel even less, she wasn't sure.

Belinda laughed. 'She's certainly got her sights set on our moody widower, but he's still too in love with his dead wife to look properly at another woman. It's tragic, and yet rather lovely than he's remained so faithful to the mother of his child, don't you think? Heart-warming loyalty to the woman he married. It's a wonderful thing.' She gave Freya a sideways glance that confirmed she was talking about their father as much as 'poor Ryan'. 'It's such a shame that Natalie was killed by her ambition.'

'She... what?'

Belinda leaned closer, as though about to share a huge secret.

'His wife, Natalie, so I've heard from a friend of a friend who knows someone who used to know her cousin, was one of those women who want it all – marriage to a handsome man, a gorgeous child *and* a brilliant career. But it's just not possible.'

'Some women seem to manage it fine,' said Freya, not wanting to argue with Belinda but feeling she should stand up for her friends, a number of whom seemed to 'have it all', as Belinda put it. They made her feel totally inadequate, but good on them for managing it.

'Hmm.' Belinda sniffed. 'Anyway, she was killed by her job.'

'What on earth did she do?' asked Freya, imagining glamorous Natalie as a spy, seducing adversaries with her stunning looks and stealing state secrets.

'She was a senior buyer for a children's clothing company.'

'That doesn't sound very dangerous.'

'Not in itself, but she was travelling to a meeting when her car was hit by a lorry. She was killed outright apparently, which is probably a blessing in the circumstances. But she wouldn't have got in the lorry's way if she hadn't been travelling to work.'

Freya couldn't hide her shock at Belinda's callous assessment. 'It was an accident, Belinda. She was allowed to have a job.'

'I suppose so,' said Belinda sulkily. 'But she left a young child motherless and her husband battered by grief for ever. It's so sad.' She glanced at her watch. 'Anyway, I'd best get on. Would you like to come to us for afternoon tea on Sunday?'

'This Sunday? Um... that would be lovely.'

Freya tried to smile, still reeling from Belinda's cruel summary of Natalie's death and already dreading the weekend. Belinda was very kind to invite her round, and it wasn't that Freya didn't care about her sister. It was more that being with Belinda was absolutely exhausting, involving, as it did, endless gossip interspersed with occasional strained silences.

'Is four o'clock all right for you?'

'I'm sure that'll be fine. Can I bring anything?'

'Just yourself,' said Belinda over her shoulder as she bustled off. 'Don't be late.'

Freya walked the long way back to Kathleen's, past the old village hall that was flanked by grand stone pillars. So this was where the village's cultural centre would be. A large poster outside proclaimed it would be officially opened at ten o'clock on Saturday morning by 'local VIPs Charles and Cecilia Epping'.

Freya made a mental note. She would bring Kathleen along on Saturday morning if she fancied it – getting out would do her good. And maybe Freya could find out more about this beautiful village that was her home for now. The village seemed serene enough, nestled on the edge of the land as it had been for hundreds of years. But there were secrets here. Freya could feel it in her bones.

17

FREYA

A small crowd of people had gathered by the time Freya reached the village hall on Saturday morning. Dozens of colourful balloons were tied to the town hall pillars and a wide red ribbon stretched between them. A canvas banner advertising the new cultural centre was flapping in the breeze.

The onlookers were being shepherded into place by Belinda, who waved at Freya in between barking orders at people to move this way and that.

'Your sister's enjoying herself,' said a low voice in her ear.

When Freya turned, Isobel was standing behind her, looking amazing in a floaty grey dress, caught at the waist by a gold belt, and grey suede boots.

'She does like organising,' said Freya, giving Isobel a warm smile. First impressions could be misleading and it would be good to have a friend in the village. She really wished, though, that she'd changed out of her jeans into something smarter.

Isobel gave a tight smile back. 'No Kathleen this morning?'

'No, I did ask her but she didn't want to come.'

'Too much to do at home maybe.'

'Maybe.'

Actually, Kathleen had very little to do at home but she'd been adamant that she wasn't particularly interested in the cultural centre or the history of the village. She reckoned she wasn't interested in history, full stop. Even though there were several historical novels in her bookcase.

Freya gave herself a mental shake. She was starting to feel like a washed-up detective, spotting clues that didn't exist. And clues to what? Kathleen not liking Driftwood House? That wasn't a crime.

'I rather thought that Ryan and Chloe might come along this morning.' Isobel was standing on tiptoe and scanning the crowd. 'Are they here?'

'I've no idea, though I don't suppose Chloe would find this very interesting.'

'Probably not,' agreed Isobel, sounding put out. 'I mentioned it to Paige but she's still in bed. She was up past her bedtime with friends a little later than usual last night.'

'Was she with Chloe?'

'I don't think Chloe was there, no. Why?'

Because your daughter is a bad influence. 'No reason. I just thought she might be.'

'To be honest, I find it hard to keep up with all of Paige's friends. She's very popular.' Isobel waved at someone on the other side of the crowd. 'Anyway, it was lovely to see you again, Freya. How long do you think you'll be staying at Kathleen's?'

'I'm not sure. It depends on how long Kathleen wants me to stay.'

'Kathleen *and* Ryan.'

'Yes, of course. Ryan and his mum are very close.'

'They are, and he's very caring towards her. Ryan is quite a remarkable man, don't you think?'

She moved quickly away, weaving her way through the crowd without waiting for an answer.

Freya watched her go, feeling unsettled though she wasn't

quite sure why.

'Ladies and gentlemen,' yelled Belinda suddenly. She nodded when a hush fell over the onlookers. 'Thank you for coming to the official opening of Heaven's Cove's brand new cultural centre. I've been involved in this ambitious project from the start and, if I say so myself, the centre is a marvellous addition to Heaven's Cove.

'Of course, Lettie and Claude are the driving forces behind it. So I'll now hand you over to Lettie Starcross to introduce our very important guests of honour.'

She did a little bob of a curtsey towards two people, presumably VIPs Charles and Cecilia Epping, who were standing behind Lettie. Freya had googled them and discovered they were local landowners who owned a very large house on Dartmoor and a pied-à-terre in London.

Next to them stood a young woman with striking red hair and an elderly man with unkempt grey hair that reached his shoulders. He was shifting from foot to foot, and seemed uncomfortable.

The red-haired woman cleared her throat nervously.

'As Belinda said, thanks so much for coming today to celebrate the opening of Heaven's Cove's new cultural centre.' Her accent was different from the soft Devonian burr Freya was becoming accustomed to – she sounded like Mavis, one of the care home residents who'd lived most of her life in London. 'For those who don't know me, I'm Lettie and I haven't been here very long, but I've already grown to love this amazing village and the people in it.'

She glanced at a handsome man with dark hair standing nearby who gave her a slow smile.

Lettie and her dashing bystander were obviously in love, thought Freya, feeling a pang of envy. Liam and Rosie were loved up, Kathleen had enjoyed a long marriage with Frank, and Ryan was still hopelessly in love with his dead wife. In contrast, her relationship with Greg had ended in disaster and it seemed they weren't even talking these days. Her text to him earlier in the week, to check out a few practical details about shared belongings, had gone unanswered.

Freya tried to stop feeling sorry for herself and listened as Lettie talked a little longer about the rich history of Heaven's Cove. Then, she thanked the man with long grey hair for lending his archives to be displayed. He looked horrified when she asked if he'd like to say anything and shook his head before mumbling, 'Nope. Nothing.'

When Lettie called Charles and Cecilia Epping forward, Freya got a good look at them for the first time. Charles had white hair and piercing blue eyes and his wife, all perfectly coif-fured hair and cashmere, looked incredibly sophisticated and rather out of place in Heaven's Cove. He seemed friendly enough but his wife cast the crowd a more disdainful look. She reminded Freya a little of Isobel.

Charles made a short and rather heartfelt speech about the importance of history and how it could impact on the present, before his wife took the large pair of scissors proffered by Belinda and cut the wide red ribbon. Heaven's Cove's cultural centre was officially open.

The crowd cheered and surged forward into the hall, with Freya following. The town hall, so far as Freya could see, consisted of a large open space with a polished wooden floor, a bar that was shuttered with a silver grille, and some doors leading off. One door had a sign above it proclaiming it to be the entrance to the cultural centre.

Inside was a large room filled with display cases and dozens of photos and documents in frames on the walls.

Freya spent some time inspecting the photos, which were of the village from decades ago and people long gone. The pictures were fascinating and made her realise that her current problems were merely a blip along the way of life. All of these people –

staring into the camera in their old-fashioned clothes – had had their own heartaches too. She hoped that they, like her, had been soothed by the ebb and flow of the sea. There was a time-lessness to Heaven's Cove that was comforting.

'Hello. You're Belinda's sister, aren't you?'

Lettie was standing in front of her. Up close, her long hair was even more of a vibrant red as it fell in curls down her back.

'I am. Well, her half-sister.' Freya was used to being Greg's wife, her father's daughter, but here in Heaven's Cove she was obviously Belinda's sister. She wondered how long it would be before she was simply Freya in her own right. 'My name's Freya,' she added, 'and I'm staying at Kathleen's opposite the church.'

'Yes, I know.' Lettie grinned. 'Everyone knows. Your sister is excited to have you here.' Was she excited? Freya felt rather mean for being apprehensive about the teatime appointment with her sister the next day. 'I hope you're enjoying having a look around and finding out more about your new home.'

'I am, and this new centre is really impressive.'

Lettie beamed. 'Thanks so much. Claude had lots of fasci-nating information stored in his cellar and it seemed criminal to hide it away rather than show it off to local residents and visitors to the village. I've been a bit nervous about the official opening, to be honest, but it seems to be going pretty well. What do you think of Heaven's Cove?'

'I'm still finding my feet but it's a beautiful village. And it has such an interesting history. I was wondering, actually...'

Freya hesitated when she spotted Belinda out of the corner of her eye. Wouldn't she be just as nosey as her sister if she tried to piece together the 'clues' that were niggling at the edges of her brain? Whatever had happened here – *if* anything had happened here – was none of her business. But she couldn't forget the sight of Kathleen, so distressed, sobbing in the early morning light.

'What were you wondering?' asked Lettie.

Freya thought of the old photo of Kathleen and did a quick mental calculation, taking into account her current age.

'I was wondering if you had anything on show from the mid-1950s to early 60s?'

'Is that a period you're particularly interested in?'

'Yes. That and... and Driftwood House. It's such a magnificent house up there on the cliff.'

'It's amazing, isn't it? I stayed there when I first came to the village last year and Corey and I still climb the cliff regularly to look at the view. Oh, there he is!'

Lettie nodded towards the handsome man who'd smiled at her during her welcoming speech. 'My boyfriend.' Her pale cheeks flushed pink as though she wasn't quite used to calling him that. 'Anyway, if you're looking for fifties and sixties info, there are a few photos on the back wall over there that you might find interesting but that's one of the time periods that's a little lacking, I'm afraid. Claude's mum collected lots of the photos, newspaper cuttings and documents that are on display here. But she had lots of health issues around that time, apparently, and her amazing hoarding habit was curtailed. Not for too long though, thank goodness, or this centre would never have got off the ground.

'As for Driftwood House, there are some landscape photos of the village from various times that show the house on the cliff. But if you're particularly interested in it, you'd do better talking to Rosie, who owns the place. This centre is a work in progress and I haven't had a chance to plot the history of the house yet, but she can probably tell you more.'

A large lady in purple-framed glasses was beckoning to Lettie from the doorway. 'I really need to go and mingle, but I hope you enjoy looking round. It was good to meet you.'

'You too,' said Freya before heading for the photos that Lettie had pointed out.

They were fascinating. The village looked much the same as now – the same quaint stone cottages and glimpses of the sea. But the fashions of women immortalised for ever on celluloid – fifties nipped-in waists and hats; sixties mini shift dresses – revealed the pictures were from another age. That and the cars – or rather, the lack of them. The tiny streets were much less clogged with traffic.

Freya realised it was ridiculous but she fruitlessly scoured the photos nonetheless for a glimpse of a young Kathleen, with her sad, haunted eyes.

Driftwood House was visible in a few of the other images. But, as Lettie had said, it was always in the distance, standing sentinel over the village, on its lonely clifftop, as it had done for generations.

Freya stepped back and stopped squinting at the pictures. While it was fascinating to see Heaven's Cove in the past, part of her was relieved that she'd found out nothing new about Driftwood House. Maybe she should just let it go, rather than letting her imagination run riot. It wasn't her job to fix whatever was bothering Kathleen. She wasn't a 'fixer' like Belinda.

She shivered and was about to leave when Lettie hurried over.

'I was thinking, I've just been given some new archive material, by the family of a lady who died recently. I haven't had a chance to go through it properly yet but would you like to take a look? I think it includes some local info from the 1950s.'

Freya hesitated. But there was no harm in looking, surely? 'That would be wonderful. Thank you.'

Freya took the cardboard box Lettie gave her and sat at a quiet table near the shuttered bar to sift through its contents.

There was so much stuff in here. Photographs of places in the village that Freya recognised, and some that she didn't. People probably now long-gone standing in front of the castle ruins, in the narrow lanes, and on the beach. There were a couple of pictures that showed Driftwood House in the background, but nothing that particularly caught Freya's attention.

She started going through the papers at the bottom of the box – old newspaper cuttings and documents from the past. Underneath the pile of papers was a small battered book, bound in red leather. Freya opened it and stared at the small, neat handwriting inside. There was a date at the top of each page. It was a diary.

The first page was inscribed with a name, Eileen Woolford, and said *1st January 1959*. Freya glanced around her, feeling as if she was spying on Eileen. Surely her family didn't mean to include something so personal in this box of local history?

Freya decided to scan quickly through the pages, searching for any mention of Driftwood House, but found nothing. The entries were fairly bland – about Eileen's children, Felicity and Andrew, and how she spent her days, which mostly involved housework and childcare. The diary came to an abrupt end on 30th March as though Eileen, busy with family life, had given up the ghost on keeping a daily record.

Freya flicked again through the pages and suddenly the word 'Driftwood' caught her eye. There it was, in an entry she'd missed. Eileen had written just two sentences about the house that so intrigued her.

Saw people from Driftwood in the village, which is unusual because they rarely venture out. I pity them.

Chills ran down Freya's spine as she carefully placed the diary back into the box. Who on earth did Eileen pity, and why? Rather than easing Freya's curiosity about Driftwood House, Eileen's words made her quite determined to find out what secrets the house on the cliff was keeping, and what upsetting hold it might have over Kathleen.

18

RYAN

Ryan stood at the bottom of the stairs and took a deep breath before calling: 'Chloe, can you come down, please? I need a word.'

When there was no reply, he called again, louder this time to compete with the music she was playing.

'In a minute,' she yelled back, above some man rapping about the challenging women in his life.

Should he be vetting his daughter's musical choices? He rather thought he should be but it was another thing that he'd let slide. He mentally added it to the 'bad parent' tally that was mounting up these days.

When there was no sign of Chloe, he took the stairs two at a time and poked his head around her bedroom door. She was lying on her bed with the music at ear-splitting volume, and her window was wide open. The neighbours would be furious.

He winced as the rapper spat out a swear word and moved swiftly across the room to close the window. Then he stabbed at Chloe's phone to turn off the music.

'No, not in a minute. Now, please.'

'Why did you turn my music off?' demanded Chloe, sitting up against the pillows.

'I want a word, and I'm not sure this is very suitable music for you anyway.'

Chloe stared at him with the same sulky expression she seemed to wear perpetually these days.

'Wassup?' she said slowly, her finger hovering over her phone, ready to turn her music back on.

Ryan momentarily contemplated ripping her Bluetooth speakers off the wall but that wouldn't convey the grown-up parental vibe he was aiming for. He took a deep breath before speaking.

'*What's up* is that I hear you jumped off Clair Point.'

Chloe moved her finger away from her phone and narrowed her eyes. 'How did you hear that?'

Isobel had told him. She'd taken him to one side in Stan's store two hours ago and had held onto his arm as she'd told him all about it. She was worried that his daughter had done something foolish and thought he needed to know.

As Isobel had described the jump, he'd experienced the kind of fear he hadn't felt since they'd lost Natalie. A raw, biting fear that churned in his stomach. It took him a few seconds to rationalise that the event in question had happened almost a month ago, that Chloe was safe and well, that her idiotic pre-teen antics hadn't got her killed.

But they so easily could have.

Fear clutched at his stomach again and he shook his head. 'It doesn't matter how I heard. Is it true?'

Chloe stared at him for a moment, as though weighing up whether lying was worth it. Then she shrugged. 'I only did it once.'

'You only did it once?' Ryan's voice was rising and he made a conscious effort to calm down. Losing his rag wouldn't help.

'Once is one time too many. I can't believe you did something so dangerous.'

'Lots of people do it,' grumped Chloe, dropping her chin towards her chest. 'Clair Point isn't that high up and it was fine. *I'm* fine, as you can see.'

'Which is more luck than judgement. Those rocks at the bottom are lethal if the tide's too low or you don't jump out far enough from the cliff. Do you remember that boy who was larking about and jumped from there just after we moved to the village? He broke his leg in three places.'

'Yeah, but he didn't die. And the tide wasn't too low and I did jump out far enough so stop stressing, Dad.'

She turned over on the duvet so her back was to Ryan, but he marched around the bed and sat down beside her.

'Why did you do it, Chloe? How could you do it? What if you'd been hurt or even...?' Breath caught in his throat and Ryan blinked rapidly, images of his daughter lying broken at the foot of the cliffs flooding his mind. 'How could you do that, after what happened to Mum?' When he stopped speaking, Chloe's bottom lip wobbled and she suddenly looked like a young girl again, the girl he often felt as though he'd lost these days. 'Please just tell me why you did it? Did someone make you?'

'No, of course not,' said Chloe, sitting up and hugging her pillow tightly to her chest. 'I just wanted to do it. To prove that I could. And I can't believe that someone grassed me up.'

'Grassed you up? We're not living in a gangster movie. The person who told me had your best interests at heart.'

'Yeah, well, that Freya woman should concentrate on looking after Gran rather than poking her nose into other people's business.'

'Freya?' Ryan was blindsided. He hadn't expected to hear her name in this conversation.

'Yeah. She acts all friendly and makes promises to stay quiet but I knew she'd tell you.'

Ryan bit down on his bottom lip. Freya – the woman looking after his mother; the woman he couldn't seem to stop thinking about these days – knew that his daughter had risked her life leaping from Clair Point and she hadn't told him. More to the point, she'd promised his daughter that she wouldn't tell him.

'Am I grounded?' asked Chloe, panic sparking in her big eyes that reminded him so much of Natalie's.

Ryan hesitated. She should be grounded for doing something so foolhardy, but the thought of being trapped in the house with a disgruntled near-teenager was too much to bear.

'Punish me however you want but don't ground me,' pleaded Chloe, literally wringing her hands. 'If I can't go to the disco, I *will* die. Properly die. Please, Dad.'

The school dance was all Chloe talked about these days. At least she seemed excited about it and it made her happy. He so wanted her to be happy after having to cope with tragedy at such a young age.

'Please, Dad,' she urged again, grabbing hold of his hand and squeezing it tight. 'Pleeease.'

'I don't know, Chloe. I guess you're not grounded, if you promise me that you'll never ever jump from Clair Point again, or do anything so dangerous.'

'Of course. I don't need to do it again.'

'What do you mean by that?'

Chloe twisted her mouth. 'Nothing. Just that I've done it and I know what it feels like, so there's no point in doing the same thing again.'

Ryan exhaled with relief, the knot in his chest loosening. 'Good. Your mum... I mean, she'd hate for you to be putting yourself at risk like that.'

He felt like a terrible parent for bringing Natalie into the conversation to berate Chloe. It didn't seem fair when she wasn't here, but sometimes he grew tired of being the perpetual bad guy.

Chloe glanced at the photo of her mother that stood on her dressing table – the last picture that had ever been taken of her and her mum together. They were making sandcastles on the beach in Cornwall, their heads bent together on their last holiday before the accident.

When Ryan dipped his head, Chloe briefly touched his hair.

'Sorry,' she mumbled. 'I didn't mean to upset you so much.'

'OK. I just want you to be well and happy, Chloe. That's all I care about.'

'I know and I'm sorry. I really won't do it again.' Chloe paused before asking softly, 'Can I put my music back on now?'

Ryan nodded. He'd leave her music choices for another time. Another day, another battle. That's how life seemed to be these days.

The music was back on before he'd even closed her bedroom door behind him.

≈

Chloe waited until her dad had gone downstairs and then turned the music down a little. Being honest, she wasn't really that keen on rap but Paige and her friends listened to it all the time. They reckoned it was subversive and she'd nodded in agreement, even though she'd had to look the word up online.

That showdown with her dad had been intense. And Chloe felt guilty that she'd worried him, though he wouldn't have known anything about her jumping from Clair Point if Freya had kept her word. It was upsetting that Gran's new carer couldn't be trusted and would lie to her actual face. It was a shame because Chloe had quite liked her. She'd cared enough to try and stop her jumping off Clair Point, but, it turned out, she didn't care enough not to drop her in it with her dad.

Chloe got off the bed, opened her bottom drawer and pushed aside socks to find the bright pink lip gloss she'd stashed there. The lip gloss that Paige had encouraged her to steal from Stan's store when his back was turned.

Chloe suddenly felt very hot, imagining her dad's face if he knew she'd become a thief. He'd definitely ground her and stop her from going to the school disco, so it was just as well Freya knew nothing about that.

It was the first time that Chloe had shoplifted and, although she'd feigned bravado with Paige and her friends at the time, she'd felt guilty ever since. Stan had been kind and given her free ice cream when she'd first arrived in the village, and he'd been really proud of the new selection of make-up in his store. She kind of wished she'd refused to steal from him.

Kristen, a new girl in their class, had refused when Paige had dared her to shoplift, and she'd paid for her defiance ever since – Paige and her friends made fun of her all the time. But Chloe couldn't help secretly admiring Kristen's bravery. And she knew that her mum would be disappointed in her – if she was here.

Chloe switched off the music that was giving her a headache, picked up the photo of her mother and sat cross-legged on the floor with it.

'Hello, Mum,' she said, stroking the woman's celluloid face.

She glanced at the door in case her dad was coming back. Talking to her dead mother had to mean she was a bit weird, didn't it? It certainly wasn't the kind of thing that she could tell Paige about. It was taking every bit of energy she had to be the kind of girl who fitted in with Paige and her friends, as it was.

Her mum smiled back at her as she always did. Her expression never changed and it never would. Even when Chloe was grown up, her mother would still be a lifeless image in a framed photograph. Familiar stirrings of longing gripped at her chest. She was beginning to forget what she'd lost as she got older. Her memories were becoming hazier by the day. But her body still felt the loss of her mum's presence. The terrible sadness had faded but an ache was still there, and Chloe hoped it would *still* be there when she was grown up. It was all that she had left of the woman who had loved her.

'I wish,' she said to the photo. 'I wish I was more like you, Mum.'

Chloe went and stood in front of her mirror, holding the picture right next to her face. Her mother's hair was dark and glossy, whereas hers glinted red in the light from the window, and it was more flyaway, like her dad's. She and her mother had the same brown eyes, but their face shape was different – her mum's was a delicate oval, like Paige's and Isobel's, whereas hers was squarer, and her cheekbones were nothing like the chiselled ones she saw on Instagram.

In fact, she looked rather more like her dad, which was upsetting. He was good-looking, if the glances from mums at the school gates were anything to go by. And Isobel was definitely mooning after him, which was kind of good and kind of gross.

But more than anything, Chloe wanted to be beautiful like her mum, rather than handsome like her dad. It was all such terrible bad luck.

Chloe gently placed her mum back in her eternal resting place on the dressing table and lay back down on the bed. She wrapped the duvet around her, closed her eyes and imagined that her mum was sitting beside her, gently stroking her forehead.

19

RYAN

Ryan poured himself a large whisky and sat on his front doorstep, watching the world go by. Actually, the only people going by were tourists heading for their hotels and B&Bs after exploring the village. Though it would be just his luck if Belinda wandered past.

She would definitely judge him if she saw him drinking spirits this early in the evening, but let her. Being a single parent was hard work, especially when those around you were no help whatsoever.

He couldn't get his head around the fact that Freya had known about Chloe's jump from Clair Point – a jump that was a potential death leap. He could imagine his daughter falling through space and being dashed on the rocks below.

He tried to ignore the horrific images flooding his mind, hoping that Freya was taking rather better care of his mother than she had of his daughter. She should have told him what Chloe had done, so he would be aware that his daughter had a death wish.

He shook his head and took another slug of whisky. A death wish? He was being overdramatic. Chloe had only done what dozens of young people had done over the years. He'd probably have jumped from Clair Point himself if he'd been brought up around here.

But Chloe was all he had. He was forty-five years old and all he had in his life was a stressful job to pay the bills, an ageing mother and a daughter who would fly the nest one day. And then he'd become old and even more lonely. Which was perhaps what he deserved.

His thoughts strayed to Isobel, who'd made it very clear that she'd be perfectly willing to take his loneliness away. Maybe that was what Chloe needed – a mother figure in her life. And she seemed rather enthralled by Paige. Perhaps he needed to stop dodging Isobel's dating offers. Who knows, maybe he and Isobel would click and he'd end up giving Chloe a ready-made family.

Ryan closed his eyes and pictured perfect, beautiful Isobel. What was he doing keeping her at arm's length? She was pushy, which could be overwhelming, but at least that showed she was keen. And he was flattered by her attention, even though he sometimes felt she saw him as a puzzle to be solved, rather than a passion to be pursued.

He was trying to picture Isobel but Freya's face kept coming into his mind. Her face turned towards him on the beach. Her eyes shining like a child's when she saw the sea lapping at the sand. The shadow of hurt that dimmed her smile when she spoke about the break-up of her marriage.

He'd been taken in by her and had started to believe she was a woman who could be trusted. But now he felt disappointed and angry that she'd lied to him by omission. Honestly, what was she thinking? She'd told her nosey sister about his mother's fall when it was patently none of Belinda's business. But she hadn't said a word about his daughter putting her life in danger and leaping from Clair Point. He had to find out why.

Ryan got to his feet, splashing golden whisky over the step.

He should calm down first before confronting Freya, but Chloe had gone to the cinema with Paige and this was his chance.

Ryan pulled the front door closed behind him and marched through the narrow lanes of Heaven's Cove towards his mother's house.

20

FREYA

Freya knew as soon as she saw Ryan standing on the doorstep that something wasn't right. His jaw was a little too tight, his smile a little too forced. But she figured that looking after a twelve-year-old girl on your own, while also holding down a demanding job, must be tiring.

'Come on in,' said Freya, wondering why he'd knocked on Kathleen's front door when he had a key. She put down the vase of yellow tulips she was holding and wiped her hands on her jeans. 'Your mum's in the front room. She was feeling a bit tired after our walk this afternoon so she's having a rest.'

'Ryan,' called Kathleen from the sitting room on cue. 'Is that you, my darling?'

'Yeah, it's me, Mum.'

Freya followed him into the sitting room and watched as he kissed the papery-thin skin on Kathleen's cheek. 'I hope you haven't been overdoing things.'

He cast Freya a sharp glance as he said it and she frowned. She thought their relationship had thawed during their visit to the beach. But he'd seen her and Belinda together just after-wards – perhaps he did think she'd told her sister about Kathleen's fall a fortnight ago. Freya inwardly cursed Belinda for not being able to keep anything to herself.

'Is everything all right?' asked Kathleen, pulling herself straighter in her favourite seat, the wingback armchair nearest the fireplace. 'Where's Chloe?'

'She's gone to the cinema with Paige, and while she's out I was hoping for a quick word with Freya, if that's all right. Maybe we could go into the kitchen?'

Kathleen frowned. 'Will you be talking about me? If so, I'd rather you did that in front of me, thank you very much.'

'I don't want to talk to Freya about you, Mum.'

Kathleen looked between them, puzzled, but then a slow smile spread across her face. 'Why don't you youngsters go out and chat? You could take Freya to the pub, Ryan. I don't think she's been to the Smugglers yet.'

'No, I'm needed here,' said Freya quickly.

'Are you? All I'm doing is sitting here, about to watch some TV.'

'What about your bedtime hot chocolate?'

'I'm perfectly capable of making myself a hot drink without doing anything disastrous,' answered Kathleen tartly. Her features softened. 'I dare say you'll be back in time for that anyway. So I insist you two young ones go out for a drink. Go on. You two should spend some time together.'

Good grief, was she trying to match-make? thought Freya in alarm. She'd definitely got the wrong end of the stick if she thought Ryan wanted a pleasant word with her. The way he kept glaring at her told her otherwise.

But Kathleen kept on encouraging in her gentle Irish lilt until it was easier for Freya to agree.

They set off a few minutes later, after Freya had changed into a dress, brushed her hair and applied a slick of pink lip gloss. She didn't need to. She could have gone to the pub in her jeans. But it was her first night out in Heaven's Cove, and the dress and make-up felt a little like armour against the telling-off she felt sure was coming.

Ryan set off at such a cracking pace, Freya found it hard to keep up with him. He said very little as they raced along. At last they reached The Smugglers Haunt, a pretty white-washed pub with a thatched roof and hanging baskets outside. Freya had spotted it on her explorations of the village and thought it looked wonderful, but she'd never ventured inside on her own.

Ryan held the door open for her but let it slam as he walked to the bar ahead of her.

'I assume you'd like a drink now we're here?' he asked coldly, raising his hand to attract the attention of the man pulling pints.

Freya frowned. Why was he being such an arse? It hadn't been her idea to come to the pub. She'd been all prepared to settle Kathleen and then have a lovely hot soak in the bath, before he'd marched in looking thunderous.

'A lemonade would be very nice, thank you, but I'm quite happy to pay for it.'

'No, you're all right. You find a seat and I'll bring it over. Maybe over there?'

He pointed at a table in a secluded corner of the pub, near a huge blackened stone hearth. A small fire was burning, even though it was spring, and Freya could feel the heat of the flames on her face when she sat down.

Ryan appeared a couple of minutes later with a lemonade in one hand and a pint of beer in the other. He sat opposite her and took off his jacket.

'It's quite hot here. Would you rather move?' asked Freya.

Ryan looked around the pub, which was half full. 'I'd rather stay here if you don't mind because I don't want us to be over-heard. It should be more private here than Mum's kitchen. She's wobbly on her feet but there's nothing wrong with her hearing.'

Oh dear. Freya groaned because she knew what was

coming, and it might mean the end of her new job if Ryan didn't believe her. She'd only spent a month with Kathleen but she'd already grown fond of the elderly woman and felt they'd built up a good rapport.

'Can I just say,' Freya said quickly, keen to get in first, 'that I didn't tell Belinda about your mum's fall in the garden. She didn't find out about it from me.'

'Oh.' Surprise flitted across Ryan's face, as though he hadn't been thinking about that at all.

'Only I wouldn't tell anyone about your mum, and I especially wouldn't tell my sister. She's not great at...' Freya tailed off, feeling disloyal for talking about Belinda, even though everyone must know what a dreadful gossip she was.

Ryan shook his head. 'I'm not here to talk about your sister.'

'So what do you...?' Freya tailed off again.

'Sometimes there are things you should definitely tell people,' said Ryan enigmatically, drawing in a long gulp of his beer. He swallowed quickly. 'Though not your sister. Not ever your sister. But at the top of the long list of things you should definitely tell other people about is their child doing something ridiculously dangerous.'

Oh no. Freya breathed out slowly as realisation dawned that her pact with Chloe was no longer a secret. No wonder Ryan was annoyed.

'I imagine you're talking about what happened on the cliff,' she said, trying to stay calm. She'd thought – hoped – that Chloe's jump was old history that would never be repeated or revealed.

'You imagine right.' His voice was cold but anger was sparking in his green eyes.

Freya winced. 'I'm so sorry. I probably should have mentioned it.'

'Do you think?' Ryan took another long draft of his beer and sat back in his chair, his eyes now glittery hard. 'Do you know how dangerous it is, jumping off those rocks into the sea?'

'Mmm.' Freya nodded miserably.

'It's a long way down and, if you manage to miss the rocks hidden under the water, there are strong currents that can sweep you out to sea. So jumping is not advisable.'

'It looked terrifying and I did try to stop her. I honestly did, but she jumped anyway.'

'You were actually there?' gasped Ryan so loudly people at the bar turned to look at them. He put his elbow on the table and shielded his face from the onlookers with his hand. 'I thought you'd heard what she'd done. I didn't know you were a part of it.' His voice was lower now, more controlled.

'I wasn't a part of it.' Freya sighed. This was going from bad to worse. 'I walked to the top of the cliff, to have a closer look at Driftwood House, and came across Chloe on my way down. She was about to jump and I tried to persuade her not to, but when she did anyway I waited to make sure she was OK.'

'That's all right then.' Ryan's mouth had set in a thin line and Freya's stomach started to churn. She could cope with him being distracted and annoyed, but this cold, hard anger was unsettling.

'I was going to tell you but Chloe begged me not to, and you have so much to cope with already. I didn't want to poke my nose in and add to the pressures in your life. Chloe solemnly promised me that she would never do it again.'

Even as she said it, Freya realised how pathetic that sounded. Believing that a twelve-year-old would behave sensibly in the future because she'd made a promise to a virtual stranger. A promise that had bought her silence.

'She hasn't done it again, has she?' she asked anxiously.

'Not as far as I'm aware, but that's not the point.'

'No, I don't suppose it is.' Freya bit down on her lip and gazed at her untouched glass of lemonade, fizzing on the table.

'It's done now and I can't change it. But I really am sorry. I made a bad judgement call and should have told you.'

'Yes, you should have. She's my daughter.'

'I know. At least, I know that now. I didn't realise it at the time when I saw her jump.'

'I get that, but when you found out who she was, why didn't you tell me or my mum then?'

It was a good question and one that Freya had asked herself since making her ill-fated pact with Chloe. Maybe she'd grown so used to keeping people's secrets, she never truly contemplated doing anything else these days.

'Well?' demanded Ryan. 'I just want to understand what you were thinking.'

'The jump had already happened and Chloe said that it would never happen again so I couldn't see the point of telling you. And I don't know anyone here, apart from Belinda, and I hardly know her, to be honest. And I didn't want Chloe to hate me, I suppose.' Freya hesitated, realising she was making herself sound even more pathetic. 'I mean, she'd only just met me, and there was no way I would worry your mum with it, and you were...'

'And I was what?' asked Ryan, leaning back in his chair.

Freya took a deep breath. 'You weren't exactly welcoming. Oh, I know why. I was parachuted in without you knowing. But I didn't realise that when I took on the job, and it was all a bit overwhelming, to be honest. I didn't expect to be living in the house of a woman I hardly know, in a part of the country that's totally unfamiliar to me at my age. It wasn't part of my plan.'

When she stopped, worried she might cry, Ryan watched her for a moment before leaning forward, his face softer.

'So what was your plan?'

Freya shrugged. 'I don't know... marriage, kids and happy ever after. Usual stuff.'

'Yeah, usual stuff.' Ryan gave a hollow laugh because, of course, his life plan had gone horribly off-track.

Freya suddenly wished that she and Ryan were back on the beach. Talking about their lives had seemed easier then, with the sun shining and the waves rolling in. But that was before he knew of Chloe's jump and her part in keeping it from him.

'So are you still hoping for a happy ever after?' asked Ryan quietly.

Freya shook her head. 'Nah. Happy ever afters aren't for people like me.'

'Me neither,' said Ryan, picking up his beer and staring into the amber liquid. He looked up and caught Freya's eye. 'So what kind of a person are you?'

Freya thought for a moment, taken aback by his question. 'A knackered one, mostly. Since my marriage ended a few months ago, I've felt... emotionally challenged and clueless.'

When she gave a tentative smile, Ryan's mouth lifted in one corner.

There was no reason to tell him all this. Why should he care that she'd felt pretty rubbish since Greg left? But he deserved some candour after her mistake with Chloe and, for some reason, he didn't seem to be as angry with her any more.

Also, she was so very tired of having no one to talk to. Her friends were busy with their own lives, and she had no family to tell – her dad was dead, her mother was distant, both geographically and emotionally, and her sister... well, her sister wasn't the sort of person you'd choose if you needed a heart-to-heart.

'I'm sorry. Losing someone, however you lose them, hurts like hell,' said Ryan softly.

'And you'd know that more than most.'

When he sighed, all the fight gone out of him, Freya glimpsed again the vulnerability that he kept so well hidden. They were a right pair. Him, widowed and trying to be so tough, and her, soon to be divorced and, at nearly forty, still getting life wrong.

She desperately wanted to know more about his life, but he went back to his beer without proffering any information and she didn't have the courage to ask.

Instead, she agreed, 'Losing people does hurt.' She rubbed a finger along the condensation on her glass. 'Greg and I hadn't been getting on brilliantly for a while but it was OK, you know? We were past the first flush of romance but we still loved each other. Or, at least, I thought we did.'

She paused so she could steady herself. This felt like the wrong way round. People usually told Freya their secrets. They unburdened themselves and usually felt better for it. But there was something about Ryan that made her want to tell him the unvarnished truth.

'Then, Greg started coming home later and later from work, and one day he said we should take a break. Like Ross and Rachel in *Friends*. Only this was real life. My life.' She closed her eyes briefly, remembering her pain and incomprehension. 'And basically, that was that. Our month-long break turned into him saying he was leaving me and wanted a divorce.'

'Is there someone else?' asked Ryan. He twisted his mouth into a grimace. 'Sorry. That's not very tactful of me.'

'It's all right.' Freya drew in a deep breath of air that smelled of hops and burning firewood. 'He's never admitted it but I think he's been having a fling with Erica, a work colleague who's always immaculately turned out. I did try to up my game but...' She glanced down at her crumpled linen dress and gave a wry grin. 'I tried to fit in with his new friends and business acquaintances and got away with it for a while, but it's hard when you're not the person they think you are.'

Ryan nodded and stared into the distance as though he was miles away. His defences had dropped again and Freya could see pain etched on his features.

'She's also younger and more attractive than me.'

Ryan's gaze flipped back to Freya. 'I think you're very attractive.'

His eyes opened wide, as if the words had slipped out without his permission, and Freya felt a blush flaring across her cheeks.

'I really am sorry that I didn't tell you about Chloe,' she said, to fill the awkward silence.

Ryan shrugged. 'I've said my piece and I guess you were in a difficult position. There's no harm done so let's forget about it. Just promise me that you'll tell me everything about my family in future. If you're looking after my mum, I need to know that I can trust you.'

'You can, and I promise to tell you everything,' said Freya, still feeling distracted.

I think you're very attractive. That's what he'd said. But he'd simply been trying to make her feel better after she'd poured her heart out about Greg. She'd never measure up to Natalie. Even immensely attractive and vivacious Isobel didn't seem to be finding it plain sailing.

'OK.' Ryan sighed again, as though he was exhausted. 'You shouldn't have to police my daughter, anyway. You're not her mother.'

Freya took a large gulp of lemonade, wondering what it must feel like to be a mother. Sometimes she ached for the children she'd never had, and at other times, when she saw friends flattened under the daily onslaught of child-rearing, she thanked her lucky stars. Would Greg still have left her if they'd had children together? She shook her head, not willing to let herself go there.

'How long have you known Isobel?' she asked instead. The question had just popped into her head.

Ryan looked up sharply. 'Since Chloe and I moved here a couple of years ago. Why?'

'I just wondered. She seems nice.'

Freya wasn't sure she was nice at all, but it seemed the best thing to say about the woman that Ryan might be about to date. Or perhaps he was dating her already.

'Yeah, she's nice.' Was she imagining it or did Ryan sound unsure too? 'She and her daughter moved into the village after she split up with her husband.'

'It seems to be a theme.'

When Ryan smiled, his eyes caught hers and Freya suddenly felt fluttery. There was no denying that he was a handsome man. But there was something more that she found compelling – a hidden depth that lay buried beneath a veneer of no-nonsense practicality. A guardedness that made his flashes of vulnerability all the more endearing.

This man has a secret. That's what her instincts were telling her, but this time they were wrong. This man simply had a tragedy in his past that continued to ripple through the years. He was a man in desperate need of affection and understanding. Her eyes moved down to his mouth and she wondered what it would feel like to be kissed by a man who wasn't Greg. What it would feel like to be kissed by Ryan.

What on earth was she doing! Freya sat up straight, grabbed her glass of lemonade and almost downed it in a few swallows. Her responsibility was to Kathleen. She needed to take care of her. And she couldn't do that if she was distracted by a ridiculous and frankly pointless crush on her son.

'Gosh, is that the time,' she said, glancing at her watch and scraping back her chair. 'I'd better get back to your mum before she starts spilling boiling milk everywhere.'

Ryan looked nonplussed at her sudden move. 'O-K,' he said slowly.

'Thank you for the drink, and I am very sorry that I kept quiet about Chloe. I truly am. I promise to keep you up to date with everything to do with your family in the future.'

'Everything?'

'Absolutely everything. Scout's honour.'

Don't do the three-finger Scout salute, Freya! Too late, she was already doing it. She burned with embarrassment and shoved her hands into the pockets of her dress.

Ryan smiled. 'Thanks. That's all I ask.'

She left him sitting in the pub, staring into his beer, and walked briskly through the village until she reached the quayside. Slipping off her shoes, she sat on the harbour wall for a few minutes, listening to the gentle slap of waves on worn stone. The sun had just slipped beneath the horizon but there was enough residual light to make out Cora Head – the headland that Kathleen had wanted to explore, rather than the cliffs of Driftwood House. It jutted out into the dark ocean, a solid shadow in the gathering gloom.

It was beautiful here, and soothing after the last half hour. Freya's breath was coming in short gasps and she wasn't sure if that was due to the brisk walking or her mixed emotions.

She was glad that Chloe's secret was out in the open. It hadn't felt right keeping information from Ryan about his daughter. And after his initial meltdown, he'd taken it quite well. In fact, in some ways, having such a frank showdown and chat afterwards had cleared the air between them. Until that moment when she'd wondered about his kissing skills.

Freya frowned, hoping that Ryan hadn't guessed what was going on in her mind. He must think she was odd for rushing off like that – what on earth was the Scout salute all about? But she'd only just split up with Greg and didn't need a rebound infatuation that could make her new life here untenable.

That's what it was, she told herself as she stood and brushed down her dress, which was even more crumpled now – a rebound infatuation that Ryan knew nothing about. And it would stay that way.

Ryan watched Freya flee – that was the only word for it – before sitting back to finish his pint. She'd rushed away from him and he didn't blame her. *I think you're very attractive.* She'd recently split up with her husband and he'd come over all flirty and inappropriate. What had he been thinking?

He hadn't, that was the point. He'd brought her here to read her the riot act about Chloe and had ended up feeling sorry for her – and guilty. Guilt, his old friend. He took a swig of his beer and contemplated buying another.

He had to admit, if only to himself, that he'd been unkind to Freya when she'd first arrived in Heaven's Cove. Not nasty, but suspicious and cold, which wasn't his usual way at all. He knew why, of course. He was surprised by her arrival and felt bad that she was looking after his mother when he couldn't. But he hadn't taken her circumstances into consideration. He hadn't fully considered that she was hurting and lost, just like him.

'Hey, Ryan,' called Ollie, who was sitting at the bar with his wife. 'Everything OK, mate?'

'Fine, thanks,' Ryan called back, forcing himself to smile. 'Just fancied a sneaky pint.' *Please don't come and join me.* 'I'm heading off in a minute,' he added, which did the trick. Ollie waved and went back to chatting with his wife. Ryan figured they'd have a nicer evening, just the two of them. He'd had some good nights in the pub with Ollie, but he wasn't great company right now.

His thoughts turned back to Freya. He was still upset that she hadn't told him about Chloe but at least she'd tried to stop the daft child from jumping. A shiver ran down his spine at the thought of his precious daughter splashing into the deep dark ocean. Another tragedy would break him, he knew that.

But Chloe was fine and had promised never to repeat the jump. And Freya had promised never to keep family matters secret from him again. And there was something about Freya and the way she'd opened up to him about her marriage and her husband – who sounded like an arse – that made him trust her and want to reassure her, because her confidence had obviously taken a hit.

Freya *was* very attractive. Not in the same glamorous, high-maintenance way as Natalie and Isobel – and Erica, presumably. Her thick hair could do with a cut and her dress looked as if she'd slept in it. But it didn't matter. Her hair curled where it hit her shoulders, her beautiful big grey eyes were full of expression, and her smile lit up her face. And her pretty, full mouth... He'd looked at her mouth as she talked about her failed marriage and wondered what it would feel like to kiss her and be kissed back.

Good grief. Ryan put his unfinished pint down on the table and got up to leave. It couldn't happen. Not considering their circumstances and after what he'd done. What he'd done to Natalie.

He'd reached the door when he spotted a group of women at a table near the far-side of the bar. One of them was Isobel, who was sipping from a very large glass of red wine. Had she seen him in the corner with Freya? Oh, what did it matter if she had?

Ryan slipped out into the night and walked through the village, lost in thoughts of his past and its effect on his future.

21

FREYA

As the gate closed behind Freya with a click, she noticed the curtains at the cottage window twitch. Belinda was looking out for her. She probably spent a lot of time peering at people going past her window, which was quite sad. Freya felt a pang of sorrow for her sister. What must her life be lacking if she had to fill it with the goings-on of others?

Her suspicion that she was being watched was confirmed when the front door was pulled open before she had a chance to knock.

'There you are, five minutes early,' said Belinda, looking very smart in a blue tea dress. 'You've inherited our father's penchant for punctuality.'

'Not so much as he got older. He was always late.'

'I wouldn't know. I never saw him,' said Belinda tartly, flushing bright pink. And Freya felt a pang of sadness that afternoon tea with her sister had already got off to a bad start.

The relationship between Belinda and their father had always been a volatile one, and they hadn't seen each other for three years before he died. Their estrangement had caused her dad great unhappiness in his final years, but Freya's attempts at a rapprochement had failed dismally. Her telephone and email pleas to Belinda to visit their father had fallen on deaf ears.

'Thank you for inviting me round,' said Freya, keen to begin the afternoon all over again.

This time Belinda smiled and ushered Freya inside. 'Well, don't just stand there. Come on in. I thought it was about time we had a proper catch-up and I'm sorry I've not had the time to do this sooner. How long have you been in Heaven's Cove now?'

'About a month,' said Freya, thinking back to how nervous she'd been the last time she'd stood in this hallway, shortly before she met Kathleen for the first time.

'Gosh, is it that long? With so many fingers in so many pies, life just runs away with me these days.' Belinda nodded towards the sitting room. 'Anyway, come and have a cup of tea. I've done a bit of baking.'

She bustled into the room and Freya followed. Jim was sitting at the table, which was groaning under a vast array of sandwiches laid out on fancy plates, and cakes piled up on silver and china stands. There was more confectionery here than the three of them could possibly eat and Freya began to regret her lunchtime toasted sandwich.

Jim gave her a wink as she took a seat, and the china tea plate that Belinda handed her.

'Gosh, this looks amazing. I feel like I'm about to have high tea at the Ritz.'

'Really?' Belinda flushed again, but this time with pleasure. 'I take after my mother, who was a talented baker, and one has to keep up appearances, even in a small village on the Devon coast. I don't like to boast but the lemon drizzle I take to village market planning meetings is famed far and wide.' She nodded at the spectacular spread. 'Don't stand on ceremony. Help yourself.'

When she bustled into the kitchen to fetch the teapot, Freya turned to Jim.

'You're looking very smart this afternoon.'

He gave a mirthless laugh. 'Belle insisted that I put on a suit. Honestly, you coming round has been like preparing for a royal visit.'

Freya glanced at her cotton trousers and jumper. 'I'm afraid I feel rather under-dressed.'

'Lucky you.' Jim pushed a finger between his neck and the collar of his white shirt. 'The last time I wore this suit was for Sofia Merchant's funeral and I think I've put on a few pounds since then.'

'Belinda really didn't need to go to so much trouble.'

'She really did.' He leaned forward. 'My wife...' He hesitated, glancing at the door. '...she wants to make a good impression on you and feels she didn't do too well when you stayed overnight. I know you've bumped into each other and chatted a few times since then, but she hasn't had a chance to pull out all the stops.'

'Why does she think she needs to?' Freya frowned. 'She was very welcoming when I stayed here. And why is she bothered about making a good impression on me, anyway? I get rather mixed messages from my sister sometimes.'

'Don't we all.' Jim gave a small smile. 'Underneath my wife's rather... bombastic manner, she's not as confident as many people believe, especially when it comes to family and particularly when it comes to you. Shhh!' He shook his head as Belinda came back into the room carrying a large china teapot.

She poured the tea and they drank it and ate cake for a while. It was strange spending time with her half-sister, thought Freya, biting into a second slice of the famous lemon drizzle cake and pitying her poor hips. Kathleen's keenness for chocolate digestives and insistence that Freya join her for elevenses wasn't great for her figure either.

'So, tell me. How is life at Kathleen's?' asked Belinda, dabbing crumbs from her chin with a white linen napkin. 'Is everything all right?'

Here we go, thought Freya. It would be an innocuous question from most people, gentle small talk or a legitimate concern. But with Belinda there was always a not-so-hidden agenda behind it: gossip. And the last thing Freya wanted was for Ryan to think she'd been talking about his mum behind her back.

'All's going well, I think,' said Freya carefully. 'We seem to have hit it off and feel comfortable in each other's company. She's a lovely woman and reminds me of some of the residents at my care home.'

Kathleen *did* remind her of the residents she particularly missed, people like Mavis, Carla and Sidney who had become almost like family. They loved living vicariously through Freya, who told them about her life outside the home and they, in return, told her their stories and secrets: how they'd come to be living in residential care and who they once were.

Freya was still regularly in touch with them on the phone. She'd spent half an hour talking to Mavis just last night and had told her all about her new life in Heaven's Cove.

'Kathleen is a very warm woman, if a little guarded,' said Belinda. 'And she's determined to stay in her cottage until they carry her out in a box. It's so fortunate you were there when she fell over, in the garden of all places.'

'That was more than two weeks ago now,' replied Freya, wondering how long it would be before her sister stopped asking about Kathleen's accident. 'If I hadn't been there, Ryan would soon have found her. Or the man next door would have heard her calling.'

'Ted? Yes, he'd soon have noticed Kathleen lying prostrate because he's quite the busybody.' Freya almost choked on her tea and Jim took an extra-large bite of his scone, but Belinda carried on, oblivious. 'Poor Ryan, having to look after an old lady as well as a poor motherless child.' Her face scrunched up in sympathy. 'What do you make of Ryan?'

She said it lightly, but Freya could see the curiosity in her eyes.

I'd quite like to kiss him. She couldn't say that. Belinda would self-combust. Freya spoke carefully. 'He seems like a very caring father. It can't be easy being a single parent.'

'Not easy at all. What an awful tragedy to befall them.'

'Indeed.' Freya took a sip of her tea and asked, equally lightly, 'Kathleen tells me that she hasn't lived that long in the village?'

'She came here several years after Jim and I moved in. It must be, what, seven or eight years since she arrived? What do you reckon, Jim?'

'About that,' Jim answered, spraying a blizzard of crumbs.

'She came here after her husband died, though I'm surprised she didn't go back to Ireland instead. It must have been very hard starting a new life in a brand new place without her husband. Though, of course, that's what you're having to do yourself, Freya.' Belinda leaned over to lay a napkin across Jim's lap. 'I've tried to find out more about Kathleen's life before she came to Heaven's Cove but she's a closed book on the subject.'

Freya nodded, sure that Belinda knew nothing about Kathleen's visit to Driftwood House as a young woman, or she would have told them all about it.

Saw people from Driftwood in the village, which is unusual because they rarely venture out. I pity them.

What would Belinda think of that strange entry in Eileen Woolford's diary? Did Kathleen, as a young woman, know the family living at Driftwood House whom Eileen pitied so much?

'A penny for your thoughts, Freya.' Belinda laughed. 'You drifted off there. What are you thinking about?'

Freya dragged her thoughts back from the past. 'Just how much I appreciate you having me over for tea and going to so much trouble. Your cake-making skills are wonderful.'

Jim gave Freya a grateful smile as Belinda launched into a long explanation of how to get the best rise in a Victoria sandwich.

Now talk had moved on from Kathleen, Freya started to relax and enjoy a sugar-high from the vast amount of cake she'd eaten. The visit was turning out to be far less stressful than she'd feared.

Belinda talked a lot about her busy schedule and about being the life and soul of the village, and Freya deflected her enquiries about her ongoing relationship with Greg. Jim said very little as he ate his way through a mountain of madeleines.

It was nice, Freya realised, sitting here talking to someone who knew her family history and shared her genes. But she missed the close sisterly camaraderie that she'd witnessed so often with her friends who had siblings. They disagreed some-times, fought occasionally, and drove each other mad, but there was an ease to their relationship that was missing in hers with Belinda.

Sometimes it seemed she and Belinda were getting on well but then a flash of hostility in her sister's eyes, quickly covered with a smile or another question, made her doubt that her sister liked her very much at all.

Freya got it. She was the unexpected pregnancy that had prompted their father to leave Belinda's mother and move in with his secretary, her mother, with whom he'd been having an affair. But it wasn't *her* fault, however irrationally guilty it some-times made her feel. She hadn't asked to be born.

'It's so lovely to have you here with us in Heaven's Cove,' said Belinda, pouring yet more tea, and Freya kicked herself for being uncharitable.

She and Belinda were sisters, and Belinda had been a great

help in bringing her to Heaven's Cove and getting her a job with Kathleen. Not all siblings were best friends, but that didn't mean they didn't like each other.

Freya took the proffered tea and smiled at her big sister. 'I'm loving being here in the village, and thank you for making it happen.'

Belinda's smile was unmistakeably genuine this time. 'That's kind of you to say. I'm glad that you're here and we can spend time together. Well,' she laughed, 'we could spend time together if I wasn't so busy all the time. But that's what happens when your community needs you.' She hesitated. 'I wonder what Greg's doing now and what he'd make of your new life. It's such a shame the two of you split up. I hate to ask, but was there anyone else involved?'

Freya sighed and bit into a slice of sticky ginger cake.

22

FREYA

Freya was worried. Kathleen hadn't been herself all day and seemed very under the weather. She'd been low for a couple of weeks. But today her gentle smile had vanished completely and she was moving slowly around the house, sunk in a deep sadness as though a dark cloud was above her head.

If Ryan was around, Freya would talk to him and ask his opinion. But Ryan had been only an intermittent visitor over the last ten days, since their visit to the pub. Freya had worried that he was avoiding her. Perhaps he'd picked up that she was attracted to him and thought it was totally inappropriate – quite apart from the fact he was a grieving widower, she was his mother's employee.

But he was crazy busy with a work project, according to Kathleen, who'd been nipping round to his house to see him and Chloe. And for the past five days both he and his daughter had been away – Ryan at a work conference in Barcelona, and Chloe taking advantage of the Easter holidays to stay with her maternal aunt in Somerset.

Freya could text him, or even call him in Spain, but what

would be the point? Kathleen denied being anything but 'tip-top' when asked how she was, and she couldn't worry him while he was away.

Anyway, what was it he'd said during their walk on the beach? His mother always got low at this time of year. Perhaps it was the change in season, from winter to spring that was affecting her. The long dreary winter had worn all of them down and summer still seemed a long way off.

But Freya couldn't shake the feeling that Kathleen's mood was specifically tied to the morning she'd found her sobbing in her bed. That was a fortnight ago now and Kathleen hadn't once mentioned it. But she'd been a little off ever since – slightly subdued and lethargic.

Today she'd been uncharacteristically tetchy and had urged Freya to 'stop fussing' when she'd tried to get her to sit down and rest. But she looked grateful when Freya lit the fire that evening, and didn't complain when Freya put a blanket over her legs. The weather had turned tonight and outside, gusts of wind were blowing squalls of rain against the dark windows.

'Shall I put the TV on for you?'

Freya picked up the remote control and started rifling through a pile of magazines to find the *Radio Times*. But Kathleen shook her head.

'No, thank you. I'll just sit here for a while in front of the fire.'

'Would you like me to stay with you?'

The elderly lady gave the slightest of shrugs. 'I don't mind. If you like.'

Freya hesitated. She'd been looking forward to reading in her bedroom and getting an early night. But she hated to think of Kathleen sitting here, miserable and all alone. Even Rocky had abandoned his mistress and was fast asleep in the kitchen.

She made up her mind. 'I'll stay for a bit, if that's OK.'

Even if Kathleen didn't want to share what was on her mind, some company might cheer her up a little.

Freya closed the door and placed the stuffed draught excluder along the bottom of it. This cottage was filled with draughts that snaked around your ankles, and the storm brewing outside made the place chillier than ever.

Kathleen was sitting in her favourite chair, by the fire, lit by the glow of the lamp next to her. She glanced across as Freya kicked off her shoes and curled her feet under her on the small sofa.

'You don't *have* to keep me company, you know.'

'I know, but I'd like to.'

'Hmm.' Kathleen went back to staring into the fire and shadows danced around the room as a silence lengthened between them. Suddenly, her head jerked up. 'I know I'm being grumpy at the moment, and I'm sorry for it.'

Freya smiled. 'That's all right. We all have bad days.'

'Yes, but that's no excuse for me to take it out on you. You've had a bad time yourself with the break-up of your marriage.'

'Splitting up with Greg was hard, but it was for the best.'

And for the first time since her husband had swept out of their apartment, taking her heart with him, Freya truly believed what she said. She'd gained a new perspective since arriving in Heaven's Cove, she realised, and some days found herself hardly thinking of Greg at all.

'Well, even if it was for the best, you don't need me being gloomy.' Kathleen winced when thunder rumbled around the village. 'We're in for quite a storm, I think, and it's not a night to be on your own. I may not have said it explicitly but I do appreciate having you here, especially in the evenings. That's when I often feel most lonely.'

'Is that why Ryan and Chloe were thinking of moving in?' asked Freya gently.

Kathleen waved her hand dismissively. 'Oh, I haven't told

them about the long evenings. I imagine Ryan's more worried about me razing the cottage to the ground or throwing myself down the stairs. They've been very good to me, but them moving in would be a disaster, don't you think?'

'I wouldn't say a disaster,' said Freya slowly, imagining a twelve-year-old stomping up and down the stairs and slamming doors.

'Merely an appalling mistake, then?' The ghost of a smile played on Kathleen's lips. 'Don't look so surprised, Freya. I'm simply being honest. I love my son but I have no urge to live with him at my age, and I can't see Chloe sitting in here of an evening to keep me company. Can you?'

'Not really.'

'Whereas, you're paid to listen to me so you have no choice.'

'I'm sure that slipping Chloe a bit of cash would do the trick.'

'You're probably right.' Kathleen settled back in her chair as another squall of rain battered against the window. She looked so done in, Freya's heart ached.

'Kathleen, I'm not sitting here talking to you because I'm paid to. I enjoy our conversations.'

Kathleen properly smiled at that. 'So do I. You're a good listener, Freya, which is a gift. There's something about you that makes it easy to open up in your company. But I'm sure you've heard that before.'

'Thank you,' said Freya, warmed by Kathleen's compliment. 'I try to be a good listener.' She grinned. 'Though my friends say my main attribute is being an excellent keeper of secrets.'

'Do you know lots of secrets then?'

'Yes, a fair few. People seem to feel obliged to tell me things. It must be my face or something. But it does them good to talk and I don't mind.'

Not usually, anyway. Freya remembered the anger and

disappointment in Ryan's eyes when he discovered that she'd kept Chloe's cliff leap from him.

Kathleen went back to staring into the fire as a fork of lightning lit up the room. 'And who do *you* talk to?' she asked quietly, in the gap before a growl of thunder began.

Freya waited for the noise to fade away before answering. 'I talk to my friends sometimes, though they're all pretty busy these days.'

She paused, not sure whether to say what had sprung into her mind. It was so very personal. But sitting here in the firelight while a storm enveloped this ancient cottage seemed to encourage the sharing of confidences. 'I also had some counselling a couple of years ago,' she added, 'after I had a miscarriage.'

'I'm dreadfully sorry to hear that,' said Kathleen.

Freya gave a sad smile. 'Me too.'

There hadn't been any pregnancies before or after. Just the one that had opened a door to a whole new shining future, before the door was cruelly slammed shut.

She and Greg had waited until their mid-thirties to try for a baby and she'd simply assumed that it would happen quickly. Her friends were all having babies and even their tales of horrendous labours hadn't put her off. But the months came and went with only the one doomed pregnancy to raise her hopes.

She'd been terribly upset, but Greg was busy with his career and didn't seem to mind being childless that much. He didn't want any medical investigations and wouldn't even consider IVF or adoption, so that was that. The counselling had helped.

'Are you all right, Freya?' asked Kathleen.

Freya did her best to smile. 'Yes, thanks. The miscarriage was just one of those things.'

One of those things that was rarely mentioned but would forever have a place in her heart.

'I'm sorry. I didn't mean to upset you,' said Kathleen when Freya went quiet. But Freya shook her head.

'No, it's all right. Sometimes it's good to talk about these things, rather than trying to keep them damped down inside.'

'Keeping painful things repressed can be so very corrosive,' said Kathleen, staring out of the dark window at the shadowy branches of the tree in the garden.

And she was so obviously talking about herself, Freya said without thinking, 'I'm always here if talking about anything would help.'

'I don't think acting as a counsellor is a part of your job description. You don't get paid enough for that,' said Kathleen, still staring into the distance.

'It wouldn't be counselling. It would be two friends talking.' Freya got up and knelt at Kathleen's feet to adjust the blanket on her legs, which had slipped.

'I've never been much of a talker.' Kathleen turned her gaze from the window. 'My family now, back in Ireland, they could talk for hours about absolutely nothing at all and they frequently did. But I was different.'

Freya sat back on her heels in front of the fire. Kathleen rarely spoke about her Irish family.

'Would you like to go back to Ireland one day, for a visit?' she asked.

But Kathleen ignored her question and leaned forward. 'Do you think talking helps? Proper talking about things, I mean.'

'Sometimes. If you pick the right person and the right time.'

'Some people tell you everything, every little slight or mishap that's happened to them over the years. Even though it's all in the past and there's nothing to be done about it now. My mammy used to say, "There's no point in crying over spilt milk, Kathleen." She was always very good at letting things go – sorrows, mistakes... people.'

Firelight danced over Kathleen's face as she let out a sigh

that made her body shudder. There was such pain in her eyes, Freya put her hand on top of Kathleen's bony fingers.

'I lost a child too, you know.' Kathleen's words were so quiet they were almost lost in the crackle of the flames. 'I lost a child and her name was Maeve.'

23

FREYA

The wind had started to howl and the flames in the fireplace began to splutter and dance. Outside, trees bent under the onslaught and the sea was whipped into towering dark waves that crashed up and over the village quayside.

But here in Kathleen's old cottage, it felt to Freya that she was at the eye of a storm. A storm that, for this elderly woman, had been brewing for decades.

Kathleen bowed her head, suddenly looking much older than eighty-three. 'Can I be confident that you won't mention this to Belinda? Can I trust you?'

'Yes, you can trust me. Belinda and I aren't close and your business is none of hers.'

Kathleen stared at Freya for a moment before nodding. 'It's odd but I trusted you from the moment I saw you. There's something about you that reminds me of my sister, Clodagh.'

Freya was touched to be compared to Clodagh, who'd given Kathleen a home when she first moved to England. Although she'd died many years ago, she was the only family member from Ireland whom Kathleen regularly mentioned.

'Did Clodagh know about Maeve?' asked Freya.

'Yes, she knew about my daughter but we rarely talked about her.'

'You don't have to talk about Maeve now, not if you don't want to.'

Kathleen gave another great sigh that seemed to come from the depths of her soul.

'But I do want to. That's the point. I'm getting older, Freya, and I have to tell someone about my daughter. Or when I'm gone, it will be as though she never existed at all. But now you know her name and that she was once here with me and she was loved.'

She turned her face towards the hearth, her white hair glowing in the firelight.

'What happened to Maeve?' asked Freya gently.

'I don't know,' whispered Kathleen, before burying her face in her hands. 'Isn't that appalling? I'm her mother and I have no idea what happened to her.'

When sobs began to shake her frail body, Freya moved close and put her arm around her shoulders. She let the elderly woman cry without saying a word, as rain streamed down the dark windows.

At last, the sobbing eased and Kathleen lifted her head. She took the clean tissue that Freya had pulled from her jeans pocket and wiped her eyes roughly, as though she was angry with herself.

Freya moved back to kneel on the floor. 'What happened, Kathleen?'

She thought back to the photo of a young Kathleen gazing across the ocean; the change that had come over Kathleen when they neared the clifftop; and Eileen Woolford's diary entry: *Saw people from Driftwood in the village, which is unusual because they rarely venture out. I pity them.*

'Did it have something to do with Driftwood House?' she asked.

Kathleen smiled through her tears. 'You're an astute one. How did you know? Was it the way I reacted when you drove up to the house by mistake?'

'It was that, and the photo I found of you on the day you fell over.'

'What photo?'

'A photo of you standing outside Driftwood House a long time ago.' Freya winced as she confessed about intruding on Kathleen's memories. 'I honestly wasn't snooping but I was looking for the antiseptic cream upstairs and it was at the back of your drawer.'

'You... you saw that picture?'

For a moment, Kathleen's face sagged and she looked older than ever. But then she shrugged. 'Oh, what does it matter, Freya? What does any of it matter? It's all too late.' She closed her eyes briefly before taking a deep breath. 'When I stayed at Driftwood House sixty-four years ago, I was pregnant.' Her voice sounded flat, as though all emotion had been wrung out of it. 'I was nineteen years old and I'd brought terrible shame on my family.'

'Why were you at Driftwood House?' asked Freya, her head reeling. 'Were you in a relationship with someone who lived there?'

'Heavens, no, child. Driftwood House was a mother and baby home back then, set up for the moral correction of fallen women like me.' The bitterness in her voice was palpable. 'They provided bed and board until we had our babies and then they took our children from us.'

Freya stopped breathing, unaware of the storm outside. The fire was dying but she made no move to add more wood to the flames. It all made sense now. The photograph, Kathleen's aversion to going too near the house, Eileen Woolford's words: *I pity them.*

'That's awful, Kathleen,' she managed. 'I can't even imagine how dreadful it was for you.'

Kathleen spoke, the flat, matter-of-fact tone back in her voice. 'I was so young and frightened and my family were appalled. They were very religious people. We lived in a small village out in the country where everything revolved around the church.

'I'd been staying up in Dublin with a cousin, helping her to run her mother's shop, when I fell pregnant. I was wooed by an older man who flattered me into believing he loved me. He promised me the world but, when I found out I was going to have a baby, I also found out they were hollow promises. He was married, you see, just to compound my sin in my family's eyes. I didn't know it at the time but he was married with a young family, and he wanted nothing more to do with me.'

Freya's heart ached for the elderly woman in front of her and the young woman she once was. 'You must have been devastated.'

'I was, and so were my family. My cousin sent me back home to Kerry, of course, but it was too much for my parents. I'd left home a naïve teenager and come back an unwed mother-to-be. My father said some dreadful things to me. Things I'll never forget.' She paused, her mind locked in a painful past. 'The local priest denounced me and arranged for me to come to Driftwood House for my confinement. It was so far away, all the way over here, and there was no risk of me bumping into anyone my family knew and bringing even more shame upon them. Out of sight, out of mind. My father told me... he told me—'

When she stopped, her head hung low, Freya clasped both Kathleen's hands in hers. 'What did your father tell you?'

Kathleen lifted her head. 'He told me that I was no longer his daughter and I would never be welcome in his house.'

'Surely he didn't mean it?'

'Oh, he meant it, all right. My father never said anything he didn't mean.'

'Did your mother go along with it?' asked Freya, aghast at the cruelty.

Kathleen nodded. 'She had no choice, but she agreed with him. I could see the anger and disappointment in her eyes. So that's how I came to be at Driftwood House on my own.'

'It must have been so frightening.'

'It was. And... they were my family. I loved them so much. I'd been horribly homesick when I was in Dublin. That's one reason I was more open to Fergal's—' She checked herself. 'The baby's father's attentions. So being cast out by my family for ever was...' A tear ran down her wrinkled cheek and plopped into her lap. 'It was too much for me.'

'It would be too much for anyone.'

Freya squeezed Kathleen's hands. She wanted to rail against Kathleen's family for sending a terrified young woman away from everything and everyone she knew and loved. But that wouldn't help. Not now, so many years later when the damage was done.

'Life was difficult at Driftwood House. We worked hard doing chores and there wasn't much kindness from the nuns who ran it.' Kathleen continued, as though now she'd started telling her story, she didn't want to stop. 'We were encouraged not to go into the village but at least we had the amazing view from up there on the cliffs. I used to sit on the grass on the rare occasions I had five minutes to myself and watch the ocean endlessly moving while I dreamed of a life for me and the child growing inside me.'

'And... what happened to Maeve?' asked Freya, desperate to know but dreading Kathleen's answer.

'I had my baby on April the sixth, at three in the morning. It was a long, hard labour with no pain relief – I believe the pain was considered a part of our punishment – but my daughter was absolutely perfect. I called her Maeve and I loved her so much. I stayed with her at Driftwood House for two weeks, until she was taken.'

The fire had died down to the glow of the embers and the room was filled with shadows. Thunder growled in the distance as the storm, now spent, swept out to sea.

'Maeve was supposed to be with me for longer than that but perhaps I was getting too close to her, too upset about what was to come. So the nuns betrayed me and our precious time together was cut short. One of them came in, an older woman who'd taken against me from the start. She told me to dress Maeve and quickly say goodbye, and that was that. They took her from my arms and I never saw her again.'

'So she was adopted?'

'That's right. They said it was for the best because I couldn't look after her. I couldn't take her back to my family, I had no job and no home, and there wasn't the support available that there is now. Perhaps it *was* for the best in the circumstances but...' Kathleen leaned towards Freya, her body in shadow. 'I've been haunted from the last moment I saw her face.'

'Oh, Kathleen, I'm so sorry.' Tears were rolling down Freya's cheeks and she brushed them away. This was Kathleen's heartache, not hers, but the story was so unbearably sad. 'What did you do, afterwards?'

'Clodagh took me in. She was working in London and living in a shared house. I stayed with her and got a job and tried to forget.'

'Did you ever see your parents again?'

'I never saw my father. I've never been back to Ireland, but my mother came to visit Clodagh in London once. I had one small black and white photo of Maeve but my mother went through my belongings and found it and ripped it up. I don't think she was a wicked woman but she thought that having no reminders would ease the pain.' Kathleen shook her head. 'She was wrong.'

The room was now in semi-darkness and Freya switched on a second lamp. Its amber glow spilled out from the corner, chasing away the shadows. She sat back down on the floor and put a hand over her mouth. She'd just realised something.

'The other morning when I heard you crying, that was April the sixth.'

'It was Maeve's birthday, and today is April the twentieth, the anniversary of the day that I last saw her. Over the years, I've learned to live without Maeve and I've had a good life in many ways. Frank was a good man and I love Ryan and Chloe, but the anniversaries are always hard to bear.'

'What about the photo I found?' asked Freya.

'That was taken on my last day at Driftwood House, by a girl I befriended at the home. Her son was taken and we said we'd stay in touch, but we never did. She sent me the photo and that was that. Maybe she didn't want reminders either. But I needed a reminder, especially after my mother destroyed the picture of Maeve. I needed something tangible to prove that I was here so long ago and my daughter did exist.'

The clock on the church tower struck eight o'clock, its chimes loud in the quiet room. Freya ran her hands through her hair, overwhelmed by the emotion of what she'd just heard.

'What I don't understand, Kathleen, is why you would come back to Heaven's Cove when it held so many painful memories for you?'

Surprise flitted across Kathleen's face. 'There was nowhere else I'd rather be. This was the only place I'd ever been with my daughter, the only place where I'd held her in my arms. Like the photo you found, being here made her more real as my memories started to fade. I've never been back to the house and I don't want to go there but it's where Maeve was born. I have no idea where she is now, but once upon a time she was there, at Drift-wood House, with me.'

'But you waited until Frank died to move here.'

'He wouldn't have wanted to come to Heaven's Cove. I told him about Maeve when we were engaged but we never spoke about her after we were married. He was a good man but a jealous and insecure one and the thought of me having a child with another man didn't sit well with him.'

'That must have been hard for you.'

'It was lonely sometimes, not being able to talk to him. But I was busy with my marriage and then bringing up Ryan.'

'Does Ryan know about Maeve?' asked Freya quietly.

Kathleen shook her head. 'No, and I don't want him to know.'

Freya closed her eyes for a moment, feeling uncomfortable. Was this another secret she'd have to keep?

'I'm sure he'd understand, Kathleen.'

'Perhaps he would but that's not a risk I'm willing to take. How can I tell him now, after he's believed himself an only child for so long? What would he think of me? I've already lost one child and I don't want to lose the respect of another.'

The thought of Ryan ever reacting in that way broke Freya's heart. She knew how much he loved his mother. It was clear to see every day, in the way he cared for her and had checked up on Freya, to make sure she was providing the best possible support.

'I'm sure he'd want to know, Kathleen,' she urged. 'He'd be sorry that you've been hurting for all these years.'

Kathleen shook her head again. 'No. What's the point in upsetting him when he's already had such upset in his life? Maeve has been a secret for so long and I can hardly bear it. I'm in my eighties now and I'll never know what happened to my darling daughter. I don't want my son to carry that burden when I'm gone.'

Freya sighed but it was up to Kathleen, even though, in her opinion, she was making the wrong decision.

'Have you ever tried to find Maeve?' she asked.

'It was never the right time to look, and what if she didn't want to know me? What if her new parents had never told her she was adopted? What if she hates me?' Kathleen shook her head. 'And now it's too late anyway. The home closed over sixty years ago, the place was run by a religious organisation that no longer exists, and I doubt they kept proper records. It all seemed a little unofficial and off the books. I have to accept that Maeve is lost for good. I suppose in coming back here a little part of me hoped that maybe she'd try to find me. Maybe she'd come back to the village if she ever found out she was born here, but she's never come.'

'I could help you to look for her if you'd like,' Freya blurted out, desperate to do something to ease the poor woman's pain. But Kathleen shook her head again.

'It's too late, Freya. Far too late.'

'I'm so sorry.'

Kathleen shrugged. 'I've made my peace with it as much as I can. I learned to live with the pain of it and the fury that she was taken. For a while, I was a very angry young woman, but that's faded over the years and now all that remains is deep sadness.' She exhaled slowly. 'Thank you for listening. I feel lighter for having spoken Maeve's name out loud to another human being and I feel blessed that you've come into my life. But please promise me that you won't breathe a word of any of this to Belinda or to Ryan.'

'I promise I won't say anything to Belinda, but secrets within families can fester and do damage. Are you sure Ryan wouldn't want to know?'

'I'm sure it's for the best that he doesn't know. So, promise me. Please. I trusted you and I need your solemn word.'

There was desperation in her eyes and a trace of fear.

Freya thought back to her promise to Ryan, that she wouldn't keep any more secrets from him about his family. But what choice did she have? Kathleen had entrusted her with precious information about her daughter, and was begging her to keep it to herself. This was about Kathleen, not Ryan or Freya or any difficulties that keeping this secret might cause between the two of them.

She nodded. 'I won't betray your trust, Kathleen, and I'm honoured that you told me about Maeve.'

Kathleen sighed with relief and patted Freya's hand.

'Thank you, child. Now, if you don't mind, I think I'll get myself off to bed early. It's been a tiring day.' She wobbled when she got to her feet but batted away Freya's attempt to help her. 'I can do this on my own tonight. You make yourself a hot chocolate and have some time to yourself. You deserve it.'

Freya watched Kathleen slowly climb the stairs. Then, she went into the kitchen and cried as the milk for her hot chocolate came to the boil. She'd shed tears over the children she'd never had, but how awful to have a child who was out there somewhere in the world but lost for good.

She felt honoured that Kathleen had entrusted her with such a painful secret, and she would keep her promise to keep it to herself. Of course she would. That's what she did.

But keeping Kathleen's secret meant keeping a huge secret from Ryan. Even though she'd given him her word, after Chloe's ill-fated cliff jump, that she would never ever do such a thing again.

It was impossible to keep one promise without breaking another.

24

FREYA

Freya didn't sleep well. That was the trouble with being the keeper of secrets. You ended up being the keeper of all the angst that went along with them.

She slept fitfully and was woken at dawn by what sounded like a baby crying. Thoroughly spooked, she got out of bed and padded onto the landing. But the wailing had stopped and, when she put her ear to the door of Kathleen's bedroom, all she could hear was gentle snoring.

Before getting back into bed, hoping to snooze for a while longer, she went to the window at the back of the landing. It looked out over the garden and onwards to the cliff that overlooked the village, and there, perched on the top, stood Driftwood House. The house that drew Kathleen to it but distressed her up close.

This morning the white building looked benign in the pale sun that was peeping over the horizon. Nowadays, it was a cosy seaside guesthouse that welcomed visitors to the village. But sixty years ago it had echoed to the cries of newborn babies and the sobs of their mothers.

How cruel the system had been back then. Freya was

grateful that times had changed and mothers were no longer parted from their children under duress. She could only imagine the heartache that Kathleen and so many others like her had quietly suffered over the years.

Freya watched the sun rise higher and score the sky with streaks of pink and gold. What had become of Maeve? she wondered. Was she standing somewhere this morning looking at the same sky? Did she have a happy life?

Her thoughts turned to Ryan and the half-sister he knew nothing about. She and Belinda weren't close, far from it. But Freya was glad they had some kind of relationship. She and Belinda shared the same genes and were joined together by a background that had shaped them both. Never knowing Belinda would have left a hole in Freya's life, she realised.

But now Freya knew about Maeve and Ryan didn't. Freya opened the window and breathed in the fresh salty air. Perhaps, she reasoned, if Maeve was never going to be found, it was for the best. You couldn't mourn what you didn't know you'd lost.

She shivered. The morning air held a trace of dampness which chilled to the bone. She made her way back to bed but didn't sleep before her alarm sounded an hour later.

Freya was cooking breakfast, feeling half dead, when Kathleen came into the kitchen. She'd put on a pretty dress Freya hadn't seen before and there seemed to be a new spring in her step as she put a glass into the dishwasher and sat at the table.

'Did you sleep well?' asked Freya, sliding a fried egg onto a plate. Kathleen loved a cooked breakfast and Freya was happy to oblige.

'Not at first. A beautiful moon came out after the storm had passed so I sat for a while looking at Driftwood House. It gave me time to think about everything. Then I slept better than I've slept for a long time. Talking to you put a lot straight in my mind, Freya.'

'I'm so glad it helped.'

Kathleen poured herself coffee from the freshly brewed pot next to her. The prospect of caffeine, lots of it, was all that was keeping Freya going this morning.

'What about you? How did you sleep?' asked Kathleen.

'Not too badly,' lied Freya, deciding not to mention the sound of a baby crying. It must have been the wind whistling round the chimney of this old cottage.

Kathleen took a sip of steaming hot coffee. 'I think I might walk into the village this morning and call in to see Ryan and Chloe. They arrived home late last night. Ryan picked Chloe up on the way back from the airport. He sent me a text first thing this morning. It's good to have them back.'

It *would* be good to have them back, thought Freya, her stomach clenching as she pictured the man with the beautiful green eyes who'd said he trusted her. It *would* be good if she wasn't now deceiving him.

Kathleen looked up from her drink. 'I truly am grateful to you for listening last night. I hadn't realised quite how much I needed to tell someone about Ma... Maeve.' She stumbled over her daughter's name as though she was unused to saying it out loud. 'My daughter is no longer a secret and I feel lighter and so much better, especially as you're going to help me.'

'Help you?' Freya put the plate filled with egg, bacon and beans in front of Kathleen and stepped back. 'Help you with what?'

'With finding Maeve. You offered to help me find out what happened to her.'

'I thought you said you didn't think that was a good idea,' said Freya slowly.

'I did but I had a change of heart as I sat looking at Drift-wood House last night. Telling you about my daughter made me realise how much I do need to find out what happened to her. It'll be easier now Frank has passed on and my parents are long gone. I don't want anything from my daughter. I don't expect anything at all. But I need to know, before I go to my grave, that she's had a good life. You can understand that, can't you?'

'Yes, of course I can.' Freya was aware of a niggling headache starting above her right temple. 'But what if you find out something you'd rather not know?'

'That's a risk and it's a risk I've never been willing to take. But I'm old now, Freya, and it's time to know the truth, whatever that truth may be. It's haunted me for long enough and I honestly don't think I can bear it any longer.' Kathleen put down her knife and fork. 'I know it's a lot to ask, but will you help me? I don't have anyone else to turn to and you young people are so much better with the internet. Perhaps there's a trace of Maeve somewhere.'

Freya turned off the hob and dropped the frying pan into the sink, her mind whirring. She'd offered to help find Maeve because she couldn't bear the thought of Kathleen being separated from her daughter – a child she'd been forced to give up, unlike Freya's own mother, who had chosen to leave her child behind. Kathleen's heartache was stirring up painful memories from Freya's own life that she'd thought long buried. But Freya couldn't turn Kathleen down. She looked so anguished.

Pushing her shoulders back, Freya nodded. 'Yes, I can help you search for Maeve. But what about Ryan? He should be told if you're actually going to look for his half-sister.'

Kathleen's mouth set in the stubborn line that Freya was starting to recognise.

'Absolutely not. Not unless there's something that's worth knowing. We might never find my daughter and I don't want to cause upset for no reason.'

'He's an adult, Kathleen, who's already coped with one of

the worst things that life can throw at you. So I'm sure he can cope with this.'

Kathleen shook her head. 'You didn't see him after Natalie died. He was a broken man and he's never been the same since, even after all this time. So I won't have him losing someone else. It wouldn't—'

Kathleen stopped speaking as the front door slammed.

'Mum, where are you?' called Ryan from the hall.

'You can't tell him,' insisted Kathleen, grabbing hold of Freya's arm and gripping so tightly it hurt. 'Please. You promised me that you can keep a secret.'

Oh, she could keep a secret all right. But the heft of this one was almost too much for her. Secrets held power – the power to surprise or delight, to hurt or harm – because they were so often bound up with primal emotions. Kathleen's tragic secret was laced through with love and fear and shame. It had cast a pall over the old lady's life, and now it risked the new life that Freya was tentatively building here. A life, she realised as she heard Ryan getting closer, that she wanted so much to continue.

But Kathleen was adamant and she'd suffered so much already.

Freya sighed. 'If that's what you want, Kathleen. But he'll have to know sometime.'

'Maybe,' muttered Kathleen as the kitchen door opened. 'Maybe not.'

'There you both are,' said Ryan, walking into the kitchen closely followed by Chloe. A newspaper-wrapped parcel was under his arm.

Looking rested, he bent to give his mum a hug at the table and caught Freya's eye as he was straightening up. His smile, bright against his sun-kissed skin, took her breath away. She'd worried that he'd been avoiding her, since she'd rushed out of the pub like an idiot. But he looked happy enough to see her now.

She smiled back but her smile was dimmed by a growing sense of guilt. If only he knew what she knew. If only he knew what she was keeping from him.

'I thought you'd like to see Chloe, Mum, seeing as she's been away for almost a week,' he said in his deep voice.

'You thought right, and it's lovely to see you too. How was your conference?'

'It was pretty boring, to be honest, but Barcelona was fantastic and I can't wait to go back. Have you ever been?' He'd addressed his question to Freya, who shook her head. 'You must go one day.'

An image of Ryan taking her hand and leading her through the ancient back streets of Barcelona popped into Freya's mind and she batted it away. Everything was getting far too complicated.

'What about you, Chloe? Did you enjoy your time with Auntie Sarah?' asked Kathleen.

'Was all right, I s'pose,' muttered Chloe, who was loitering in the doorway. Ryan was still smiling, but his daughter most definitely was not.

She grunted a few more words to her grandmother and scowled at Freya, who frowned. What was wrong with Chloe? She hadn't seen her since Ryan had confronted her about the cliff jump. But it wasn't her fault that her father had found out. And Ryan had assured her he'd told Chloe that she wasn't the 'bad guy' who'd blabbed.

Freya's shoulders slumped. She wanted so much to fit in with this family. She liked them, perhaps more than was sensible at times, and she was starting to feel at home here. But none of them were making it easy. And now there was Kathleen's new bombshell...

'It really is wonderful to see you both. You're out very early,' said Kathleen, with a loaded glance at Freya, who pulled herself together and fetched a coffee cup for Ryan.

'I went to the harbour to buy fish for lunch and I got extra in case you both fancied some plaice. Chloe was up and about and I reckoned she'd like to see her grandmother.'

He'd reckoned wrongly, thought Freya, moving the parcel of fish from the table onto the draining board. Chloe had moved to stand by the back door and was staring into the garden, as though she'd rather be anywhere but here.

'Come and sit with us, Freya, and have a coffee,' said Ryan, ignoring his surly daughter.

'In a minute. I'd better get the fish in the fridge and the washing up done first.'

'Can't you do that later? Come and sit with us.'

When Ryan smiled, Freya's stomach did a flip, but whether through attraction or guilt, she couldn't be sure. She'd promised not to keep anything from this man and, while she could just about square keeping Kathleen's sad story a secret, now she would be actively taking part in trying to find his half-sister – the half-sister he knew nothing about.

'Thanks but I'd really better get this fish into the fridge or it'll smell the place down, and I don't want the water to go luke-warm before I tackle the greasy pans.'

'Sure. That makes sense.'

Ryan turned back to his coffee but not before Freya had caught a flash of disappointment in his eyes. But even if he liked her now, he certainly wouldn't when he found out what she was doing.

Though maybe he'd never know. Freya would help Kathleen to look for Maeve but if her lost child was never found, Ryan would be none the wiser.

Freya was ashamed when hope surged through her. Ryan would only remain oblivious to what was going on if Kathleen never discovered what had happened to her daughter. And that was too high a price to pay. Even if Maeve had completely vanished, could Freya keep quiet about a woman who should be so important in his life?

Freya had come to Heaven's Cove in search of a fresh start, but life right now seemed more complicated than ever. Her headache had started banging and Chloe was still scowling at her from the back door.

Freya opened Kathleen's medicine cupboard in search of paracetamol and surreptitiously downed a couple of tablets while Ryan was telling Kathleen about his trip to Spain. Chloe spotted what she was doing and narrowed her eyes but said nothing.

Freya got herself a coffee and sat down at the table, only half listening to Ryan and Kathleen's conversation. She was beginning to wish she'd never got up at all this morning.

25

CHLOE

Honestly, Freya had such a cheek! She was sitting there, like she owned the place, simpering at her father. She'd even said hello to Chloe when she and her dad had come into the room, as though everything was OK between them. But she was a liar. A liar who'd told tales about her jumping from Clair Point, after she'd promised that she never would.

Her dad had told her he didn't want to say who'd grassed, but it wasn't Freya. But he would say that, wouldn't he? No one else knew except Paige and her gang, who'd never have said anything. Her dad just didn't want her causing a fuss with his mother's new carer.

Chloe, standing next to her grandmother's back door, started drumming her heels against the wooden frame. And the disapproving glance her father gave her made her drum even louder. She was so tired of being told what to do. She was tired of being shipped off to an aunt she hardly knew so her dad could go to stupid Spain. But most of all she was tired of feeling... she wasn't sure quite how she was feeling these days. Everything seemed very confusing. But she knew she didn't like it.

'Chloe, love, do you think you could be a bit quieter over there?'

Her grandmother's words pierced Chloe's bad humour and, with a loud sigh to signal her displeasure, she set her feet firmly on the vinyl tiles. They'd become marked over the years and the kitchen was shabby – nothing like Isobel's new, modern kitchen with its sleek lines. That was like a celebrity kitchen on MTV. This one was more like a shabby kitchen in the boring dramas that her dad watched.

Chloe sniffed. The plaice her dad had dragged her out to buy this morning was in the fridge but the kitchen still smelled of fish. Fish, and burned toast, and old lady. Chloe gnawed at the inside of her cheek, feeling guilty.

Her gran was always kind to her and Chloe loved her, but she seemed a lot older and more gaga these days. So much so, she needed Freya to move in and look after her. Chloe gave Freya another scowl for good measure and was rewarded with a frown. Good. She knew what she'd done. And she had a headache if the pills she was popping were anything to go by.

'Right, well, we'd better get on. Chloe has got homework to do before the Easter holidays are over.'

When her dad got to his feet, his fingers brushed Freya's. It looked like an accident but Chloe narrowed her eyes. They both knew it had happened. Her dad looked weird and Freya, too. Her gran was shovelling bacon into her mouth and hadn't noticed a thing. But then she was oblivious to most things these days. Did that mean she would die soon? Fear clutched at Chloe's stomach as her thoughts ran away with her, and she swallowed hard.

'See you, Gran,' she said, as kindly as she could.

'It was lovely to see you both.'

Kathleen grabbed Chloe's hand as she walked past and pulled her in for a hug. If Paige had been around, Chloe would have shrugged her off but she let herself be held for a moment.

Her gran's body was warm and reassuring and sometimes Chloe imagined it was her mum with her arms around her.

Her mum wouldn't make her go out for walks and get stressy about her doing her homework. Or freak out about her jumping from Clair Point. Actually, Chloe wasn't one hundred per cent sure about that but she liked to think that her mum would be more laid back than her dad. Her mum would fight her corner. Her mum would understand why nothing made sense sometimes.

Chloe felt tears prickling her eyes and pushed away from her gran. Sometimes it was best not to think about what you were missing.

'Nice to see you too,' she muttered, following her dad out of the kitchen, being careful not to look at Freya at all.

Outside, the wind had picked up and it was freezing even though it was supposed to be spring. Chloe began to regret not wearing her thick coat but she shook her head when her dad asked if she was cold. It was only when he'd advised her to wear her thick coat that she'd decided to wear her thin jacket instead.

Deep down, she knew that was foolish. She knew she was the one suffering for it, not her dad. But she felt that she needed to hit out at someone or something these days, and her dad was the one constant who would put up with her crap.

They were walking past the quay, with the roof of their cottage in sight, when Chloe spotted Paige and Isobel walking towards them. Her heart started beating faster because she needed to be ready to see them. Out of the blue, before she'd had time to settle herself, they could be overwhelming.

'Ryan! I haven't seen you around for a while,' said Isobel, who was looking amazing, as always. She'd dyed her hair snow white – the same colour as her gran's, actually – and it made her look like a model.

'I've been to Spain for work. There was a conference in Barcelona.'

'I didn't know that.'

Isobel's reply made Chloe blink because she so did know that. Chloe had told Paige about it a week ago, while Isobel was there too.

'It looks as though Spain really suited you. A tan makes you even more devastatingly handsome.'

When Isobel winked at her dad and touched his arm, Chloe fought down the conflicting emotions that were tumbling through her. She liked to imagine having Isobel as a stepmother and Paige as her sister. That could happen, couldn't it? And it would be pretty cool. Mostly. But Jade at school said her mum called Isobel a flirt and a gold-digger, which didn't sound good. And Chloe didn't want her dad to be hurt, even though he was, like, totally annoying all the time.

'How's Freya?'

Isobel's question took Chloe by surprise. Why was she asking about Gran's carer? Her dad looked a bit taken aback too.

'She's fine, I think,' he answered.

Isobel smiled. 'That's good. I wondered how she was settling in and thought something might be wrong. Last time I saw you both, you were deep in conversation in the Smugglers Haunt.'

Chloe glanced at her dad, who hadn't mentioned anything about taking Freya to the pub.

He smiled back at Isobel. 'Everything's fine. Mum suggested that Freya and I have a quick drink while we discussed some family stuff.'

Trust Gran to suggest something lame like that.

Isobel felt the tips of her long fingernails with her thumbs. 'So it was kind of a work meeting.'

'That's right.'

'Hmm. And how are you, Chloe?' asked Isobel, breaking into her thoughts.

'Fine, thank you,' mumbled Chloe, feeling caught out. She

often felt uncomfortable around Isobel, she suddenly realised. Maybe it was because her perpetually flawless make-up and shiny white-blonde hair was such a contrast to Chloe's skin, which was increasingly spotty these days, and her hair, which looked lank even when it was freshly washed.

'Where are you two off to?' trilled Isobel.

'We're heading home. We've been to see my mum.'

Chloe winced because that made it sound like she was a little child who'd been visiting her gran.

'Now what I really wanted to ask is... what are you like with sheds, Ryan?' asked Isobel, fluttering her long eyelashes.

That was a bit left field, thought Chloe, and her dad obviously agreed. He frowned.

'Um... sheds?'

'Only mine lost part of its roof in that dreadful storm last night and I wondered if you might be able to patch it up for me. To stop the rain coming in. I would ask my ex but, unlike you, he doesn't have the muscles for it.'

Her tinkly laugh went straight through Chloe. She was definitely flirting with her dad, which was both gross and exciting. Gross because she couldn't imagine her dad kissing anyone, and exciting because if Isobel did hook up with her dad, that might give her brownie points with Paige.

She looked at Paige but she was staring at her dad, with an amused expression on her face. He was wearing his weird yellow jumper again, the one the colour of mustard, and there was a hole in the shoulder. A hot rush of shame flooded through her, making her cheeks burn. She was ashamed of her dad, and ashamed of herself for feeling that way.

'I guess I could come round and have a look at it,' said her dad.

'Wonderful! And don't forget that I'm happy to help Chloe get ready for the school dance which is fast approaching. Only a fortnight to go!' Her long nails caught in Chloe's hair when

Isobel ran her hand across her head. 'You want to look your best, don't you, darling? A school disco – how exciting! At my school discos, we used to snog in the corner with the fit boys from the upper sixth.' Snog? No one said 'snog' any more. Chloe winced inside but her dad was smiling. 'So it's a date, Chloe. We'll see you on dance day at six o'clock?'

Chloe hesitated. Did Paige want her company? She didn't look too unhappy about it, and help with getting ready was much needed. She had a new dress that she'd chosen from a shop in Exeter while her dad hovered self-consciously outside the changing room. But it didn't look that nice. No doubt, Paige would look stunning. She'd shown them a photo of her dress, which was silver and sparkly with little spaghetti straps.

'You can get ready at home if you'd rather,' said her dad, giving her arm a squeeze.

But Chloe had made up her mind. 'That would be great, thanks.'

Maybe Paige and Isobel could make her sparkle too.

26

FREYA

It had seemed like a good idea at the time but now Freya wasn't so sure. Having found nothing relevant online about Driftwood House's past, going to the house itself seemed like the obvious next step. But Kathleen had insisted on coming and she was looking more nervous by the second.

'Are you sure about this?' asked Freya, for the third time since they'd left the house in Ryan's car. They'd just trundled up the shockingly pot-holed cliff road and were parked with Driftwood House in front of them and the sea all around. 'I can take you back home, or you can sit in the car and wait for me.'

Kathleen looked out of the passenger seat at the water, which was grey with white-crested waves, and shook her head.

'I want to do whatever's necessary to find Maeve. I've had no involvement in her life since the moment she was taken from me, so this seems the least I can do.' She shifted in her seat and stared directly at the white-washed building in front of her. 'I've been drawn to this building for decades and terrified of it too. When we took Chloe out for picnics, I always suggested the beach or Dartmoor or a different headland. There are too many memories up here. But it's time to face my fears, don't you think?'

'Maybe. Maybe not.' Freya gently touched Kathleen's shoulder. 'It's not a defeat if you wait here for me. I can go to the house on my own and see what information I can find.'

She crossed her fingers because going on her own would be better. Not only would it be less upsetting for Kathleen, it would also give Freya some breathing space. Since she'd agreed to help find Maeve five days ago, Kathleen had asked on the hour every hour if there was any news. And her face fell every time when the answer was no.

But Kathleen took a deep breath and pulled her shoulders back. 'I know you're trying to do what's best for me, Freya, but I've avoided this for long enough. I need to lay my ghosts to rest, so let's get on with it, shall we?'

A blast of wind swirled around the inside of the car when she pushed open the door and levered herself out of the passenger seat. Freya watched her walk off slowly across the cliff, towards the house. She admired Kathleen for facing up to her demons, but what can of worms might she be about to open? She thought again of Ryan, blissfully unaware of what was happening here, high above the village. He would hate her involvement in it. Freya, shaking her head, got out of the car and followed Kathleen.

A large sign said DRIFTWOOD GUESTHOUSE and, even on a grey day, the house looked welcoming. It was surrounded by wild flowers scattered across the clifftop. The view was magnificent, the village was tiny far below, and the sea stretched as far as the eye could see.

Freya recognised the front door from the old photo she'd come across in Kathleen's bedroom. The heavy wooden door was weather-beaten and looked original. She imagined the younger version of the woman beside her, imagined her standing right here, her heart broken and aching for her child.

The child she wouldn't see for sixty years, or perhaps never, ever again.

Freya placed her hand on Kathleen's arm, to steady her, and knocked on the door.

'How long has this place been a guesthouse?' she asked, hoping to ease Kathleen's nerves while they waited for the door to open.

'Not that long. Only since last summer. Rosie inherited the house after her mother died last year and decided to take in paying guests. According to your sister, the business has been doing well, though I dare say it's been quieter over the winter months. When storms roll in, it can get very bleak up here.'

Freya shivered, imagining black storms sweeping in from the sea and engulfing the house along with the pregnant women and grieving new mothers inside.

The door was suddenly pulled open by a young woman in jeans and a sweatshirt. Her clothes were covered by an apron and there was a white streak of flour on her cheek.

'Hello,' said the woman, a note of surprise in her voice. 'Kathleen, how lovely to see you up here.' She glanced at Freya and frowned. 'Is everything OK?'

'Fine, thank you, Rosie,' said Kathleen, before Freya had a chance to speak. 'Freya here is interested in the history of Heaven's Cove and she wanted to see your historic house for herself. You're an amateur historian and absolutely love Driftwood House, don't you, Freya?'

'I... um, yes, I do.'

'And she wants to find somewhere for family and friends to stay when they visit.'

'That's right.' Freya nodded, wondering when Kathleen had become so proficient at lying. She always blushed an unflattering shade of fuchsia when she told untruths but Kathleen's skin remained pale. Maybe keeping a secret for decades had taught her how to lie well.

'It's nice to meet you, Freya,' said Rosie, wiping her hands on her apron. 'I've heard a lot about you.'

'Been talking to Belinda, have you?' muttered Kathleen.

Rosie grinned. 'Look, why don't you come in and have a cup of tea?' She pulled the door open wide. 'I've just put some cakes in the oven because I've got a full house of guests from tomorrow, and I was about to take a break.'

'That would be lovely, if you're sure,' said Freya, stepping into the hall.

'Definitely. Come on into the kitchen.'

Rosie walked away, across the light, bright hallway with its black and white floor tiles. Freya looked back at Kathleen, who was still standing on the doorstep.

'Do you want to go back to the car?' asked Freya gently.

Kathleen shook her head, her jaw tight, and stepped across the threshold. She looked around her at the hallway with its wide staircase, and a grandfather clock in the corner.

'This looks much the same,' she murmured, her eyes on the door that Rosie had just disappeared through. 'So much the same.' She cocked her head as though listening to an echo of the past.

'Would you ladies prefer tea or coffee?' asked Rosie, poking her head around the kitchen door.

'Coffee for me, please,' said Freya, taking hold of Kathleen's arm and gently guiding her towards the kitchen.

As it turned out, the chat with Rosie was very pleasant. Freya immediately took to the woman, probably a decade younger than her, who had worked so hard to turn her family home into a guesthouse. There was something about her – a gentleness and sense of contentment – that was endearing.

Kathleen sat quietly at first but gradually got involved in the conversation, which Freya gradually steered onto the house itself.

'This is an amazing place and in such a fabulous location.'

'Thank you. I love it here.' Rosie smiled and brushed hair from her eyes, the diamond engagement ring on her finger glinting in the light. 'It's been my haven since my mum died last year.'

'Kathleen told me about your mum. I'm so sorry.'

Rosie gave a sad smile. 'I still miss her. Of course I do. But I'm happy up here, on top of the world. She still feels close and I talk to her, if that doesn't sound too weird.'

Her cheeks flushed and Freya leaned towards her.

'It doesn't sound weird at all. My dad died years ago now but I still talk to him all the time. Even when I'm sure he'd rather be enjoying some peace.'

When Rosie gave a grateful laugh, Freya wondered if they might become friends. If she stayed in Heaven's Cove long enough.

'Do you know much about the house's history?' she asked.

'Not really. I keep meaning to find out more because the documents I was given when I took on the place are pretty sketchy. All I know is that my mum lived here from just before I was born, it was lived in by the Starcross family for a while in the 1930s and 40s, and some religious organisation took it over for a while in the 1950s.'

'Really?' said Freya, sensing Kathleen stiffen beside her. 'Do you remember their name?'

'It was something strange. Something like the Godly Women's Group. Maybe they felt closer to God up here, closer to the sky. What was it now? It was a very odd name.'

Rosie thought for a moment while Freya glanced out of the back window, at the sea to the right and the swathes of country-side rolling into the distance on the left. It was a heavenly location, all right. But she could imagine the mothers' unbearable sorrow leaching into the very walls of this house when their children were taken.

'It's strange to think of a religious organisation taking over the house,' said Freya, worried that she was pushing the subject too far. Kathleen shot her a concerned glance, but what else could Freya do? They had no other leads to go on. 'I wonder where they went when they left the house?'

'I have no idea,' said Rosie, pouring another cup of tea. And if she wondered why Freya was showing such an interest in an obscure group, she didn't show it. Instead, she found some biscuits and chatted about Heaven's Cove with Kathleen before turning to Freya.

'I heard on the grapevine that you're Belinda's sister but I must say you don't look very alike and, on first impressions, you don't seem very similar either.'

'We're not very alike. Belinda is my half-sister so we didn't grow up together and we hardly know each other, to be honest.'

Part of her felt a bit mean, distancing herself from Belinda. But it was the truth.

'That's a shame. It's sad when families lose touch. But you'll be able to make up for lost time now you're in Heaven's Cove.'

'We will,' agreed Freya, though she and Belinda hadn't spent any proper time together since her visit to Belinda's home for afternoon tea. Should she be making more of an effort and inviting her sister to the pub one evening? They were lucky to have each other, really, when some people had been torn away from their families. She glanced at Kathleen and made a mental note to be a better sibling.

Rosie smiled and turned to Kathleen too. 'You haven't been here since Mum died and the house was refurbished, have you? Did you come up for the opening of the guesthouse? That whole afternoon was a bit of a blur and I'm not one hundred per cent sure who was here and who wasn't.'

Kathleen looked up from studying her cup of tea. 'I didn't come to the opening. In fact, I've never been here at all.'

'Never ever? Would you like to look around? I can give you the grand tour if you'd like. And it would give you a better idea of the facilities if you've got family who might want to stay, Freya.'

Freya blinked, momentarily confused. She'd forgotten that was a reason Kathleen had given for her interest in the house when they'd arrived.

'I can tell it's a lovely guesthouse and I'm not sure we have the time for a tour right now,' said Freya quickly, but Kathleen was already getting to her feet.

'We can spare five minutes. That would be lovely, Rosie, if you don't mind.'

'Are you sure?' Freya's eyes locked onto Kathleen's. 'You said you had things to do in the village this afternoon.'

'I'm quite sure,' she replied with a straight gaze. 'Everything else can wait.'

She followed Rosie from the kitchen and only Freya noticed Kathleen's hands balled into tight fists, as though she was about to go into battle.

Rosie led them through the house, from the conservatory on the ground floor that overlooked acres of land rolling towards Dartmoor, to the guest bedroom tucked away under the eaves of the house.

Rooms were bright with big windows that let in the extraordinary light up here on top of the cliff, and everything was sparkling clean. It felt like a happy house today, thought Freya, in spite of its history. Perhaps the people who had lived and loved here over the last sixty years, once the religious organisation had moved on, had helped to balance out the sorrow.

Kathleen said very little while Rosie was showing them round but she lingered in one bedroom that overlooked the ocean. Was this where she'd last been with her daughter, where her little girl had been ripped from her arms? A glint of tears in her green eyes gave Freya her answer.

The bedroom was warm and welcoming with paintings on the cream walls and a colourful quilt across the single bed. But

Kathleen shivered as though she'd slipped back through time and saw the room as it once was.

Rosie had moved onto the landing and Freya joined her and made small talk about the village far below, giving Kathleen time alone with her memories. They chatted away about nothing much at all while, a few feet away, an elderly woman relived the heart-breaking moment that had haunted her life.

Rosie broke off from telling Freya about the village's monthly market when Kathleen walked slowly out of the bedroom.

'Are you OK, Kathleen?' she asked, a furrow appearing between her big brown eyes. 'You look very pale. Do you need to sit down?'

When Kathleen didn't answer, Freya linked her arm through the old lady's and caught hold of her hand. 'I expect you're tired, aren't you? You said you didn't sleep too well last night and lack of sleep can catch up with you.'

'That's right. I had a terrible night. Awful,' agreed Kathleen, giving Freya a grateful glance as she grasped onto the white lie.

'In fact, I'd better get you home so you can have an early lunch and maybe catch forty winks this afternoon.'

'That might be best. But thank you for showing me around your lovely home, Rosie. It's quite different from how it was.'

Rosie glanced at Freya and there was a beat of awkward-ness. How did Kathleen know how the house had been before if this was her first ever visit?

Please don't say anything. Freya didn't believe in telepathy but maybe Rosie caught the plea in her gaze because she smiled kindly at Kathleen. 'I've enjoyed having you both here and I hope you feel better after your nap. Broken nights are such a pain.'

Kathleen gulped in a lungful of fresh air when she and Freya stepped out of Driftwood House, as though she'd been holding her breath since they'd arrived. She started walking across the flower-strewn grass but, before Freya could follow her, Rosie put a hand on her arm.

'Can you wait a moment?' she asked, going to a large chest in the hall, opening the bottom drawer and taking out a black ring binder. She quickly leafed through its contents.

'Ah, I thought it was in here, and I almost got the name right. Look.'

She pushed the binder into Freya's hands. It was open at a yellowing list that someone had typed out on an old-fashioned typewriter – the sort that Freya's mum had used when she first became a secretary. It was a list of past owners and tenants at Driftwood House.

Freya ran her eye down the list. There were gaps but there, listed from 1957 to 1960, was The Godly Society for the Support and Education of Young Women. The first clue that could lead them to Maeve.

She repeated the name in her mind to make sure it was lodged in her memory. Though it wasn't a name she was likely to forget, due to the sheer hypocrisy of it. The support and education of women? It was a sick joke.

Freya bit down the anger that was bubbling up inside her and handed the binder back to Rosie. 'That's quite a mouthful of a name. Thanks for checking.'

Rosie shrugged. 'You're welcome. I thought the list might be in here and you seemed keen to find out more.'

She wanted to ask why. Freya could see it in her expression. Rosie knew there was more to this morning's visit than met the eye, but she was willing to help anyway. Freya decided that she liked Rosie very much indeed and Liam was a very lucky man.

Freya ran across the clifftop to catch up with Kathleen, who was doggedly walking towards their car. The wind had dropped but grey clouds were massing on the horizon and a bank of mist was rolling in across the sea. A lone seagull swooped low over Freya's head.

'Rosie seems lovely,' said Freya.

'She is. She lived abroad for a long time but came home after her mother's death. She's engaged to a local farmer.'

'Liam, isn't it? I met him briefly when Ryan showed me the beach. He seemed like a very nice man.'

'He is. He was a bit of a Jack the Lad once upon a time, but he's settled down now and he and Rosie make a wonderful couple.'

They'd reached the car, and Freya opened the passenger door and helped Kathleen inside. Then she slid into the driver's seat but didn't turn the ignition. The rolling sea mist had obliterated the horizon and almost reached the land.

Freya shifted round in her seat towards Kathleen. 'Were you OK going back to Driftwood House? I was worried about you when you came out of the bedroom.'

'I felt wobbly when the memories came rushing back. I thought I knew every little detail but there were things I'd forgotten over the years. When I was back in that room, I could feel the weight of Maeve in my arms again and remember her milky smell. It was so long ago but it felt like it was happening all over again.'

She stared through the windscreen at the impressive house in front of them. 'It was hard. I won't lie. But I'm glad I went back to Driftwood House again. I've been staring at it from my bedroom for the last eight years. It's been the first thing I've seen in the morning and the last thing at night. It's almost been taunting me, but now I feel that I've laid that particular ghost to rest. Though it's a shame Rosie didn't know the name of the organisation that ran the mother and baby home. I can remember so much about that time but the name has gone.'

'I wouldn't be surprised if your mind hadn't deliberately blanked it out. The whole thing was so traumatic.'

'Maybe. Ah well, it's gone for good. And so is Maeve.'

For one fleeting second, Freya considered not telling Kathleen that she now knew the name of the organisation that had mistreated her so cruelly. She could keep the lid on this can of worms. Maeve would remain a secret and no one would be hurt.

No one apart from Kathleen, who would go to her grave not knowing if her beloved daughter was alive or dead.

Freya took hold of Kathleen's hand. 'I've got something to tell you. As we were leaving, Rosie showed me a list of people who used to own Driftwood House. For four years in the fifties it was The Godly Society for the Support and Education of Young Women.'

Kathleen blinked once, twice, then she pulled in a deep lungful of air and smiled. 'That's it,' she said, her eyes shining. 'So. Now we can find out what happened to Maeve.'

'Perhaps, but it was a long time ago. I'll see what I can find out about them and if they kept records.' Freya paused. 'Before I go any further, are you quite sure you want me to delve deeper into this?'

Kathleen looked through the windscreen at Driftwood House, which was starting to blur in thick sweeping curls of fog. The roof was a ghostly outline between land and sky and the windows were grey and blank.

'I'm sure,' she said softly.

'And are you still sure that you don't want to tell Ryan what's going on?'

'I'm very sure about that, too.'

'I don't like keeping secrets from him.'

Kathleen gently pulled her hand from Freya's and linked her fingers in her lap. 'Neither do I, and I know I'm putting you in a difficult position but this might come to nothing and then he'll never need to know about Maeve. Or what I did.' She kept staring out of the window into the mist. 'I'm sorry, Freya, that you've been dragged into such a tricky business, but please don't say anything.'

'All right, if that's what you want.'

With a heavy heart, Freya did a three-point turn over the scrubby grass and started bouncing down the pitted track, towards the village. The car lights caught tendrils of mist twisting in the air ahead of them. Behind them, Driftwood House was swallowed by fog and disappeared completely.

27

FREYA

Freya closed the lid of her laptop and leaned back against the kitchen chair. This was hopeless.

She was running her fingers through her hair when Kathleen shuffled into the room. She'd been complaining of pain in her hip ever since she'd marched across the uneven clifftop a week ago and Freya had made her an appointment with her GP for the coming Tuesday. In the meantime, she'd found an old walking stick under the stairs that Kathleen, after a short war of wills, had agreed to use.

'Any luck?' asked Kathleen, lowering herself onto a chair with a wince and balancing the stick against the kitchen table. Rocky immediately jumped onto her lap and started purring loudly.

'I'm afraid not. The Godly Society seem to have disappeared off the face of the earth.'

'And their records along with them,' murmured Kathleen.

'It looks like it, I'm afraid. Maybe the society was short-lived and badly run.'

'Like I said, the whole thing seemed rather secretive and strange back then and maybe my instincts were right.' Kathleen drummed her fingers on the table. 'Is there anything else we can do?'

Freya shrugged. She'd been searching online and making phone calls for days. She'd scoured social media for people called Maeve but just a first name wasn't enough to go on, and she'd contacted myriad organisations including the local council and government agencies. She'd also found the adoption contact register and added Kathleen's name, in case Maeve wanted to search for her. But they'd had no luck. And without Maeve's new surname, what more could she do?

Freya closed the lid of her laptop. 'The problem is, we're not even sure that Maeve is still called Maeve and even if she is, we don't know her last name. And we can't post your story anywhere in the hope someone might have information, or try to get a newspaper to cover it, because you don't want to publicise it.'

'Definitely not.' Kathleen shivered. 'It's my business and no one else's. Even something vague might link back to me.'

'And if it's too vague, it wouldn't help anyway.'

'So that's that, then. Maeve will remain unfound.' Kathleen's face crumpled as though she was about to cry. But she sniffed and took a deep breath to compose herself. 'Perhaps, at the end of the day, that's best for her. Perhaps she'd rather never know the mother who gave her up.'

Freya's heart broke for this woman who, more than half a century later, still wanted what was best for the daughter she'd known for only two weeks. Was there still a way to reunite them?

She laced her fingers together and rested her chin on her hands. 'There is one other possible option. From what I've read online, some people seem to use a detective agency or tracing agency that reunites families, but that would cost money.'

Kathleen stared at Freya for a moment. 'How much money?'

'I'm not sure. I can find out if you're interested. Some of them provide an intermediary service too, to act as go-betweens if people are found, but there's no guarantee that they'd find Maeve.'

'They probably wouldn't, but at least I'd have tried everything I could. I have some savings and what am I saving my money for? Ryan and Chloe will benefit from the sale of the cottage when I'm gone.' Kathleen thought for a moment. 'I'd like you to go ahead with it.'

'If that's what you want, I can make a few calls to see how it works.'

'Thank you. I don't know what I'd do without you.' Kathleen put her hand on Freya's before pulling it away sharply. 'Oh, I can't have any agency names popping up on my bank statement. I don't want anything linking their name with mine. Would you be able to pay for the search and I can reimburse you?'

Freya closed her eyes briefly. It sounded like a perfectly reasonable request. But Kathleen's determination to hide any evidence of their search meant she was getting increasingly involved in what felt like a deception against Ryan.

'That'll be OK, won't it?' urged Kathleen. And she sounded so desperate, Freya nodded.

Three days later, an agency had been found, a very pleasant employee had spoken on the phone to Kathleen, bank payments had been set up on Freya's account, and the search for Maeve was almost underway.

Freya re-read the email from the agency, confirming the arrangements, and tried to make sense of her conflicting emotions. She was excited for Kathleen that they might be closer to finding her long-lost daughter, and desperately worried that they would. There was no guarantee of a happy reunion, and what would Ryan think when he found out about his half-sister, and of Freya's involvement in her return?

I promise to tell you everything. That's what she'd told Ryan in the pub. And they'd got on better ever since. Chloe was still sullen on the infrequent occasions that she called in, but Ryan was warmer and seemed to seek out her company. The end of her month-long trial in the job had come and gone more than three weeks ago, and Freya felt entwined in Kathleen's life.

Rather too entwined, in some ways.

Freya read the email for a third time and clicked 'send' on her return email instructing the agency to go ahead. The search for Maeve was on, and who knew what the consequences would be?

28

CHLOE

It was the day of the school dance and Chloe could think of little else. She'd washed her hair this morning and the toothpaste she'd dabbed on her chin last night seemed to have done the trick. The angry spot she'd discovered with dismay was far less red. She gently touched it to see if it felt less sore.

'Chloe!'

When Chloe spotted Isobel and Paige walking towards her, she resisted the urge to dodge into a side street. She couldn't risk Paige thinking she was nervous around her and telling the girls at school. Or, even worse, not letting her sit with her tonight. Chloe had banished her 'scaredy cat' tag by jumping from Clair Point and she really didn't want to have to do that all over again.

'Chloe!' said Isobel again, as if she was surprised to see her there, even though Chloe was only two streets from home.

'Hello, Isobel.'

Chloe smiled at Paige, whose smile in return seemed half-hearted. Had Chloe upset her in some way? She'd thought she was making headway with their friendship, but Paige could blow hot and cold. It was very confusing.

'How are you?' asked Isobel. 'Are you excited about the

disco tonight?' She gave Chloe a brief look up and down. 'You're looking very nice.'

There was definitely a slight hesitation between 'very' and 'nice', Chloe decided, her stomach plummeting. Why had she chosen to wear shorts this morning? A chilly breeze was blowing off the sea – it definitely wasn't shorts weather – and her legs were pale as milk bottles. And, she suddenly realised with a hot flush of shame, she'd thrown on a cardigan as she'd left the house. It was warm and cosy, but it was also vomit-green and hand-knitted.

Isobel was looking her usual immaculate self in neat capri trousers that grazed her skinny ankles, wedge sandals and a silky baby-blue top. Paige was wearing fashionable jeans with holes at the knees and a black logo-ed sweatshirt, whereas Chloe was in an old-lady cardigan knitted by her gran. She shrugged the knitwear off her shoulders, and fanned her hot cheeks.

'Wow, it's suddenly got really hot.'

Was that a smirk from Paige? Chloe was torn between wanting to cry and a sudden urge to kick Paige in the shins.

'How's your father?' asked Isobel, fluttering her eyelashes, which were so thick they had to be false. 'He did a marvellous job of mending my shed but I've hardly seen him in the fortnight since. I'm beginning to think he's avoiding me.' She laughed as though that would be ridiculous.

'He's all right, I think. He's gone round to see Gran but I didn't feel like going.'

'So where are you off to?'

Chloe thought frantically. She was actually heading for the beach. She liked to sit on the sand and enjoy the gentle slap of the waves nearby. It gave her time to think about things and made her feel calmer. But would that sound a bit lame to Paige?

'I'm on my way to the ice-cream parlour,' she lied.

It was obviously the right answer because Paige nodded.

Sometimes the older boys from their school hung out there so it was deemed an appropriate place to go.

'Are you still coming round to ours before the disco to get ready?' asked Isobel, studying her nails, which were long and polished letterbox-red.

Chloe swallowed. She'd thought – hoped, just a tiny bit – that Isobel had forgotten her offer. But she did need some help with getting ready, if she wasn't going to end up a laughing stock with Paige and her friends.

'If you don't mind, that would be good.'

'You're welcome. Paige will be glad of the company. You girls can get excited together. Isn't that right, Paige?'

'Yeah, definitely.'

When Paige gave her a smile – a proper one this time – Chloe felt warm inside. She would bond with Paige this evening and the dance would be amazing. Her mum would never see her in her new dress but Isobel and Paige would. And who knew? Maybe Isobel would be her stepmum one day and she and Paige would be sisters.

If her dad did more about it, that is. Sometimes Chloe thought he wasn't really interested in women any more because of what had happened to Mum. But he seemed to be interested in Freya.

Stupid Freya would ruin everything, thought Chloe. And she'd started acting weird and dragging her gran into her weirdness as well. The two of them were looking at Freya's laptop the last time Chloe called in, and her gran had slammed down the lid as though she'd been looking at porn or something.

'We'll see you after tea then,' said Isobel, walking off and gesturing for Paige to follow her.

Chloe watched them go, imagining what it would be like to have them as her stepfamily – if Freya kept out of things. Though, to be honest, she wasn't sure she really wanted what she feared Freya would ruin, anyway. Everything was very confusing and being a twelve-year-old girl was totally pants, she decided.

Eight hours later, Chloe was staring at herself in Isobel's magnifying mirror and Isobel was standing behind her with a thoughtful look on her face.

'Let's see what we can do here.' Isobel picked up a lock of Chloe's hair before dropping it abruptly. 'It's a shame we haven't got the time to sort out your hair colour.'

Chloe burned inside with shame. Some of the people at school made snarky remarks about her red hair, but she'd never heard an adult be nasty about it before.

'Don't worry,' said Isobel, picking up a huge make-up bag and unzipping it. 'Make-up can work wonders. It'll certainly cover up the spots that are under the skin on your chin.' Chloe ran a finger self-consciously along her jawline. 'And I'll certainly do my best to make you look like your poor mum. I saw her photo when I dropped off the jacket your dad left behind after mending my shed, and she really was a stunner.'

'I don't look anything like my mum.'

Chloe was hoping that Isobel might contradict her but she nodded. 'It's a shame, but never mind. We'll see what we can do.'

It's a shame.

Chloe blinked furiously so she wouldn't cry as Isobel moved the mirror out of her reach and started to layer primer onto her skin. Maybe Isobel could work a miracle and make her look halfway decent. She didn't want to look terrible next to Paige.

Ten minutes later, Isobel stepped back with a smile of satisfaction and placed the mirror back in front of Chloe.

'There you go. I can see your mother in you now. What do you think?'

Chloe stared into the mirror and blinked again. She hardly

recognised the person looking back at her. Her face was smooth with foundation, her cheeks were rosy pink and a thick black line beneath her lower eyelashes made her eyes look less nondescript. The coatings of mascara Isobel had expertly applied had thickened her lashes, and her lips had been painted a deep red. As the finishing touch, her hair had been scraped back into a bun that sat high on her head. She looked so different. She didn't look like herself at all. But that was the point, wasn't it? She *did* look a little more like her mother. And yet...

Chloe was still staring when Paige bowled into the room.

'Wow! Chloe, you look totes amazing!'

Did she? Chloe smiled into the mirror and a stranger smiled back. Yes, she did look amazing! Paige and Isobel thought so, and Paige looked great in her sparkly dress. Chloe was regretting the boring dress she'd bought with her dad now. It was too late to change that, but at least her face looked more interesting – even if she did get a jolt of surprise every time she looked in the mirror.

'Thanks so much, Isobel. That's brilliant,' said Chloe. 'I'd better get home and get changed.'

'Oh, I thought your dad was going to call in to collect you,' said Isobel, looking put out. She smoothed down her hair although there wasn't a hair out of place.

'I don't know why you didn't bring your dress with you,' said Paige, pouting at herself in the mirror over Chloe's shoulder.

'I forgot.'

That was a lie. Chloe would never admit it but she wanted her dad to see her all dressed up, when it was just the two of them. It felt important to share that moment with him for some reason, even though fashion had passed her dad by. Quite what her mum had seen in him, she wasn't sure. Then she felt annoyed with herself for thinking that. He was a good man and a good dad. She loved him. And he'd be proud of her, looking so grown-up and so much more like her mum, the woman he still adored.

'What's your dress like?' asked Paige, narrowing her kohl-rimmed eyes. 'Did you get it online from ASOS?'

'No, I got it from a shop in Exeter.' Chloe deliberately didn't name the store, worrying that it wouldn't be deemed fashionable enough. 'It's quite a simple dress, really. Nice, though. It's blue and it's got flowers on it.'

'Flowers?' Paige curled her lip. 'You can borrow my navy high heels, if you like. That might rescue it.'

Chloe grinned. Paige had an extensive shoe collection – most people did, actually, compared to her one pair of sensible school shoes, one pair of summer sandals, one pair of wellies and one pair of trainers. She'd been planning on wearing her sandals, which were pretty, but she'd love to wear Paige's shoes instead. That was what true friends did, wasn't it, lend each other clothes and shoes?

After leaving Isobel's, she walked home through the back streets, Paige's shoes swinging from her hand. She didn't want to bump into one of her classmates in the village and spoil the surprise. They'd be amazed that the ugly duckling had become a swan. Her mum used to read that story to her when she was little.

She let herself into the cottage quietly. Her dad was in the kitchen, whistling along to the radio as he washed up, and it was comforting to hear him banging the pots and pans.

She slipped upstairs and changed into her dress before inspecting herself in the mirror on the back of her door. Wow, she certainly looked different. She still wasn't sure about her dress, but her face was something else. Tentatively, she touched her flawless cheeks and peered at her heavily made-up eyes. She liked how she looked, didn't she? It was just the fact that she looked so different – so much better – that was making her nervous. It was excitement rather than nerves, she decided. And she couldn't wait for her dad to see her.

She called out to him as she went downstairs and stood waiting for him in the sitting room, with a big smile on her face.

'Are you back from Isobel's?' asked her dad, wiping his wet hands on his trousers as he came into the room. 'How did it go?'

His smile faltered and froze when he saw her. 'Good grief.'

Good grief? Was that good? He was obviously amazed at how brilliant she looked. Chloe twirled slowly on the spot.

'What do you think? Do I look fabulous?' He was still staring at her with his mouth open. 'Dad? What do you reckon?'

When he continued to stare without saying anything, Chloe started to feel nervous. Why was he being so weird? She *did* look fabulous. She was almost sure of it.

'Say something, Dad!'

'What have you got on your face?' he asked.

'Duh! It's make-up.'

Chloe knew she sounded insolent but he wasn't reacting the way she'd expected. The way she'd hoped.

'I can see it's make-up. Rather a lot of make-up, by the look of it.'

'Not really.' Chloe shuffled her feet into the carpet. 'Isobel and Paige said I look nice. They said I look amazing.'

'You can't go to the school dance looking like that,' said her dad flatly.

Looking like that? Chloe's stomach plummeted into the borrowed shoes that were already pinching her toes.

'What do you mean? It's a disco, Dad, and I want to look nice.'

'But you don't.' When Chloe gasped as though she'd been slapped, her dad rubbed his hand across his eyes. 'What I mean is, you always look nice, Chloe. You look lovely as you are but not like this, not with so much make-up on. You're only twelve. It's not...' He searched for the right word. '...appropriate.'

'Of course it's appropriate. Everyone wears make-up when they're twelve.'

'No, they don't.'

'Paige does.'

'Paige isn't everyone, and what Paige does is up to her and Isobel. What happens in this house is up to me and I'm telling you that you're wearing too much make-up and you can't go out like that.'

Chloe could feel herself getting hot. 'I can,' she shot back.

'No, you can't, Chloe.' He took a deep breath. 'Look, I don't want to argue about this. I know you're looking forward to the dance and I want you to have a good time. But you need to take some of that make-up off first.'

'Isobel won't like it if you make me clean my face.'

'I don't care what Isobel likes.'

'And Paige will never talk to me again.'

'Of course she will.'

'She won't,' wailed Chloe. Why did he have to ruin everything? 'She'll say I'm a loser and I do everything my dad says.'

Her dad took another deep breath as though he was trying to keep his temper. 'I'm afraid you do have to do what I say while you're living under my roof. But you'll still look wonderful if you take some of the make-up off.'

'No, I won't,' shouted Chloe, resisting the urge to stamp her feet. That was what she did when she was a toddler and it would only justify her dad's argument that she was too young for make-up.

'Please don't shout, Chloe. Let's talk about this like adults.'

Chloe put her hands on her hips. 'One minute you want me to be an adult and then you say I'm a child. You can't have it both ways, Dad. It's not fair. And the only reason you don't like my make-up is because I look like Mum.'

'You don't look anything like your mother.'

Tears sprang into Chloe's eyes as she looked at the photo of her mum on the mantelpiece. So even her dad thought she looked nothing like her beautiful mother. Even her dad thought she was ugly.

'Chloe.' Her dad sank onto the sofa and patted the seat next to him. 'I'm sorry. I'm not handling this very well. Please let's sit and discuss it. I know you don't want us to argue over this.'

'Well, you're wrong,' shot back Chloe. 'You don't know anything about me. Nothing at all. I wish Mum was still here. She'd understand. In fact, I wish you'd died instead of her.'

She hadn't meant to say that and she watched with horrified fascination as colour drained from her dad's face. She'd thought that was just a saying – something people used to explain how upset someone was – but her dad's face really had changed colour. He looked chalk-white, as if he'd seen a ghost.

Suddenly the house seemed full of people who were no longer there and the room was stifling. She had to get away. With a sob, Chloe turned and rushed into the hallway. She wrenched open the door and ran into the street, her stupid shoes that didn't fit properly slipping and sliding on her feet. And she kept on running, as her dad called to her through the open sitting room window.

29

FREYA

When Freya heard the front door slam, her heart started to beat faster. It was either Ryan or Chloe, both of whom provoked a maelstrom of bittersweet emotions these days.

Chloe's visits to her grandmother were increasingly rare, and Freya missed her. She felt surprisingly protective of the girl who was growing up without a mother, just as she had. But when their paths did cross, Freya often ended up wishing that they hadn't. Chloe was so surly and obviously resented her being in her grandmother's home.

Her relationship with Ryan, on the other hand, had improved and she looked forward to his visits now. He'd often sit and chat for ages about this and that, and she loved watching his handsome face as he got more animated and started flinging his arms around.

'That's his Irish heritage,' Kathleen had told her. 'My family couldn't communicate if they sat on their hands. My brother Kiernan was the worst. He once knocked a full pint all over the local priest when he was in the middle of one of his tall tales.'

She didn't say if it was the same priest who'd denounced her when she was pregnant, but Freya sincerely hoped it was. Kathleen had started talking more about her life in Ireland since sharing her secret about Maeve and Freya loved the stories.

Just as she loved spending time with Ryan – or would have if she wasn't drowning in guilt as the search for Maeve went on.

It was Ryan who bowled into the kitchen, and her breath caught in her throat. He was wearing a baggy Aran jumper in soft cream that Greg would dismiss as scruffy, but it suited him perfectly. He was tall and craggily handsome and secretly vulnerable. Freya felt her heart hammer even more.

'Hi, Ryan.' Her smile of greeting froze on her face when she saw his expression. He looked distraught. 'What's on earth's the matter?'

'Is Chloe here?' he asked, ignoring her question.

'No, I'm afraid not. What's going on?'

'Nothing.' Ryan winced. 'Everything. We had an argument and I said some things and she said...' When he stopped, unable to continue, Freya caught hold of his arm and led him to the table.

'Sit down and tell me what's happened.'

He sat and put his head in his hands for a moment. Freya had an urge to stroke his salt-and-pepper hair, which was shining ash-grey in the light from the sun that was starting to dip below the horizon.

'Tell me what's upset you,' she urged again, gently.

He lifted his head, his eyes weary.

'I've handled a situation badly, so incredibly badly, and now Chloe has run off and I've no idea where she's gone.'

'Perhaps she's at Isobel's.'

He shook his head. 'I rang there on my way here and she's not turned up. Heaven knows what Isobel thinks is going on. I was so agitated, I must have sounded deranged.'

'I'm sure Chloe will be back soon,' said Freya, hoping she was right.

Ryan shook his head. 'I'm not so sure. I hurt her feelings and we argued, and she told me...' He swallowed. 'She told me that she wished I'd died rather than Natalie.'

'Oh, I'm so sorry.' Without thinking, Freya reached out and covered the back of his hand. He turned his hand slightly and interlaced his fingers with hers. His skin felt warm and his fingers soft. 'She'll come back. I'm sure of it, and she didn't mean what she said. She loves you.'

'I love her too. I just wish I wasn't such a rubbish dad.'

His beautiful green eyes held hers and she leaned towards him. She wanted to comfort him so much. But he pulled his hand back and looked away at the sound of footsteps in the hall.

'Please don't tell Mum,' he pleaded. 'There's nothing she can do and I don't want to worry her.'

Another secret! Freya wondered if she might reach a tipping point one day, when all the many secrets stuffed into her head over the years would come bursting out like a flood. But she nodded. 'Of course not. But where would Chloe go?'

'I don't know.' He pushed back the chair and got to his feet. 'Sometimes she goes to the castle ruins with friends. I'll have a look there.'

'I'll come with you. I can help you search and—'

'No! Please stay here like normal. Otherwise Mum will wonder what's going on.'

Freya bit her lip, wanting to do what was best but desperate to help Ryan find his daughter. 'OK,' she agreed reluctantly as the kitchen door opened.

'Ryan,' said Kathleen, shuffling in with her stick and frowning. 'I thought it must be Chloe slamming the front door like that. You're going to crack the glass one day.'

'Sorry, Mum.'

'Why are you here? I thought you'd be taking Chloe to the dance or the... what do young people call it these days? Rage or rave or something?'

'It's still called a disco,' said Ryan, his hand already on the kitchen door, ready to rush away. 'I'm about to take Chloe but came round to—' He came to an abrupt stop.

'He came round to drop in some information he had for me about Dartmoor,' said Freya, pointing at the leaflet on the dresser that she'd picked up earlier that day from the tourist information office. The game was up if Kathleen had noticed it earlier, but she nodded.

'That was kind of you, Ryan.' She looked between the two of them. 'Are you two planning a day out together, then?'

'Maybe,' said Ryan, giving Freya a grateful look.

'That would be lovely because Freya loved Dartmoor when she went with me. Why don't you take her next weekend? I can keep an eye on Chloe. You can take a picnic.'

'Look, I've got to go, Mum. Love you,' said Ryan in a rush. He paused only to kiss Kathleen on the cheek before, with a final glance at Freya, hurrying into the hall. Kathleen winced as the front door slammed shut again.

'I can see where Chloe gets her penchant for closing doors rather loudly.' She yawned. 'I'm feeling tired so I might sit and watch some TV for a bit. There's an old Elvis film on that's good fun.'

'While you're doing that, I think I might go and get some air,' said Freya, grabbing her cardigan from the back of a chair. There was no way she could sit here twiddling her thumbs while Chloe was missing. 'If that's OK with you, of course?'

'Absolutely,' said Kathleen with the hint of a smile. 'If you rush, you might catch Ryan up, if you were wanting to see Chloe in her dancing frock.'

Outside, Freya breathed in the briny scent of the sea and thought about where to look for Chloe. She hated to think of her on her own and distraught. Heaven knows what the argument had been about, but it sounded pretty nuclear.

She tried to remember what being twelve years old had been like for her. It had been a difficult time for lots of reasons and, though specific memories were hazy, she could still remember the discontent and confusion that had led to her slamming doors one minute and crying in her bedroom the next. Being twelve wasn't much fun, especially if you were missing a mother.

Pulling her cardigan tightly around her, against the wind, Freya set off into the village. As she neared the village hall, she spotted balloons strung up on the pillars and heard the thud of loud music. A huddle of youngsters was outside, waiting to be checked in for the dance. The girls in their party dresses and boys in smart trousers and white shirts made Freya feel sad. Chloe should be with them, feeling excited about the night ahead.

It must have been a dreadful falling-out for her to have said something so unkind to her dad. And it would soon be getting dark. The sun, partly hidden by cloud, was nearing the horizon and shadows were already lengthening.

Where on earth could Chloe be? Martha at the care home had gone walkabout one evening and was almost hypothermic when she was found wandering in her nightdress. But Chloe was young and it was a chilly evening in May rather than a freezing evening in January, Freya told herself sternly. There was no point in panicking.

Suddenly, Freya remembered that she'd spotted Chloe a couple of times sitting alone on the beach. She'd cut a solitary figure and Freya had let her be, not wanting to intrude. Maybe she'd gone there? It was worth a try.

Freya hurried along the lane that led out of the village. Lights were coming on in Liam's handsome farmhouse as she rushed past, and spits of rain licked at her face.

By the time she reached the edge of the cove, the wind was picking up and gritty grains of sand were whipped into her face.

The grey water was curling into waves that pounded onto the shoreline and the beach was deserted, save for one figure sitting alone, facing the ocean.

Freya slipped off her shoes and walked towards Chloe, her toes sinking into the cool sand. Chloe was sitting motionless, her knees pulled up to her chest, with a pair of blue shoes discarded on the sand beside her. She turned when Freya reached her.

'Do you mind if I sit down with you?'

'Whatever,' said Chloe sullenly.

Freya tasted salt spray on her lips as she sat on the sand and glanced at the young girl beside her.

She hardly recognised Chloe – her hair was pulled into a tight bun that dragged the skin at the sides of her face, and her beautiful glowing skin was covered in foundation. There were rosy apples on her cheeks and a thick dark shadow on her eyelids.

The make-up had clearly been expertly applied and it made Chloe look older, and bland. She looked like just one more of the many done-up-to-the-nines young women that Freya saw on Instagram – aside from the tear-tracks of mascara now trailing down Chloe's cheeks.

Surely, this must have been what the argument was about. Freya could understand Ryan being shocked by his daughter's sudden transformation and the situation then escalating. She felt shocked and she wasn't Chloe's mum. She wasn't anyone's mum.

'I think the dance has started,' said Freya, her arm almost brushing Chloe's.

'I'm not going.'

'That's a shame.'

'Yeah.'

They sat for a minute, both staring at the sea, which was choppier than Freya had ever seen it before. A churning grey mass of water stretched to the horizon, tipped by white foam that was blown by the wind and danced in the air.

'Your dad's looking for you,' said Freya after a while.

Chloe swivelled round in the sand until she was facing her.

'Did my dad send you?' she demanded.

'No. He's out looking for you because he's worried about you. But he doesn't know you're here.'

'How did you know?' she asked, narrowing her kohl-lined eyes.

'I've seen you here a couple of times, sitting on your own.'

'I don't like being spied on.'

'I wasn't spying, Chloe. I sometimes walk to the beach myself to spend time on my own and I just happened to see you.'

Chloe stared at Freya for a moment before picking up a handful of sand and letting it trickle through her fingers. 'I like to sit and think sometimes and it's peaceful here.'

'It *is* peaceful, especially when the weather's not so good and there aren't loads of tourists about.'

'Yeah. The girls who've lived here for ever don't really appreciate the sea. Paige says it's boring and she only comes to the beach when it's hot and sunny. But I like it best when there's no one else here and the sea is wild. It makes me feel closer to nature and... and people.'

She clamped her lips together as though she hadn't meant to say so much, and stared back at the ocean.

'Does it make you feel closer to your mum?' asked Freya gently.

Chloe nodded, her bottom lip wobbling. Freya shuffled closer until their arms were pressed together.

'It's hard missing your mum, isn't it? I know a little how it feels.'

That caught Chloe's attention. 'How do you know?' she demanded. 'Is your mum dead too?'

'No, my mum's still alive. But she left to go and live in Greece when I was ten years old.'

'Did she leave you behind?'

'She did.'

'Hmm.' Chloe thought for a moment. 'Greece is, like, ages away.'

'It's about one thousand five hundred miles away. I used to get my dad's big atlas book out and work out the distance from where I was to where my mum was. And it's a long way.'

'That must have been horrible,' said Chloe, flinching when a screeching seagull swooped above her head. The sun was obscured by thick grey cloud and the bird was a dark shadow in the lengthening gloom.

Freya swallowed as she nodded, feeling an old rush of hurt and pain. The memory of her mother choosing to leave her behind was one she rarely dwelled on these days. But it was suddenly there, in the forefront of her mind.

Although the choice was as much hers as her mother's. Her mum, madly in love with a man from Greece whom she'd met at work, was leaving her dad and wanted to take Freya with her.

But Freya, seeing the devastation on her father's face, just couldn't leave him behind. By insisting she would stay with him she'd hoped her mother would change her mind and stay with them both in England.

But her plan had spectacularly backfired.

'Why did she go to Greece?' asked Chloe in a small voice almost drowned out by the crash of the waves.

'She wanted to marry a man who came from there and live with him instead.'

Her mother had left to start a new life, and their mother-daughter relationship had never fully recovered. Her mum had married the Greek man after divorcing Freya's father, and Freya had gone over for the wedding. But the trust between them had gone, along with Freya's easy confidence in the world. If one of the people you loved the most could disappear from your life like that, the world must be a very scary place. Chloe must be scared.

When Freya put her arm around the young girl's shoulders, Chloe leaned into her.

'What was your argument with your dad about?' Freya rested her cheek against Chloe's soft hair.

'He went totally ape about me wearing make-up to the disco, and then he said... He said I looked nothing like my mum.'

'Ah. I see.' Freya paused for a moment before asking, 'Who did your make-up?'

'Isobel,' answered Chloe, sniffing as a large teardrop plopped onto the sand. 'She said she was trying to make me look more like my mum.'

Freya felt in her pocket for a clean tissue and handed it over as she tried to control the anger bubbling up inside her. What on earth had Isobel been thinking?

'Do you like my make-up?' asked Chloe, lifting her head. Her eyes were red-rimmed with crying and black eyeliner had joined the mascara sliding down her face.

'To be honest, it probably looked better before you got upset.'

'Probably.' Chloe scrubbed her hands furiously across her face, spreading black trails further across her cheeks.

'I think what your dad was trying to say was that you don't need to wear lots of make-up.'

'I do. I need to look like my mum.'

'Why?' Freya took hold of Chloe's shoulders. 'You look like you and I'm sure that's what your mum would want.'

'I don't want to look like me.'

'Really? I'd have killed for lovely thick auburn hair when I was your age. It's really eye-catching, especially when it glints a fierce red in the sun. It looks so much better than my mousey mop.' Freya tugged at her hair, which was being whipped around her face by the wind.

'I don't like being different. I'd rather be like Paige, but she thinks I'm an idiot.'

'Do you want to be like everyone else? That sounds pretty boring to me. You're not like Paige, and that's fine. You don't need her approval to be who you are. Just be yourself and stand tall and proud!'

Too much? Freya winced inside at her rallying cry but Chloe gave a small grin.

'I still think I look better with make-up on.'

Was that a question or a statement? The slight rise in intonation at the end of her sentence made Freya think the former.

'A little bit of make-up for a special occasion is fine. But you don't need a lot. In fact, too much make-up detracts from your fabulous features.'

Chloe gave a laugh laced with disbelief. 'I wish.'

'No, honestly. You have the most amazing cheekbones.' Freya ran a finger lightly across the girl's cheek. 'And your eyes are a beautiful colour.'

'They're brown,' said Chloe flatly.

'They're more amber, with flashes of deep green. And your skin absolutely glows – I've noticed it before.'

'You're just saying that.'

'I'm really not. I wouldn't lie to you, Chloe.'

Chloe's eyes darkened. 'You said you wouldn't tell Dad about me jumping off Clair Point, but you did.'

'No, I didn't. I didn't say a word to your dad about it. Well, not until he tackled me about it in the pub, but he knew all about it already. Is that what you thought, that I'd gone back on my word and told your father?' Chloe nodded. 'Is that why you've been a bit off with me lately?'

Chloe nodded again. 'I thought you'd lied and told on me.'

'Well, I promise that I didn't, even though I wish I'd never said I'd keep it quiet in the first place. Your dad wasn't very happy with me when he found out about Clair Point from someone else and realised that I'd known all along.'

He was so angry, remembered Freya, wondering how upset he would be if he knew of the even bigger secret she was keeping from him. Keeping quiet about a child doing something rash that had passed without incident was nothing compared to staying schtum about a long-lost half-sister he knew absolutely nothing about.

'Sorry,' said Chloe, her apology almost lost in the sound of the encroaching tide.

'It's all right. Why don't we get off this beach and you can go to the dance.'

'I can't go now. It's too late.'

'No, it's not. It's only just started. You're wearing a lovely dress, which is a little sandy right now, but all you need is a tidy up. Come back to your gran's and I can get you sorted. It won't take long.'

Chloe turned and stared at Freya. 'Why would you do that? I've been horrible to you.'

'Because I think you'll have a good time if you relax and let yourself, and I like you, Chloe.'

Chloe smiled properly at that, and her next words warmed Freya's heart. 'I like you, too.'

'Come on then.' Freya stood up and pulled Chloe to her feet. 'Grab your shoes and let's go.' The two of them started walking across the sand. 'You'd better ring your dad on the way home and tell him that you're OK. He's really worried about you.'

Chloe came to a sudden standstill. 'I can't talk to Dad. I said something terrible to him – something that I didn't mean. Something about him and Mum, and I can never take it back.'

'Whatever you said, he still loves you, Chloe. So give him a call and let's get to your gran's. We can go the back way so none of your friends will see you.'

'Thanks. I'm glad you found me.'

Chloe pushed her hand into Freya's as the two of them walked across the sand.

30

RYAN

Ryan only fully relaxed when he spotted Chloe and Freya walking towards the village hall. He'd been terrified when Chloe ran off that history would repeat itself – he would lose her and it would be his fault. Even Chloe's phone call on the way back to his mum's hadn't been enough to banish the dread. But here she was, walking side by side with Freya.

The two of them looked comfortable together, at ease in each other's company. But Chloe's face clouded over when she saw him. She stopped for a moment and Freya bent to say something in her ear before she marched over.

She stood in front of him, hands on her hips and head bent. 'I'm sorry, Dad,' she said, her bottom lip wobbling.

'It's all right, Chloe. I'm sorry, too.'

When she stepped into his arms, he pulled her close and closed his eyes. What would he do without her? She'd saved him when his despair after Natalie's death had been overwhelming. They'd saved each other.

'I didn't mean what I said,' she murmured into his shoulder.

He squeezed her even tighter. 'It's all right. Let's forget all about it. We both said things we didn't mean.'

When he released her, she stepped back towards Freya, who was standing watching them both.

Much to Ryan's relief, Chloe looked very different from the last time he'd seen her. She was still wearing the pretty dress they'd bought together in Exeter. But the thick make-up was gone, replaced with a touch of lip gloss and a little mascara, and her hair was released from the tight bun and was falling in red waves around her shoulders. She looked like his daughter again. She looked beautiful.

'You look absolutely amazing,' he said, giving her a wide smile.

Chloe beamed. 'Freya helped me to get ready and we had a good chat about things. She's all right, really.' A shadow passed across her face and she glanced back at Freya. 'I feel better like this. More like me. But I'm still worried that Paige and Isobel will be cross after they spent ages getting me ready.'

'How you look is up to you,' said Freya. 'Just tell Paige that you and your stylist had a re-think and decided that the natural look is far more in fashion these days.'

Chloe giggled. 'Paige has got more make-up on than I had.'

'Well, that's up to her. Just be proud of who you are, and have a brilliant time. And that new girl, Kristen, you told me about – perhaps you could check that she's having a good time too and not feeling left out?'

'I will. Love you, Dad, and thanks, Freya. You're the best.'

With a wave to both of them, Chloe skipped into the hall, which was filled with the sound of music and youngsters' excited chatter.

Ryan watched her go before turning to Freya.

'Are you some kind of miracle worker?'

'What do you mean?'

'My monosyllabic daughter not only apologised to me, she also smiled and said she loves me.'

'She does, whatever she said to you earlier,' said Freya

simply, her face glowing in the light spilling from the hall. 'She's twelve and full of hormones and conflicting emotions. I was a mess at her age, and a total pain to my dad. I was gawky and geeky. It was hell, believe me, but my dad survived and I came through it OK.'

'More than OK,' said Ryan, noticing for the first time how Freya's hair, shining gold in the light, framed her delicate face perfectly. She looked flushed and hassled and untidy, in her blue jeans and T-shirt – and completely lovely. There was a vulnerability in the way she twisted her hands together as she spoke, and a fresh-faced beauty in the tilt of her chin when she smiled at him. And she was kind. Kind enough to find his lost daughter and, as well as making her feel better, to encourage a rapprochement between the two of them. She was wonderful.

Ryan swallowed hard. There was no point in having feelings for Freya because it would only lead to a broken heart. He didn't deserve to be happy, not after what he'd done.

'Are you all right now?' asked Freya, taking a step towards him. 'Chloe really didn't mean what she said, you know. She was just upset and sounding off.'

'I know.' Ryan briefly closed his eyes, pushing Chloe's words away. She might not have meant them, but he'd never forget them.

A noisy group of revellers wandered by, heading for the Smugglers Haunt, and they gave him an idea. He didn't fancy going back to an empty house and the storm clouds had cleared, leaving an inky black sky filled with stars.

'Do you fancy grabbing a drink and sitting on the quayside, away from all the noise? It's an inadequate thank you for finding Chloe and helping to rescue her – rescue both of us.'

When Freya hesitated, Ryan suddenly hoped that she'd refuse. Heaven knows he shouldn't have asked her. He was being impetuous and that was a bad idea when Freya was involved.

But Freya nodded, a smile lighting up her face. 'Why not? Your mum's dozing in her chair after all the excitement of Chloe turning up, so she won't miss me.'

Ten minutes later, they were sitting on a bench at the quayside, Ryan with a plastic glass of real ale in his hand and Freya with a gin and tonic. The slap of the water could just be heard above a low *thump-thump* coming from the village hall.

'Claude won't be happy about all the noise,' said Ryan, glancing at a tiny cottage behind him. 'Have you met Claude, our local eccentric?'

'I saw him at the opening of the cultural centre. He looks like an interesting man.'

'He is, and he's a good sort. Lots of the archive material at the cultural centre came from him. He and Lettie, who set up the centre, make a good team. She hasn't lived here that long but she's fitted in really well.'

Why was he talking about people whom Freya hardly knew? he wondered. Displacement, he decided with a flash of clarity.

He thought back to the therapy he'd had shortly after Natalie's death. It had never properly helped him because he'd never truly said what he was feeling. He'd talked endlessly instead about the practical logistics of keeping his job going while bringing up a child as a single parent. His therapist had branded it 'displacement', right before Ryan gave up therapy for good. What was the point when he already knew what was bothering him and it could never be changed?

He made an effort to refocus and raised his glass. 'Here's to you, Freya. Thank you for finding Chloe and for knowing how to make her feel better. Thank you for persuading her to wipe off all that awful make-up. And thank you for helping my mum. I haven't seen her so happy in ages.' He shrugged. 'I misjudged you when you first arrived. I was off-hand and suspicious and possibly a little pompous, and I'm sorry about that.'

'No apology needed.' Freya placed her half-drunk gin on the floor, at her feet. 'To be honest, I rather misjudged you too.'

'Let me guess. You thought I was a grumpy old man.'

'Um.' Freya twisted her mouth. 'That wasn't exactly what I thought.'

'It's what Chloe thinks, or so she tells me. That, and wishing I was dead rather than her mother.' He gave what he hoped what a sardonic smile, to take the sting out of her words.

'She really didn't mean it. She was just...'

When Freya hesitated, Ryan touched her arm. 'She was just what?'

'She was upset that you said she was nothing like Natalie.'

He winced. 'Did I say that? I can hardly remember what I said, to be honest. Of course she's like her mum. I see Natalie in her every day, in the way she walks and talks, and I'm so glad about that. I was just horrified by what Isobel had done to my daughter's face.'

'You'd better get used to it. No doubt, Chloe will wear lots of make-up one day.'

'And that'll be fine when she's thirty. Nah, maybe forty.' Ryan smiled, feeling comfortable with Freya. Far more comfortable than he'd ever felt with Isobel, who always seemed to have some hidden agenda. She always wanted some DIY jobs done, or she was angling for a lunch invitation or needing advice. Isobel had a polished façade and he wasn't sure who she really was. But with Freya, he got the feeling that nothing was hidden. Every hurt she'd ever suffered was there in her big grey eyes for all to see.

He suddenly hated everyone who had hurt her over the years and, being spontaneous again, he leaned forward and brushed his lips across her cheek. Her hand flew to her face, to where he'd kissed her.

'Why did you do that?' she asked, staring into his eyes.

'I don't know. To say thank you?'

When Freya didn't move, her hair gleaming under the harbour lights, he lifted his hand and brushed her fringe from her eyes. He could hear his heart beating as feelings and longings he thought he'd put aside for ever washed over him. Just one kiss. Would that be so wrong?

He'd done a terrible thing in his past, to Natalie. But surely he didn't deserve to be unhappy for ever?

'Hello. What are you two up to, sitting out here in the dark?' Isobel's loud voice made him jump. 'Is there room on there for another little one?'

Without waiting for a reply, Isobel plonked herself down on the end of the bench next to Ryan, and her thigh, in tight black trousers, pressed hard against his.

'We were discussing Kathleen's care,' said Freya levelly, shuffling further along from Ryan.

'Is that right?' Isobel's voice, heavy with sarcasm, made Ryan wonder what she'd actually seen.

Perhaps it was just as well that she'd arrived when she had. What had he been thinking? Kissing Freya, even on the cheek, wasn't a good idea. She hadn't moved away when he touched her hair. But even if he hadn't totally misjudged the situation and she wanted him to kiss her, it wasn't fair on her because she had no idea what kind of a man he was. He couldn't take a relationship any further and she deserved better after her failed marriage.

'Did you find Chloe in the end?' asked Isobel. 'Is she at the dance now?'

'Yes, she's there,' Ryan answered.

'You sounded rather upset when you called to ask if she was still with me and Paige.'

'We'd had an argument about how much make-up she had on and she stormed off for a while.'

'Really?' Isobel sat back with her arms folded. 'Gosh, Ryan. You're not an old fuddy-duddy who objects to make-up, are you?'

'I don't mind make-up and it was good of you to help Chloe get ready but she had rather a lot on for a child of twelve, don't you think?'

He tried to keep his voice level. Isobel had been trying to help, and the fact that it had all gone disastrously wrong was his fault really for handling the situation so badly.

'What do you think, Freya?' asked Isobel. 'Where do you stand on make-up? I've noticed you hardly wear any so I'm guessing you're not a fan.'

Was that a subtle dig at Freya? She shrugged next to him. 'I can understand Chloe wanting to wear make-up. I was the same at twelve. But I don't think she needs to wear too much. Her natural beauty shines through.'

'Hmm.' Isobel sniffed. 'So you obviously found her in the end, after her walkabout.'

'Freya came across her at the cove and persuaded her to go to the dance,' said Ryan.

When he smiled at Freya, Isobel leant across his legs, her breasts brushing against his chest. 'That was kind of you, Freya. Looking after Kathleen *and* Chloe too. You're an absolute treasure and certainly worth your money. You're becoming so much more than the paid help.'

Ryan bristled on Freya's behalf, but before he could say a word, she got to her feet.

'And as the paid help, I'd better be getting back to Kathleen,' she said levelly. 'She likes her hot chocolate around now and I often have one with her. Goodbye, Isobel.' She nodded at Ryan. 'Bye, Ryan. I hope Chloe has a lovely time at the dance.'

'I'll walk you back to Mum's,' he said, about to get to his feet. But she shook her head.

'No, thank you. It's not far. You stay here with Isobel.'

'Thank you for everything,' he called after her. But she'd already disappeared into the darkness without looking back.

Annoyance surged through him. 'You were quite rude to Freya there.'

'Was I?' asked Isobel, pouting as she looked up at him with her big blue eyes. 'I was complimenting her, actually. I called her a treasure, which she obviously is. I think you're still a little overwrought after what happened with Chloe. It's hard, I know, but you need to move with the times and accept that Chloe and Paige are growing up.'

Ryan shuffled along the bench. He didn't really feel like talking to Isobel after the way she'd spoken to Freya. But she was right about one thing. Chloe *was* growing up – and the thought terrified him. How could he keep her safe when she was out on her own in the world? How could he protect her from being hurt like Natalie?

He steadied himself before asking: 'I know the girls are getting older, but it's good to let them be children for as long as possible, don't you think?'

'I guess so. Honestly, heaven only knows how you'll react when Chloe brings home her first boyfriend. I don't envy him.' Isobel laughed before tilting her chin towards the night sky. 'Look at all those lovely twinkly stars up there. It really is incredibly romantic out here.'

And with that, she flung her arms around his neck and pressed her lips hard against his.

Ryan pulled away, breathing heavily. 'Stop, Isobel. It's very public here and this is all a bit sudden.'

He couldn't deny that when Isobel had first shown an interest in him, he'd been flattered. And it *was* very romantic here, with the inky sky scattered with stars and waves washing gently against the quayside. But this wasn't what he wanted.

'Sudden? Do you really think so?' Isobel's mouth lifted in

one corner. 'You've been attracted to me for quite some time, Ryan. You can't deny it.'

'You're a very attractive woman but—'

'But you feel guilty about your wife,' Isobel interrupted, rolling her eyes. 'Look, it's lovely that you were so devoted to Natalie.' She ran a finger along the sensitive skin on his inner arm. 'Truly lovely, and it makes you even *more* attractive, to be honest. Caring and empathetic and vulnerable and all that. But it's been a few years now, Ryan, and it's time to move on. You don't deserve to feel guilty.'

Isobel was so wrong about that, but not for the reasons she suspected.

Ryan stood up quickly and shook out his legs.

'I'm sorry, Isobel. I'm just not ready. It's nothing to do with you. You're a wonderful woman, I'm sure, but—'

'Oh, please, another "but"?' Isobel sounded rather put out, but then she smiled, her lipstick smudged from their kiss. 'Of course. I understand. You need a little more time but you should know that I'm not the type to give up so easily.'

She made him sound like a challenge. A man who didn't succumb to her charms. A puzzle to be solved.

'Having rejected me so cruelly, will you at least walk me home?' she asked, pouting prettily.

'Of course,' said Ryan, because what else could he do? There was an awkward atmosphere between them now, and he was still bristling at Isobel's rudeness to Freya. But he couldn't leave a woman alone in the dark when she'd asked for his company. He was a mess but he wasn't a total heel.

Isobel linked her arm through his as they walked past the village hall that was still pulsating with music, and through the cobbled streets. He left her at her front door and walked back to his cottage, his mind filled with thoughts of Natalie, Isobel and Freya.

31

FREYA

Freya woke early, roused by the screeching of seagulls on the thatch above her. Pale dawn light was creeping beneath her curtains, and a glance at the clock on her bedside table showed it was only six o'clock. Kathleen wouldn't be stirring for at least an hour.

Freya pulled back the curtains. Shadows around the church were being chased away by the sun, which she could glimpse peeping above the horizon. Heaven's Cove was reborn as it was every day, fresh and new.

Slipping on her jeans and a sweatshirt, she crept down the stairs, pulled on her trainers and let herself out of the front door.

Heaven's Cove was at its best first thing, before tourists arrived to jam the narrow streets and drop ice cream on the cobbles. Freya was an incomer too. But, she realised, she'd already grown to love this village which had nestled for centuries where the land met the sea, the past and present meeting in its ancient lanes.

The smell of fish got stronger as she got close to the quay. A fishing boat had pulled up against the stone and men in thick woollen jumpers were unloading their catch, whistling to themselves under the pale sun that was creeping higher into the lightening sky.

Freya walked on to the edge of the village, to where the land rose up steeply. This was the way to a cliff that the locals called Cora Head. Freya had considered walking up to Driftwood House but she'd avoided going up there since her visit with Kathleen. She already felt stressed enough this morning without adding sadness into the mix.

The path wound through trees until she emerged at the top of the open headland. A bench had been placed in a prime spot and Freya sat down after glancing at the small plaque attached to it: *IN LOVING MEMORY OF IRIS STARCROSS.*

Who was Iris Starcross? she wondered, gazing out across the ocean. It was such an unusual surname, she must be related to Lettie Starcross, who'd opened the cultural centre. Did Iris once sit here and take in this magnificent view?

The sky was scored with wide streaks of rose-gold as the sun rose higher, and the ever-moving water below was such a pale blue, it looked almost like quicksilver. Freya took in a deep breath of fresh air and felt her body relax. So much had happened recently. There had been so many changes, it was hard to take everything in. And then there had been last night...

Freya thought back to Chloe's tear-stained face and another shiver of sympathy ran through her. It was hard enough being twelve years old without having to cope with the loss of your mother *and* peer pressure. At least she had a loving father to guide her.

Freya had deliberately kept her thoughts away from Ryan. But now, for a moment, she let herself picture his face when he'd leaned towards her to kiss her cheek. For one crazy moment, she'd thought he was going to kiss her full on the mouth. She'd hoped he was going to kiss her full on the mouth.

But Isobel had arrived and the moment had passed. *The moment!* Freya laughed into the early morning air. What on earth was she going on about? She was imagining things. Ryan's kiss on the cheek had been nothing more than a thank you kiss: a thank you from a relieved father for helping his daughter.

Freya, as Isobel had so eloquently reminded her, was the paid help, and Ryan didn't want to properly kiss her. He didn't want to properly kiss anyone except Natalie, or maybe women like Isobel who reminded him of his glamorous wife.

She glanced down at her well-worn jeans and thought back to Isobel's black trousers last night. They were tailored, tight, and looked brand new, as did her scarlet figure-hugging jumper, which matched her carefully outlined lips.

Freya wasn't sure she'd ever used lip liner. A touch of mascara, blusher and lip gloss were the most she usually managed. Isobel, in comparison, was always glamorous, as was Natalie from the photos she'd seen of Ryan's wife. That was the sort of woman he preferred, even though seeing Chloe in full-on slap had freaked him out. Which wasn't surprising. Freya felt again a rush of irritation towards Isobel for misjudging the situation so entirely. Or was she annoyed with Isobel because she was so much more Ryan's type?

Freya stared at Heaven's Cove, far below. Farther away, she could just make out Driftwood House, high on the cliffs that edged the other end of the village.

None of this is my business, she told herself sternly as a seagull swooped overhead. Ryan and Isobel could do whatever they wished and it was nothing to do with her. She was merely a paid carer, and one who happened to be hiding a huge secret from her employer's son.

What a mess! There was no news as yet about Maeve, which wasn't surprising as it had been only a couple of days since the agency was first tasked to find her. But that hadn't stopped Kathleen from frequently asking if there were any updates. And, as the search went on, she was still adamant that Ryan should never know. Being the keeper of secrets absolutely sucked, thought Freya, squinting at a blur of colour that had just appeared at the top of the headland.

Her heart started beating faster when she realised it was Ryan. He was in jeans and didn't look as though he'd brushed his hair since getting out of bed. Freya tried very hard not to picture him in bed, one bare muscular arm thrown across the duvet.

'Hi there,' she said lamely when he got closer. 'Couldn't you sleep either? This is quite a coincidence, you and me bumping into each other up here at' – she glanced at her watch – 'six thirty in the morning.'

'Not really,' said Ryan, folding his arms and looking out to sea. 'I followed you.' He grinned sheepishly. 'Sorry. That came out rather stalkery. What I mean is, I was opening my curtains and saw you going by and wanted to make sure you were all right after last night's excitement with Chloe.'

'I'm fine. Thank you,' said Freya, still feeling flustered. Her fair hair was being blown by the breeze and she hoped, for a moment, that Ryan would lean forward, like last night and brush it from her eyes. She breathed in deeply, inwardly berating herself. *He's not interested in women like you.*

'Have you left Chloe at home on her own?' she asked.

'No, she's having a sleepover with a girl called Kristen.'

Freya grinned because that was brilliant news.

'I think that might be something to do with you?'

'Not really. Chloe mentioned that Kristen's a new girl at school who's finding it hard to settle in so I suggested that she might look out for her.'

'It seems to have sparked a new friendship.'

'I hope so. Chloe knows what it's like to be the new girl and, from what she was telling me, it sounded like Kristen might be a little less... hard work than Paige. How did she explain to Paige about her lack of make-up?'

Ryan grinned. 'Oh, she blamed me, big-time. She said I'd

insisted that she clean her face immediately and that was why she ran off. I think she might have said that I attacked her with a wet flannel.' He shrugged. 'Paige was shooting me daggers when I went to pick Chloe up, and she didn't look best pleased when Chloe went off with Kristen and her mum. Though she probably thinks Chloe can't bear to be at home with such a dreadful dad.'

He smiled again, but the pain in his eyes caught Freya off-guard.

'You're a good dad,' she assured him.

'Not all of the time.'

'You're doing the best you can.'

'It's not always good enough, though, is it?' He gave a mirthless laugh. 'Pay no attention to me. I have a horrible tendency to feel sorry for myself sometimes.'

'That's not surprising. You've been through a lot.'

'So have you.'

Freya smiled. 'I don't think a broken marriage equates to losing your wife in such a tragic way.'

'It's not a competition,' said Ryan gently. 'It all hurts.'

Freya had never seen this side of Ryan before. He seemed deflated, as though all the confidence had gone out of him. He pulled his shoulders back and turned his face towards the sun rising above the ocean. 'You were really great with Chloe last night.'

'Thanks. Our relationship has improved now she knows it wasn't me who told you that she jumped from Clair Point.'

'I did tell her it wasn't you.'

'She thought you were being economical with the truth, to avoid her taking against her grandmother's carer. But I think now she's actually starting to like me.'

'We're all starting to like you,' said Ryan gruffly.

He turned from the sea and reached out his hand. *Step back! Stop this before it starts!* said a little voice in her head. But she didn't move as he cupped the side of her face in his palm, his skin warm against her cheek.

'Freya?' His voice was ragged, his face pained.

The crashing of the waves against the headland and the cries of circling seagulls faded away as Ryan dipped his head and kissed her on the mouth.

She'd wondered what it would be like to kiss a man who wasn't Greg. She'd imagined it would feel much the same, but it didn't. Ryan was taller and his body more wiry when she leaned into the kiss and put her arms around his neck. His kiss was more urgent than the perfunctory pecks she and Greg had exchanged for months before their marriage ended. He wanted her. But he didn't know she was keeping a secret from him.

The moment she had the thought, Ryan pulled away as though he could read her mind.

'I'm sorry,' he gasped. 'I shouldn't have done that.'

'It's all right.'

Freya touched his arm, but he moved away, seemingly angry now. What on earth was going on? Ryan was a master of mixed messages. Did he want to kiss her or not?

'It's not all right. I shouldn't have kissed you and led you on for nothing.'

'Why do you say for nothing?'

'We can't have a relationship, Freya.' He closed his eyes for a moment and shook his head.

'Why? Because I work for your mother?'

'No, that's got nothing to do with it.'

Freya felt her stomach plummet. She'd horribly misjudged the situation and he was just like Greg. Why on earth would a handsome widower like Ryan be interested in a mess like her? She'd seen the photos of Natalie and she'd heard the stories of how wonderful she was. There was no way she could ever measure up.

'I understand.' She swallowed hard. 'You feel guilty about

Natalie and about being with someone else who isn't her, someone who's so different from her. I understand. It's OK.'

She turned to go, but Ryan caught hold of her arm.

'Please don't go, Freya. Not like this. I do feel guilty about Natalie but it's not what you think. You're the first woman I've had real feelings for since Natalie died, but I'm not the man that you think I am.'

Freya shook her head. 'I have no idea what you're talking about.'

Ryan looked out to sea, the muscles in his jaw moving, as though he was coping with huge inner turmoil.

'Can I trust you?' he asked.

Freya heard an echo of his mother saying the very same words to her and shivered. She was already keeping more confidences than she could cope with, but Ryan looked so troubled.

'I can keep a secret,' she told him, just as she'd told Kathleen before him.

'What about your sister?'

What about Ryan's sister who's out there somewhere? Freya shook her head to get rid of the thought.

'Belinda is my half-sister, and I don't tell her anything, believe me. She and I share a father, but that's all. I don't share secrets with her. I promise you.'

Ryan walked to the edge of the land and looked down at the waves pounding into the rock below. Freya moved to stand beside him.

'The reason I feel so guilty all the damn time is because...' He closed his eyes briefly and, when he opened them again, they shone with tears. 'Natalie is dead because of me.'

Freya's breath caught in her throat. That was the last thing she had expected Ryan to say.

'How can that possibly be true?' she asked gently. 'Your mum mentioned... she said it was an accident.'

He sighed. 'Yes, that's what everyone says. It was an accident, pure and simple. A tragic accident. She was driving to work and the sun was in the lorry driver's eyes when he pulled out into the path of her oncoming car.'

'If it was an accident, how could you possibly be to blame?'

Ryan began to tap his foot on the grass. Tap, tap, tap, as though his agitation was too much to contain.

'Natalie and I had argued before she left the house that afternoon and she was upset. So upset that her concentration was shot to pieces. Who's to say that she wouldn't have anticipated the danger and seen the lorry earlier if she'd had her mind fully on the road?'

'It's hard to anticipate a lorry pulling out in front of you. You don't know that it would have made any difference at all.'

'That's the point. I don't know, and it's the not knowing that's killing me.'

'What had you argued about?'

Ryan paused, his face a mask of pain. 'I'd just told her that I wanted a divorce.'

Freya could hardly believe what she was hearing. 'Ryan... I don't know what to say. From what your mum's told me, I thought you were so happy together.'

Ryan smiled sadly. 'Natalie had many wonderful qualities, but Chloe and Mum have an idealised version of her. She and our relationship – the way we were together – have become almost perfect in their minds, and I've gone along with it. That's the last thing I can do for her. Natalie and I didn't live near Mum then so she wasn't aware that our relationship was imploding. And Chloe was too young to really know what was going on. She knew we were arguing, but that was it. No one knew that we'd grown apart and our marriage was about to end. And what would telling them the truth achieve now that she's gone? Chloe has lost her mother.'

'I get that. I do. But Chloe's trying to live up to an idealised version of Natalie and doesn't feel that she can ever be good enough. She'll never be enough to fill the gap that Natalie has left in your life.'

'Is that what she thinks?' Ryan wobbled, alarmingly close to the edge of the cliff, and Freya grabbed his arm and pulled him back.

'Please be careful. Chloe and your mum need you.'

She needed him too. The more she spent time in his company, the more that truth was seeping into her brain.

'They don't know about my guilt over Natalie's death. They don't know it was my fault.'

Freya held his gaze. She could hardly bear to imagine the torment he'd suffered over the last four years. It broke her heart.

'Ryan, it wasn't your fault,' she said slowly and clearly. 'I'm sure your grief at losing Natalie in such an awful way, and the pain of seeing Chloe without her mum, has built it up in your mind. But people argue and marriages break down all the time. I know that more than anybody, and sometimes it's because people want different things in life and grow apart. You're not to blame for Natalie's death. It was an accident – a dreadful accident which has scarred everyone who loved her. But you don't need to feel guilty. I promise you.' This time it was Freya who stood on tiptoe and cupped her hands around his cheeks. 'You owe it to yourself and to Chloe to be happy again.'

Freya could sense the conflict being played out in Ryan's mind. He so wanted to believe her and unshackle himself from the guilt that was dragging him down. But guilt had a way of holding on tight.

Time seemed to stand still as they stood on the headland together, Ryan's skin warming beneath Freya's fingers. Then his shoulders dropped and he let out a sigh that sounded, to Freya, like relief.

'I feel so fortunate that you've come into our lives,' he whispered, catching her around the waist and pulling her in close.

This time his kiss was soft and gentle and she melted into his body, feeling tingles down to her toes.

He pulled away from her. 'I didn't mean to tell you the truth about my relationship with Natalie, but you have a way of drawing out people's secrets. It's a gift.'

A gift or a curse. Ryan smiled, but Freya's smile in return was forced. In all the emotion of the last few minutes, she'd managed to ignore the big family secret she was guarding. He'd told her about Natalie, and she so wanted to tell him about Maeve in return, but it was Kathleen's secret to tell. Freya had given her word not to tell a soul, and she couldn't break her promise.

But keeping that promise meant there was an invisible wall between her and Ryan, a wall built of deceit. She needed time to think.

Freya glanced at her watch. The sun had risen higher in the sky and the village was starting to wake up. Cars, looking like Matchbox vehicles, were negotiating the narrow lanes and tiny stick-like figures were thronging on the quayside.

'I'm sorry but I have to get home before your mum gets up. She'll wonder where I am.'

Ryan hung his head. 'Do you think badly of me now?'

He looked like a small child who'd done something wrong and Freya's heart and resolve melted.

'Of course I don't think badly of you. I feel sorry that you've lived with guilt that's so unwarranted for such a long time. You're not a bad man, Ryan. Quite the opposite, in fact. You're a wonderful dad and son.'

And brother. It was on the tip of her tongue but she couldn't betray Kathleen's trust. She was in too deep and couldn't get out.

'So, what about us?' Ryan lifted his head and held her gaze. 'I don't want to complicate everything.' He winced. 'Let's be honest, I *am* complicated and you're coming out of a marriage and you're vulnerable and you deserve better. I shouldn't have kissed you but it's all I've wanted to do for a while now.'

Freya's mind was a whirl of emotion. This complicated, lovely man wanted her.

'I thought you and Isobel... She's very keen on you and...' Freya trailed off when Ryan shook his head.

'Isobel thinks she's keen on me but... she's not you, Freya.'

'I thought that was maybe a good thing,' said Freya, raising an eyebrow. But Ryan shook his head again, more vehemently this time.

'I don't feel about Isobel how I feel about you. I haven't felt this way in what seems like forever. You've bewitched me, Freya, and it's scary.'

'It's scary for me too,' whispered Freya, her breath taken away by his words.

He leant over to rest his forehead against hers. 'So what do we do now?' he murmured, his words warm on her cheek.

'I don't know,' whispered Freya, desperately trying to work out a way forward that didn't involve betraying Kathleen's trust.

'If you don't want this, I—'

'No,' interrupted Freya, her mind still whirring but sure of one thing. 'I'm not so vulnerable that I don't know my own mind, and I know that I want to be with you.'

Had she said too much? A slow smile spread across Ryan's face.

'You want to be with me?' He straightened up and gently ran his fingers through her hair. 'In that case, we could take things slowly and see what happens.'

Freya swallowed, determined not to complicate matters even further by throwing herself back into his arms. 'What about your mum? I work for her so wouldn't it be inappropriate?'

'I don't think so. My mum has really taken to you, Freya, and I'm sure she'd be happy for us. But she doesn't need to know yet anyway, not if we're just seeing how things go. What do you think?'

'I think... I think we could take it *very* slowly, maybe,' replied Freya, standing perfectly still while her mind raced ahead. Taking it slowly was perfect. It would give her time to get her head around the dilemma she faced and to find a way to solve it. She looked at the handsome, vulnerable man who'd just opened his heart to her. She so wanted to solve it.

Ryan nodded, the sky above him scudded with wisps of white cloud. 'Let's see how this goes, then.'

Ryan sat on Iris's bench watching as Freya reached the trees that led down towards the village. She looked so slight, a tiny figure on the huge headland. She turned briefly to wave at him and then she was gone.

He turned his gaze towards the sea and stretched out his legs. He could still taste Freya on his lips and feel her in his arms. Tears prickled the corners of his eyes. It had been so long since he'd felt this way.

He felt elated. Warm inside and lighter. The guilt he'd carried for so long was still there but it had eased. Telling another person – trusting Freya enough to tell her – had robbed it of its power.

She hadn't recoiled from him or condemned him. Instead, she'd let him kiss her and she'd kissed him back. She'd told him he wasn't a bad man. And her understanding and acceptance had redeemed him. She'd brought some peace into his life.

A red fishing boat chugged into view and he watched as it approached the harbour, screeching seagulls following in its wake. Ripples spread across the sea until the water looked like silver silk being ruffled by a gentle breeze. The sun was catching cottage windows in Heaven's Cove, making them sparkle and the sky was turning from milk-white to china blue.

Everything looked brighter. Even the grass growing at his feet was a more vibrant shade of green than he'd ever noticed before. Ryan looked around him, feeling as if he was waking from a long sleep.

He was still scared. Scared that this feeling was fleeting, scared that whatever he and Freya might have would peter out rather than grow. But they would take it very slowly. She'd seemed happy with that. And whatever happened, she'd given him this precious gift – even if only for a little while, the world around him was ablaze with colour and no longer a guilt-ridden grey.

32

FREYA

Freya gazed out of her bedroom window at the village green that was edged with primroses and red campion. Beyond the patch of greenery stood the church whose clock chimed on the hour, day and night.

At first, the chimes had roused Freya from sleep and made her heart beat faster as they echoed across cottage rooves. But now, it was a comforting sound in the night – all was well in Heaven's Cove, as it had been since the church was built seven hundred years ago.

Freya had only been in the village for two months but she was already very sure that she never wanted to leave. Especially after the last two weeks, which had passed in a blur of clandestine meetings and stolen kisses with Ryan. She pictured him in his moth-eaten, mustard-yellow jumper and smiled to herself.

True to their word, they were taking things slowly and keeping their fledgling relationship from Kathleen and Chloe for the time being. So there had been a walk hand in hand on the beach in the rain, two trips to a remote country pub a few miles from Heaven's Cove, and an evening snuggled in front of the TV when Kathleen had an early night.

It would all be wonderful, Freya mused, going back to her laptop, if only she could be completely herself with Ryan. But with the search for Maeve ongoing, and him none the wiser, she was always holding a part of herself back.

'So this is where you've been hiding.'

Freya jumped up from her desk, startled by her sister, who had suddenly appeared on the landing.

'I didn't hear you arrive,' she said, closing the lid of her laptop. In between daydreaming about Ryan, she'd been browsing information about mother and baby homes and was feeling shaken by the sorrows she'd uncovered.

'Kathleen saw me walking up the garden path and let me in,' said Belinda, marching into the room. 'I thought I'd say hello seeing as you bailed on our trip to the pub last night.'

'I'm sorry I postponed but I had a headache and needed an early night.'

Don't blush or she'll know you're lying! Freya told herself, though she feared it was too late. She *had* bailed on Belinda and didn't like telling untruths, but their visit to the pub last week hadn't gone too well – her sister's barbed comments about Freya's mother and their shared father had grown wearying after a while.

So the prospect of spending two hours in Ryan's company last night instead had been too enticing to turn down.

She still felt guilty though, and Belinda looked far from convinced.

'Hmm,' she said, pursing her lips before her eyes settled on a piece of paper poking out of a folder next to the laptop. 'What's this?'

Freya muttered a curse under her breath. She'd printed out some information about adoption and mother and baby homes while the search for Maeve continued. She pushed the paper back into the folder but not quickly enough to escape Belinda's eagle eye.

'You're not thinking of adopting, are you?' she asked, wrinkling her nose. 'I don't mean to be rude but you're a bit long in the tooth. Polly in Sheep Street adopted at about your age. Her little boy is four now and Polly looks dreadful. Totally washed out, poor woman.'

'I was looking at an interesting article, that's all,' said Freya, feeling for poor, exhausted Polly.

'An article about adoption?'

'That's right.'

'And what's this?'

With a shiver of horror, Freya realised that she'd left a print-out about mother and baby homes on the bed, along with the old photo of Kathleen standing on the clifftop.

Freya made a grab for the photo but Belinda was there first. The woman had lightning reflexes when she sensed gossip in the making. She held the picture up to her face while Freya tried to grab it from her.

'Heavens, is that...? It's Kathleen as a young woman. The birthmark is unmistakable. And is that Driftwood House?'

Freya snatched the picture from her and shoved it, together with the print-out, into the folder.

Belinda turned to Freya, a strange look on her face. 'You're being very peculiar this morning. Oh, good grief. Our father didn't have more children, did he? Are we awash with adopted brothers and sisters out there?'

Freya hesitated, tempted to lie again. But Belinda already had a poor opinion of their father and it didn't seem fair to malign him with fathering lots of unknown siblings.

'As far as I'm aware, you and I are Dad's only children.'

'Are you sure?'

'No, I'm not sure.'

Freya thought her dad had been faithful to her mum throughout their marriage. But he'd been unfaithful to Belinda's mother in the first place, so who knew for sure?

'But you're not looking for siblings?'

'No, I'm not and I have no reason to think that there are any other siblings out there. It's just you and me.'

'Thank goodness for that.' Belinda let out a sigh of relief but then frowned. 'So if that's the case, why are you so interested in mother and baby homes that went out with the ark? And how come Kathleen was in that photo? Was she here in Heaven's Cove years ago? She kept that quiet.' Her eyes opened wide. 'Oh! Oh, I see!'

'What do you see?' demanded Freya, feeling panicky.

Belinda went to the door and, after looking up and down the landing, closed it quietly.

'Are you doing this for Kathleen?' she whispered.

'I don't know what you're talking about,' said Freya, opening the desk drawer and pushing the folder inside it. Cold dread was seeping through her.

'I always thought there was something strange about Kathleen,' said Belinda, sitting down heavily on the bed. 'Something a little off. She was sad about her husband dying, of course. But I always felt there was something more.'

'Her daughter-in-law being killed in a car accident, perhaps?' gabbled Freya, going hot and cold because Belinda knew. The biggest gossip in Heaven's Cove knew Kathleen's deepest secret.

If only Kathleen had called up the stairs to say that Belinda had arrived. She'd have had time to tidy everything away. But Kathleen had been kind and sent her sister straight up.

'Obviously the accident was very sad,' murmured Belinda. 'But there's always been something else. I have a nose for these kinds of things.'

'A nose for other people's tragedy?'

Belinda drew a sharp intake of breath.

'There's no need to be unkind, Freya.'

'No. Sorry.' Freya ran a hand through her hair, wondering

how best to handle this and prevent Kathleen's secret being blabbed around Heaven's Cove. Belinda was only guessing what had gone on and she would embellish it until it bore little relation to the truth. But the damage would be done. 'All I meant is that people's private business should remain private,' she said firmly.

A deep line appeared between Belinda's eyebrows. 'Of course. And I'm the soul of discretion.' The sheer hypocrisy of the woman took Freya's breath away. 'But tell me, are you looking into something for Kathleen?'

'No, I'm not,' lied Freya, as calmly as she could, hoping that her cheeks weren't burning again and giving her away. 'You've got the wrong end of the stick, Belinda. It's nothing, and you can't go around making wild claims all over the village.'

'I wouldn't dream of it.'

'Any unfounded gossip would hurt Kathleen, and I don't believe you want to do that.'

Belinda stared at Freya for a moment before shaking her head. 'I care a great deal about Kathleen and wouldn't want to do anything to upset her. And if you say there's nothing in what I'm surmising, I'll believe you and won't mention anything about it.' When Freya continued to stare, she shrugged. 'Not to anyone.'

'You promise?'

'If I have to,' she huffed.

'Properly promise,' added Freya, not wanting to push the point but desperate for reassurance that her gossipy sibling wasn't about to start blabbing about Kathleen's heartache all over Heaven's Cove. If Ryan heard about it from someone in the pub... A shiver curled itself around Freya's heart.

'Of course I properly promise,' said Belinda, looking seriously put out. 'How old are we, ten? I promise from one sister to another. Though...' She wrinkled her nose. 'If there's nothing in it, it really wouldn't matter what I said, would it?' She raised her hand when Freya opened her mouth to speak. 'OK. I'll keep it to myself.' She raised an eyebrow. 'Even though "it" isn't anything at all.'

Freya tried to smile, but she was still feeling panicky. A secret adopted child was gossip gold to Belinda. Poor Kathleen would probably have given birth to triplets by the time her sister was through with it.

'So when are you going to be free to meet up?' asked Belinda, flinging the door open wide now she realised that Freya wasn't about to spill any beans.

'I'll have a word with Kathleen and see when she doesn't need me. You will remember that you've solemnly promised not to say anything to anyone about Kathleen, won't you? It's absolutely nothing.'

She was overdoing it. She knew she was. But Freya was panic-stricken at the thought of betraying Kathleen's trust, and Ryan finding out that way.

'You're implying that I have the memory span of a goldfish, Freya. I won't say anything about' – she put the next word in air quotes – '"nothing". But can I say that the truth is written all over your face. You're absolutely hopeless at keeping secrets.'

Belinda really had no idea, thought Freya wryly.

Her sister paused in the doorway. 'You've grown quite fond of the old lady, haven't you?'

'I have, and that's why I don't want her to be hurt by anything.'

'Oh, do stop labouring the point. I won't mention anything to anyone. And don't leave it too late to arrange an evening out with me. I am in demand, you know, what with fundraising for the village hall ongoing, and raising awareness of the new cultural centre, and chairing the parish council.'

Freya sensed a way to claw back some ground from Belinda.

Flattery got you everywhere, right? 'You're like a mini celebrity in Heaven's Cove,' she told her, trying to sound upbeat.

'I suppose I am,' Belinda purred, as Freya had known she would, her attention diverted. 'Well, I'd better leave you to finish all the top-secret things you were doing. I'll see myself out.'

33

FREYA

Once Belinda had swept from the room, Freya sat slumped at her desk with her head in her hands. She'd thought life couldn't get more complex – keeping Maeve a secret from the man she was falling for was complicated enough. But adding Belinda and her loose lips into the mix was potentially disastrous. Kathleen, already on edge waiting for news of her daughter, would be furious. Or distraught, which would be far worse. Freya groaned softly.

The cheerful yells of youngsters playing at the tiny primary school around the corner floated in through the open window. And she heard the front door open and close when Kathleen went to have lunch with a friend in a village café. But Freya didn't lift her head until her mobile started ringing, jolting her back to life.

She answered without looking at the caller information. It was probably a cold call, in the middle of the day.

But it wasn't anyone trying to sell anything.

'Hello, Freya,' said a chirpy voice on the other end of the line. 'It's Derek here. Derek who's heading the search for Maeve.'

Freya nearly fell off her chair.

'Hi... hi! Hello. Yes, we've spoken before.'

'How are you?' he asked cheerfully. 'I imagine it's lovely by the sea on a day like today. I've always fancied living by the beach myself. It must be like being on a constant holiday.'

'Yeah, it's great,' said Freya, sounding slightly curt but keen to move away from small talk. Derek had to be ringing for a reason.

'Is Kathleen there?' he asked.

'I'm afraid not. She's gone out for lunch. Can you speak to me instead?'

In the background, Freya could hear papers being shuffled. 'Kathleen has given permission for you to be involved at every step, and she gave your number as the best one for contacting her so...'

Come on, Derek. Freya realised she was holding her breath as he sighed. Why was he sighing? Sighing couldn't be good, could it?

'I have mixed news,' he said, putting her out of her misery. 'Using our contacts I've managed to track down paperwork from the organisation who ran the mother and baby home in Heaven's Cove in the fifties. And from that, via various records, I've been able to ascertain the whereabouts of Kathleen's daughter.'

Freya jumped to her feet and sat down again. 'You've found Maeve?' she whispered.

'We have indeed and we've passed on the letter that Kathleen wrote in the event that we were able to locate her.'

'So she's read Kathleen's letter?'

'She has.'

'But that's wonderful.' Tears sprang into Freya's eyes. Kathleen had laboured for hours over that letter, which was filled with explanation and love, never knowing if her daughter would read it. 'So what happens now?' she gulped. 'Will Maeve make contact with her mother?'

Derek paused. 'I did say that the news was mixed, I'm afraid. Maeve has received the letter and spoken with our intermediary and she says she bears no ill will towards her birth mother, but she doesn't wish to pursue any contact at this time.'

'None at all.'

'I'm afraid not. She was quite clear about that.'

Disappointment washed over Freya. Kathleen's daughter had been found but she and her mother would never meet.

'At least I can tell Kathleen that she's alive.'

'She most definitely is.'

'Does she live in this country?'

'I'm sorry but I'm not comfortable giving out information without Maeve's permission.'

'Is she well?'

Derek paused again before answering. 'As far as I'm aware, she is. Look, I'll put what information I can in an email for you to show Kathleen, and she can give us a call if she'd like to. Though I'm afraid I can't really answer questions because my hands are tied. I am sorry.'

'I understand, and thank you so much for finding her. Knowing that her daughter is alive and well will mean the world to her.'

After Derek rang off, Freya sat with the phone in her hand for ages. This was massive news and she felt like shouting it from the rooftops: *Maeve has been found!* Kathleen would be delighted, she was sure – but there was a sting in the tail, a sting that would wound her deeply.

Two hours later, Freya was sitting on the bottom stair when Kathleen turned her key in the lock and stepped into the hall.

'My goodness,' she said, placing her walking stick against

the wall. 'Have you been sitting there waiting for me?' She frowned when Freya nodded. 'There's nothing wrong with Ryan or Chloe, is there?'

'No, they're fine.' Freya stood up and stretched her legs. She'd been sitting on the stair for the last twenty minutes and had grown stiff.

'Belinda isn't still here, is she?' Kathleen peered into the sitting room. 'I thought I heard her calling out a goodbye before I went out with Maureen but my hearing's not what it was. Just so long as she's not going to leap out of a corner at us. With Belinda, you never know if she's listening in somewhere. Sorry. I know she's your sister.'

'Half-sister,' murmured Freya, her thoughts on the momentous news she was about to impart. News that would change Kathleen's life. 'Take your jacket off and come and sit on the sofa for a minute?'

'Why?' Kathleen walked slowly to the sofa without taking her jacket off and sat down. Her breath suddenly started coming in short gasps. 'Have you heard something about Maeve? Is there news?'

'There is.' Freya crossed the room and closed the door. Belinda had definitely left the building but Kathleen's talk of eavesdropping in corners made her nervous. 'While you were out, I took a call from Derek, who's been looking for Maeve. He told me something amazing. Maeve has been found.'

'Oh.' Kathleen's hand flew to her mouth. When she said no more, Freya sat beside her.

'Are you all right?'

'I'm fine.'

Kathleen didn't look fine. Her skin had blanched and her hands were trembling in her lap. Freya covered Kathleen's hands with hers.

'Is she well?' asked Kathleen, quietly. 'Is she happy?'

'I don't know much, I'm afraid. But Derek said that she's well and she's read your letter.'

Kathleen's green eyes filled with tears. 'She's read it? So she knows what happened now. She knows that I didn't give her up because I didn't care.'

'She knows, Kathleen. She knows exactly what happened and how heartbroken you were and still are. She knows that you've always loved her.'

Kathleen hung her head, breathing deeply. After a while, she asked softly, 'Is her name still Maeve or did her adoptive parents change it?'

'I don't know for sure but Derek called her Maeve so I assume that her name's still the same.'

'I hope so,' murmured Kathleen. 'Her name was the only thing I was ever able to give her.'

She turned to Freya, her face transformed. She looked younger and full of hope. 'But this is marvellous, isn't it? My daughter's been found.'

Freya took a deep breath, hating that the rest of the news she had to tell would destroy that hope. 'I'm afraid it wasn't all good news,' she said gently. 'Maeve has read your letter and she said she has no bad feelings towards you. But she doesn't feel able to meet you.'

Kathleen's face fell. 'Not ever?' she whispered.

'Not at the moment. But this must have all come as quite a shock to her. Maybe she'll change her mind in the future.'

'And maybe she won't. Or she'll change her mind when it's too late. I'm eighty-three, Freya. Time isn't on my side.'

'I know.' Freya stroked the old lady's hands, feeling helpless. 'We know nothing about her life and the sort of woman she's become, but if she's anything like you, she'll want to do the right thing.'

'The right thing for me or for her?'

'Maybe they're the same thing.'

Kathleen gazed into the cold fireplace. 'No, the right thing for Maeve is to get on with her life, don't you think? The only life she's ever known, without me in the background upsetting the apple cart. I've only ever wanted the best for my daughter and if that's what Maeve wants, then it is for the best.'

She turned back to Freya, her face resolute. 'I know that Maeve is alive and well and I know that she's read my letter. That's enough, Freya. That has to be enough.'

'You're amazing, Kathleen. Do you know that?' said Freya, on the verge of tears herself.

'Come on, my girl.' Kathleen was now the one to pat Freya's hand. 'Don't upset yourself. This is good news. I can rest easy and be at peace knowing that both of my children are safe. And I know now that I was right not to say anything about her to Ryan.'

'Is it still right not to tell him?'

'I'm sure of it. How can I tell him that he has a sister after all these years, but he and she will never meet or have any kind of relationship? I want to save him from that. It's knowledge that will eat away at him.'

Just as it would still eat away at Kathleen, for all her fine words about being at peace with Maeve's decision.

Freya bit her lip. Perhaps Kathleen knew best. What Ryan didn't know couldn't hurt him. And it couldn't hurt Freya's love affair with him.

A wave of relief washed over her. She was falling hard for Ryan and he seemed to feel the same way. She would always know about his sister but she could keep Kathleen's secret search, and the part she'd played in it, from him. She'd feel guilty for all time. Of course she would. But it was for the best. Kathleen was right and everything would be fine.

A dreadful thought hit Freya. Everything would be fine, just so long as Belinda kept her promise to keep quiet.

34

RYAN

Ryan looked up from the box file and ran his fingers through his fringe.

'Are you sure you paid the plumbing insurance, Mum? And the house insurance, too?'

Kathleen looked up from her knitting. 'I'm not sure. I can't remember everything.'

She sounded curt, which was very unlike her. Ryan frowned. She'd been rather out of sorts for a few days. Tired and distracted. He'd found her last night, sitting in the dark, staring into space.

'Is everything all right, Mum?' he asked.

She didn't pause from her knitting. 'Absolutely fine,' she replied, as she always did. If her arm was hanging off she'd never complain. His mother was made of stern stuff. Sterner than him, he often thought. Her needles stopped clicking. 'Isn't there anything about the insurance in the file?'

'No, afraid not.' Ryan puffed out his cheeks at the reams of documents thrust into a battered manila folder. 'Your filing system could do with an update.'

Maybe insurance payments were being made via direct

debit, he thought, opening the laptop he'd brought with him and logging into his mother's bank account. She preferred to go into her bank in the nearest town, rather than bank online, but he had her login details and she relied on him if she got into a financial muddle.

She also relied on him for repairs around the house, but the latest plumbing issue was beyond him. A professional was needed, perhaps even a new boiler, and there was no point in her paying out if her insurance would cover it.

'Hey, Ryan. I didn't hear you arrive.'

Freya walked into the kitchen with the washing basket balanced on her hip and picked up the peg bag.

Ryan glanced at the woman he couldn't stop thinking about. He could hear his own heartbeat pounding in his ears.

'Hi, Freya. I've called in to help Mum sort out the plumbing,' he said, keeping his voice steady for his mother's benefit, and resisting the urge to leap from his chair and pull her into his arms.

They hadn't told anyone of their burgeoning relationship yet, not even his mum. They were still taking it slowly, although taking it slowly was slowly killing him.

'That would be great.' Freya dropped the peg bag on top of the wet clothes. 'The water temperature is very unreliable. It went freezing cold when I was in the shower this morning.'

'That must have been a nasty shock.'

'It was.' Freya raised an eyebrow as she smiled. 'I'm surprised you didn't hear my screams.'

Their eyes locked as Ryan tried not to imagine Freya in the shower. He swallowed and glanced back at his laptop. Whose idea had it been to take it slowly in the first place?

He clicked onto his mum's current account and started going through recent outgoings, glancing every now and then through the open back door into the garden. Freya was out there now, hanging out his mother's washing. She'd grown so fond of Freya. What would she do without her? What would he do?

Ryan had lots of work to finish, and he'd promised Chloe that he'd pick up the ingredients for a chicken curry. But he was happy here, with Freya popping in and out of the kitchen.

She was always on his mind and he could still feel her lips from the kiss they'd shared last night. He hadn't felt this way since long before Natalie died.

Ryan ran a finger gently across his mouth. He was turning into a love-struck idiot. One of the 'dweebs' that Chloe mentioned so dismissively. But it was good, he realised, to feel something other than sorrow and guilt. It was good to feel desire.

It wasn't all plain sailing. Freya was easy to talk to and easy to trust. But there were complications on both sides. He had an often stroppy daughter and the guilt he was still working through, and Freya was just coming out of a marriage and currently working for his mum.

Neither his mum nor Chloe knew what was going on – at least, he didn't think his mum knew. She could be quite astute at times. He glanced at her but her head was bent over her knitting needles. It was best they didn't know for now – he and Freya had agreed to keep their relationship quiet for a little longer, while they got to know each other better.

Plus, if he was being honest, he wasn't one hundred per cent sure how she felt about him. She always looked happy to be with him but sometimes she seemed distant. As though she was holding something back.

He stopped scanning through his mother's account and watched Freya while she pegged out a sheet and stood back to admire the clean washing blowing on the line.

Something about her took his breath away. Sometimes, when she caught his eye and gave him a smile, he found it hard to breathe. And when she looked upset, he wanted to wrap his arms around her and chase away everything bad in the world.

This amazing woman had appeared out of nowhere. A few weeks ago he didn't know she existed, and he'd managed without her. But now his life was changing for the better.

You know nothing about her. That was what Isobel had said about Freya when she'd called by to drop off Chloe yesterday. He hadn't mentioned her but Isobel had given her opinion all the same. *I feel I have to say something because I'm worried about you and your mother. She's pushed her way into your family. Don't you think it's a little suspicious?*

He'd defended Freya and made it crystal clear he didn't want Isobel spreading rumours about his mum's carer around the village. But Isobel could be a loose cannon so who knew what she was saying? He really didn't want Freya hurt by idle gossip.

Ryan went back to his laptop, and found what he'd been searching for amongst the debits on his mother's account.

'Here it is. You paid the plumbing insurance six weeks ago, so I'll give them a call.'

'Whatever you think is best.'

There it was again. His mother sounded flat and not right. The low mood she often suffered at this time of year should be lifting by now. She'd seemed much better a few weeks ago.

He was about to close down the banking website when his eye was caught by a payment made by his mother a couple of weeks or so ago. It was a sizeable sum. And it was paid directly to Freya.

Ryan frowned. Freya's bed and board were included in her role with his mum and she also received a monthly payment. That was being paid regularly into her account but this sum was extra. He looked back through his mum's accounts and his breathing quickened when he noticed another payment to Freya.

'Is everything all right?' His mum put down her knitting and stared at him. 'You've gone a funny colour.'

He tapped his fingers on the table. 'What are these payments to Freya?'

'She has to be paid, Ryan. She doesn't look after me for nothing.'

'I don't mean that money. I mean the extra payments that have gone to her.'

'What extra payments?' Kathleen picked up her knitting again, a pink stain spreading across her cheeks.

'You've paid money – extra money – into Freya's bank account, and it's a sizeable sum.'

'Mm-hmm.'

Ryan frowned. His mother was being evasive.

'Can you tell me what those payments were for?' he persisted.

'This and that.' His mother shrugged. 'I can't quite remember.'

'You must remember, surely.'

Kathleen studied her knitting for a moment before she replied. 'It was to cover the cost of my art supplies. Yes, that was it. When Freya went into Exeter, she picked up some things I needed.'

'Art supplies?' He checked the bank statement again in case he'd got it wrong. 'This money is for far more than a few canvases and pots of paint. And you haven't done any painting in ages.'

'I've started again so I need to stock up, and these things cost far more than you think.'

'Can I see your new paintings?'

'Not yet,' she told him, focusing intently on the ball of pink wool nestling in her lap. 'They're not fit to be seen yet.'

She was lying. He was sure of it.

Freya bundled back into the kitchen, the empty laundry basket in her arms. She smiled at them.

'Is everything OK?'

'I'm not sure. I was checking something in Mum's bank account and noticed some extra payments to you.'

Freya's smile faltered and she glanced at Kathleen, who piped up, 'I told Ryan that you'd got me some art supplies when you went into Exeter.'

'Is that what happened?' asked Ryan, feeling awkward for asking but something felt very wrong here.

'Mmm. That's right.' Freya turned to place the empty peg bag on the windowsill. When she turned back, she didn't catch Ryan's eye. 'What would you like me to cook you for tea, Kathleen?'

'What are my options?'

'There's some fish left or I could rustle up some pasta. Would you and Chloe like to join us?'

Ryan looked at his phone, which had just beeped with a text from Chloe.

Where are you? I want chicken curry.

'I promised Chloe I'd cook for her tonight, but maybe some other time. Thanks.'

He got up and gathered his things together. The atmosphere in the room had shifted and his head was spinning.

On the way home through the narrow lanes, questions tumbled through his mind. Why was his mother being so secretive and paying out money to Freya? The two of them had shared a look when he'd questioned the finances. Was there something between them that he wasn't aware of? And the worst question of all: did Freya have some sort of hold over his mother?

You know nothing about her. Isobel's words sounded in his

head. *I'm worried about you and your mother. She's pushed her way into your family.*

He'd dismissed Isobel's suspicions at the time. Of course he had, because he trusted Freya. He'd started to feel... He wiped his hand across his face, which felt hot even though the wind against his skin was cold. He knew so little about her background. He'd been charmed by her down-to-earth attitude and apparent vulnerability. But what did he really know about her – the woman who'd waltzed into their lives just two and a half months ago?

He wandered round the grocery store, deep in thought. Then, he let himself into his cottage and put away the chicken and spices he'd bought.

'When's tea gonna be ready?' Chloe shouted down the stairs. 'I'm starving.'

'Not long,' he shouted back, but he sat down at the table rather than starting to cook. He'd told Freya the truth about his relationship with Natalie. He'd let his guard down and trusted her with things he'd never told anyone else. But had he got things horribly wrong?

35

FREYA

Freya was polishing the sideboard in the sitting room. The rich mahogany was sparkling clean and smelled of beeswax, but she was planning to polish it until it positively gleamed. Just like she'd cleaned the kitchen floor until it was so germ-free she could eat her dinner off it. And the shower had never been so shiny.

She had to keep busy because Ryan knew. He knew that something odd was going on. He was suspicious yesterday about the money Kathleen had paid into her account.

Of course he was. Art supplies, indeed! Kathleen's made-up reason had been laughably inadequate, though laughing was the last thing on Freya's mind. The thought that Ryan might suspect she was fleecing his mother made her go hot and cold.

Keeping occupied was the only thing stopping her from marching round to his house and telling him everything she knew about Maeve. That and Kathleen's pale face when Freya had said again this morning that Ryan should be told. Kathleen was still insistent that her son was better off not knowing that he had a sister out there somewhere.

They'd argued in the end because both of them were tired

after hardly sleeping. Freya kept picturing Ryan's puzzled face checking Kathleen's bank account whenever she closed her eyes, and Kathleen was done in by Maeve's rejection, even though she'd never admit it.

Her polishing arm was starting to ache but she kept on going, trying hard not to cry. There was no solution she could see that ended well.

If she said nothing, Ryan would suspect her of stealing from his mother. He would sack her and hate her. But if she told him the truth against Kathleen's wishes, she'd be betraying the elderly woman's trust and he would still hate her for keeping the truth from him all this time.

Either way, keeping secrets had messed things up big-time.

Freya stopped manically polishing when there was a rap on the door that echoed through the cottage.

'It's the post,' called Kathleen, coming down the stairs. 'I saw Alan coming up the road.'

Freya got to the door before Kathleen and, when she opened it, Alan was standing on the doorstep, his knobbly knees poking beneath the hemline of his shorts.

'Afternoon, ladies,' he said cheerily. 'I've got a recorded delivery letter here for you. Are you going to sign for it, Kathleen?'

Kathleen signed her name in spidery writing and thanked Alan, who went off, whistling tunelessly.

She turned to Freya, the large cream envelope in her hand. 'Who would send me a recorded delivery letter? The postmark is...' She peered at it closely. 'I can't make it out.' She suddenly thrust the letter at Freya, her green eyes huge in her pale face. 'Open it for me, please.'

Freya slid her finger under the envelope flap and took out the paper inside – one thick cream sheet, covered in large looping handwriting. Freya turned the letter over, her heart hammering.

'Oh.' Her hand went to her mouth.

'What is it?' urged Kathleen.

Freya looked at the elderly woman standing in a pool of sunlight that was spilling through the glass in the front door.

'It's a letter from your daughter.'

They both stared at the letter which had the power to change Kathleen's life for ever – a letter from the daughter she had mourned for years and thought lost for good.

'Here, Kathleen. You should read it.'

Freya handed the precious sheet of paper over and, holding it as though it might burst into flames at any moment, Kathleen walked into the sitting room.

Freya sat on the bottom stair, giving Kathleen some privacy, and her thoughts turned, as they often did, to Ryan, who was unaware of the potentially life-shattering letter his mother was about to read.

'Freya, please come in here,' called Kathleen, her voice querulous.

When Freya went into the sitting room, Kathleen was standing by the window. The sheet of paper was still in her hand.

'I can't read it,' she said, holding the paper towards Freya. 'I'm too scared about what it might say. Can you read it to me? Please.'

Freya took the letter and started to read aloud, Kathleen wincing as though every word hurt.

Dear Kathleen,

This is a hard letter to write. At first, when I was contacted to say you were looking for me, I felt overwhelmed and, being totally honest, not sure that I wanted to be in touch. I was told by my parents from an early age that I was adopted, and I often wondered about you. But as I got older, I assumed that you had another family and had moved on with your life, and that I should do the same. I thought you must have forgotten about me.

But now I've heard about the circumstances of my adoption, and have had time to take it in, I know that my story is very different from the one I'd imagined. I'm so sorry that you had to go through such heartbreak as a young woman and I want to reassure you that I had a very good adoption and was brought up by a loving family. I hope that will bring you some comfort. My mum sadly died five years ago but my dad is still alive and well, and I have an older sister who, like me, was adopted by our parents. I'm married to a wonderful man called Robert and we have two grown-up daughters, Tara and Holly.

I'm told that you'd like to meet me. I'm not sure whether that would be a good idea, but my daughters have suggested that you might like to write to me. If you would, my address is at the top of this letter. I see that you live in Heaven's Cove in Devon. I visited Heaven's Cove once, about seven years ago, when Robert and I were touring Devon. We sat on the village green and had a picnic. It's a beautiful village.

I wish you all the best, Kathleen, and assure you that I have no bad feelings towards you.

Yours,

Maeve

Freya carefully folded the paper. 'That's a lovely letter, Kathleen. What do you think?'

Kathleen shook her head. 'Maeve was in Heaven's Cove seven years ago. I must have been here in this cottage while she was sitting just there, in front of the church.' She looked out of the window. 'And I never knew.'

'But now you do know that she's alive and she's well and she sounds happy. She has a lovely family and you have two more grandchildren.'

'And she has no bad feelings towards me.' Kathleen's eyes shone with tears. 'I know that's what Derek told us but I didn't quite believe him. But this is proof, isn't it? My daughter doesn't hate me, Freya, for what I did.'

'She understands that you had no other choice.'

'But she doesn't want to meet.'

'Not yet. But she says you can write to her. That's a start, isn't it? A chance to find out more about each other and build bridges.'

'Where does she live? I didn't see.'

Freya looked again at the letter and smiled at the symmetry that linked these two women. 'Maeve lives in Ireland, Kathleen, not far from Dublin.'

Kathleen gasped. 'She went back home then, in the end.' She took the letter that Freya held out to her and pressed it to her heart. 'Oh dear,' she said suddenly, moving away from the window. 'Ryan and Chloe are coming up the street. They're back from their trip to Exeter already and they're coming here.'

Freya's heart began to flutter. 'That's a good thing. You can tell Ryan about Maeve, now that she's been in touch.'

'I don't want to tell him yet,' said Kathleen, shaking her head.

Freya groaned quietly. 'But you have to, surely.'

Even though telling Ryan the truth was unlikely to end well for her. While Kathleen's confession would explain the mystery payments she'd made into Freya's bank account, it would also reveal Freya's part in keeping Maeve's existence from him. But whatever the consequences, he deserved to know the truth at long last.

Freya tried again. 'I know it's hard but Ryan is Maeve's brother and he should know what's going on. He should know that she exists.'

But Kathleen's mouth had set in that familiar stubborn line. 'No, I'll wait to see if Maeve will agree to meet me before I say anything. And I can't see Ryan like this. Can you tell him that I'm lying down or something?'

'I don't think—'

'Please,' said Kathleen as they heard the front door open and Chloe's voice floated into the room.

'Gran? Where are you?'

'You can't keep this from him for ever,' urged Freya in a desperate whisper. 'I know you're scared about telling him. I know it's been a secret for so long, it's hard to say the words, but it needs to be said.'

'He doesn't need to know yet,' retorted Kathleen. 'Perhaps if Maeve does agree to meet me, he can be told then.'

A stubborn old bird. Wasn't that how Belinda had described Kathleen before their first meeting? She'd been right on the money, Freya decided, stepping into the hall and closing the sitting room door behind her. Ryan and a sulky-looking Chloe were standing at the foot of the stairs.

'Is everything all right?' she asked. 'How was Exeter? Did you enjoy it?' Her voice sounded over-bright and Ryan gave her a questioning glance.

'We spent a couple of hours there but Chloe got bored.'

'That's because it was pretty boring, Dad.'

'Boring seems to be your favourite word these days.' He turned back to Freya. 'Where's Mum? I thought I might take her out for a drive, seeing as I took the day off for Chloe's inset day. Chloe can go and see Kristen, which is what she really wants to do.'

This was so awkward. Freya hated lying.

'I think your mum's lying down at the moment. Shall I bring her along to yours once she's up and about? She shouldn't be long.'

'Is she feeling unwell?'

'No. Nothing like that. She's fine. Totally fine.' *Stop speaking!* urged the voice in her head. 'Just tired,' she finished, wishing the ground would open up and swallow her.

'O-K,' said Ryan slowly. 'We can go home and unpack the picnic we never had. Apparently Chloe doesn't eat meat any more.'

'Meat is murder,' said Chloe, skipping up the stairs towards the bathroom. 'I won't be a minute.'

The bathroom door slammed shut behind her and silence fell over the cottage. Ryan looked at his feet, dark shadows beneath his eyes that were dim in the gloomy hallway. He was tired. Neither of them spoke and the silence lengthened.

'Look,' he said, glancing upstairs at the closed bathroom door. 'Before Chloe comes back, I need to know what's going on between you and my mother. Only there was the money thing yesterday and I thought I saw Mum looking out of the window when we came up the road and... I don't know what to make of you, Freya. I thought we had something. It's felt so right over the last couple of weeks, but now I'm not sure I know you at all.'

He folded his arms across his chest as Chloe, who'd just appeared at the top of the stairs, opened her eyes wide.

Being the keeper of secrets was definitely a curse, thought Freya. People telling her their innermost confidences had made her feel warm and useful over the years. But sometimes they pushed their secrets onto her whether those secrets were welcome or not and then expected her to accept the consequences. It was time to stop.

'Come with me,' she told Ryan, walking towards the closed door to the sitting room. 'Your mother has something to tell you.'

36

RYAN

The first thing Ryan noticed was that his mother wasn't in bed at all. She was standing at the window, looking out into the distance. A rush of disappointment flooded through him as he realised that he *had* seen his mother at the window and Freya had been lying.

The second thing he noticed was the look of surprise on his mother's face when she turned round and saw him. Even though she must have heard him and Chloe in the hall.

There was a peculiar charged atmosphere in the room and no one said a word. It was as if the room was frozen in time. Ryan had stumbled across something of great magnitude, he could feel it, but he had no idea what was going on. He hoped his mother hadn't had another of her impetuous ideas.

The spell was broken by Chloe barging into the room behind him.

'Hello, Gran. What's going on? Freya said you were in bed, asleep. Are you all right? You look like you've been crying. And there's no loo roll in the bathroom.'

Ryan peered closer. His mum's eyes were red-rimmed.

'What's going on, Mum?' he demanded. 'And what's that?'

He nodded at what looked like a letter his mum was clutching to her chest.

Suddenly, Freya brushed past him and walked into the centre of the room.

'You haven't told him,' she said, 'but you need to.'

An echo of Freya arriving to look after his mum sounded in Ryan's head. His mother hadn't told him about that until she had to. Was there someone else she was planning on moving in? And what was Freya's involvement in whatever this was? Why was his mother putting money into her account?

Freya took hold of his mum's arm. 'Kathleen, sit down by the fire, and Ryan, sit on the sofa. You two need to talk.' She raised her hand to silence his mum, who had started arguing. 'There have been too many secrets in this house for far too long and, quite honestly, I'm not prepared to be in the middle of it all any longer. So start talking and we'll all face the consequences.'

His mum sat as she was told. 'Sit down, Ryan, love,' she said flatly.

Ryan could feel his heart beginning to hammer in his chest. Why did he need to sit down? The last person to advise him to sit down had been the police officer who'd arrived on his doorstep to break the news of Natalie's accident. He said the same to his mother as he'd said to the ashen-faced police officer all those years ago.

'I don't need to sit down. Just tell me, whatever it is.' His mother sighed and glanced at her granddaughter. 'Does Chloe need to leave?' he asked, wondering what on earth his mother was about to say.

'No, this affects Chloe as well so she should stay. Perhaps I should have told you a long time ago, but I never felt I could. I didn't want you to hate me too.'

'Hate you? Why would I possibly hate you?' Now Ryan was scared. 'Tell me.'

His mum closed her eyes for a moment. 'I lied to you, Ryan.

I'm sorry, but I lied to you. I came to Heaven's Cove when I was a young woman.'

He didn't know that, but what did it matter if she'd visited the village many years ago?

Ryan shrugged. 'OK.'

'I came here to stay at Driftwood House for a few months when I was a young woman.'

'I see,' said Ryan, though he didn't see at all. So she'd had a holiday in the village when she was younger? So what?

'Driftwood House wasn't a guesthouse back then.'

'Did you know the people who owned it? Is that why you stayed there?'

'No.' His mother took a deep breath. 'All those years ago, Driftwood House was a mother and baby home.'

'A mother and baby home? Why were you staying in...' Ryan stopped, his mind racing ahead. 'What exactly are you saying?'

'I'm saying that I was there, to give birth.'

Ryan shook his head, hardly believing what he was hearing.

'How old were you?' he managed to say. He was aware of Chloe, in the corner of the room with her mouth open. And Freya, who'd gone to stand beside her.

'I was nineteen years old, not that much older than Chloe, and absolutely terrified. I grew up in a small village in rural Ireland, as you know, and the stigma of being an unmarried mother was huge back then, but not as huge as the shame I felt, and still feel.' She stumbled over her next words. 'My parents sent me away to have my baby.'

'Why did they send you to Heaven's Cove?'

'They had links to the religious organisation that ran the mother and baby home here. And, best of all, Devon was a long way away from their neighbours with the twitching curtains.'

'How long were you there?' The question came from Chloe.

Kathleen smiled sadly at her granddaughter. 'A good few

weeks and then, on April the sixth, at three in the morning, I gave birth to a little girl. She looked a lot like you when you were born. I called her Maeve, after my grandmother.'

'What happened to Maeve?' asked Chloe, in a small voice.

'She was a beautiful child and I loved her but, after two weeks, I had to let her go.'

'Did you give her away?' asked Chloe, as Ryan tried to process what he was hearing.

'Yes, I did, though I didn't want to. I had no way of caring for her.'

'You could have got help,' said Chloe. 'Olivia at school, her big sister doesn't have a husband but she had a baby and they all live together now.'

Kathleen smiled at her granddaughter. 'Times were different then, Chloe. My family didn't want me to bring Maeve home and there was no proper help for women like me.'

'That's sad,' said Chloe.

'How come you've never told me before now?' blurted out Ryan.

He had a big sister out there. A half-sister he'd never known about. He glanced at Chloe, who was biting her nails, a thoughtful look on her face. Should she be hearing all of this? To be honest, she seemed to be handling it better than he was.

'I didn't know how to tell you,' said Kathleen. 'It was a big dark secret at the time and it carried on being a secret for so long, it seemed impossible to say anything.'

'Did Dad know?'

'Yes. I told him when we were engaged but we never spoke about it again after our marriage. I never spoke about what had happened to anyone really until I spilled it all out to Freya. Though she'd already found the photo so she knew something wasn't right.'

Ryan had forgotten Freya was there. She was standing so close to the wall, it was as if she wanted to meld into it. Her gaze flicked from Kathleen to him and back again. She couldn't look him in the eye.

'What photo was that?' he asked coldly.

'Freya found a photo of me at Driftwood House that was taken just after I'd given birth to Maeve. Just after I'd given her up. Freya wanted me to tell you about Maeve, Ryan, but I swore her to secrecy.'

'When did you find the photo?'

Even though Ryan had asked Freya directly, she still didn't look at him when she answered.

'The day of your mum's fall in the garden, when she hurt her knees. But I didn't know what it meant at the time. Your mum only told me about Maeve on the night of the storm.'

The storm? That had happened a month ago – after she'd promised never to keep anything about his family from him ever again.

'But now she's been found,' said his mum, waving the letter at him. 'Freya helped me to find Maeve and now she's written to me. Look.'

When Ryan didn't move, Chloe took the letter from her grandmother and passed it to him. He read the words slowly, taking in the curve of the woman's handwriting. It was an emotional letter – thoughtfully worded and caring. But he could hardly believe that the woman who'd written it – a total stranger – was his sister.

'How did you find her?' he asked, handing the letter back to Chloe. She might as well read it too.

'We used a detective-type tracing agency because I couldn't track down any records about Maeve's adoption,' said Freya. 'That's what the payments you questioned were for. Your mum paid me and I paid the agency.'

A tiny glimmer of relief in Ryan's chest that Freya had come by his mum's money legitimately was quenched immediately by the knowledge that she'd kept yet another secret from him. This one even bigger than his daughter's leap from Clair Point.

Freya had arrived in Heaven's Cove less than three months ago but she'd turned his life upside down in so many ways.

'Do you hate me, Ryan?' asked his mum.

Her words felt like a punch. How could she ask such a question?

'Of course I don't hate you, Mum,' he assured her, kneeling at her feet. 'Why would I? I can't imagine how awful it's been for you all these years.' He brushed away the tear that was snaking its way down Kathleen's papery skin.

'I thought you'd hate me for not telling you a long time ago that you had a sister.'

Ryan breathed out heavily. 'I wish you'd felt that you could tell me, Mum. I wish you'd told me before—' He paused. *Before you told Freya.* That's what he wanted to say. *Before you told the woman I was falling in love with.* But instead he took hold of his mum's hand and said simply: 'I'm just glad that you've told me now.'

'It'll be all right, Gran.' Chloe rushed over and grabbed Kathleen's other hand. 'I don't hate you either,' she blurted out. 'I don't hate anyone. Well, there's a boy at school who throws pencils at the backs of people's heads. He's pretty horrible, actually, but I don't even hate him.'

'That's good to know,' laughed Kathleen through her tears. 'You mustn't tell anyone about all of this, Chloe. Is that all right?'

Chloe nodded. 'Of course.'

Ryan put his free arm around his daughter's shoulders. She was being so grown up about the whole surreal situation. He had a sister, an older sister he'd never met. He was reeling from that information, and then there was the sucker punch on top – Freya had known all about her.

This time Freya met his gaze when he looked at her. She

was still standing by the wall, with her hands clasped together and her eyes huge in her pale face. He had an urge to put his arms around her and rest his head on her shoulder, to seek comfort from the woman he'd trusted. But everything was different now.

'Do you think you could leave us alone?' he said, his voice sounding flat and cold. 'We have a lot of family business to discuss.'

'Of course.' She swallowed and blinked quickly, as though she might cry. 'I'll go upstairs.'

When she went into the hall, Ryan followed her and closed the sitting room door behind him.

'It might be better if you go out for a while, actually.'

'If you'd rather.' She turned to face him, anguish etched across her features. 'Ryan,' she said quietly, 'can we talk? Please.'

'I don't think there's anything more to be said.'

'Please. Let me explain.'

The longing in her eyes would have broken his heart, if it wasn't broken already.

He beckoned for her to follow him into the kitchen. 'Explain what?' he asked coldly. 'Why you lied to me?'

'I didn't lie.'

'It's just weasel words, Freya.' He lowered his voice, remembering that sound carried in this small cottage. 'You didn't lie to my face, but you lied by omission. You kept a huge family secret from me after you promised to tell me everything. And I told *you* everything.'

When his voice faltered, Freya took a step towards him.

'Your mum begged me not to tell you.'

Freya was crying now but he had to harden his heart. He couldn't let her slip under his defences again.

'I don't care. You and I, we...' But there was no more 'we', not after this. He shook his head. 'I can't do this. I have to go and talk to my mother.' He turned on his heel and hurried back into the sitting room.

A few moments later he heard the front door open and close as Freya walked out of the cottage and, he realised, out of his life.

37

RYAN

'You poor man.' Isobel stepped into the hall as soon as he opened the front door and threw herself into his arms. 'I can't believe you're having to deal with this on top of everything else,' she muttered into the side of his neck.

Ryan stepped back and gently pulled Isobel's arms away. Chloe was standing by the kitchen door, watching them with her mouth open. 'Are you all right?'

'Me? I'm fine but are *you* all right?' Isobel shook her head. 'What a shock.'

A cold shiver went through Ryan. What did she know? Taking hold of Isobel's arm, he led her into the sitting room and closed the door. Outside, a gentle breeze was lifting the leaves of the tree in his garden, but in here, the air was quiet and still.

'What do you mean about a shock?'

'I mean it must have been a terrible shock when you found out.'

'When I found out what?' asked Ryan slowly, although he knew what Isobel was going to say.

'When you found out that you had a long-lost sister, of course. It must be devastating to discover that everything you thought was true in your family was a lie, and I can't believe that your mother kept it from you. Surely, you deserved to know.'

Ryan sat down heavily on the sofa. 'How did you find out?'

Isobel shrugged. 'It was the only topic of conversation among customers in Stan's store when I nipped in to buy a few groceries this morning.'

'So everyone knows?'

'Not everyone, but a fair few people in Heaven's Cove. You know what this place is like for gossip.'

Oh, he knew exactly what Heaven's Cove was like. He was known as 'the sad widower' for ages after he and Chloe moved in, and Belinda had kept patting his shoulder and asking him about Natalie, wanting every juicy detail.

Belinda! The thought that Belinda must be the source of the gossip was like a punch to the gut. Because if Belinda knew, she could only have found out from one person – Freya.

There were things about Freya he didn't know, but he'd believed her utterly when she'd told him she could keep secrets. She'd kept his mother's secret, even from him. He could almost forgive her for that because she was being loyal to his mother. But this final betrayal was too much. Once he'd found out about Maeve, she must have let something slip to her sister.

Isobel was looking at him strangely. 'It's not so bad, you know, having a baby out of wedlock. Everyone does it these days. Sex outside marriage is totally fine.' She stroked his arm. 'It's just the deceit, isn't it? The not being told about it when Freya obviously knew everything all along. That's what people are saying,' she added, when he raised his head and stared at her. 'Freya knew and didn't tell you. But now she's gossiping with her sister and it's spreading all over the village.'

'I don't think she would do that,' he said, desperate for it not to be true.

'Ryan.' Isobel sat beside him and took his hand in hers.

'You're a very trusting man. Too trusting for your own good. Freya arrives out of the blue and moves in with your mother. And then she worms your mother's secrets out of her and upends your life. Who else knew about your mum's secret love child? It really is time she went and then life can get back to normal. You and I can get back to normal. I know that's what you want.'

Ryan stood up, shaking off Isobel's hand. Isobel taking the opportunity to flirt while passing on gossip about his family left a bad taste in his mouth. But nothing could top Freya's betrayal.

'I need to go and see her,' he said, hoping Isobel wouldn't notice the wobble in his voice.

'No, you don't. Send her an email telling her she's sacked and you never want to see her again. Surely she's packing her bags already anyway.'

'This needs to be done face to face.'

Ryan went to the door and wrenched it open. Chloe was standing in the hall.

'Did you hear all of that?' he asked wearily.

'No, of course not,' huffed Chloe. 'I wasn't listening in. I'm on my way to my bedroom, actually.'

Isobel walked past her, without saying hello, and paused at the front door.

'I'm here for you, Ryan, when you've sorted things out,' she announced. 'I'm always here for you.'

She swept out, leaving a scent of exotic spices in the air.

'Why did Isobel come round?' asked Chloe as the bang of the front door echoed through the house.

Should he tell her? She'd heard enough unsettling things yesterday from her grandmother. But it was surely better hearing it from him, than hearing the rumours flying around the village.

He took a deep breath. 'It seems that people in the village are gossiping, about your gran and about Maeve.'

Chloe's hand flew to her mouth. 'How do they know?'

'That's what I want to find out. I'm going to see Freya.' He'd reached the front door when he paused and turned back. 'You didn't tell anyone, did you, Chloe?'

'No, of course not. You made me promise not to.'

'It's just...'

'I didn't tell anyone, all right?' Chloe was almost shouting.

'It's just that I trusted you and...'

'I didn't say anything, OK? I swear on Mum's life.'

When her bottom lip began to wobble, Ryan felt guilty for distrusting her, even for a moment. He knew his daughter far better than Freya who had, as Isobel so rightly pointed out, arrived out of the blue and upended his life.

He pulled his daughter to him and gave her a tight squeeze. 'I'm sorry, love. Will you be all right on your own for half an hour while I go to Gran's?'

'Yeah, I'll be fine.' Chloe let herself be hugged for a moment before stepping away. 'But I don't think you should go. Seeing Freya won't do you any good. I don't want you to go, Dad.'

Ryan hesitated at the front door. Maybe Chloe and Isobel were right. Thankfully, he hadn't seen Freya when he'd called round to check on his mother this morning, and he didn't need to see her now.

He could send her an email, terminating her job, and she would leave without him ever setting eyes on her again. His mother wouldn't be happy about it, but he and Chloe would move in with her instead. And soon it would be as if Freya had never set foot in Heaven's Cove at all.

'Come on, Dad. Just stay here,' urged Chloe.

Ryan shook his head. 'I need to speak to Freya, face to face. This won't take long.'

38

FREYA

Freya was at her bedroom window when she saw Ryan approaching the cottage. She was glad he was coming round to speak to his mum again. Kathleen was relieved that her secret was out and had forgiven Freya for forcing her hand. But she was still upset that Maeve didn't want to see her.

Ryan must be all over the place too. Finding out about his long-lost sister must have come as such a shock. And then there was her betrayal on top. That's why she was keeping out of his way. He'd made it very clear yesterday that their relationship was over.

Freya blinked away her tears and glanced at her half-filled suitcase on the bed. She'd be so sad to leave this place but she'd made a total hash of everything.

Kathleen didn't want her to go. She said she felt lighter now that Ryan knew about Maeve.

But Freya knew she couldn't stay. Ryan would adjust to the idea of having a sister and he'd forgive his mother for not telling him. That was the kind of good man he was. But how could he forgive her for breaking her promise and keeping such momentous news from him? Secrets and promises. They'd been her downfall.

Ryan had reached the house and she heard a murmur of voices in the hall below her. It was good that they were talking. Perhaps Ryan could help Kathleen to build bridges with his sister. Perhaps one day there would be a happy family reunion. Not that she would ever know.

Freya went back to folding dresses that she'd never worn into the case and tried to imagine her return home, back to the empty apartment that was still on the market. Greg would think she'd failed at starting a new life without him, as indeed she had.

She froze, bent over the suitcase, when she heard footsteps coming up the stairs. Kathleen's slow, light tread was familiar, but there was a heavier tread alongside it. Ryan was coming upstairs with his mother. Was he coming to see her? What was the point? It would only be painful for both of them.

Freya closed the suitcase and sat on the bed, trying to steady herself as the footsteps got closer. There was a soft knock on her door.

'Come in,' she said quietly.

As Kathleen and Ryan walked inside, Ryan's eyes flicked to the case and then back to her.

'There you are,' said Kathleen, her face creased with anguish.

Freya got to her feet, worried that such an emotional time was proving too much for a woman in her eighties. 'Are you all right, Kathleen? Do you need to sit down? You look like you've seen a ghost.'

'Everyone knows,' she said shakily.

'Everyone knows? What do you mean?'

'Maeve, my daughter, is the talk of Heaven's Cove,' said Kathleen, sitting down slowly on the bed. 'Isobel has just told Ryan all about it. Everyone knows about me and my stay at

Driftwood House. It's the sole topic of conversation in Stan's store. My business is all over the village.'

Freya's hand went to her mouth. 'Oh, no. I'm so sorry.'

'Why are you sorry?' asked Ryan.

She frowned, feeling confused. 'That's what people say when someone has had bad news. How did—' She stopped, suddenly realising what their expressions were telling her. 'Do you think that I told Belinda? I would never tell her. Never, though...'

She thought back to Belinda barging into her bedroom and seeing the mother and baby home print-out on the bed, and Kathleen's photo.

'Though, what?' asked Ryan, sounding more cold and distant than ever.

While she was packing, Freya had thought it wasn't possible to feel any worse about all that had happened. But now her stomach clenched with added anxiety and guilt.

'Belinda came into my bedroom a few days ago and saw some information about adoption. She guessed some of what was going on. But I swore her to secrecy.'

'You swore *Belinda* to secrecy?'

When Ryan raised his eyebrows, his face a picture of sarcastic disbelief, Freya felt like crying. Kathleen had gone very quiet.

'She promised me,' said Freya softly, as much to herself as to Ryan and Kathleen. 'She promised me, one sister to another.'

Kathleen started sobbing, her shoulders shaking up and down.

'Mum, it's all right.' Ryan sat down beside her. 'It'll all blow over in a few days. You know what it's like around here.'

'I'm sorry,' said Freya again, pushing her feet into her shoes. Then she left the room without looking back. There was someone she had to see.

39

FREYA

'Freya, how lovely to see you.' Belinda's smile faded and she frowned when Freya stepped past her into the hall, without a word. 'Come in, why don't you? If you're looking for Jim to fix something for Kathleen, you're out of luck. He's about to go shopping for some hacksaw or other he needs to repair the attic. Honestly, these old cottages look quaint and charming but they're an absolute money pit when it comes to maintenance.' She paused when Freya stood looking at her. 'Is something the matter?'

Oh, something was definitely the matter. But now she was here, Freya didn't know where to start. She'd rehearsed a speech all the way from Kathleen's cottage. But nothing quite summed up the gravity of what her sister had done.

'You're being very peculiar,' tutted Belinda. 'Are you all right?'

'Not really,' Freya managed.

'Oh, dear. Is Kathleen all right?'

'She's upset.'

'Really?' Freya despised the eagerness in Belinda's voice

when she urged: 'You'd better come and sit down and tell me all about it.'

'Why on earth would I tell you anything?'

Belinda's frown grew more pronounced. 'You're not making any sense, Freya. Are you unwell?'

'No, I'm not unwell. I'm simply tired of you interfering in other people's lives, in *my* life. You shouldn't do it, Belinda. People get hurt.'

That wasn't as eloquent as the speech she'd rehearsed and she'd just blurted it out. But it summed up the anger Freya was feeling.

'I don't hurt people,' bristled Belinda, taking a step back. 'What exactly are you saying?'

Freya tried to calm down because losing her temper wouldn't help.

'I'm *asking* if you told people that Kathleen was searching for her adopted child. I know you put two and two together and knew what was going on.'

'I did put two and two together because it was pretty obvious. Kathleen seemed agitated and you went all cloak and dagger when I saw the article you were reading and then there was the photo. But I promised you that I wouldn't tell a soul.'

Freya shook her head. 'You did promise. That's true. But I know you, Belinda, and I've been told that you can't keep anything to yourself.'

'Then you've been misinformed because I kept Kathleen's secret as I said I would,' said Belinda icily.

'If that's true, how on earth did half the customers in Stan's store this morning know all about it?'

'Someone must have told them.'

'Exactly.'

'And that someone wasn't me. It must have been someone else.'

'But no one else knew. No one who would have risked Kathleen's happiness by spreading it around the village.'

'So are you saying that I'm lying?'

Freya shrugged. 'I'm saying that you just can't help yourself, Belinda, because you're a dreadful gossip. You have to be the centre of attention with the juiciest information to share, the head of the committee, the person with her fingers in every pie. You're self-centred and judgemental and you have a bad word for everyone.'

Freya stopped, breathing heavily. She hadn't meant to say all of that but she couldn't bear Belinda's constant gossiping and low-level antagonism any longer. This time her sister had gone too far. This time, she'd hurt people that Freya cared about and had helped to turn Ryan even more against her. Freya bit down hard on her bottom lip to stop herself from crying.

'And you're Little Miss Perfect, are you?' Belinda pulled herself up tall, her nostrils flaring. 'Let's drop the pretence and stop playing happy sisters, shall we?'

'If you like,' countered Freya, with more confidence than she felt.

'The truth of it is, you ruined my life. When Dad walked out on me and Mum it was the worst day ever. We thought he'd miss us and come back, but then you came along and that was never going to happen. At least your mother disappeared out of our lives when she ditched Dad and went abroad. But you didn't. I couldn't believe it when you stayed with him.'

Freya blinked. Belinda was going way off-topic but that wasn't surprising. Their relationship had always been a powder keg, just waiting to be ignited.

'Wow, I got the feeling you didn't like me much but I didn't realise quite how much you resented me.'

'You stole my father,' said Belinda bitterly. 'What do you expect?'

'I didn't "steal" anyone, and it was a long time ago,' countered Freya. But Belinda's face had crumpled into a scowl.

'It doesn't matter how long ago it was. You feel guilty about it. I can see it in your eyes sometimes when we're talking.'

'That's because you make me feel guilty by telling me your mum has never recovered. You seem to forget that I was only a child in all of this.'

'So was I.' Belinda was almost shouting now and Jim suddenly appeared at the top of the stairs, carrying a hammer.

'Is everything all right?' he asked, looking between them with a puzzled expression. 'What's going on?'

Belinda continued as though he wasn't there. 'I was a young teenager when Dad walked out, not much older than Chloe, and left with a mother so depressed she could hardly get out of bed in the morning.'

'I didn't realise it was that bad.'

'No one did. No one cared. Mum's never been the same since and I'm the one who's left still picking up the pieces.'

'I'm sorry. I truly am. But it doesn't take away from the fact that your gossiping ruins people's lives,' said Freya, torn between sympathy for her sister and anger about what she'd done to Kathleen.

'Belinda, what have you been saying to people now?' asked Jim. He sighed loudly as he walked down the stairs, trailing dust from the attic.

'Absolutely nothing. I did as Freya asked and kept Kathleen's secret quiet. Though I might as well have shouted it from the rooftops if I'm going to be blamed for telling people anyway. You both believe me, don't you?'

Jim glanced at Freya. When both of them said nothing, Belinda shook her head. 'I see. My own husband and sister think I'm a dreadful gossip and a liar to boot. At least I know where I stand.'

With that, she turned and marched into the sitting room, slamming the door behind her.

'What has she done this time?' asked Jim quietly, placing the hammer on the hall table.

Freya shrugged. It was all around the village anyway. 'She told people that Kathleen was looking for the baby daughter she had when she was a young woman. The daughter she gave up for adoption.'

'Oh, Lordy.' Jim briefly closed his eyes. 'How did she know about it?'

'I was helping Kathleen to find her daughter, and Belinda saw some information about it when she was in my bedroom. I asked her to keep it to herself but...'

'But keeping quiet is hard for my wife.' Jim puffed out his cheeks. 'Are you quite sure it was Belinda who spread the gossip?'

'It couldn't have been anyone else, Jim. I'm sorry.'

Jim nodded. 'Is Kathleen very upset?'

'Kathleen and Ryan are upset, and so am I. I feel responsible for Kathleen's news being the talk of the village.'

'You're not responsible, Freya.' Jim bowed his head for a moment. 'Living with Belinda isn't easy, you know. She gets some things terribly wrong and causes friction. It's been the same all the years we've been married. But I do love her, and she loves you too, in her own way.'

He blushed, as though talking about feelings was too much for him.

'I don't think Belinda loves me at all and she doesn't like me much either. She's made that pretty clear.'

'I think you're wrong about that.' Jim glanced at the closed sitting room door. 'I'd better go and have a word with her and sort out this latest mess.' He opened the front door to show Freya out but stopped, with his hand on the door latch. 'Did Kathleen find her lost daughter?'

'Yes, Maeve has been found.'

'And she's safe and well?'

'Apparently.'

'I'm glad to hear it, and I hope Kathleen and you will be able to forgive my wife.'

He waited, presumably for Freya to agree that she would forgive his wife's toxic gossiping. But she couldn't, not even to make lovely, blameless Jim feel better. This time Belinda had gone too far and had done more damage than she would ever know.

'Bye, Jim,' said Freya, blinking back tears when she realised this was probably the last time she would ever see him.

She was leaving Heaven's Cove and would never return. She'd never see Belinda again – her sister would make sure of that. Or Chloe and Kathleen. Or Ryan, who was so disappointed in her.

Freya almost ran through Belinda's tidy garden and across the cobbled road. She needed to get back to Kathleen's cottage so she could finish packing. So she could leave behind everything, and everyone, that she'd grown to love in this beautiful village.

40

CHLOE

Freya, rushing down the road from Belinda's cottage, didn't notice Chloe. But Chloe, sitting on the sea wall, saw her – the woman who had upended her family's life.

It was hard to believe that one small woman could cause so much havoc. But since Freya had arrived, her gran had gone totally off the rails and turned from a sad old lady in hand-knits into some kind of secret-wielding stranger. And her dad, so close to getting it on with Isobel and thereby making Chloe and Paige almost sisters, had gone all moony instead over the hired help. That's what she'd heard Isobel calling her, anyway.

It was weird. Chloe should want Freya to leave and never come back. But she didn't, she realised, watching Freya furiously wipe tears from her cheeks. She didn't want her to leave Heaven's Cove at all.

But she is going and it's all your fault. Chloe ignored the little voice in her head, just like she was refusing to think about swearing on her mother's life that she'd told no one about Maeve. It was OK to swear on someone's life when they were gone anyway, wasn't it? And there was no point in feeling bad about the current situation. It was too late to change anything.

Chloe gazed at Driftwood House, high up on the cliffs, and thought about how her family's lives had changed since Freya had appeared.

Freya had been kind over the whole make-up debacle. Her dad had seemed almost happy for the first time ever, with Freya around. And her gran had a new spring in her step since Maeve had been found.

It was also pretty cool finding out that your boring old gran had a whole secret life that no one knew about. Imagining her gran as an abandoned pregnant woman had blown her mind, mostly because it meant she'd had sex with a man who wasn't Grandad. But it was exciting, nonetheless.

But fancy not knowing where your daughter was for well over sixty years. Chloe drummed her heels against the stone. That put her make-up meltdown, and the subsequent hour when her dad didn't know where she was, well into perspective. Not that he would see it like that. He still went pale if she so much as looked at a lipstick.

Chloe pictured the bright pink lip gloss still stashed in her dressing table drawer. The lip gloss that Paige had encouraged her to steal.

You're not like Paige, and that's fine. You don't need her approval to be who you are.

That's what Freya had told her when she'd found her on the beach, before the school dance. Chloe remembered Freya's kindness that night, as a wave swelled against the wall and water splashed onto her bare feet.

Freya wasn't as glamorous as Isobel, but she was more gentle and kind... and better for all of them. Chloe suddenly knew with startling clarity that's what her mum would have thought, too. She had a sudden memory of sitting on her mum's knee, having her hair brushed, and it was so vivid it took her breath away.

But now her mum was gone, and Freya would soon be gone

too. Life would get back to the way it was. The way that Chloe had wanted it to be. Isobel and her dad would properly get it on, and maybe get married and she and Paige would become sisters. Just like Chloe had wanted. Once upon a time.

She suddenly knew what had to be done, whether it was too late or not. Getting up from the sea wall, she rubbed her wet feet on the pavement and slipped on her sandals. Then she half-walked, half-ran to the beach before she could change her mind.

The sand was almost deserted, thanks to today's unpredictable weather which had put off most visitors. But a small huddle of girls and boys were sitting by the rockpools, as Chloe knew they would be. Paige, normally never one for the beach, had accepted an invitation to a lunchtime picnic on the sand from Chantelle at school.

Chantelle was in the year above them and Paige spent a lot of time unsuccessfully trying to impress her. Their relationship was very much like her own with Paige, Chloe realised with another flash of clarity. Doomed from the start.

'Hey, Chloe! You made it after all,' called Paige as Chloe got closer. Chloe's resolve began to falter when everyone stared at her, but she made herself carry on walking towards them.

'Can I have a word?' she asked Paige, as she reached them. That's what grown-ups said when they needed to broach something difficult. That's what her dad said when he wanted to tell her something that he thought she wouldn't like.

'Sure. Do you have something interesting to tell me?'

Paige smirked at her friends before following Chloe across the beach, towards an opening in the rocks that formed a shallow cave. The cave filled with water at high tide but the tide was low this afternoon.

'What is it then?' asked Paige, giving her friends a jaunty wave.

Chloe ducked into the cave and Paige followed. In here, it

was gloomy and there was a chill in the air. But it was out of earshot of the others and they couldn't be seen.

Chloe took a deep breath, knowing with a sinking feeling that it was too late to back out now.

'I want to know if you told everyone,' she said in as courageous a voice as she could manage.

'Told everyone what?' asked Paige, using the same sulky tone of voice she often used with her mum.

'Did you tell everyone about Maeve, my gran's long-lost daughter? Did you say anything about her to anyone else?'

Paige shrugged, her face thrown into shadow by the few rays of light that reached this far into the cave. 'I might have mentioned it to Chantelle last night and my mum. Why?'

Chloe's heart sank. Irrationally, she'd hoped she was wrong and Paige hadn't let her down.

'Why?' repeated Paige, kicking at the wet sand under her feet. 'Hurry up. I want to go back to the picnic.'

'I told you about Maeve in confidence. I told you it was a secret, but now I've heard it's all round the village.'

'Oops.' Paige's laugh bounced off the damp rock that surrounded them. 'What can I say? Chantelle has loose lips, I'm afraid.'

'So do you.'

Chloe blinked. Had she really said that? To Paige, of all people? Paige seemed taken aback too. She laughed again, uneasily this time.

'I don't think you want to be saying that kind of thing to me.'

Chloe wasn't sure she wanted to either, but it had to be said. She knew that now.

'You promised me that you wouldn't tell a soul.'

'Chill out. I only mentioned it to Chantelle.'

'Who mentioned it to someone else and now everyone knows. You know what people are like round here.'

Paige's eyes glittered in the filtered light. 'Are you ashamed of your gran, or something?'

'No, I'm absolutely not ashamed of my gran. But I'm ashamed of myself that I trusted you. Well, that won't happen again.'

Chloe stopped speaking. She had the most peculiar sensation that she was standing outside herself, watching as she burned everything to the ground.

Paige took a step closer. 'Don't you want to be my friend any more?' There was a sneering tone to her voice.

'I'm not sure that I do.'

'But who'll be your friend if I'm not? No one likes you, you know.'

Chloe blinked at that but kept going. 'Kristen likes me.'

'Aw. Poor little Kristen who cried when she lost her pen? Boo hoo.'

Paige balled her fists and rubbed them beneath her eyes, her face twisted and ugly.

Chloe took a deep breath. 'Kristen's new to the school and finding things difficult, but she's very kind and I like her.'

'I'm kind.'

'No you're not. You're not kind to Kristen or to me or to anyone.'

'Yes, I am.'

'No, you're really not.'

Chloe pushed past Paige and emerged from the cave, blinking in the light.

Paige called after her, 'Hey, wait up.'

But Chloe kept on walking across the sand, her breath coming in short gasps. Behind her, she could hear Paige shouting, 'Hey! Come back here now, Chloe! I said come back! We can still be friends.'

Chantelle and her gang by the rockpools stopped what they

were doing and stared. But Chloe kept on walking as Paige called out again across the sand.

There would be hell to pay for this, no doubt, but it felt good to be who she really was for a change. Though, she realised with a sickening churning in her stomach, if she'd thought calling out Paige was hard, the next bit would be even harder.

41

FREYA

'I don't want you to go,' said Kathleen, pushing out her bottom lip. 'I don't care what Ryan says and I don't care if people in the village know about Maeve now. Not really. She's been a secret for long enough. And you didn't tell them anyway.'

Freya sighed. This was hard enough as it was without Kathleen begging her to stay. She'd grown so fond of Kathleen over the last few weeks, but the elderly woman would be better off without her.

She stopped filling her suitcase and turned to Kathleen. 'I didn't tell anyone about Maeve but Belinda did. And she only knew about her and what was going on because of me. If I hadn't been here, she wouldn't have come into the house and seen the information that tipped her off.'

'And if you hadn't been here, I would never have found Maeve in the first place,' retorted Kathleen, folding her arms. 'I want you to stay, Freya.'

'I know, and thank you. I'd like to stay too, but it's too difficult. I can't be in the same village as Belinda. It wouldn't be fair on either of us. And I also can't be...' She paused, her throat tight.

'You can't be in the same village as my son?' Kathleen shook her head. 'You're good for him, Freya. Oh, I'm not daft,' she continued when she saw Freya's surprised expression. 'Anyone with half a brain can see that you two have been... carrying on, we used to call it.'

Freya tried to laugh but it sounded more like a sob. 'There's no getting past you, Kathleen. But after all the trouble I've caused, I don't think Ryan can forgive me.'

'Oh, Freya. I'm so sorry that me being pig-headed over telling him about Maeve has sparked all of this. I should have told him long ago, you were right. But you stood by me and now Ryan blames you.'

When Freya gulped, tears streaming down her face, Kathleen stepped forward and took her into her arms. 'Oh, my darling girl. What a terrible mess we're all in.'

Freya put her head on the old lady's shoulder and wept. This was how it had felt to be held by her mother as a child.

'Gran!' Chloe's voice sounded in the hallway, followed by the thump of the front door. 'Where are you?'

'Good grief,' said Kathleen, releasing Freya from her embrace. 'That child never closes a door quietly when she can slam it.' She called out towards the door. 'We're up here, love, in Freya's bedroom.'

There was a thundering of feet up the stairs and Chloe bundled into the bedroom. She looked at the suitcase on the bed and folded her arms.

'You can't leave,' she said. 'You have to stay here with my gran and me and my dad.'

Freya shook her head. This was making everything so much harder.

'I'm sorry, Chloe, but I have to go. I'll help your gran find someone else who can provide the support she needs.'

'But someone else won't be you.'

When Chloe's bottom lip started to wobble, Freya pulled

her into a hug. She was going to miss this awkward, wonderful young girl so much.

'Chloe,' she murmured, her cheek resting against her beautiful red hair. 'Things haven't worked out here for me, or for your family. I'm so fond of you all, but how can I stay when a relative of mine who lives in the village can't be trusted to keep your family business confidential? How could you ever trust me? Your dad knows that I have to go.'

Chloe pulled away, scrubbing at the tears on her cheeks. 'But it's not you that can't be trusted,' she blurted out. 'It's me. That's why I'm here, so I can tell you. I'm sorry but it's me.'

'What are you saying, child?' asked Kathleen.

Chloe spoke quickly, as though it was taking all of her courage. 'What I'm saying is that it wasn't Belinda who blabbed about your secret, Gran. It was me, and I'm really, *really* sorry.' She burst into noisy tears.

'It was you who told everyone?' Kathleen sat down on the bed, on top of the dresses waiting to be packed.

'Not everyone,' sobbed Chloe, her shoulders heaving under her thin T-shirt. 'I only told Paige but she told Chantelle from school, and Isobel. And I swore on Mum's life to Dad that it wasn't me who'd told, but I lied. I didn't want him to be disappointed in me, after Isobel came round and said that everyone in the village knew about Maeve.'

'But why did you tell Paige?' asked Kathleen, her face a picture of confusion.

Chloe was sobbing too hard to reply so Freya stepped in. 'I reckon you told Paige because you thought it would make her like you more. Is that the truth?'

'Yes,' gulped Chloe, her breath coming in gasps. 'Paige is popular and fashionable and pretty, but she hasn't got a secret auntie who's appeared out of nowhere. I told her not to tell anyone, and she promised. But now she's told people and now Freya hates her sister, and Dad hates Freya, and he'll probably end up marrying Isobel and I'll have to live with Paige, who's never ever going to be my friend again. And now you two and Dad hate me as well.'

When Chloe's sobs reached a new high, Kathleen got to her feet and put her arms around her granddaughter.

'I could never hate you, my darling girl,' she murmured with such tenderness that Freya's eyes began to fill with tears again.

'I could never hate you either,' said Freya, stroking Chloe's shoulder. 'It's all right. You made a mistake and trusted the wrong person.'

'I know and I told her that. I told her I didn't want us to be friends any more. She should have known that Chantelle wouldn't keep it to herself.'

Chantelle or Isobel? wondered Freya, thinking back to Isobel's barbed comments to her. Perhaps she'd realised that Freya was an obstacle between her and Ryan. If it was Isobel, she'd struck the fatal blow to any relationship that Freya and Ryan might have been able to salvage.

'I'm so sorry, Gran,' gulped Chloe.

Kathleen patted her granddaughter's back. 'Ah, don't upset yourself, child. There's nothing to be sorry about. Maeve has been a secret for far too long. Maybe it's time everyone knew about her, because I love her too, like I love you and your dad and your grandad.'

'And you don't hate Freya any more?'

'I never hated Freya.'

'Dad hates her now.'

Chloe's words were like a spear to Freya's heart. Kathleen gave her a sympathetic smile. 'Your dad doesn't hate Freya. But thanks to me being pig-headed, it's all gone wrong. See? Adults make mistakes too and have to live with the consequences.'

'Having a baby wasn't a mistake, was it?'

'What, Maeve?' Kathleen kissed the top of her granddaughter's head. 'No. She was never a mistake, even though I acted like she was a shameful secret for years. I feel more at peace now I've told the people I love all about her.' She kissed Chloe's head again. 'Will you tell your dad that you told Paige about Maeve, so he doesn't blame Freya?'

'He'll be so upset and disappointed that I lied to him.'

'So don't tell him,' said Freya, staring out of the window at the church and the green which had become so familiar to her over the last couple of months.

'I have to tell him,' said Chloe, her voice muffled against Kathleen's shoulder.

'No, you don't. Not if it will upset him.'

'But he'll go on thinking you're the reason everyone knows Gran's secret.'

'I'm leaving later today anyway so it makes no difference what your dad thinks of me. So just go home, give him a hug and tell him that you love him.'

Freya had thought she was through with secrets. But this one was healing, rather than corrosive. And it was one last thing she could do for Ryan and Chloe – a small penance to say sorry for making such a mess of things.

'What do you think, Gran?' asked Chloe, a hint of hope in her voice.

'I don't think Ryan needs any further upsets or disappointment,' said Freya. 'Do you?'

Kathleen's eyes met Freya's over the top of her granddaughter's head. 'He's already had his fair share. That's true enough. But surely you could stay in Heaven's Cove if he knew the truth?'

Freya hesitated. She so wanted to stay. But discovering that she'd known about Maeve had destroyed Ryan's trust in her. And she couldn't bear to go back to the cool, distant relationship they'd had when she first arrived in the village. He wouldn't want her looking after his mother now, anyway.

Freya shook her head. 'I don't think so, Kathleen. Life here has become far too complicated. You see that, don't you?'

'I do, but I'm sad that I'm helping me to find Maeve has led to this.'

'It is sad,' agreed Freya, blinking back tears. 'But whatever's happened, I don't regret helping you to find your daughter. You needed to know that Maeve is alive and well.'

When Kathleen stretched out her hand, Freya took hold of it. She was going to miss this wonderful, feisty woman too.

'So do I need to tell Dad what really happened or not?' asked Chloe, pulling back from her grandmother.

Kathleen shook her head. 'Freya's right that it's probably kinder to leave things as they are, if she's leaving anyway. You didn't mean for Paige to tell anyone. I love you, Chloe.'

'I love you too, Gran.'

Chloe burrowed back into her grandmother's arms and it was such a tender family scene, the tears in Freya's eyes spilled over and ran down her cheeks. How she wished she had close family like this. All she had was a mother over a thousand miles away who wasn't that interested in her life, and a half-sister she'd recently argued with.

Oh heavens! Freya was so caught up in the drama unfolding before her, it had only just sunk in that if it was Chloe who'd blabbed about Kathleen's secret that meant...

'I have to go,' said Freya, grabbing her handbag and rushing to the door.

42

FREYA

'Please let Belinda be in,' muttered Freya to herself as she dodged tourists in the crowded lanes.

It had been hard to hear that Chloe had been the person who'd shared Kathleen's secret. But there had been a surge of relief when Freya realised that Belinda wasn't the culprit, followed by a wave of guilt. The guilt she often felt with regards to Belinda was amorphous and not warranted – she knew that. It was their father who'd made all the decisions that had impacted on their lives. But this guilt was sharp and real.

Freya worried that Belinda was out when no one answered the door, but it was suddenly pulled open by Jim. He looked over his shoulder before stepping outside into the garden and pulling the front door to behind him.

'Hello, Freya. I'm afraid Belinda is indisposed.'

'Is she in, Jim? I just need a quick word. That's all.'

He frowned. 'I don't know how to put this nicely, Freya, but I'm afraid she doesn't want to see you.'

Of course her sister didn't want to see her. She'd accused her of lying and ruining people's lives.

'Please, Jim,' pleaded Freya. 'I need to apologise to Belinda.

I've found out that she wasn't the person who told people about Kathleen's adopted daughter.'

'Wasn't she?' Jim blinked with surprise, then he smiled. 'Well, that's very good to know. You'd better come inside, then.'

Freya followed him into the hall and he beckoned for her to go with him into the sitting room.

Belinda was standing with her back to them, looking out of the window at the ocean.

'What did she want?' she asked, turning round. 'Oh.' Her hand flew to her mouth. 'You let her in.'

'I did and I'd like you to give the woman a chance. I think you'll want to hear what she has to say.' Jim shrugged. 'I'll leave you both to it while I nip to the shops for the milk I forgot this morning.'

'Can't you stay?' asked Belinda.

But Jim had left the room, closing the door behind him, and Freya heard the front door open and shut.

Neither woman moved. The room was stuffy and quiet, apart from the far-off shouts of young children on the sea wall.

'Are you all right?' asked Freya, to break the silence.

'Yes, thank you. You?'

'Yes, I'm fine, thanks.'

'Good.'

Silence ensued again as Freya wondered how two sisters had reached this point of estrangement, when in reality they had so much in common. She took a deep breath.

'I'm here to apologise, Belinda. I've found out that you kept Kathleen's secret, as you promised you would, and didn't blab... I mean, tell anyone else about it.'

'Not even Jim,' said Belinda, her arms folded across her bosom. 'I didn't even tell my own husband.'

'I'm sorry.' Freya shook her head. 'I made a terrible mistake in accusing you and I apologise from the bottom of my heart. I hope you can forgive me.'

Belinda glared at Freya for a moment but then all the fight went out of her. She seemed to shrink in front of Freya's eyes.

'Oh, do sit down. I'll forgive you if you'll forgive me in return.' Freya sat on the sofa as ordered but Belinda stayed standing by the window. 'It took guts coming back and saying you were wrong.'

'I was a bit nervous, to be honest, in case you bit my head off. You can be a bit scary.'

'Can I?' Belinda frowned. 'No one has ever said that to me before.'

'Probably because they were too scared.'

There was a stunned pause before Belinda burst out laughing. 'At least families can say what they really think.' Her laughter stopped as quickly as it had begun. 'I don't mean to be scary.'

'I'm sure you don't. It's just that you're quite... forceful in your opinions sometimes. I guess that's why you're involved in so many things in the village.'

'Heaven's Cove would grind to a halt without me,' opined Belinda, before biting her lip. 'Or that's what I like to think. I dare say they'd all manage perfectly well without me.'

'I doubt it.'

'Hmm.' Belinda looked unconvinced. 'You didn't believe me when I said I hadn't said anything about Kathleen's secret past. I believe your words were: "You're a dreadful gossip."'

Freya winced. 'Sorry. I shouldn't have said that.'

'Maybe not. Or maybe it's the truth. I've been thinking about what you said. All of it.' She hesitated before asking: 'Is that how people see me, Freya – a scary interfering old gossip? The sort of woman that my mother would call an old battle-axe?'

'Not a battle-axe, no. But you do talk a lot about other people's business.'

'I suppose I do, but their lives tend to be rather more exciting than mine.'

Belinda looked out of the window for a moment, at the branches of the tree in her garden swaying in the breeze blowing off the sea. Then she turned back to Freya. 'I like to feel needed, you see. I like to believe that I'm at the centre of this village and in control of what happens here. I like to feel that people respect me and that I'm worth something.'

Freya hesitated before saying: 'Is that because you didn't feel you were worth anything when Dad left and went off with my mum?'

Belinda frowned. 'That's quite a stretch, Freya. I don't hold with all this psychological claptrap. There's nothing in it at all.'

But her eyes glistened and Freya's heart melted when two large tears tracked their way down her cheeks, leaving white trails in her make-up. She dabbed at them with a tissue from her pocket.

'Belinda, what Dad did wasn't fair to you or your mum, and he paid for it when my mum left him.'

'I was glad, you know.' Belinda bit her lip. 'I was all grown up by the time your mum went, but I was still glad he was suffering like we'd suffered. I was so busy feeling vengeful, I didn't really take in that you were a child who'd lost your mother just like I'd lost my father. Isn't that awful?'

Freya shrugged. 'You were a child who was damaged by someone you loved who should have protected you better. I'm really sorry that Dad left you and your mum. And I'm sorry that it's had such an enduring effect on your mother.'

'Me too, but it's not your fault, is it? It never has been.'

'Neither of us are to blame.'

When Belinda bent her head, Freya saw her as the child she once was, mourning the loss of a father who had begun another family without her. Freya got up, walked to Belinda and put her arms around her. At first Belinda was stiff as a board but then she softened and let herself be held. The two of them stood there, sisters united by the past and the future yet to come.

'Is everything all right?' asked Jim, popping his head around the door, a plastic litre of milk in his hands. 'Oops,' he said, catching sight of the two sisters hugging. Then he smiled at Freya over the back of his wife's head. 'I'll leave you to it.'

Belinda was the first to pull away. She wiped her eyes and gestured for Freya to sit down again. This time she joined her on the sofa.

'Can I tell you a secret?' she asked, sitting ramrod straight with her legs crossed at the ankles.

Freya groaned. 'Do you have to? I'm just about through with secrets. They tend to cause nothing but heartache and pain.'

'This one won't. My secret is merely that I'm always rather desperate to impress you.'

'Why?' Freya laughed. 'Why do you care what I think?'

'I care because you're my sister and the only family I have left, apart from my mother and a couple of cousins I don't get on with.'

'You don't need to impress me, Belinda. I'm impressed already. You have a lovely home, you're a stalwart of the village, and you've been married for years to a wonderful man.'

Belinda's mouth lifted in the corner. 'He is rather wonderful and he puts up with a lot. Jim is very loyal. What about you, Freya? Are you going to stay in Heaven's Cove? I'd really like you to.'

'I've grown to love this village, but no, I'm not staying. Ryan and I...'

'Are the two of you an item?' asked Belinda, her eyes shining. But before Freya could open her mouth, Belinda's face clouded over. 'I didn't mean to ask that,' she said quickly. 'It's absolutely none of my business. Actually, I've been thinking... maybe I should resign from some committees.'

Freya, impressed with her sister's new grasp on discretion,

shook her head. 'God, no, Belinda. If you start resigning, the village hall will close, the monthly market will fold and Heaven's Cove will very possibly slide into the sea.'

When she grinned, Belinda grinned back. 'Are you teasing me, Freya?'

'Isn't that what sisters do?'

'I don't know. I don't feel that I've ever really had a sister before now.'

'Me neither. But let's try to change that, shall we?'

'I'd like that,' said Belinda, sniffing and fishing in her pocket again for the tissue. 'I'd like that very much.'

The sisters sat side by side in silence, enjoying each other's company, as moss-green waves curled outside the window towards the shore.

'Don't tell anyone,' said Freya quietly, after a few minutes, 'but Ryan and I were an item for a little while.'

'I knew it!' Belinda punched the air, before turning to Freya. '*Were* an item? So you're not together any more?'

'No, things didn't work out.'

'Hmm.' Belinda self-consciously placed her hand on her sister's knee. 'That's a shame. I'm very sorry.'

'Me too. And I'm glad you know, but you can't say a word about it to anyone!'

'My lips are sealed,' said Belinda, drawing her finger across her mouth. 'I promise you, one sister to another.'

And this time Freya believed her.

43

RYAN

'Stop being such a dick, Dad.'

That stopped him in his tracks. Ryan turned to face his daughter, who'd just informed him that she was the one who'd talked about his long-lost sister. There were so many emotions coursing through him right now: anger, disbelief, sadness, and a stabbing disappointment that she'd let down both him and her gran. Good grief, she'd even sworn on her mum's life that she hadn't said a word about Maeve.

He breathed out slowly, trying to stay calm. 'I think you're the one in big trouble here, Chloe, and being rude to me isn't going to help you.'

She gave the sigh of a woman twice her age. 'I don't care what you do to me. You can ground me for a month if you like. I deserve it. But you're in far more trouble than I am.'

'What on earth are you talking about?'

'You know,' she said, tilting her chin towards him, just like Natalie used to do when she was challenging him about something.

It was strange. He could think about Natalie these days without the crushing guilt. He was starting to remember the good times they'd had together, rather than always focusing on her final moments.

Chloe got off her bed, put her arms around him and gave him a hug. It was so unexpected, it took his breath away. He was still upset with her for gossiping about Maeve and lying to him but he put his arms around her anyway. Chloe's hugs were hard won these days and he'd take them as and when he could.

'You're an idiot,' she mumbled into his chest.

'Why?' he asked, wondering how a good father would deal with this situation.

She looked up at him, her arms still around his waist. 'Freya really cares about you. She cares so much, she said I didn't have to tell you it was my fault everyone knows about Maeve.'

'Why would she do that?'

Chloe rolled her eyes. 'Duh! She didn't want you to be upset and disappointed in me. She was more concerned about you and me getting on than what you thought about her. She said she was leaving later today anyway so it didn't matter.'

Freya had done that for the two of them? After he'd accused her of being the reason that Maeve was the talk of the village. He rubbed a hand across his chin, a jumble of so many emotions right now, he couldn't even begin to unpick them.

'But you came home and told me what you'd done anyway.'

'I didn't want to. I knew you'd be upset with me, but I don't want Freya to leave like that. She'll be getting a taxi to the station really soon and you're letting her go.'

'You don't understand what's been going on,' said Ryan flatly.

Chloe moved away from him, her face flushing pink. 'That's what all grown-ups say when they don't want to explain things. But I can totally see what's going on. You're sad after Mum died so you'd rather be on your own for ever but that's stupid. Freya tried to please everyone and keep everyone's secrets but ended up making everyone cross. That's also stupid. So you belong together. I can tell you really like each other.'

Ryan's mouth dropped open, then he started to laugh. Out of the mouths of babes.

'I thought you wanted me to hook up with Isobel.'

'Nah, she can be a bit mean and her daughter's a cow.'

'Is that right?' Ryan was going to have to tackle Chloe's language but now wasn't the time. 'Freya's much nicer,' continued Chloe. 'She was kind to me and to Gran.'

'And to me,' said Ryan, thinking back to how she'd listened to him at Cora Head and made his world brighter. How she'd kissed him, but now he would never kiss her again. He suddenly found it hard to breathe.

'Go on, Dad,' said Chloe, opening her bedroom door. 'If you go now, I bet you'll catch her.'

Ryan was running. The last time he'd run like this he was sixteen and being forced to do the two hundred metres by a sadistic PE teacher. He wasn't sure that his knees could take it these days. But he had to see Freya.

She'd gone to have one last look at the sea, his mum had told him when he'd rushed into her cottage. Freya's suitcase was packed and waiting in the hall for the taxi that was booked in an hour's time.

Ryan hated that Freya hadn't told him about his long-lost sister. But he hated the thought of her leaving even more. His life had been a mess since long before Natalie had died, and it was time to sort it out. If he hadn't left it too late.

The beach was empty apart from a couple of dogs careering across the sand and their owners following behind, wrapped up against the strong wind that was whipping the waves into peaks. Had he missed her?

Ryan's heart leapt into his mouth when he spotted her on

the rocks where they'd sat together on her first sunny visit to the cove. Such a lot had happened since then.

She was staring out to sea and didn't notice him until he sat down beside her. The cold of the rock seeped through the denim of his jeans. Freya must be freezing in her cotton trousers and thin sweatshirt.

'What are you doing here?' she asked, her voice low and flat.

'Mum said you'd come to have one last look at the sea.'

Freya nodded. 'I'm going to miss it.'

'I saw your suitcase in the hall. You're all packed and ready to go.'

'That's right.' She wrapped her arms around her waist for warmth.

'Where are you going? You're not going back to Greg, are you?'

'I didn't think you'd much care what I was doing.'

She didn't say it unkindly but her words cut through him more than the cold wind ever could. It was killing him to think that she might go back to her husband, the man who didn't think she was good enough for him.

'I'm not,' she said quietly, her words almost snatched away by the breeze. 'Greg has moved on, and so have I. He's not right for me.' She twisted on the rock to face him. 'Why are you here, Ryan?'

'I had a heart-to-heart with my daughter, who told me that she was the one who talked about Maeve. She told Paige, who told her mum and Chantelle. But I think you know that already.'

Freya frowned. 'She didn't have to tell you. I'm leaving anyway so it doesn't make much difference.'

'It makes a difference to me.'

He paused, remembering his daughter's ashen face as she'd told him the truth. And his growing realisation that it was possibly Isobel who'd talked about his long-lost sister and then blamed Freya for being indiscreet.

'I'm sorry that I blamed you for talking to Belinda about Maeve.'

She shrugged. 'I didn't deliberately tell Belinda but I was careless and she put two and two together after seeing the information in my bedroom.'

'I know. But she didn't tell anyone.'

'No, she didn't. I asked her not to and she didn't say a word. Not even to Jim.'

'Blimey.' Ryan began to reassess his opinion of Belinda.

'I'm kind of glad that you know the truth,' said Freya, watching a child's discarded red bucket bob in the waves. 'But I hope you're not too disappointed in Chloe. She was trying to impress a friend and didn't mean any harm. She's a brilliant kid and she really loves you and Kathleen.'

'I know.'

Freya smiled before glancing at her watch. 'I need to go. The taxi will be here soon and I want to have time to say a proper goodbye to Kathleen.'

'My mum will miss you,' said Ryan, feeling his throat tighten.

'I'll miss her too.' Freya bit her lip, looking close to tears.

'Then stay.' Ryan grabbed hold of Freya's hand. 'Please.'

'I can't,' said Freya, but she let her hand stay resting in his. 'What's brought about this change of heart?'

'My daughter gave me a good telling-off and she was right. She said that I'm stupid and so are you so we obviously belong together.'

'Is that right?'

Freya began to laugh. It melted into the whoosh of waves on the sand and the calling of seagulls above their heads and was the most beautiful sound he'd ever heard.

She stopped laughing, her face serious again. 'I've caused nothing but trouble since I arrived.'

'You're a good person, Freya, and you were trying to do the best by my mum. She put you in an impossible situation and she realises that and is sorry for it. But look how our lives have improved since you arrived. Mum and Maeve are in touch, and Chloe is making new friends at school and doesn't care so much about Paige's approval. They both need you.'

'And what about you?' asked Freya, staring into his eyes.

'Me? I've gained a sister, I've shed lots of the guilt that's haunted me for years, and I...' He swallowed, about to say something that he'd thought he'd never ever say again. '...I've fallen in love. So why don't you stay?' He grinned. 'Just for a month and we'll see how it goes?'

For a moment, Freya didn't move and he thought all was lost. Then she turned and put her arms around his neck.

'I can't bear the thought of leaving your mum and Chloe, and you.'

'Is that a yes?'

'Yes,' she said, kissing him hard on the mouth. He put his arms around her waist and lifted her off the rocks and pulled her down onto the sand. It was absolutely freezing and the tide was coming in and one of the dog walkers was staring at them, but he didn't care. Freya was in his arms and that was all that mattered.

Freya wasn't sure how long they'd been kissing. Time seemed to stop when Ryan lifted her onto the cold sand and pulled her close to his body. All she knew was the pressure of his warm lips on her mouth and his hands in her hair – until the encroaching tide broke the spell.

'Oof!' she squealed, sitting bolt upright as the edge of a

wave bubbled around her shoulder. The water was absolutely freezing.

'Quick,' laughed Ryan, jumping up and pulling Freya to her feet. They ran further up the beach, hand in hand, shedding sand with every step. 'Are you OK?'

'I'm fine,' said Freya, grinning at the man who'd stolen her heart, before waving at the dog walker who was still staring at them. 'You do realise that you and me making out on the beach will likely be all round Heaven's Cove by the end of the day?'

'I don't care. But do you? Would you rather keep our relationship – us – quiet for now?' he asked, biting down on the lip she'd kissed only moments ago.

'No,' replied Freya, looking into his beautiful green eyes. 'I'm happy to tell anyone who wants to know. I'm tired of keeping things – amazing things like this – quiet. I think the time for keeping secrets is long gone, don't you?'

A slow smile lit up Ryan's face as he nodded. His fingers brushed sandy hair from her forehead, his touch making her melt. And then he bent his head to kiss her again.

EPILOGUE
KATHLEEN

They were all here – Ryan and Freya standing, hand in hand, with their backs to the sun, a sea breeze ruffling their hair, and Chloe in her blue dress. The only person missing was Maeve. She'd been missing all these years, but she would soon be here.

Chloe gave Kathleen a thumbs-up and Kathleen gave her a warm smile in return. When she'd realised that Chloe had put on her best dress for the occasion, it had almost broken her. But she'd kept it together and she would keep it together throughout this. Maeve wouldn't want to meet a blubbering mess. Kathleen was surprised that she'd agreed to meet at all – it had taken weeks of careful bridge-building – and she was determined not to blow it.

Kathleen was under no illusion. She wasn't Maeve's mum. That was the woman who had adopted her and loved her and given her a happy life. But she *was* Maeve's birth mother and that special link to her daughter could never be broken.

Kathleen realised that she was biting her nails and laced her fingers. She wanted to look her best for her daughter. She'd already checked twice that she hadn't tucked the back of her dress into her knickers, and Freya had painted her nails a pretty pink and helped her to put on some make-up. First impressions counted and Kathleen wanted to make a good one.

It was strange being here, on the doorstep of Driftwood House. The same place where she'd stood as a young woman, in the prime of her life but broken-hearted. And now, more than half a century later, she was back – this time towards the end of her days – and life had turned full circle. The baby that was taken from her was returning, but she wasn't a baby any more.

Suddenly Kathleen was overwhelmed with sorrow for the years missed. The birthdays and holidays, the grazed knees and cuddles, the books read at bedtime and the shared confidences.

'There's no point thinking like that,' she murmured under her breath. 'This is your second chance. Be grateful for it.'

'Are you talking to yourself, Gran?' asked Chloe, grabbing her hand. 'You don't need to be scared because we're here with you.'

'Thank you, darling, but I'm not scared.'

Yet her heart started hammering when Chloe pulled her hand away and pointed into the distance. 'Here comes a car. She's here.'

As the taxi laboured up the potholed track to the top of the cliff, Kathleen's mind went to what had happened over the last few weeks, since Maeve had sent her first letter.

Chloe seemed happier now she was no longer chasing after Paige's approval, and she and Kristen had become close. Isobel still flirted outrageously whenever she saw Ryan but she'd switched her affections to a fisherman in the next village.

Ryan didn't mind because he was so clearly in love. Kathleen glanced at her son and smiled. He was so much happier these days and more like the son he used to be when Chloe was young. And she had Freya to thank for that. Freya, who had appeared in her life out of the blue and transformed it for the better. Freya, who loved her son and her granddaughter, and was becoming like a daughter to Kathleen herself. Even Belinda had calmed down with her sister in the village and seemed to be gossiping far less these days.

'It's her, Gran. She's in the taxi.'

Kathleen walked forward as the taxi pulled to a halt in a cloud of dust, leaving her family behind. She had to see her. After all this time, she had to see her daughter.

The door of the taxi opened and a middle-aged woman slowly got out. She leaned down to pay the taxi driver and turned into the wind. That was when Kathleen caught sight of Maeve for the first time in over sixty years.

The woman in front of her was taller than she was, with red hair cut short into the nape of her neck. Kathleen had two shocks – Maeve was no longer a child. Of course she wasn't. And she looked so very much like her aunt Clodagh, Kathleen's sister, it took Kathleen's breath away.

The taxi turned round and drove off back down the cliff as the two women looked at each other.

'Hello, Maeve,' said Kathleen, her words carried in the wind. 'Thank you for being here.'

'Hello.' Maeve smiled. 'How could I not come?'

Kathleen walked towards her daughter and almost stumbled in her haste. Maeve put out her hands to catch her and the two of them embraced as seagulls circled overhead and waves far below boomed as they hit the cliff-face.

This was her baby, her little girl. Kathleen felt Maeve's arms tighten around her and she finally felt at peace.

A LETTER FROM LIZ

Dear reader,

That's it! You've reached the end of *The Girl at the Last House Before the Sea*, and I really hope you enjoyed the latest goings-on in Heaven's Cove.

If you did and would like to keep up to date with all my new releases, just sign up at the following link. Your email address will never be shared and you can unsubscribe at any time.

www.bookouture.com/liz-eeles

I loved writing this book and giving Freya and Ryan a happy ending – Chloe too, who'll no doubt keep her dad and stepmum (I don't think it'll be too long before they tie the knot) on their toes. I especially enjoyed writing about Kathleen, a character I created after coming across the heartbreaking, true-life tales of women who'd had to give up their babies decades earlier. In my story, I was able to reunite Kathleen with her child, and writing the epilogue was my favourite part of the whole book.

If you were touched by Kathleen's tale, or had fun escaping to Heaven's Cove for a few hours, I'd be so grateful if you could write a review. I'd love to hear what you think, and your views might help new readers to discover my books for the first time.

This might have been your first visit to Heaven's Cove. If it was and you'd like to go back, there are two other standalone novels in the Heaven's Cove series that you might like – *Secrets at the Last House Before the Sea*, and *A Letter to the Last House Before the Sea*. And there will be more to come!

When I'm not making up stories, I can often be found on social media, and I love hearing from readers. You can get in touch on my Facebook page, through Twitter or Instagram, or via my website. The links are below.

Thanks, again, for choosing to read my book,

Liz x

www.lizeeles.com

facebook.com/lizeelesauthor

twitter.com/lizeelesauthor

instagram.com/lizeelesauthor

ACKNOWLEDGEMENTS

After writing a whole book, you'd think that penning the acknowledgements would be a piece of cake. But, ironically, I'm finding it hard to put into words just how grateful I am to all the people who've given me the opportunity to write this book and see it published.

There are lots of people to thank: everyone who works so hard for my publisher, Bookouture; my editor, Ellen Gleeson, whose encouragement and judgement I value and trust; my family and friends who are always interested in and supportive of my writing; and everyone who takes time out of their day to read my books, including this one.

A very big THANK YOU from me to all of you.

Printed in Great Britain
by Amazon